An Alluring Brew

My Lady's Potions, Book 3

Katherine Lyons

ARE YOU SIGNED UP FOR DRAGONBLADE'S BLOG?

You'll get the latest news and information on exclusive giveaways, exclusive excerpts, coming releases, sales, free books, cover reveals and more.

Check out our complete list of authors, too!

No spam, no junk. That's a promise!

Sign Up Here

www.dragonbladepublishing.com

Dearest Reader;

Thank you for your support of a small press. At Dragonblade Publishing, we strive to bring you the highest quality Historical Romance from some of the best authors in the business. Without your support, there is no 'us', so we sincerely hope you adore these stories and find some new favorite authors along the way.

Happy Reading!

CEO, Dragonblade Publishing

Additional Dragonblade books by
Author Katherine Lyons

My Lady's Potions Series
The Love Potion (Book 1)
The Truth Serum (Book 2)
An Alluring Brew (Book 3)

Rogues Gambit Series
Rules for a Fake Fiancé (Book 1)
Rules for a Bastard Lord (Book 2)
Rules for a Wicked Wager (Book 3)

Chapter One

"WHAT WAS THAT about?"

Maximillian Palo, Earl of Artanges, tried to make his voice sound casual as he pried into the prince regent's private affairs. Spying on Prinny was always difficult, but tonight the ruler was being especially grumpy.

"You know Lord Benedict," Prinny said with a dismissive snap of his wrist. "Always something. It can wait until tomorrow." He plucked a candied plum off a nearby tray and ate it with sloppy adoration.

They were having a casual evening in the prince's private house, and the royal clearly had no interest in any affairs of state. Nevertheless, a messenger had appeared and insisted on delivering a message straight into Prinny's hand. It was only because Max was near enough to recognize Lord Benedict's handwriting that he became interested.

Lord Benedict never bothered Prinny with anything except urgent matters. Add that Max had caught a single word writ large and he couldn't stop himself from poking further. That word had caught his attention as a boy when his uncle had returned from the far east with treasures of silk, tobacco, and a silver filigree box so fine that the best English silversmiths could not begin to imitate the design.

That word had settled deep into his bones later when a school friend ventured to the same land and come back with exotic—and erotic—tales of the far away country. Thanks to Reggie's stories,

Max's interest in China blossomed into a secret obsession. He couldn't go there himself. His responsibilities in England prevented it. But oh, he was fascinated by everything that word whispered.

China.

Lord Benedict had sent a message about China, and the damned regent was too lazy to pay any attention to it.

"Is something happening at the Foreign Office?" Max pressed. That's where Benedict worked as second in command to Lord Castlereagh. Together they formed the bulk of England's relationships with every other country on the planet, including those they were at war with. "Has Napoleon done something annoying?"

Max already knew that wasn't the case. Castlereagh wanted Prinny as far away as possible from the war with Napoleon. Indeed, Max's orders—or strong suggestion from Castlereagh and Benedict both—were to interest the Regent in anything *except* the war effort. Which suited Max fine because his interest was fixed firmly on the Orient.

No fool, Prinny snorted. "As if he would message me anything about that. No, this is about an unofficial delegation."

The damned man was being coy now just to toy with Max. He knew of Max's interest. "A delegation from China, perhaps?" Max pressed.

"Unofficial. Of no importance. I am free to ignore them."

"Ignore them!" Max exclaimed, knowing now that the prince was indeed playing with him. Prinny had nearly as much interest in Chinoiserie as Max did. It was one of the few things that created their friendship, though their conversations were mostly about gossip and politics, in that order.

"I suppose," Prinny drawled, "that I could allow you to be here when I receive them." He gestured vaguely at the throne room. "Tomorrow."

"When?"

"Who knows when the ships come in? Could be morning,

could be during supper." Prinny grinned. "You'll just have to stay through the night to make sure to be here."

Max groaned, knowing he was incapable of resisting the lure. Even if he was excruciatingly tired of carousing until all hours with the prince. Even if he was bored to tears with the courtesans that constantly tried to attract him with overblown airs. And even if another morning with a sore head was going to be death of him. The prince wanted his company and was willing to bribe him with an interesting bit of Chinoiserie to keep him there all night.

"Very well," Max said as he gestured to his empty glass. "How would you like to pass the time until then?"

Prinny grinned, knowing he had won. "I think we should discuss the idiocy of your father's latest speech in Parliament."

Max chuckled. Attacking the Tory party was one of Prinny's favorite pastimes. "I cannot in good conscious entertain you with tales of my father's stodgy, boring, ridiculously old-fashioned conservatism. He is, after all, my father and a highly respected duke."

"Indulge me."

Max did. It was the easiest thing he'd done all day. Unfortunately, it continued nearly to dawn.

GONGGGGGGGG.

Max jolted awake, his head pounding and his eyes gritty.

"Bloody hell," moaned a voice near him.

Max needed to squint to see his oldest friend Christopher, the Earl of Bloomsbrook, tightened into a ball on the nearest settee. The man slept just like he had twenty years ago when they'd both arrived at Eton with knobby knees and a mutual terror of the aggressive older boys. Last night, his friend had joined the party after midnight and was now looking worse for the wear. He was gray beneath his straw-like hair which stuck out in every direction.

"Was that a gong?" the man rasped.

How the hell would he know? Max rubbed the grit out of his eyes. Damn it, his back was killing him. What had he slept on? And what was that nauseating smell? Ugh. *He* smelled like cheap perfume.

Gonggggggg.

There it was again. Beneath the echoing, he could hear the murmur of anxious footmen and nervous secretaries. Good lord, Prinny must be beside himself with fury.

Then he remembered. The Chinese! A Chinese delegation was coming today and apparently, was already here. Max pushed to his feet, ignoring the way his temples throbbed.

"What time is it?" Christopher mumbled.

"Time to watch Prinny murder an impertinent delegation," Max retorted. He had better hurry over to moderate any royal grumpiness. Max tugged on the bellpull then tried not to groan when a servant appeared with barely contained excitement.

"Yes, my lords?"

"Who is making that sound?"

The boy bounced slightly where he stood. "A whole group of Chinese, my lord. With a gong and a litter closed up with silk curtains."

Gongggggggg.

Chris moaned. "Why won't they stop?"

"They say they'll bang it until the prince himself greets them."

"Bloody impertinent," Max grumbled. "Ringing a gong in a royal's private palace."

"They're Chinese," Chris said as he finished off a half glass of leftover wine. "What do they know about how things are done?"

Max didn't answer. He was in need of some personal grooming. Fortunately, there was a place for his toilet and a footman nearby who attempted to repair Max's appearance. It wasn't possible. Not completely, but together they fixed the worst of the damage. Max was debating the need for a quick shave when the gong rang again.

This time the sound truly did bother him. It was loud enough to wake the dead, which meant Prinny would be out soon, ready to chop off someone's head.

"Come along," Chris said as he banged on the door. "Prinny's up."

Max finished with his cravat and headed out, easily keeping pace with the shorter earl. They followed the sound of the thrice-damned gong into the ante chamber of the throne room. The place was stuffed to the gills with Chinese. Two thick-armed men stood front and back between the poles of a curtained palanquin. They were the bearers of the litter which must have been heavy because they were opening and closing their hands as if unused to that kind of work. Two more big men stood behind and another two in front looking like officials. One carried the hand gong. And at the head of them all, grinning at the spectacle, was a gruff sea captain. At least that's what was suggested by the braid on his lapels and the cutlass shoved into his belt.

Oh hell, the second official was about to bang that gong again.

Gonggggg.

The sound reverberated in Max's skull hard enough to make him recoil. But then he looked at Chris and couldn't suppress his grin. Both of them were anticipating a dinner tonight regaling friends with this tale.

"Stop that noise!" growled Prinny as he at last made it into the room. The prince looked like he'd just pulled on a dressing gown. The royal hadn't even bothered with shoes, and his face was slick and slightly green. They had consumed a great deal of…well, everything last night, and the prince did not enjoy early morning surprises. Even if it was after noon.

When the gong continued to reverberate, Prinny waddled forward, grabbed the offending brass, and ripped it out of the Chinese man's hand.

"What the devil is this about?" the royal demanded as he tossed the offending instrument aside. One of Prinny's footmen scrambled to catch it and silence the brass note as it clanged against the wall.

The captain cleared his throat, pulled off his hat and bowed to the prince. "Your Highness, my name's Captain Pugh, and I've been sailing between England and China since I was a boy. It's a right good living, Your Highness, and I've made friends, so to speak, so when the Wong patriarch needed a ship to deliver his gifts, he picked me. It was an honor, Your Highness—"

"Yes, yes, man. Get to the point or I'll have you hanged." Prinny dropped onto a settee and glared balefully about the room.

"Er...yes... Well—"

Before the captain could say anything more, the lead Chinese official stepped forward, his silk robes flapping about his feet. He looked ridiculous to Max's western eyes, especially the pointed red hat and the long black queue that descended down his back, but the man clearly took his position very seriously as he unrolled a parchment horizontally between his two hands.

Whatever was written was unintelligible to Max's eyes. From his place against the wall, he could see some of the thick, black strokes of Chinese characters. They appeared like very beautiful, very ordered chicken scratch, though he'd learned to identify a few characters over the years. The official spoke loudly in Chinese with unexpected bursts of volume in his already stentorian voice. And when he was finished, every foreigner stomped his feet, first left then right, then both together before they clapped left fist into right palm and bowed before the prince.

It was an impressive sight. Max appreciated the colorful out-fits and the attempt at discipline. But it was merely an attempt. Even he could see that they weren't true military. The bearers wore similar loose black shirts and pants, but the styles weren't identical. Neither did the men stand straight while waiting, but slumped and shuffled their feet. But they all wore impressive short swords and had the muscles to wield them. It may look odd to him, but that was part of the fun.

After all, he was in a royal home witnessing something few westerners ever had and that alone made this moment exciting. Especially since they had yet to see who was inside the palanquin.

Meanwhile, Prinny rubbed his temples as he grumbled. "What did he just say?"

The captain bowed again, his smile appearing to fade a bit. "This is a delegation from the Wong cohong, Your Highness."

"The what?"

"They're a merchant family, your highness. Very important. They sell tea and silks to us and are part of the governing body that oversees exports."

Prinny narrowed his eyes. "So they're merchants, not the Chinese king."

"Yes, your highness. Not the Chinese emperor, but still a powerful family. Very important to the Chinese trade. The Wong patriarch is on the governing body and works closely with the Hoppo."

"The hippo?"

"Hoppo, Your Highness."

Prinny held up a hand and glared balefully at Max. "Can you explain this?"

Yes, but it was complicated. "Hoppo is a title, like prince or…" He shook his head. "It doesn't matter. These gentlemen are here from a leading merchant family."

The captain nodded. "The Wong cohong, my lord. They express their greeting and respect for the prince in, um, very complimentary terms. He impresses them with his health and prowess. His great power and wisdom."

Doubtful. Prinny wasn't impressing anyone right now with his sweat damp skin and his baleful eyes, but such was the language of diplomacy. And not surprisingly, Prinny wasn't in the mood to accept such insincere worship.

"What does he want, Max?"

The captain turned to the official and spoke in quick Chinese. Even Max could hear how badly garbled his language was when compared to the Chinese official, but apparently the meaning got across.

The official declared something very loudly. It was shorter than the other statements and he punctuated it by snapping the edges of the scroll together before he gestured to the guards.

Max didn't need the captain's translation.

"He has gifts, your highness."

"Well, bring them on," Prinny groused, but Max could see the gleam of interest in the royal's eye.

Two guards behind the palanquin gathered things from a basket in the back of the litter. The first unrolled a bolt of bright yellow fabric, heavily embroidered. He spread it out before the prince. The other man came forward with a lacquered box that he opened. Inside were silk pouches filled with something aromatic. Several somethings, no doubt, and Max's nose twitched as he tried to sort through the scents.

"Silk, your highness," intoned the captain. "The finest. Imperial tea, meant for kings and emperors. Tobacco as well."

Prinny wrinkled his nose. "Not very much," he groused. "Bring it here." A pair of footmen rushed to do the prince's bidding, but Max could already see that the silk was of excellent quality. Likely the tea and tobacco as well, though as bribes went, this was a rather pitiful showing. Prinny seemed to agree, though he wasn't disposed to liking anything right then. In the end, he waved the gifts aside as he dropped his chin on his hand.

"Is that all?"

The captain cleared his throat. "Er, one more thing, your highness."

The Chinese official started speaking again. His voice lowered into more lilting tones. His hands gestured expansively, and he dropped his head as if in awe. Then he paused with his head bowed and hands outstretched as he waited for the sea captain to translate.

"The Wong cohong offers your highness a gift most dear to the patriarch's heart. A gift that demonstrates the level of his respect and begs you to appreciate the cost to his soul."

"What is it?" Prinny grumbled. If only the Chinese had arrived later in the day. Normally, Prinny would love the pageantry of such a moment.

The captain turned back to the official. He spoke in his thick Chinese with a quick kind of urgency. The bowed official flushed red at the words, but he continued his performance. He backed away from the palanquin. The two bearers walked to the windowed sides and put their hand to the curtains, but they stood still.

No one moved.

"Well?" Prinny pressed. "Why aren't they opening it?"

"I think they're waiting for the gong," Max said.

The second official walked over to the footman and tried to take the gong, but the royal servant wouldn't release it. It was an awkward tug-of-war until Prinny grunted.

"Oh, let him have it. Just don't hit it hard."

The footman released it, and the official turned, lifting the gong with a pompous gesture. He raised the mallet, but the captain was quick to speak in Chinese. Max guessed that the man said something like, *not too loud! The prince has a headache!*

With a grimace of annoyance, the official struck the gong—somewhat softly—and right on cue, the bearers ripped out the curtains. They pulled the fabric away as if it were tissue paper. And there, sitting with her head held high and all sorts of dangly things waving about her face, was a Chinese princess. Or someone who looked very much like a princess.

Max narrowed his eyes, trying to sort face and form through the colorful make up. Her face was powdered white, her lips bright red, and her eyes darkened with kohl. She neither smiled nor looked around. Indeed, she might have been a statue except for the way a large quantity of red beads swung around her face.

Both officials stepped forward and extended an arm. The

woman stood slowly as she stepped out of the palanquin. She moved with exquisite care and some awkwardness. Probably because she was tottering on odd sandals that raised her up an extra half foot.

Max was watching her face as she moved, as much as he could see through the swinging beads. Was she revolted by the prince? Was she anxious or frightened? What would it be like to travel all the way from China to be presented to a hungover prince in a dressing gown?

She walked in tiny, careful steps, so her exit from the palanquin was excruciatingly slow. She was dressed in red silk with gold embroidery. Her hands were hidden inside the massive sleeves, and her head was bowed. She seemed a delicate creature, dwarfed by the weight of fabric, headdress, and the two officials hovering on either side of her.

Eventually she made it halfway to where the prince sat, then the official on her left lifted the gong and banged it again. Oh hell, that thing had to be thrown into the rubbish. Max's temples throbbed every time the thing sounded, and Prinny couldn't feel much better.

But before the prince could order the blasted thing away, the primary official started intoning grand Chinese words. Such ponderous weight he put to every syllable. Then he paused and looked at the captain.

"This is Wong Xiao Yihui, revered daughter of the Wong patriarch. She's...uh, beautiful, smart..."

The official spoke more, his words lengthy while the captain clearly struggled to translate.

"Poetic. Godfearing. Um, has elegant hands?" He looked at his hands as if they held the answer. Then he smiled at the prince. "She's got a good...um, healthy body for babies, I think. I don't really know all his words, but she's a prize, your highness, a very good woman."

Prinny frowned as he looked at the people arrayed before him. "Yes, I see she's a woman. Is she going to dance for me?"

"Um, no, your highness. She's the gift, you see." He twisted his hands together and bowed once before his next words. "They mean her to be your wife."

Prinny stared. "My wife?"

"Yes, Your Highness."

To his credit, the prince did not react. Neither did anyone else until the room seemed to pound with the silence. And all Max could think was that his sister was going to laugh and laugh at this story when he told her tonight.

Finally, Prinny rolled his eyes. "Max, explain to them that I'm already married."

"I think they know that, Your Highness," Max said as he took another step forward. He was trying to get a better look at the woman. What did she think of being presented as a gift to the corpulent prince? "It's a common practice in China. Gifting women, that is, and taking multiple wives. I'm told the emperor has a thousand."

Prinny gaped at him. "A thousand?"

The prince stared at the woman who did an acceptable job of not tottering on her bizarre footwear. It was simple fantasy. Prinny couldn't take another wife. It was scandalous enough that he had a mistress everyone knew about. Putting a random Chinese woman into his house could not happen, but it was clearly fun to imagine. Didn't every man have a Chinese princess fantasy?

In the end, though, sanity prevailed. "I cannot accept a woman as a present like she's a horse or something. Good God, can't you explain that to him?"

Max turned to the captain. He didn't know what he could add to the conversation, but he tried, speaking in a low tone. "You know this will not work."

"But it has to, my lord," the captain shot back.

"Why?"

Unfortunately, Prinny was too impatient to wait for an answer. "Never mind, Max. Thank him for his generous offer, but I cannot accept. The Chinese might keep women like stray cats, but the Crown does not. I suggest they take her back to the hippo people—"

"The Wong cohong."

"Whomever. And—"

The ring of steel being pulled from a scabbard cut off the prince's words. Indeed, it silenced everyone after a gasp of alarm. Max tensed. He knew the sound, but it took him a moment to figure out who was drawing a weapon in a royal home.

The nearest palanquin bearer had his sword out and pressed it to the Chinese woman's neck. His arm was extended, and a simple pull would slice her throat open.

Just like everyone else, Max gaped in shock. What had seemed like a fun display of pageantry had abruptly changed in tone. Especially since the two palace guards in the room abruptly lifted their guns and pointed them at the Chinese delegation.

Good God, they couldn't shoot people in here! Half the servants would be caught in the crossfire, not to mention himself and the poor woman.

And when the hell had they gotten guns?

Meanwhile, Prinny was reacting in the way of all sane people. "What the devil is he doing?" he squeaked. "Put those things away!"

The captain abruptly lost his grin as he turned to the official. He spoke in rapid Chinese and pointed to the sword, but none of the Chinese moved, least of all the woman. Damnation, why wasn't she having hysterics? She stood there as if insensate.

Again, the official spoke, his tone and expression appeared regretful. He even bowed before the prince, but when he straightened the sword was still at the woman's throat.

"Well?" the prince demanded.

"He says that she is a gift to you from the great Wong cohong. She is the daughter of the Wong patriarch himself."

"Then why does he want to kill her?" Prinny demanded, his voice ratcheting higher. "We don't kill people in England. Not on my marble floor!"

"She is a gift, you see," the captain said, clearly sweating as he tried to explain. "Her task was to gain your favor. If you reject her, then she has failed. And failure... Well, you can see they don't tolerate it very well."

Prinny stared at the tableau in front of him. "I'm supposed to take her as a mistress or they'll kill her? Right here?"

"It's your favor they want, Your Highness. The emperor has issued an edict restricting the cohongs. There's to be only two merchants, you see, rather than the dozens we have. It's a bad deal for us. We need more cohongs to keep the prices down. But the emperor issued his edict, and now the Wongs are trying to be named one of the two—"

"*Max!*"

Max stepped forward, trying to condense a complicated trade situation into as few words as possible. "A merchant family is trying to bribe you into working exclusively with them."

"By giving me a wife I can't have."

"Yes."

"Are they idiots?"

"They have different customs, Your Royal Highness."

"But why bribe me?" Prinny pushed forward on his seat, his expression tight with annoyance. "It's the Chinese side. I don't get to pick the Wongs or anyone else."

The captain stepped forward, his expression eager. "Very wise, but you could influence things." He raised his palms in a supplicating gesture. "You could say that the British will only trade with the Wongs."

And no doubt the captain would benefit greatly from such a situation. He probably had a favored relationship with the Wongs. He certainly would if he managed this. But Prinny's snort showed he wasn't fooled.

"Why would I do that, Captain? We need more people selling to us, not less."

"They're called cohongs."

"Wong, hong, I don't care." He sent a glare over the entire room. "They should send their bribe to the East India Company! The Crown doesn't handle the trade. You lot do!" Presumably, Prinny meant the sea captains who actually managed the cargo. "Tell him that!"

The captain turned to the official and spoke in halting, awkward Chinese. The official didn't seem to take it well. His skin turned dark, and his mouth tightened in a hard line. When he finally spoke, his words were curt and challenging.

"Um, begging your pardon, but he says, um—"

"What?"

"He said that you're the king."

Prinny pursed his lips. "I'm not the king yet," he groused.

"Er, yes, but he knows you're regent for the king. So…" The captain shrugged. "You're the acting king as it were."

"But I don't control the East India Company. I have nothing to do with that."

That wasn't true. Half the business of the Crown was to manage trade routes. Indeed, one might say that it was nearly the entirety of what they did beyond going to parties and the like. They'd just been less than successful lately with China. Hence the current situation where merchants thought they could grab a piece.

Meanwhile, the captain continued to wheedle. "Begging your pardon, but he says, as king, you can make a decree. You can say, England will trade with the Wong cohong."

"Because they sent me a woman?"

"Yes."

"And they'll kill her if I refuse."

"Yes. On account of you rejecting her."

"Damned barbarians."

The captain nodded. He seemed to be shrinking into himself as he realized that there were guns pointed in his direction, too. "It's the way they do things there. And you can interfere. You just have to make a decree."

"It's not how we do things," Prinny snapped. It was a useless gripe. And damn it, unless something changed quickly, there was about to be a bloodbath right here.

Max didn't think deeply about his next action. He certainly knew it could be dangerous. But no one else—Prinny included—seemed to see a solution and he did. He regretted that he had to do it hungover and unshaven, but some things couldn't be changed.

Max crossed the last of the way around until he was even with the woman. She appeared oddly relaxed for someone about to get her throat cut. He glanced at the captain.

"Tell them I just want to look at the, um, offering. We can't have the prince accepting a false gift, as it were."

"Oh no, my lord. She's pure and everything. Me and my men were kept away from her all during the trip. Most of us weren't even allowed to look on her."

"I'm sure you acted exactly as you ought." He glanced back at room at large, but mostly at the guards. "Everyone stay calm. I'm just having a look. Nothing dangerous at all."

The captain explained things to the Chinese official while making *stay calm* gestures. Max blocked him from his thoughts. He was more interested in the girl and the sword pressed to her throat.

He approached slowly. His gaze took in the extended sword arm. To his dismay, the man holding it appeared rock solid. No wavering. No trembling. One swift pull backwards and the girl would be bleeding on the floor.

Max smiled weakly at the man. There was no reaction. He slowly raised his hands toward the woman's face.

There were a whole lot of beads to either side of the woman's face, and more still dangling in front of her eyes. He gently wended between the dangling things to touch her face. Her eyes were downcast, but at his gentle pressure, her gaze came up to meet his.

Beautiful. Long lashes surrounding dark eyes. The kohl

around them accentuated a shape that drew him in. Her face was powdered white, her lips blood red. It was theatrical paint, as far as he could guess, but she was exotic to his eyes. And he was man enough to like it. Until he looked closer at her eyes.

She was drugged.

Her pupils were dilated, her demeanor completely placid. He supposed if he were going to kill a girl in front of a prince, he'd make sure she was barely lucid. In truth, he was surprised she was able to stand.

"Hullo," he said.

She narrowed her eyes as if sorting her way through the fog. Her gaze sharpened as she took in his features and her nostrils flared as she breathed. Then she swallowed and her eyes widened in surprise.

"Stay still," he said.

He didn't know if she understood English. Probably not, but he hoped his tone would calm her. She had to feel the sword at her throat. Indeed, he felt her tense and her breath catch.

"Don't move," he stressed. "I'll get you free."

Her gaze locked on his and she remained quiet. What discipline! He doubted he could be so calm.

He shifted his stance, keeping his hands near her face. "She is indeed lovely."

"Doesn't mean I can marry her!" Prinny cried, appropriately so.

Which meant it was time for him to act.

Chapter Two

YIHUI EXPECTED TO die today. Or perhaps she hoped for such an end because concubine to a white king was not the life she wanted.

After her failed escape yesterday, she knew Lao Gu would find a way to punish her. She knew, even if they did not, that the English were not as stupid as the Chinese generally believed. Even the English captain had doubts that this scheme would succeed, but Lao Gu was determined to use her to flatter the king. Then he expected to embed himself in the English court as the concubine's master.

She thought it ridiculous, but what did she know of the plans of men? Nothing. And so she had tried to escape last night and failed. Then they had broken her feet, fed her opium for the pain, and she had willingly embraced it.

When a woman had no future, she would take whatever escape she could.

Then an Englishman dared break her from her daze.

His voice caught her first. There was a richness to how he spoke, low and yet still compelling. Like a drumbeat calling her forth. She couldn't understand why she responded. Yet come forth she did, her gaze focusing on his blue eyes.

"Stay still," he said. She understood him perfectly but was not predisposed to any man commanding such a thing. Nevertheless, she obeyed merely to gain time. She had to know what was happening around her.

She replayed in her thoughts what had been no more than a slipping of time in a wash of pain. But now she knew, she felt, and she accepted her coming death. Hadn't that been her preference? And yet the feel of the sword at her throat made the reality of it all too much.

She began to panic.

"Don't move. I'll get you free."

Free? He would free her? No man promised such a thing, but what else could she do? Her captors would not help her. This man with blue eyes spoke with a voice that called her to awareness. What choice did she have but to hope?

But the blade was there pressed against her throat. She dared not breathe, not swallow, not totter on her throbbing feet.

The Englishman turned his face from her, robbing her of the steadiness of his gaze. She wanted to reach for him, but her body was heavy and slow.

"She is indeed lovely," he said.

"Doesn't mean I can marry her!" the English king retorted.

"As to that…" he began, then he shoved her.

His push landed hard, right in the center of her chest. While she flew backwards, he chopped down on the wrist holding the sword. It was hard to see with the beads clattering in front of her eyes, but as soon as she could focus, she saw him standing with the sword against…too many others.

He had gotten her a reprieve, but it was short-lived. The others were coming for him with swords drawn. He adjusted. Indeed, he'd leaped to a position in front of her, half standing over her legs. At his back was the palanquin, so at least there was defense on one side, but it would not last.

Meanwhile, the fat king was clapping his hands as if this were a performance.

"Good show, Max! Good show!"

"I'm afraid I can't maintain it, Your Royal Highness. Not three against one. You'll need to find another solution. Quickly, if possible."

Yihui looked around, trying to find a way to escape. The blue-eyed man had provided the distraction. All she needed to do was crawl away. But she was surrounded on all sides as the ship captain started pleading with the king.

"If you would just accept the present, then that will be all that is required. Bring her into your household for a time. You don't have to marry her. The Wongs have to go back to China eventually."

There was panic in the man's voice and a desperation that Yihui would find satisfying if she had enough attention to spare. As it was, she could only cower behind the blue-eyed man and hope he found an answer.

Meanwhile the English leader grunted in obvious disgust. "As if I didn't already think of that. I can't be seen to take a Chinese woman as my wife by anyone. Even in pretense. It makes me a liar, and I won't have it."

"But Your Royal Highness—"

The English king stood up. Thanks to the raised dais, he towered over the captain and even Yihui could see his irritated expression. "Why can't people think?" He looked at her blue-eyed protector. "Thankfully, we have another solution. Max isn't married. He already offered to help. Got a sword for it and everything. Max, you take the girl, and honor is satisfied. Then it's your fault if the hippo isn't satisfied."

Yihui sorted through the people. The blue-eyed man was named Max. And his ruler had just commanded him to marry her?

"I can't marry her!" Max snapped. "I'm going to marry Lady Kimberly of Tillgrave."

The prince took a step down from the dais. "Have you offered for her yet?"

"No, not exactly, but—"

"It's a royal command. She'll understand."

Like bloody hell she would. He'd already mistreated Kim, starting from when he'd been thirteen and bragging about things he had no business saying. And had never done either. There was no way she'd understand this!

"Besides," continued Prinny, "you've always been interested in China. And someone in your family works with the East India Company, yes?"

Yes. And Max had peppered his uncle with a million questions over the years, but none of what he'd learned would help now. "That doesn't mean—"

"Figure it out." Prinny waved to the captain. "Tell him that his lordship, the Earl of Artanges, future Duke of Fernbury, will accept the girl on my behalf. Honor is satisfied." The leader grinned, then burped. "So that's done," he said as he started to turn away.

"Your Highness!" Max called as the guards began to advance on him again. "This isn't going to work."

"It's an excellent solution. Captain, tell them before Max gets skewered."

Yihui heard the panicked back and forth between the ship captain and Lao Gu. They both realized that there would be no royal favor for either of them unless they could force it on the blue-eyed Max. She wanted to warn him of their plans, but she knew better than to speak up. Her only hope was to remain quiet and slip away while the men argued.

But where could she go? Ru and Yan—the captors she'd nicknamed Pervert and Weed—stood just beyond the circle of Max's reach, each smacking his lips at the possibility of gutting the barbarian. She knew how cruel they were. If she made it to their side, they wouldn't help her. She, on the other hand, would be happy to kill them if she got hold of a weapon.

And then she ran out of time. Lao Gu called off his men while the captain smiled at Max.

"They've accepted your terms, my lord," the captain said with clear relief in his voice. "Provided that they are able to see to the girl's proper accommodations."

The king stopped halfway out the door. "Well of course

they'll be proper. Max, you have enough room in your house, don't you?"

"What? But—"

The English leader was losing patience. His voice was hard. "You don't have to get a priest today. Look into the hippo thing. There's no need to rush until you know it's important." He grinned as if he were a boy playing a mischievous prank. "No one will be upset. It's a royal edict.

"To marry?" Max let his sword arm drop far enough to look less aggressive. Then he addressed the captain. "Is there any way to refuse this gift?"

The man shook his head. "You can, but they'll kill her. It's their way of showing that they mean business. She's a bribe. And if you refuse their terms, they won't think twice about murdering her and me." Yihui knew his worry was about himself. Their whole scheme had been idiocy from the beginning. "It can be a lawless land, my lord. I wouldn't want to make it more dangerous for us."

The king shook his head. "Barbarians! Very well. Max will marry her."

"But—"

The protest was left dangling as the prince departed with a wave, the onlookers chuckled with grand amusement, all while Max slowly lowered his sword. She could see the dawning realization on his face. Was his life a joke to them? Yes, it was. Did his wishes mean nothing? Correct. How would he live now that he knew he was insignificant? As she did, with fury and the sweet dream of revenge.

He looked to her, his eyes wide with shock, and she felt a connection with him. Women, at least, were accustomed to being used in men's games. Obviously, this was new to him, and he seemed like a child whipped for the first time.

The impression didn't last long. A moment later he gathered his dignity. He straightened his shoulders, tightened his jaw, and headed straight to her.

"Are you all right?" he asked. "Do you speak English?"

"Do not touch her!" Pervert barked in Chinese, but his meaning was clear, and Max stilled before reaching her. His blue gaze was shrewd as he took in Pervert's measure. The guard might take great pleasure in harming a weak woman, but he would not fare so well beneath the white man's withering glare. Better yet, if Max were a typical man, he would take out his anger on the guard, and Yihui could not wait to see it.

Except this white man was not typical. He dismissed Pervert with a disdainful curl of his lip as he addressed her. "I should like to take you to my home now," he said, his words slow. "We can sort this whole thing out better there. Do you understand?"

She nodded. Her command of English was adequate before she'd left China. Then she'd spent every moment of the six-month trip learning the language, so now she could understand nearly everything.

She opened her mouth to respond, but Lao Go blustered forward, stepping between her and the Englishman.

"No touch!" he barked in English. "No touch!"

As if he cared anything for her purity. But with his sudden push forward, Pervert was able to bend down and roughly pick her up. He jostled her foot by accident or out of spite, but either way she cried out as white hot pain shot through her entire body.

"Hush, bitch," he growled in her ear. "Or I will drop you on your feet."

The feet that he had taken great pleasure in breaking.

She white-knuckled through the pain, thankful for the remaining bits of opium in her body. Her dream of revenge kept her from screaming again as she envisioned the chi—the energy life force in his body—draining away until he was a wasted hulk.

They knew—because she had told them—that she could do these things. That her grandmother ran a shop selling curses, and she had learned from the woman's knee.

"I will die very soon, Yan," she whispered, giving voice to her fantasy. "My ghost will haunt you. I will eat the chi of your feet and cripple you ten times what you have done to me."

"Shut up," he snapped, his hands tightening painfully on her arm. "Or you will die now."

"Please kill me now, Yan. I do not want to wait for my revenge."

She'd frightened him. His expression wavered as she stared at him. He knew she spoke in earnest. With two broken feet, how was she to survive? Best to die now.

Except Max was suddenly there before them, his expression dark.

"You will take care!" he snapped. He looked like he wanted to grab her out of Pervert's hands. She would have gone willingly, but the ship captain stepped in between.

"She must go back in the palanquin, my lord. How else can she go to your home?"

"Do it carefully," he snapped.

"Of course, my lord. Of course."

The English lord stepped back, his expression wary. Yihui smiled as she meted out a bit more revenge.

"Yes, Yan. Put me in the litter carefully. Otherwise, my ghost will chew on your balls before your feet."

He set her very carefully in the wood cage. She resolved to eat his chi anyway. Every aspect of her body throbbed with pain. So hard not to howl at the knowledge that she might never walk again.

The others continued to talk. She didn't want to hear their babble. Her life was over now that she couldn't run to safety. What did she care what they planned?

But one could only fixate on pain for so long. Despite her will, she heard what they were saying.

"Well, how the devil did they get her here?" demanded the white lord.

"In a donkey cart, my lord. We couldn't very well walk her through the streets of London."

"Like so much cargo?"

"Yes, my lord."

"And you think that's more dignified than sitting in my carriage?"

The captain shrugged. "It's the Chinese way."

It wasn't the Chinese way unless one wanted to make a show of privilege and didn't have a carriage. Did these Englishmen think the streets of Peking were clogged with men carrying palanquins?

"Seems remarkably uncomfortable," the man grumbled.

Lao Gu, the obnoxious sycophant, sniffed his outrage. "She is an exalted lady! It is an insult to treat her as anything less!"

"That's what I'm trying to do!" Max grumbled. "Very well. Put her back on the donkey cart. I'll follow in my carriage. And Chris—" He pointed at another white lord leaning against the wall. He was clearly amused by the whole situation. "Ride ahead and tell my mother what's happened."

The man straightened off the wall with a *must I?* expression, but rather than express it, he bowed with a mocking kind of flourish. "Capital," he drawled. "I shall be in a prime place to see their faces."

"Break it gently," Max warned.

"Not possible," returned his friend with a jaunty wave.

Pain was eating at her concentration. The bearers took their positions and lifted up the small palanquin, dipping and swaying her seat as they adjusted. To think she'd once wished to ride in one. What a foolish child she'd been. She pressed her arms against the cheap wood and prayed they didn't drop her.

They left the palace as they'd come, with unsteady steps and the annoying bang of a gong. Then she was trussed up on the back of a donkey cart to sit in the hot sun while the foul stench of the city made her nauseous. Everywhere there were sound and smells, foreign sights, and the wretched beat of the sun. Once, she would have been fascinated. She would have drunk in every aspect of the world about her as she looked for advantage.

Today, she simply wanted to die. And if possible, to take

these evil, wretched men with her.

She closed her eyes and fantasized about killing them, but something else slipped into her thoughts. She wasn't even sure if it was an opium dream or a memory, but it captured her attention more clearly than violence.

Eyes the color of a blue flycatcher songbird. There was a softness to them, like dark feathers, and yet undeniably blue. She'd never seen eyes that color and they sang through her thoughts, pushing aside other things until everything became soft.

His eyes had brought her out of her daze and forced hope upon her. Even now when she wanted to sink into thoughts of death and revenge, they pushed her to wonder about other possibilities. Would he help her escape? Or was it all yet another mirage?

Chapter Three

E MMALINE'S GAZE WANDERED past the high back on the settee in their drawing room, through the glass panes of the windows, over the iron gate, and out to the street where occasionally someone would pass. A fashionable couple out for a stroll. A dog or a cat chasing something best not examined closely. Something, anything, to change the sameness of her days. Days which were supposed to be filled with delight and excitement at this most wonderful time of her life.

Ha!

"Emmaline! Are you listening to me?"

"Yes, Mama."

"You have no idea what I just said—"

"You are the most brilliant woman in all of London and your compatriots are stupid. They dress badly, set their hair in the wrong way, and say the most idiotic things. If only they would listen to you, then everyone would be much better off, but they are too stupid to know your value." She turned her head until she was looking directly at her mother's pinched, red face. "Did I miss anything?"

"You impertinent wretch!" her mother screeched, tears flooding her eyes. "How could you say such an awful thing to me? After everything I do for you! My every waking thought since the day you were born..."

The words went on. A litany of martyrdom. Emmaline had known she would pay for speaking so bluntly to her mother, but honestly, how many hours of her life had been wasted sitting listening to her mother's endless complaints? She was sick of it, sick of the days of her life ticking away to no point whatsoever. Much more of this and she would take to her paints to draw endless black lines of frustration over the canvas.

This was her third Season in London, and what was she doing? Exactly the same things she'd been doing in the country. Exactly the same thing she'd been doing nearly her entire life when she couldn't escape into her paints. She was sitting and listening to her mother complain.

Her mother was outright sobbing now, fat tears streaming down her face. Bloody hell, if this went on much longer, then the woman would take to her bed and make everyone miserable for the rest of the week. It wouldn't make a difference to Emmaline. She was always miserable as she catered to her mother's every whim, but there was no reason to make the staff suffer.

Still, it was excruciatingly hard to voice the words. She did it anyway. She waited for her mother to draw breath, then rushed her words.

"I'm so sorry, Mama. I'm out of sorts. This is my third Season, and no one has looked twice at me." That wouldn't be enough to ease her mother's mood. She had to go one step further. The words that felt like hot coals in her throat, but she forced them out. "Will you help me, Mama? I have no idea what to do to attract a man!"

That was a lie. She knew exactly how to attract a man. After all, she'd been doing it her entire life. All she had to do was hang on their every word, just like she did with her mother. She listened to the erstwhile suitor, focused on whatever he wanted, and gave it to him. Did he want praise? That was easy. Did he want someone to agree with his opinions and add on to his complaints? She could do that in her sleep. Did he want witty cruelty aimed at someone he considered beneath them? To her personal shame, she had done that as well even to the point of being cruel to a servant here or there. But she'd always felt wretched afterwards and so had sworn off that particular man-enticement.

In truth, she'd sworn off all her false tricks. They were exhausting to maintain, and worse, they were boring. And that's where she was: bored with everyone in her life because they were so self-involved that they never once looked beyond their narrow perspective to see anyone else. To see *her*. And she would not shackle herself to a lifetime of…well, of being married to the worst characteristics of her mother.

Meanwhile, her mother sniffed three times, each louder than the last. It wasn't until the fourth sniff that Emmaline realized she was being inattentive.

"Oh, Mama! Did you want me to get you a fresh handkerchief?"

"Well, seeing as how I've soiled this one and half my dress—"

"I'll fetch one immediately."

She rose from her chair feeling like her shoulders were carrying an anvil apiece. When she finally gained her feet, she looked outside again, wishing for something to look different. Then froze when it did.

Was that Christopher? Arriving on a horse as if he'd rode hells to leather from God only knew where? Good God, the horse was heaving for breath!

"Mama, is that—"

"Whatever has happened? His cravat is a mess! And there are wrinkles all over his clothes."

Yes, Lord Christopher looked done in, though that was how the man usually appeared after a night at Carlton House. She knew because Max and Chris often came here after a night carousing with the prince.

"He hasn't shaved," she muttered. "He usually does that before coming here." She knew that because she never, ever forgot what Lord Christopher looked like. She hadn't since she first met him eight years ago when he had spent a summer with them in the country. And he, the cur, had completely ignored her. She'd run through all her adolescent wiles—twice—to no avail.

Something was different about him today. Certainly, the sun still turned his straw locks gold, his legs still ate up the ground with athletic ease, and his broad shoulders still looked strong enough to hold up the sky. But today there was an extra measure of excitement. A grin—or was it a grimace?—that dismissed the exhaustion from his face and gave his step extra urgency.

Her mother made it to her feet and together they stood at the parlor door. It wouldn't do for them to appear to wait for him, so her mother liked to pretend she was just stepping through the parlor door when the front door opened.

They waited three heartbeats for the knocker to sound. And another three for their butler Chiverton to pull the door open. And then Mama took two delicate steps into the hallway, speaking as if in the middle of a conversation.

"I won't forget how Miss Appleton drank up all the punch last time. Very declasse—" She made a little gasp. "Why Lord Christopher! When did you get here?"

The man bounced toward them, his eyes alight with anticipation. "Good morning, Your Grace!" He kissed her hand with exquisite flourish. "And Lady Emmaline, you are a vision."

He went to kiss her hand, and more fool her, she was already holding it out to him. Why couldn't she stop throwing herself at him? "It's afternoon, Lord Christopher," she said with a dampening air. It was uncalled for, but she was out of sorts today and he was an easy target simply because nothing she did ever touched him.

"Is it?" he drawled. "I hadn't noticed. I was too busy, you see, managing an influx of Chinese into Carlton House."

"Chinese!" her mother gasped, grabbing his lure with both hands. "I must know more!"

"Indeed, you must," he said, "for you are directly involved."

"Me!" Mama cried, as she pressed her hands to her bosom. "But whyever would I—I mean, I don't know—You must explain at once!"

He leaned forward. "I shall explain everything, but first you must direct every spare room in the house to be aired and readied for guests. Every one, including, I suspect the servants' quarters. I fear you shall need every bed. And notify your cook. Once the news gets out, I expect you shall have visitors aplenty and must feed them tarts or tea or something."

"Visitors!" Mama exclaimed with breathy enthusiasm. "But the Season has barely started. We've only attended one ball and—"

"You shall be the talk of the *ton*, I fear. This shall be a nine-day sensation."

"A what!" Alarm filtered into the woman's tone. It was a delight to be a one-day sensation, but nine days? That was a little much.

"You see…" he said with a dramatic pause, but Emmaline had had enough.

"Oh, spit it out!"

He arched a brow in her direction. Her mother did, too, although the woman added a stern admonishment. "Emmaline, what has happened to your manners?"

What had happened? What always happened. Lord Christopher showed up and acted as he always did—like a damned fool—playing into everyone's worst traits. In her mother's case, it was her sense of the dramatic, and so he held them both enthralled as easily as any magician on stage. But if there were things to be done, scandal to be managed, then they needed to know it without all the folderal. And so she would tell him in no uncertain terms. But instead of chastising him, she blurted out her fears.

"Has something happened to Max? Is he hurt?"

"Or is it his reputation?" her mother gasped. "Did he do something outré at Carlton House?"

That fear was almost laughable. What would be considered outrageous at Carlton House? The place was already infamous.

Lord Christopher's expression softened, as did his voice. "Max has certainly stepped in it, but he is not hurt. At least not until

Lady Kimberly finds out."

"Finds out what?" Emmaline demanded.

The horrible man rocked back on his heels, straightened to his full height, and pitched his voice so that everyone—including the servants—would hear every word. "The prince has commanded that Max marry a Chinese concubine!"

Emmaline stared at the man. He didn't appear crazy. Indeed, he appeared exactly like himself with an impish grin and dancing eyes. She knew he was smarter than he appeared, knew that he loved knowing things that others did not, and most important of all, she knew that he was not one to lie or create dramatic falsehoods just for the attention.

Which meant he was not lying about this.

But…what?

And that appeared to be exactly the reaction of every other soul in the room, including her mother.

"I'm sorry?" Mama said.

The servants just gaped.

Lord Christopher drew breath to speak, but Emmaline held up her finger right before his eyes. He focused on her and she matched his bright expression with a narrowed look of her own.

"First, what must we do?"

He took a breath. "I told you. Air the rooms. All of them. Now."

Emmaline nodded, then turned to Chiverton. He was standing there as slack-jawed as everyone else, but he snapped back to himself when she called his name.

"Mr. Chiverton, please do as his lordship suggested. Air the guest room—" This was their London home and so they only had one. "And do we have any extra beds upstairs?"

"One, my lady, for a footman."

"Get that ready as well, if you would."

"Right away, my lady." Then he turned and with an echoing sniff mobilized the staff lingering in the front hall.

Meanwhile, Emmaline turned back to Lord Christopher.

"How much time do we have?"

He shrugged with a rather distracting shift of his broad shoulders. "I have no idea. Max was commanded to bring the girl here and marry her or at least appear to. The snooty official was declaring that he must see that her accommodations are adequate to her status."

Mama pounced on that. "What *is* her status? Is she a princess?"

"Er, no. Merchant's daughter, I believe."

Mama blinked in confusion. "My son—a future duke—has been given a royal command to marry a merchant's daughter?" Her voice rose in outrage with every word.

"Well, I gather he's a rather important merchant. Or at least trying to be."

Mama pressed her handkerchief to her forehead. "I believe I am going to be ill."

"Then you are sharing your son's feelings exactly, I expect. Oh," he said, snapping his fingers as if he just remembered something urgent. "It all has to do with your relation in the East India Company. Max will likely have a great deal of questions about that."

"What relation? No Artanges works. Don't be insulting."

Lord Christopher raised his hands as if to say, I am only repeating what the Regent said to Max. That was a lie. He was doing what he always did. He dropped hints and half thoughts, then waited to see what information would spill out. If nothing did—as in this case—he merely passed it off as something he overheard. If something delightful came out, well then, he was in the perfect position to hear all the juicy details.

In short, it was a marvelous way to garner information while still appearing like a halfwit. Part of Emmaline admired the subtle manipulation, once she had caught on to the way of it. The larger part of her damned the man for the subterfuge. He was not stupid, and he shouldn't work so hard to appear as such.

"Lord Christopher," she said impatiently, "what was going on when you left Carlton House?"

"Oh yes, that's what I was saying. Max was busy trying to get the whole entourage over here. It's quite a crowd and they have to carry her on a palanquin—"

"A what?" Mama asked.

"It's a—"

"A litter, Mama. Like the Romans used to be carried around in," she said as she pushed her parent toward the parlor. "Lord Christopher, you can give more details in the parlor, yes? While I see to some tea for us all."

Christopher turned to her like a dog scenting at treat. "Tea? Perchance—"

"And some strong coffee for you. Plus a few sandwiches. Yes, I know."

"You are an angel, Lady Emmaline."

"False flattery," she drawled. "Exactly what every girl longs to hear."

"Emmaline!" her mother exclaimed. "Such a thing to say!"

Emmaline didn't have to respond because she was already headed for the kitchen. Unfortunately, she wasn't far enough away to miss her mother's next words.

"Don't mind her, Lord Christopher. She's out of sorts because she's afraid she won't take this Season. It's making her irritable, and me miserable!"

Oh good God. She wasn't afraid she wouldn't take. She was afraid there would be no gentleman worth the effort of getting caught. After all, she was the daughter of a duke. She was intelligent, reasonably fair of face, and possessing an acceptable dowry. Several someones would undoubtably try to win her affection, just as they had for the last two Seasons. But not a one was worth a second look.

And true to Mama's perverse nature, she blamed Emmaline for the problem and not every single boring, stupid, and rude gentleman in London.

Emmaline made it to the kitchen only to find it abuzz with

gossip. It was quickly silenced when she appeared, but she knew someone would ask soon enough. Sure enough, their chef Mr. Gaudreau nodded to her.

"Is it true that I shall have to cook for a regiment of Chinese, my lady? If so—"

"I hardly think it will be that many," she said. "But for now, you should expect a few more for dinner."

He frowned at her. "A few more," he deadpanned.

"Yes—"

"How many is a few more?"

"I don't know as yet, but I promise to send word as soon as possible."

"And what shall I feed them, my lady? What do they eat?"

She had no bloody idea. "Whatever we eat, I expect. 'When in Rome' applies to them. They're here unexpectedly, therefore they shall eat what we do. At least until we are told differently."

The man thought about it for a moment, then gave a regal nod. "Very well, my lady."

"Excellent, and in the meantime—"

A young woman's voice interrupted. "Tea service for you and the duchess," said their housekeeper Mrs. Pizzi. "Coffee for Lord Christopher," she said as she added it to the tray. "I'll send sandwiches up directly."

"I am most grateful," Emmaline responded. She waited while a footman gathered up the large tray then began to precede him up the steps. But just as she set her foot on the step, a maid ran down the stairs crying out in excitement and alarm.

"They're 'ere! A whole lot of them Chinese. And ain't it a si— " The girl drew up short when she saw Emmaline. "Oh blimey. Pardon me, milady. I didn't see you there."

No point in chastising the girl for improper decorum. To be honest, everyone was twitching to get upstairs and see the sight. Herself included.

"Well, then," she said as she started up the stairs. "Bring the tea service and sandwiches and let's have a look."

Chapter Four

MAX WAS CLOSE to strangling the lead Chinese official who had finally deigned to introduce himself. He apparently wanted to be called Wong Mandarin which was not his name but some sort of title that meant big man or important man. Most likely the latter because the mandarin certainly enjoyed his consequence. Even Max's father—the most pompous duke imaginable—rarely wanted such deference.

But until Max knew the exact lay of the land, it did little harm to play into the obnoxious man's ego. No matter how much it irritated Max.

Once Chris had departed, Max focused on moving everyone to his home in Grosvenor Square. For the mandarin and the captain who acted as translator, nothing but the plushest carriage would do. The woman, however, had her litter awkwardly raised onto a donkey cart and unceremoniously left there, She looked like an elaborately dressed monkey in a cage. Or a prisoner on her way to the Tyburn gallows.

"I insist she sit inside the carriage with us," he told the captain. "That cannot be comfortable for her." She'd be breathing the London dust without even a cushion to ease the jolts.

"Aw milord, that's kind of you to think that," the captain said, "but Chinese women are kept separate, you see. It wouldn't be right for her to sit with us in the carriage—"

"Her own carriage, then—"

The mandarin interrupted with a quick flurry of Chinese and

some imperious pointing. Apparently, the man wanted to get on their way. Max guessed he was getting hot under his heavy robes and wished to sit in the dark carriage. And no thought whatsoever to the girl already wilting up there as she slumped in her seat.

"She cannot stay up there—" he began, but the captain shook his head.

"Best not to argue, milord. They're particular about their ways and easy to insult. She's used to this, I'm sure. Don't give it any more thought."

Impossible. He quickly leaned into his carriage and grabbed two of the squabs. Let the mandarin sit on hard wood. The donkey cart was wide enough for Max to leap up into, and so he did. Then he pulled open the palanquin door and offered the woman a cushion.

Her eyes widened at his presence, and then she nodded as she understood his offer. But it took her forever to stand up, her knuckles turning white as she gripped the hard wood to push herself upright onto unsteady feet.

Good lord, how much opiate had she eaten? She could barely stand.

He quickly set a cushion, then helped her down. He didn't want to shut the door on the small palanquin but was afraid she'd tumble out if he didn't. Then once she was situated, he put the second cushion beside the palanquin. It was uncomfortably hot with the sun beating down, but he wasn't going to let everyone in London think she was a prisoner or a carnival show. If he, as an earl and a future duke, sat beside her, then that would shield her from gossip. Perhaps.

Or he was a complete fool because no matter what he did, the tale would go through London like lightning, and then out to the rest of England.

Meanwhile, the captain watched with his jaw agape. "My lord!" he finally cried. "What are you doing?"

"I'm sitting up here with my guest." He could not force himself to say "fiancée."

"But you'll be—"

"If you are about to suggest that I would see to my comfort over my guest's, then you are grossly mistaken." He pinned the mandarin with a heavy stare. "And anyone who does otherwise with the beautiful, honorable, and exalted daughter of the great Wong patriarch should be severely disciplined."

Naturally the captain flushed a dark red. "Of course," he said. "Most appropriate."

"I suggest you translate that exactly to the mandarin," he said. He didn't give the man a chance to respond but looked back to the row of hackneys brought in to carry the Chinese guardsmen. They had all piled in as soon as possible, probably to avoid being ordered to carry the litter again. Everything looked ready behind him, so he looked ahead to his coachman.

"As soon as you're ready, Mr. Jenkins."

He had the pleasure of seeing the mandarin, his face flushed with embarrassment, scramble into the carriage before it departed without him. The captain jumped in as well, and the ridiculous parade began.

And then, finally, he had the opportunity to speak privately with the woman. First things first.

"Hullo. My name is Max. Do you speak English?"

She nodded and pressed a hand to her chest. "Yihui."

Excellent! "A pleasure to meet you, Yihui," he said formally. And then his words failed him. How exactly was he to proceed? "Do you understand what has happened?"

She opened her mouth to answer, and then the cart lurched beneath their feet. They both braced themselves, and Max silently prayed they'd stay upright. "Damned streets are filled with ruts," he muttered. Then he flashed her a rueful smile. "This is not the best way to see my country."

It was hard to tell with the white rice paint on her face, but he thought she had gone pale. Her hands were still braced on the litter, her knuckles showing white as she breathed with steady control.

"Are you hurt?"

Her eyes opened slowly and she nodded. Good God, what he had originally thought was the dull affect of opium was actually pain.

"Where are you hurt? What did they do?"

"My feet," she said. "Broken."

"They broke your feet? Why?" He couldn't see her feet now. He could only remember her high sandals, but he had no reason to doubt her.

"Last night. I tried to escape."

"So you are a prisoner."

"Lao Gu and the captain. Liars. They kept most of the bribe for themselves."

He couldn't care less about the silk or spices. "Are you the daughter of—"

"No. No." She was speaking more clearly now, her voice strong and steady. "My father sold me to the Wong patriarch to pay his debts." She leaned forward, gripping the edges of the palanquin window as she pleaded with him. "Do not let them near me. They will kill me—"

"You are safe with me."

"You cannot trust what they say!"

Obviously, but there were still diplomatic issues to sort out. He couldn't just throw them into the street on her word alone. He didn't know how much official standing they had with the Chinese government.

"I will not trust them—"

"You cannot let them know what I told you. You cannot—"

Another rut had her gripping the litter again, and he dared cover her small hand with his own as the donkey cart steadied.

"You are safe with me," he said. "I promise."

She looked at him and he read a mix of hope and desperation in her eyes. What could she have endured during the six-month voyage to England? The possibilities were as varied as they were horrifying.

"How did you learn English?" he asked.

"I knew some before. Then I practiced on the boat." She lifted her chin as if daring him to doubt it. "I am very smart."

"I can see that." So many questions he wanted to ask. Who was she really, what had her life been like? But they were nearing his home. Their opportunity for private conversation would soon end. He had to suppress his curiosity in favor of learning the most pressing matters. "What do they want?"

"Lao Gu convinced the Wong patriarch that this is the best way to win favor with the English king. He expects to live expensively as my protector." The venom with which she said "protector" was obvious. "He will rob you in every way."

"And the captain?"

"He has favored trade status with the Wongs. If the bribe works, he will have much of the silk trade from China."

"But he's English. He knows Prinny can't take a wife."

"He knows England wants to please China."

It was true. The Chinese had no interest in English goods. The market for Chinoiserie, however, was as strong as ever. If it weren't for the opium, the Chinese would shut their borders to the English completely. Indeed, they had tried to do it several times already.

Meanwhile Yihui pressed forward. "He will tell you to write a good letter to the Hoppo. Agree, then write one saying terrible things. Say they beat women and kill children for sport. Tell them—"

"Is any of that true?"

She looked away, but her chin didn't lower. "They bought me. They broke my feet!" Her gaze went to his. "There was another girl, too. She died, and they threw her overboard!"

"Did they kill her?"

She shook her head. "Fever. It is how I was allowed out. I knew medicines to treat the sick."

"You know medicines?"

Her head snapped up. "I know very many medicines. I was

important back home! Many patients!"

He doubted that. Important people weren't sold by their fathers to cover debts. But he didn't argue with her. Now was not the time to discuss her skills. They were arriving at his home, and he would need to manage a diplomatic incident without giving his mother a heart attack.

Already people were lined up on the street, watching their very strange procession. God, what a ridiculous spectacle. His father was going to be furious. As a duke and the leader of the conservatives, his father despised anything that grabbed popular attention, especially if it ridiculed their family. Max shuddered, imagining the cartoons already being drawn about this. But that was a problem for later. Right now, Max had to focus on Yihui and how to help her.

He studied her, his thoughts spinning as he took in her face and form. She wore a great deal of make-up, all of it very dramatic. He couldn't deny how very interesting that made her appear. White skin, red lips, dark eyelashes swept up into her black hair.

"I won't anything happen to you," he vowed.

"*Shi shi*," she said. "Thank you."

Pride surged in his chest, an irrational protectiveness welling through him. She was a foreign woman offered as a bribe and then threatened by her captors, and yet she had the wherewithal to hold her dignity around her like a shroud. Good lord, it made him feel like a knight of old, pledging service to a captured queen. Especially when she smiled at him, hope sparking in her glorious eyes.

Then there was no more time as they climbed Grosvenor Street toward the ducal residence. He gave her an encouraging smile, then hopped out of the donkey cart before the thing even stopped. He quickly crossed to the base of the walkway, then directed everyone as they arrived. The mandarin and the captain came out first. He handed them off to his butler, directing Chiverton to set them in the parlor.

The donkey cart stopped next, and he directed the guards to lift up the litter and carry her into the house.

"She's the honored guest," he told Chiverton. "See that she is treated as such." Then he glared at the men awkwardly maneuvering the palanquin. "The guards, however, leave the second she's set down. Have the captain instruct them. They must fetch her luggage, but they are not to come inside the house again. Get some footmen to keep them out if you have to."

"I understand, my lord," Chiverton intoned, and Max had absolute faith that it would be done. He couldn't get rid of the mandarin or the captain—yet—but the guards were another matter. He would not be polite to people who had just moments ago threatened her life, unless, of course, international relations required such a sacrifice. But until he was so instructed, he would banish them from her presence with the quickest dispatch. This had the added benefit that if he didn't see them, he couldn't order them arrested and hanged for drawing weapons in the palace.

Once that was accomplished, he supervised the awkward lifting and carrying of the palanquin inside. The guards seemed to be getting better at it. There were no terrifying dips and sways. Max never had to rush forward to save her, though he twitched with the need.

Eventually, they made it inside and he turned his attention to the gong bearer and another guard who made to enter his home as if they belonged there. He blocked their entrance by the simple act of standing in the middle of the walkway and glaring them back. And he had the pleasure of hearing the other guards grumble as Chiverton got them out of the home. A few minutes more glaring and pointing saw the extraneous souls riding away in hackneys.

Good riddance.

"Ah-hem."

Max winced. That sound was his mother waiting to address him. And just how was he to explain that he'd finally become engaged? She'd been planning his wedding to Lady Kimberly since they'd been betrothed when he was four.

"Max, dear," she called.

"Yes, Mother?" he said as he turned to address her.

She stood in the doorway awaiting his attention with all the regal aplomb of a duchess. Elegant as usual, but her flushed cheeks and pursed lips showed her displeasure. Chris stood a half-step behind her, his grin showing unseemly delight at this fiasco. Far be it for the man to be useful and entertain the mandarin. Christopher would always be where the action was, a quiet observer who would remember every salacious detail. His memory was uncannily exact in such things.

"Max, why is there a cage in the middle of my hall? The servants are tripping over the thing."

He frowned. "Well, get it out of the way. Put it in the stable."

Her brows rose. "With the girl inside?"

It took him a moment to realize that no one had thought to let Yihui out of the palanquin. That couldn't possibly be true. Chiverton was not that much of an idiot. But Chris's nod told him that it was true.

Cursing under his breath, Max pushed his way into the house. Damn it, there she sat—upright, thank God—in the middle of the foyer. Was this normal? Did Chinese women just sit in hallways until they were needed?

"Did no one help her to the parlor?" he demanded, rounding on their butler. "Good God, Chiverton, I would think you could manage the basics of—"

"They said she had to be carried! Said she can't walk. And I…" He gestured helplessly. "They said it must be their people or no one. My lord, I don't know anything about greeting a Chinese princess!"

She wasn't a princess, but he didn't argue. She had the entourage of one and his normally unflappable butler appeared rather…er…flapped.

"Max—" his mother began. "Lord Christopher has been telling me the most extraordinary tale."

"It's all true," he said. Chris was selective about the details he shared, but they were always accurate. Max stepped past his mother and went to the front of the palanquin.

No one had even opened the door.

With a polite smile, he opened the door and extended a hand to her. "Miss Wong, if you would accompany me to the parlor, I believe some refreshments are on their way."

Her gaze hopped between him and the Chinese official. She was clearly terrified and working hard to contain it. "You're safe. I swear," he said in an undertone.

He saw relief and terror fighting in her eyes, but it was completely locked down when the captain spoke.

"She's not coming out because she's not allowed to walk. Not more than a step or two. It's their custom."

Or maybe it's because her feet were broken. He was about to turn on the bastard and speak his mind, when she grasped his hand. "Not yet," she pleaded. "They fight. Swords."

He winced. He'd gotten rid of all the guards, but the captain still had his sword and who knew what the mandarin hid beneath his robes. Even if Max could defend himself—maybe—his mother and sister were here, not to mention a score of servants. This was not the place for a violent altercation. And so he nodded to Yihui, swallowing down his fury until a more practical time.

He turned back to the captain. "If she cannot walk, then how is she supposed to function?"

"Their ladies—the highborn ones—got to be carried. That's why they bring all those guards. They do the lifting and hauling, so to speak."

"I sent them back to your boat to get her luggage."

"Aye, my lord. I saw that."

But he hadn't seen fit to explain before? "Captain, you are beginning to irritate me. I suggest you fix that immediately."

The man straightened in outrage, but if he thought to strut about in a ducal household just because he spoke Chinese, then he was sorely mistaken. Especially since Max knew that Yihui spoke English.

Meanwhile, he solved the problem. No one could object to her fiancé carrying her, and so he leaned down and picked her up. It was awkward, to be sure. The palanquin was so small he could barely fit his shoulders in it. But she helped him with a surprisingly strong grip. She took hold of his shoulders and settled into his arms.

His first impression was that there was a solidness to her belied by her small stature. She was slender for a woman, but he felt muscles flex powerfully beneath the fabric as she pulled herself upright in his grip. And damn those clacking beads that dangled between their faces.

And surprise of surprise, her breath was sweet. That was a rarity even among the elite.

Crossing into the parlor, he set her carefully on a cushioned wingback chair. It was his father's favorite seat, but Max felt it appropriate for her as the seat of honor. The thing made her appear very small, but she sat tall. And when he offered her tea, she took it with small, unsteady hands.

Was it the drugs or terror? Either way, he had to get her out of here as soon as possible.

"Well," said his mother as she entered the parlor, "now that everyone is comfortable…"

Max looked up to his mother. He hadn't been seated, so he had no need to rise. The captain, of course, understood English custom, so he leapt immediately to his feet. The mandarin, however, did not know he was supposed to stand at the entrance of a lady. The obnoxious man continued to drink his tea without even looking up.

It was made even worse when his sister entered the room. Her expression was genial. Emmaline was always kind, but her eyes widened at the mandarin's obvious rudeness. Meanwhile, the captain grew uncomfortable in the growing silence.

"Begging your pardon, Your Grace, but he doesn't understand. As a general rule, the Chinese women serve. The men don't stand."

"Really?" his mother responded, her tone icy. "And if he were meeting with the Empress of China?"

The captain's eyes widened in horror. "He won't kowtow to you, Your Grace. Not outside of China."

"I gather kowtowing is some sort of polite behavior? A bow of sort?"

"Yes, Your Grace. Only it's done on the knees."

"I see. But he won't do it to me because…?"

"You're not the Empress of China."

"And because he doesn't respect our customs or believe that he must perform any type of courtesy to me. Correct me if I'm wrong, doesn't he serve a merchant?"

"Er, yes, Your Grace. The Wong cohong—"

"And does he carry a title?"

"Not as you mean, Your Grace."

She nodded slowly. The mandarin at last sensed that he was the topic of conversation. He turned his head slowly, a single eyebrow lifted in query. Max's mother returned it with one of her own. And when she spoke, her words were chilly.

"Why is he here then?"

The captain shifted awkwardly on his feet. "I believe he must see—"

"Don't guess. Ask him."

"Er, yes." The man turned to the mandarin and spoke quickly—rather urgently, in fact—to the mandarin. The man responded, his tone as cool as the duchess's, and Max felt his lips curve in a smile. There was nothing more entertaining than watching his mother put down a man who richly deserved it.

Ignorant of what was coming, the mandarin gracefully made it to his feet—not to bow, but to nod imperiously to the duchess as if directing a servant. Then he spoke in clear tones which made the captain pale in horror. There was more conversation, but the mandarin didn't repeat himself except to stare coldly around him as if the room was no more acceptable to him than a pigsty.

Given that his mother had decorated this room herself, the man couldn't have been more insulting if he tried.

"Begging your pardon, Your Grace, but the mandarin says, um, he has indicated…"

"Do tell me his exact words."

"Er, he, um, he said that he will inspect the miss's room now. Um, to see that it is acceptable."

"Of course," his mother said with an arched brow. "And what else?"

"Er—"

"Try to be exact."

"Exactly? Well, he said that his accommodations had best be of the finest quality or he shall report the insult. That, um, the Wong cohong will not share commerce with any country that gives him insult."

Max wasn't surprised at the man's nerve. He clearly had a backwards sort of logic that offered a bribe at the same moment he demanded overwhelming deference. This nuance wasn't lost on his mother either.

"Max," she drawled, "have we, as a family, ever heard of the Wong cohong before today?"

"No, Mother."

"And had the prince heard of them?"

"He did not appear to."

"Very well." She gestured to their butler. "Chiverton, please show the mandarin to his accommodations—"

"Yes, Your Gr—"

"—in the stable loft. I'm sure a bed could be made for him there, yes?"

Chiverton didn't so much as blink. Indeed, he bowed and intoned, "Yes, Your Grace."

It was the captain who choked, though Max thought there was a gleam of appreciation in the man's eyes. Nevertheless, the captain was forced to try and moderate the insult. Max didn't care to tell him that any objections would fall on deaf ears.

"Er, Your Grace, he is tasked with seeing that the lady, um, performs appropriate to her, um, role, so to speak."

"Her role?"

"Her wedding, Your Grace. He can't go home until he sees that. And he'll carry tales. England enjoys good commerce with them. Silks, Your Grace. Some that, uh. Well, the tea and spices are top notch..." His voice trailed away beneath her withering stare.

"Do you know, Emmaline," his mother began.

"What, Mama?"

"I find I prefer good English cotton. So much more comfortable. I believe I shall make it popular." Her gaze skipped over the mandarin to the wingback chair. "Max, do help Miss Wong to the guest bedroom. I believe she would prefer to rest."

The captain shifted uncomfortably. "He, um, will want to inspect her room. So he can report back."

The duchess waved an airy hand. "By all means. Show him her bedroom and then show him his." And with that, she departed the parlor.

Max did his best to hide his grin. He was well aware that he might regret his mother's impolitic reaction. After all, Prinny had given tacit support to the man. The prince might view an insult to the mandarin as an insult to the Crown. But for the moment, Max appreciated his mother's absolute confidence in the management of her household.

And so he was smiling as he once again scooped up Miss Wong. She hissed as if in pain, but the sound was quickly silenced as she pressed her face—clacking beads and all—into his shoulder. In return, he settled her more securely against him and found she fit nicely in his arms. Indeed, holding her like this was unexpectedly delightful.

Sadly, there was no time to revel in the feelings as—for the second time that day—he found himself in a strange procession. Chiverton led the way, walking as if he were in Windsor Castle. Max came next, careful not to step on the trailing swaths of Miss

Wong's dress. His sister was behind him, gesturing to the mandarin that he should follow her. He did with his nose lifted into the air. Then behind them all trailed the captain, with every appearance of wanting to escape before he had to explain about the stable.

The bedroom was freshly cleaned and aired, the fabrics done in soft yellows, and the bed was large enough to please a royal. Max set Yihui down carefully in a chair by the window and heard her sigh as her feet stretched out beneath her gown.

He did a doubletake at the sight.

Her feet were so tiny! They appeared barely the size of his fist, tightened down by silk ribbons that seemed strained to near bursting. The outline was of a strange, blunted shape, and he couldn't tell if it were the ribbons or something else that created that impression. Had her feet been snapped in half? Horror choked him.

She must have seen him looking as she twitched her skirts down, her eyes canted away in embarrassment. Then before he could say anything, the mandarin bustled in, shouting as he stepped in front of Miss Wong.

Max reared back, if only to give space between him and the man's tobacco-laden breath. Then the officious man waggled a finger before Max's eyes.

The captain rushed forward. "Begging your pardon, but he says you cannot see before the wedding. It is improper."

"To see what? She is fully clothed."

"Her feet, milord. They do put a great deal of stock in feet."

Then they shouldn't have broken them. Max folded his arms to keep himself from strangling the man. He had to get these people out of here so he could order a doctor. But his uncertain diplomatic position kept him silent. As well as the captain's sword. Though he did glance at Emma.

"I think you and Mother should stay back," he said in an undertone. Emma nodded her understanding, and she and his mother stepped away. Then he heard Yihui's breath increase in fear. Odd that he could be so attuned to her.

"I won't leave you," he said quietly, and he had the satisfaction of hearing her exhale in relief.

Meanwhile, the mandarin made a show of inspecting every corner of the bedroom. He opened the wardrobe and sniffed in disdain at the modest robe and slippers set there for guests. He tested the strength of the window and even looked under the bed as if for rodents. And every moment that he spent there increased Max's desire to wring the man's neck.

Eventually the mandarin finished. Speaking through the captain, he declared the room adequate. He agreed to be escorted to his accommodations, and Max was happy to follow. He couldn't wait to see the man's reaction when he was escorted to the stable. Even Chiverton displayed an expectant smile.

He waited to leave, though, making sure everyone departed. Then he turned to her. "Shall I carry you to the bed?" he asked. "Should I call for a doctor?"

She looked up and he thought her lips curved in a smile. Maybe. He really wished she'd take off those damn beads.

"No. Thank you." Then she glanced at the door. "No one will come? I will be alone?"

"No one." He smiled reassuringly, inordinately pleased that they could communicate. "I will return soon so we may speak." And with that, he bowed deeply and stepped out of the room, shutting the door behind him.

Now on to dealing with the mandarin.

He rushed down the hallway, picking up the tail end of the procession that was now descending the stairs. He got halfway before he pulled up short.

There, framed in the doorway, stood a very statuesque, very tight-lipped Lady Kimberly. His other fiancée.

Damnation. He should have taken the time to shave.

Chapter Five

MAX FELT HIS entire body tighten with guilt. In one flash, he saw the ridiculous display that surrounded him and knew that he had done the one thing that he'd sworn to never do again. He'd dragged Lady Kimberly into a scandal.

He watched her green eyes widen as she took in her surroundings, then saw her skin pale to a grim shade of gray. She was a private, quiet woman, and whatever gossip she'd heard that brought her to his door was now confirmed by the parade of people coming down the stairs straight at her.

And then, true to her aristocratic bearing, she straightened her shoulders, lifted her chin, and arched a single brow in his direction. It both demanded an audience and threw the coming debacle at his feet.

Hell.

"Good afternoon, Max," she said in cool tones as he made the main floor. "I apologize for not sending word earlier. I wondered if I could have a moment of your time."

He nodded, his gaze going to the mandarin who appeared confused. The man was clearly torn between giving her a respectful bow and demanding she curtsy to him. Worse, the foyer was choked with servants standing around gaping. Chiverton was clearly not in control of the staff.

Meanwhile, Lady Kimberly, pitched her voice a bit louder. "My lord, you have not introduced me to your guest."

He winced. He should not need to be reminded. He'd been

drilled in proper behavior since he was a child, just as she had. It had been repeated ad nauseum for exactly this kind of moment when one was so confused as to become lost in the weeds. Proper etiquette was a godsend, and she was reminding him of it as any future duchess ought.

It was still immensely aggravating.

He straightened, then strode forward. Taking her hand, he bowed before her. "Lady Kimberly. I'm so pleased to see you."

A lie, of course, but a polite one and therefore forgiven. She smiled as she dipped into a shallow curtsy. Then he turned to gesture to the mandarin.

"Pray allow me to introduce the Wong Mandarin. He has been charged with the care of a lady who is resting upstairs. Prinny himself asked me to see to her comfort."

Thanks to the captain's hurried communication in Chinese, the mandarin slammed his fist into his palm and bowed before her. Obviously, this was a Chinese greeting, and Kimberly curtsied in response.

"I am pleased to make your acquaintance, sir," she said. Then everyone waited as the captain translated.

The mandarin responded in Chinese with a bold look in Kimberly's direction. He even held out his hand as if he were the king himself asking her to walk with him.

And that raised Max's hackles.

"What, exactly, did he just say?" he demanded.

The captain blushed. "Er, well, he asks if the lady is to accompany him to his chamber. B-begging your pardon, my lady," the man stammered. "It's common in his country to, um, reward service and, um, please guests in very specific ways. Not every family, of course, but the Wongs have become renown for such…um, things. It's what he expects. He assumes it's you or at least you're the one who will acquire—"

Max held up his hand, the gesture nearly violent. "Please remind him that he is in England now, and such *assumptions* are impertinent." He glanced at Kimberly. "I think the library would be the perfect place for our conversation." He glanced at the nearest footman. "See that tea is brought there directly."

Then he held out his arm and escorted her there. Recalled to his duty, Chiverton managed to rush ahead to open the library door. And then, as was appropriate, he left the door ajar. They weren't officially engaged, so propriety demanded a chaperone or at least an open door. Her maid followed at a respectful distance and took a seat in the hall chair set for exactly this situation.

Then he watched as Kimberly took a deep breath and settled herself on the settee. He noted the stains on her skirt and the faint whiff of dog that surrounded her. Her greatest love was for the canines in her life. Indeed, her fascination had brought her a medical understanding far superior to many veterinarians.

"Whose animal is ill?" he asked. The aristocracy often sought out her advice with their sick dogs.

"My cousin's. Oscar is at the end of his life, and Mary Ann is beside herself."

He nodded. "I'm sorry. It's always hard to see a beloved pet pass."

She took his sympathy with a grateful nod but then went straight to the point. "Out with it, Max. Quickly, please. Before half the *ton* finds an excuse to visit."

"I think they're already outside," he groused. In their short moments in the hall, he'd glimpsed no less than a dozen people "strolling" by.

She nodded but didn't comment. She would not be put off the mark with a delaying tactic. And neither could he soften the coming blow.

"Prinny has commanded me to marry a Chinese bribe. Some diplomatic thing that I mean to ferret out." He quirked a brow at her. "He said you'd understand."

Predictably, she did not.

"Damn it all, Max, I told you this would happen."

He threw up his hands, and his voice was heavy with sarcasm. "You told me that I would be forced to marry a Chinese bribe?"

She pushed to her feet, her fury making her twitch as she paced tight circles about the room. "I told you that carousing with the prince would land you in trouble. When Prinny drinks, he does all manner of erratic things."

"He wasn't drinking yet!"

"Then he had the blue devils, just as you do now." She stomped forward until she met him nose to chin. "I told you, Max. I *told* you that you could not embroil me in scandal again. You made me into a loose, fat girl before—"

"That was years ago! I was thirteen and an idiot."

"And yet the taint remains years later. I cannot weather another scandal."

"You exaggerate."

"Do I?" She dropped her hands on her hips. "Do I understand that you are now royally engaged to a Chinese bride?"

"She's a *bribe,* and I don't yet know if this is a ruse. It could be over the minute we get rid of the mandarin, but even so, I don't like the appearance of accepting a bribe." He shook his head. "Kimberly, they were going to kill her right before our eyes—"

"*Max!*"

"What?"

"We are not discussing *how this happened.* I need to know how to *manage it* before—"

The knocker sounded loud enough to reverberate back here in the library. The *ton* was arriving. They both stared at the door then back at each other.

"I need a plan of action," she said.

"What plan?" he retorted. "I am to see the woman settled and get rid of the man. After that—"

Emmaline stuck her head into the library door. "Keep your voices down!" she hissed. Then she sent an apologetic look at Kimberly. "I am so sorry," she said. "I cannot imagine how difficult this must be for you."

Max snorted. "For her? I'm the one who is supposed to marry

a stranger!"

"You're an idiot," Emmaline said to her brother before she turned back to Kimberly. "I'll keep the biddies away for as long as I can. Mother will help after her restorative. You know how much she enjoys her upset nerves. She'll likely make a dramatic entrance in twenty minutes or so. But after that—"

"I will endeavor to be quick," Kimberly answered. "Thank you." Then she turned to face Max. "Is it true? She's an opium eater?"

He jolted. "Where did you hear that?"

She threw up her hands. "It's what is said about all the Chinese."

He winced. It could be true. Or more likely, Yihui was fighting horrendous pain from broken feet and may or may not have had opium to fight the agony. "I have only just met her. She told me they broke her feet."

Kimberly appeared to absorb that information with a frown. "Have you sent for a doctor?"

"I have to get rid of the mandarin first. Otherwise, he'll interfere with everything."

She nodded. "Did you truly sit on a donkey cart with her?"

"I couldn't very well leave her up there alone. She looked like she was headed for Tyburn."

"Of course not," she muttered, and he couldn't tell if she was being sarcastic or genuine. "Exactly how direct was Prinny's command?"

"Explicit."

"And did he mean it?"

Max shrugged. "Maybe. I may be able to talk him out of it once I understand the particulars." He rubbed his chin. "I need to speak with Lord Benedict. He'll know the details of our relationship with China."

Benedict was high up in the Foreign Office and Max's unofficial superior. If anyone could help him out of this quagmire, it would be Benedict.

Meanwhile, Kimberly dismissed Lord Benedict with a wave of her hand. She'd never cared about the business of nations.

"What do you want me to do?" she asked.

He stared at her. "Kimberly, I don't know that there's anything to do. I've sent an urgent message to Lord Benedict. I'm doing my best to get rid of that toady mandarin. Yihui is upstairs alone as she wanted—"

Kimberly rolled her eyes. "Not that! The way I see it, I can either wait patiently by your side playing the wilting Ophelia until I drown myself for lack of attention—"

"Wilting what?"

"—or I can throw you over in a fit of pique and be done with you all together."

She visibly shuddered at her words. They both knew how much she despised the social whirl. Their engagement had never been announced, and yet everyone had expected it since they were both small children. If she were to publicly cast him aside, then she'd have to enter the Season for real. She'd have to go to parties and look for a suitable husband, all at an age when most of her peers were at home with their second or third child.

"Kimberly, don't be hasty. Let it wait for a few days."

She glared at him. "Do you understand how long I have been waiting? You should have proposed years ago."

He dropped his hands on his hips. "You know why I didn't. Lord Castlereagh himself asked me to stay in Prinny's inner circle. England needed someone with a level head to keep Prinny from his worst excesses."

"I would never stop you from going to Carlton House!"

"Prinny prefers to entertain with bachelors, not dull men with leg-shackles on them." He dropped his weight onto the desk. "Those are his words, not mine."

"And now you are engaged to a Chinese opium eater."

"That wasn't my fault!"

"But it was predictable. This or some other disaster, and you know it."

He pressed his lips together. He knew it was the truth. She'd warned him of it three years ago when he'd told of her Castlereagh's request. One could not remain in Prinny's intimate orbit without getting pulled into one scrape or another. Naturally, as a future duke, he would be forgiven whatever mishaps befell him, but she was in a more precarious position. As the daughter of an earl, she was an acceptable wife to him, but her title had neither prestige nor great wealth. Given that she was not considered a *warm* person like his sister, scandal would inevitably slide off of him then splat on top of her.

It wasn't fair, but it was the truth of their positions. As was the fact that he should have proposed to her years ago. Indeed, if he had been a "proper son," as his mother put it, they'd be married and have a couple heirs already in the nursery. It was only his promise to Lord Castlereagh that had kept him from doing his duty by her. They'd begged him to act as a brake to Prinny's impulsive behavior. And in order to do that, he'd had to remain a bachelor.

But now he had to fulfill his promise to her. It was the only honorable thing to do. So he pushed off the desk to cross back to her. He gathered her hand in his and squeezed her fingers.

"Kimberly, I have every intention of fulfilling my promise to you."

She gripped him back. "Max, I am five and twenty. That is much too old to be searching for a husband. If not for our understanding, I would already be called an ape leader."

"I will call out any man who dares utter such a thing."

She rolled her eyes. "It's not the men who say it. Or at least not until their mothers and sisters say it first."

"A few more days," he pleaded. "I shall resolve everything and then we can announce our engagement." He flashed her a grin. "In this, *Prinny* will have to understand."

They both knew that Prinny understood only what he felt like understanding, and Max could no more force the royal than he could sprout wings and fly. The real question was whether

Max would marry her anyway despite royal displeasure.

"I have been faithful to you, Max," she said firmly. "I have done as you and your parents asked. I have stood by you when your friends called me fat—"

"I didn't mean—"

"For it to happen," she finished for him.

What he'd actually said—and his friends had repeated—was that her breasts were as plump as bowls of treacle and just as tasty. He'd been thirteen, and boys tended to say such things. But what had been a youthful boast by him had tainted her as a fat, loose girl who was not fit to be a duchess. He'd been an idiot, and he'd apologized profusely for his stupidity. At the time, she'd forgiven him, and yet she still brought it up whenever she was angry at him.

"But it did happen, Max, and I forgave you. I refused good marriage offers from men who would have given me a fine life."

"You will be my duchess—"

"And I have waited while you dance upon the prince and do things that you should have outgrown by the time you began shaving." She didn't say it, but her gaze went to his unshaven cheeks.

"Kimberly, I am playacting. If you could know what excesses I have prevented—"

"None of much importance, I wager," she snapped. "If it were not you, it would be someone else. The prince is not without wit or discretion of his own. He uses you as an excuse to stop his wildest impulses."

Max shook his head. "You have no understanding of what it means to keep Prinny happy."

"I am not being unreasonable," she countered.

"Neither am I! I did not expect to be saddled with a Chinese girl." And now they were simply repeating themselves.

"Max—"

Her words were cut off as a roar sounded throughout the whole house. It was the mandarin's voice, and he was clearly furious.

"Damn it," Max cursed. "I had meant to stop him in the stable, not bring it back here."

They listened as feet thudded up the stairs. The bastard must have escaped Chiverton and was now running up to Yihui's room.

"Go," she said, though he was already headed out the door. "I'll put on my Ophelia face and sit in wan, devoted, patience."

This time Max did roll his eyes. "I am not Hamlet!" he snapped. And he was grateful that she didn't remark at how very Hamlet-like that outburst was.

Chapter Six

YIHUI SAT IN a chair, her head pressed against the window and her feet throbbing in agony. She wanted to lie on the bed but couldn't move across the room to accomplish it. They'd broken her feet and now how was she going to survive?

Her eyes drifted closed, but she was too frightened to rest. Her ears were attuned to the noises in this house, to the sound of restless feet, to anything that might signal danger. She heard nothing alarming, and for that, she was grateful to the blue-eyed Englishman.

She'd known men in her life who were kind. Decent men who treated their servants with honor, even the women. They spoke kindly and paid their bills. She knew one who had a laugh like a summer breeze and another who winked when he found something funny, which was often. Never had she expected to meet one in England, and yet somehow she had.

Even when she couldn't completely follow the spoken word—English accents were variable and strange—she could see from observing Max that he was a good man. Unfortunately, she had no faith that a good man could manage in this world. They inevitably got crushed by something. One could not care for everyone and still maintain a safe world for oneself. He had to have limits and when something went wrong, she, as the foreigner, would be left out in the cold.

And yet, that did not stop her from imagining his smile and remembering the strength in his arms as he carried her. He was powerful in body and pleasing to her eye. Funny how even the strangest physical appearance became appealing when set on a kind man. She'd always thought the English to be big, ungainly apes who smelled bad. Instead, she found Max strong, his hair intriguing, and his smile captivating.

But only a fool relied on a stranger with a charming smile. Her best hope was to rid herself of her captors—both Chinese and English—and make a life for herself however she could. But first, her feet had to heal. As soon as the door had shut behind Max, she had untied her binds, rebroken what had begun to heal crooked, and prayed that she was never again alone with any of her Chinese captors.

For a while the pain overwhelmed her, and she allowed it. She had lost everything, so if she wallowed in despair in this strange yellow room, then who would blame her? She would count on Max's promise of safety for a little bit.

The commotion roused her from her despair. Someone's fury, someone else's dismissal mixed into her dream, or perhaps they shaped her dream by pulling up horrific memories. Six months on board the English ship had not been easy. Pain, fever, stench. The memories set her heart racing with terror even before her door banged open.

She jolted awake with a cry, only to have fear choke off the sound.

Lao Gu stood framed in her doorway, his face contorted in fury. He pointed a harsh finger at her as he spit out his venom.

"You have failed, fat-foot bitch. We leave now."

She recoiled, and in her fear, she pressed down on her feet. Agony shot through her body.

She cried out, the pain whiting out everything else until her head snapped to the side. It was a moment before she realized he'd slapped her. She hadn't even felt the blow because the pain in her feet was all-consuming. Instinct and long custom made her throw up her arms to shield her face, but the one blow was all he intended.

He towered over her, glaring down at her unbound feet.

"You have destroyed your own chances," he growled. Then with deliberate cruelty, he set his boot upon her nearest foot and pressed down.

She screamed as pain exploded through her body. She struck out with little thought beyond trying to hurt him back. She knew where a man's organ was even when covered by layers of clothing, and she had strong hands to grip the thing until he squeaked like the pig he was.

She found it.

She clenched down as best she could, tightening and twisting as she poured all her pain into what she did. But it was not enough.

He threw himself backwards and his tiny jinjing slipped away.

"Gutter dog! I will tie you down and laugh as the foreigners grunt on you."

She hadn't the strength to fight him. And when she looked for help, she saw Weed and Pervert maneuver into the room. They were carrying her trunk of clothing, but they dropped it with a heavy thud on the floor. Fear and pain choked her. Other times, she'd had words to throw at them. Curses and threats from her ghost if no one else, but she was disoriented and exhausted. In short, she was broken, and now she was no more than the animal they named her with no voice beyond a howl.

"Take her," Lao Gu ordered.

Weed advanced while Pervert cracked his thick knuckles. She heard herself whimper and cursed herself for sounding so weak, but there was nothing she could do to change what was about to happen.

Until someone else changed it for her.

Suddenly, Pervert was thrown against the wall. All she'd seen was a white hand slip around and grab his shirt, then drag him aside. Weed barely turned his head before he received a blow to the face.

Max.

He moved into her view like a warrior god. His face wasn't even distorted into fury. It was simply hard, cold, and implacable as stone.

She thought him beautiful.

He hauled Pervert backward by the neck, tripping the guard on purpose or by accident. Whatever he intended, Pervert went sprawling out the door where other white men grabbed him.

She hoped they killed him.

Meanwhile, Lao Gu grabbed her by the hair. She fought, but she could get no leverage. Her feet would not take any weight, and she had no control with her head jerked back and forth.

She saw Lao Gu draw his knife. She knew he meant to slit her throat. How many times had he threatened it? At least twice a day, but this time she believed him. This time, he had nothing left to lose and so she fought as an animal—with teeth and claws and every scrap of strength in her body.

She saw it happen as one must in a fight. The action seemed slow to her eyes and yet so large as to fill her whole vision. Max gripped Lao Gu's arm despite the nearness of the blade. He twisted it with a savage grip, his knuckles white as they passed in front of her eyes. He made a sound full of dark fury—one that seemed to match and strengthen her own—and then his other fist plowed upward in a hard cut that snapped LaoGu's head back.

Her tormenter flew backwards, the knife clattering from his hand. It landed near her feet hard enough to slice a dark line in her swollen flesh. She scrambled for it. This was the first weapon to come to her. The first time she could strike at the man who had reduced her to an animal.

So she acted like one. She grabbed the knife and plunged it straight into his heart. Blood welled up, thick and ugly. She knew its scent, knew its potency. And then, she gripped the handle with both fists and twisted.

Let the blade shred his black heart. And let his ghost pay for the crimes he committed.

"I curse you," she said as she twisted the knife. "I curse you," she repeated as it turned again. "I curse you to suffer under one such as you."

It wasn't elegant. It wasn't even clever. But her grandmother had taught her how to curse with the power of all victims, and so she spun the words out now as she had been taught. She did not use her own weak qi, she called upon all the women who had died on the boat, the ones he had maimed and she'd treated, the ones who could never speak because of what he had done to them.

"Take him," she called to them. "Take him and find peace, Su Lan." She named the girl who had died on the boat. Then she named others who had been harmed by men in power. "Yuan Fu, Cai Jian, Xiao Xi…" She named every girl she had ever treated who had reason to curse a man. And she balled them all up in her mind and set them upon Lao Gu. And she didn't stop until a white man's large hand gently pulled her away.

It took a great deal of strength for him to stop her. Indeed, he couldn't do it until she was pushed back upon her feet and pain shot through her mind. It interrupted her chant, and she collapsed. She felt her body drop into his hands as he struggled to manage her weight.

"What…feet?" he demanded. She couldn't understand all the words, but his expression of horror was enough. He pointed to her swollen, ugly feet as he rounded on the others. "What…her feet?"

"The dog needed small feet!" bellowed Weed in Chinese.

Pervert didn't deign to answer the demand. He cursed the white men as he fought against the two men holding him. It didn't save him.

And indeed, while he drew breath to begin again, she finally found her voice. "I curse you now with their names. When they are done with Lao Gu, they will come for you." Just as Lao Gu had done to her, she raised her hand and pointed at each of them. Blood dripped from her fingers, and she had the satisfaction of seeing them both go white with terror.

They knew, because she had told them, that her grandmother was skilled with curses. That all the women in her family knew how to turn ghosts into spirits of vengeance.

She grinned at them and threw the same names at them. "Eat their spirit!" she cried. "Have them, Su Lan, Yuan Fu, Cai Jian…" She kept repeating their names. She said them while Weed and Pervert stopped struggling with the white men. She threw names like daggers until they twisted out of the white men's grip and ran.

She heard them scramble down the stairs. She heard their ragged breath and rapid feet as they fled the house. And still she cursed them until her voice was hoarse and her energy spent. And in that moment, she lost all the power within her.

Her last word before she lost consciousness stayed in her mind and echoed in her body, clinging to her because it was all she had to give.

"Curse."

Chapter Seven

MAX'S GORGE ROSE up, all but choking him. Blood was everywhere. He breathed it in the air, saw it pouring across the carpet, and he swore he could hear it in his haggard breath. His body shuddered with horror, and yet he couldn't make himself move. Yihui had collapsed at his feet. He should pick her up. He should do any number of things, but the blood… The knife… The dead…

What was he supposed to do?

"Chiverton!" his mother called. "Why is everyone standing there?"

Embarrassing that his mother's voice was the one thing that could break him from his frozen shock. Max whipped around and pointed directly at his butler. "Keep her away!"

His butler blinked, snapped his arms to his sides in a butler salute, then turned immediately to the side. "Your Grace, pray allow me to bring you some soothing tea. Things are about to get very upsetting, and you really shouldn't be in the thick of it."

Things were *about* to get upsetting? Max looked to the lovely yellow counterpane that his mother had bought in Yorkshire. With barely a grunt of regret, he stripped it off the bed. The fabric would be soaked through in a moment, but he had to cover the mandarin with something. God, how much blood was in a body?

"Max, Mother is very distraught…" His sister's voice wavered as she spoke. "Oh heavens. Oh… Oh…"

He looked up to see his sister's blanched face as she stood in the doorway. Damnation, he hadn't wanted her to see this. As fast as possible, he threw the coverlet over the body.

"Emmaline—" he began, but he didn't know what he wanted to say. The two of them had always relied upon each other, but this… This was something he wanted to spare her.

She visibly started at her name, and then their gazes met across the room. "Is she…?"

"What?"

"How many b-bodies, Max?" she whispered.

It took him a moment to understand her question, but then his sluggish brain finally caught up. "She passed out."

Guilt washed through him. He should have been worried about her. He *was* worried about her, but he'd never seen… He'd never…

"We need another room for her," he said as he squatted down. He didn't want to hurt Yihui as he lifted her up. He gathered her gently into his arms. This time he felt the dead weight of her and worry all but choked him.

"She can have my bed," his sister said. "And, um, perhaps Kimberly could help?"

Lady Kimberly here? In this? Good God, no!

She must have read his expression because she shook her head. "With Miss…with the woman," she said pointing to Miss Wong's feet. "That doesn't look good. And, um, Kimberly has helped with medical…um… things." She swallowed and took a step forward, but Max stopped her. He didn't want his sister one step closer to this disaster.

"Your room," he said. He settled Yihui in his arms. He didn't even know her full name! What was wrong with him? Engaged by royal decree and he didn't know what to call her. These were the thoughts that circled through his head as he tried to distract himself. She was covered in blood, and he was little better. Everything he wore would need to be burned.

He felt her breath against his neck and felt better. Then he saw her deformed feet in the mirror. Thank God she was insensate. She'd told him that they'd broken her feet, but somehow the reality of it was so much worse. He couldn't imagine what she'd suffered on the boat. She had literally twisted a knife in the mandarin's chest. What would push a person to do such a thing?

He straightened to his full height before he realized that three footmen stood in the doorway like frozen trees.

"Rees, bring water and towels to Emmaline's bedroom. Mitchell, ask Lady Kimberly if she would assist. Atkins, send someone for a doctor and then find the Watch."

Emmaline twisted around to stare at him. "The Watch? Must we? Half the *ton* is strolling outside. And the rest will be knocking within the hour!"

Did she think this could be hushed over quietly? "There are rules, Em. When a Chinese delegate dies in your bedroom, the rules must be followed!" And those rules included calling law enforcement. In London, that meant summoning the Watch, as they were the ones who policed the city.

She nodded as she backed out down the hallway. "Of course," she muttered half to herself, half to him. "You're right, of course. We must do this properly."

As if there were a proper way to handle this!

He cradled Yihui close, taking care as he maneuvered her out of the bedroom. He didn't want to bang her feet and, truthfully, he had no idea if she had other injuries. What had she suffered?

He settled her head against his shoulder. Tenderness suffused him. He grabbed onto that emotion. He needed it as a buffer against the ugly feelings still roiling within him. Better to make sure she was properly cared for than allow guilt and horror to drown him.

A few more steps, and he was inside Emmaline's bedroom. Then he lay Yihui down gently, wincing as he saw blood smear across the rose counterpane. He adjusted her head on the pillow and gently tugged her black hair aside. Long thick strands, silky soft against the linen. She must have discarded her beaded headpiece when she washed away the make-up.

There was blood on her skin now, a dark smear that he tried to wipe away with his handkerchief. It didn't work because there was blood on his own hands, smears on his white handkerchief, and…

He swallowed and shoved those thoughts aside. She was a beautiful woman, he realized. Her face was a well-formed oval, her nose nicely rounded at the tip, and her mouth had a sweet bow shape magnified by the red paint still on her lips. She had been sorely used, and he vowed to do everything in his power to see that she was taken care of going forward.

He didn't examine this overwhelming vow. He needed it to focus his thoughts. He was her rescuer from a horrendous situation. That was a noble role for him, one that fit his youthful fantasies, where he'd been a pirate captain rescuing a Chinese princess. Indeed, it gave him the energy to face the next few hours. He was no longer the victim of international politics and a prince's whims. He was an active participant in the world around him. One who was determined to protect an innocent girl now under his care.

That was what he chose to do. This was his decision in a life that was restricted on every side. And in this way, he found control.

"My lord?" a female voice interrupted. It was Mrs. Pizzi their housekeeper. "If you could step away for a moment, we can make her more comfortable."

He looked over his shoulder. Mrs. Pizzi was followed by his sister's maid who carried a large tub of water and several linens.

Nodding, he stepped back from the bed, though his hand stayed as long as possible on Yihui's arm. "Thank you, Mrs. Pizzi. Be as gentle as you can."

"Of course, my lord—"

"Did you call a doctor?" Lady Kimberly interrupted as she stepped into the room.

Max winced at the woman's clipped tone. "Yes—" he began,

but she cut him off.

"Best to call a surgeon. The doctor won't be able to do anything with those feet."

His attention abruptly sharpened on her. "Why would you say that?" he demanded. Yihui deserved the best treatment he could afford. And he could afford a very great deal.

"Because surgeons handle broken bones. And those feet…" She shook her head. "If she were a horse or even a dog, we would have to—"

"She's not an animal!"

Lady Kimberly shot him a frustrated look. "No, she's a woman who will want to walk again. Best get a surgeon who has seen many injured laborers. People who must walk again or starve. How many broken bones does a doctor see in his day?"

Not many. Doctors treated agues and the vague ailments of the aristocracy. And though they knew how to set bones, Kimberly was right. A surgeon set many bones every week. And he would also know if the damage were too severe, and amputation was the only way to prevent death.

He didn't want to imagine it. Indeed, he couldn't force himself to contemplate the possibility, but he would not compromise care just because he felt squeamish at the thought. Looking over Lady Kimberly's shoulder, he gestured to Chiverton who hovered in the hallway.

"Send a footman to whomever Lady Kimberly suggests."

"Immediately, my lord," Chiverton said. "And the Watch has arrived, as well as several guests. Visitors, my lord, to see the duchess."

Gawkers, gossips, and snoops. "Send them away. Tell them Her Grace is not well."

"Yes, my lord."

Max straightened his jacket while his thoughts finally dropped into order. "I'll see the Watch in the Library."

"Yes, my lord."

"And when my father arrives, do not under any circumstance

allow him upstairs. Not yet."

At the mention of his father, every soul in the room gulped audibly. Not a one of them had realized that his father would descend on the household the moment he heard of the commotion. As the head of the conservative party, his father would be the first to be told of any royal gossip. He would have learned of Max's impromptu engagement and be headed here in fury. Especially since he was the one who had declared that Max marry Kimberly, the daughter of his closest political ally.

The man would likely come home in a rage. No one wanted him to arrive to find the Watch in their home and a bloody corpse upstairs. Though how they were going to prevent that was beyond him.

Either way, it was up to Max to manage it. Meanwhile, Emmaline looked like she was going to be ill.

"It's all I can do to keep Mama out of it," she whispered. "Papa's going to have an apoplexy."

Not if Max could help it. He squeezed his sister's arm as if she were his compatriot in a war, and indeed, they both felt as such. "Leave Papa to me." He looked to their butler. "Chiverton, send another footman to the House of Lords. Have him suggest, delicately of course, that Mama is overwrought, and father should take dinner at his club."

"Right away, my lord."

Emma met his gaze with a shrug. "It might work."

It wouldn't. The man was already on his way home, but it was the only play Max had. And with that thoroughly depressing thought, Max squared his shoulders and headed for the stairs. Best not to look in the guest bedroom. Best not to smell the air. Best not to remember—

But he did. And in that moment, his sister caught his elbow.

"Max!" she cried. "Max!"

He blinked, startled to realize that she'd had to call him several times. "Yes?"

"Before you see the Watch," she said gesturing at him.

"What?"

"Max, look at yourself! You need to change your clothes before you go downstairs. Mama's visitors are still there."

He looked down at his blood-stained clothing. Was that what was important now? Changing his clothes instead of seeing to the dead Chinese official or finding out if the lady would have her feet amputated? Splotches of blood on his—

"You wore those clothes yesterday and it shows."

No, that wasn't in the least bit important now, but it was what had to be managed. Everything must be done in the proper order, after all. With a clipped jerk of his chin, he headed to his bedroom. Then he stopped and snapped his fingers at the nearest footman.

"Send another footman for Lord Benedict. Emphasize that it's urgent."

If Max had to deal with the Watch and his father, then he'd damn well have Lord Benedict standing beside him. And the man had better know something about Chinese politics.

"Right away," Chiverton said with a bow while Max headed straight for his bedroom.

His valet met him the moment he entered the bedroom. "Quickly, my lord. Your clothes are ready, and I've got every-thing prepared for a shave as well."

Of course, he did. Because clearing off his whiskers would magically save the day.

Max had barely stripped out of his jacket when he heard the front door open. The bellow carried through the air a moment later. "Where the devil is my idiot son?"

"I'm right here, Father, washing blood off my hands," he muttered. Then he stretched his chin toward his valet. "Shave as quick as you can. Just don't slice my throat."

He'd leave that honor to his father.

Chapter Eight

MAX RUSHED DOWN the stairs, his cheek still stinging from his valet's rushed scrape. It wasn't the man's fault. Max had been pulling on a fresh shirt at the same moment, and that had not gone well. He prayed he wasn't bleeding all over his attire.

Once on the main floor, he saw his father seated on the chair everyone called his throne. Emma was with him, valiantly trying to delay the man with sweets.

It wasn't working. Though he pretended to listen to her babble on about Mama's nerves, his attention was focused on the parlor door while he sat slapping his newspaper against his thigh. At least Christopher had made himself scarce. Max's friend was the one man guaranteed to ignite father's temper.

That wasn't his father's fault. Chris enjoyed constantly poking at the man's politics. In truth, Chris liked poking humorless people until they broke, and in the duke's case, that meant making fun of conservative politics. But now wasn't the time to inflame the situation, and so Max was grateful for his friend's absence.

Determined to keep everyone calm, Max sauntered into the parlor as if he'd just arrived from an afternoon's stroll. "Hullo Father," he said. "Thank you, Emmaline," he added, pressing a kiss to her cheek. "You're a treasure."

"And don't you forget it," she said with an extra-wide glare. "Mama's upstairs resting. The servants are deployed as instructed."

He grinned, always finding it funny when she used military language.

"And in the library?"

"The Watch."

Max nodded. "I will speak with them directly."

No fool, their father bolted to his feet. "The Watch? What the devil—"

"Not something you should be concerned with," Max said with a jaunty wave. "Come if you must"—he knew his father would—"but since you haven't any idea what's been going on, pray do let me handle it."

His father harumphed. "I know a Chinese gentleman has expired in one of our bedrooms."

"That's true—" Max began.

Emmaline interrupted. "But it isn't the whole story."

"*Maximillian!*"

Damn it, his father was in no mood to be fobbed off. "Yes, Father?"

The man's eyes narrowed, and he abruptly pulled out his handkerchief. Then he closed the distance to his son in two long strides and firmly brushed it across Max's jaw. The white linen came back bloodied.

The duke looked at Emma. "Sack his valet immediately."

"Yes, Father."

It would do no good to argue that it hadn't been Moore's fault. By his father's estimation, any valet who allowed his master to appear in public in anything less than perfection was a man who didn't deserve the position.

Fortunately, Emma saw Max give a slight shake no. She knew not to obey the command. In fact, she would likely whisper to Moore to keep out of sight for a while.

"A disgrace. An absolute disgrace," their father muttered, referring to Max and not his poor valet.

Max responded as he always did. He grinned and gave yet another jaunty gesture that covered the wince. "Right-o," he said, sounding more like an idiot the longer his father glowered at him. "The library."

He spun on his heel and walked at a speed his father would not match. The man was as hale as a horse, but he believed in a decorous pace no matter what the situation. That allowed Max a moment to enter the library, scan the four Watchmen who waited for him, and address the one who appeared to be in charge.

"Good afternoon, gentlemen. I am sorry you must deal with this ghastly business, but I'm sure it can be handled quickly if we all work together."

"Oh, yes, milord," the man said with a slight bow. "I'm Sergeant Berry and I've already seen to the bulk of it. If you could recount what happened, we'll get this wrapped up."

Max nodded. He took a moment to lean back against his father's ponderous desk and feign an insouciance that he didn't feel. He was well aware of his father's dark glower as the duke entered the room. Max summarized his day in short, clipped sentences, skipping over his engagement, leaping to Miss Wong's recovery upstairs, and focusing on the mandarin's brutality.

"I've seen 'er feet, my lord," the sergeant agreed with a sad shake of his head. "And there were plenty of witnesses to say that he had a knife to her throat. It's self-defense to be sure. I'm afraid I can't keep it out of the paper, but there'll be no trouble from us."

"Thank you."

"I've given your butler the name of someone who can help with the body, my lord—"

Right. Max fought the shudder that went through his body. "Good thinking, Sergeant."

"And if I may, there's a home for young ladies that might have room for her. Madame Sabate runs a private rooming house—"

"Madame Sabate?" Max interrupted, his voice growing colder as his blood heated. He knew of the infamous courtesan and guessed exactly what the true purpose of her home for young ladies was: a training ground for new courtesans. Indeed, Yihui's exotic looks would garner a pretty penny from lustful aristocrats who wanted to try an out of the ordinary kind of girl.

"Yes, my lord. She runs—"

"I know who she is and what she runs," Max snapped.

But the damned man would not back down. "It's the best future for her, my lord, assuming she survives. She'll make good money if she's trained right."

Max wanted to toss the man bodily from the house, so furious was he at the suggestion. But a future duke couldn't be seen throwing the Watch out of the house. That would add fuel to the gossip flame. So instead, he focused his mind on the other thing the man had said.

"What do you mean, 'Assuming she survives?'"

"Oh well, my lord, I was upstairs when…" The man fumbled with his notebook as if he'd written something in it. "Well, I heard the doctor and the surgeon conferring. Lady Kimberly as well."

"Conferring about Miss Wong?"

"Yes, my lord. She's got a fever, growing worse by the second. And those feet…" He shook his head. "Well, it seems to me that it might be best if she passes. And if she doesn't, then what's she to do with those feet? Madame Sabate can train—"

"You will not mention that woman again," Max said, his voice a low growl.

The man squared his shoulders. "I'm older than you, my lord, and seen a bit more of what happens to these girls. And your mum, the duchess is in quite a state. If you sent the miss away—"

"The miss, as you call her, is my fiancée by royal decree!"

The sergeant's head bobbed up and down. "Well, yes. I had heard that, but seeing as how it's become a bungled affair an' she's not likely to survive—"

Max hadn't realized he'd stepped to tower over the man until he saw the sweat beading on the sergeant's pate. "I do not require your assistance in the care of my fiancée."

"O-of course not. I-I only thought to help—"

"Is that all?" he bellowed.

"Er, yes, my lord." He turned to his men who all bobbed their heads in equally silly fashion.

"Then I bid you good day," Max said.

Chiverton was on the mark, popping open the library door with an imperious air. "This way, gentlemen," he intoned.

The Watch scrambled away. That was one thing done. Next, Max needed to go upstairs before the leeches could do something stupid. But he didn't make it out the door before his father's firm hand gripped his arm.

"Have you taken leave of your senses?" the man growled in a low enough tone that no one else would hear.

Max turned to his father and deadpanned his answer. "I'm quite sure I have. I watched a man get a knife to his chest today. If you don't want to smell his blood while you sleep, I suggest you spend the night at your club."

"Chiverton's handling that," his father returned. "Why do you claim this Chinese gel? Do you plan to go into mourning when she dies? Do you mean for us to pay for her funeral rites?"

"Prinny himself—"

"Will understand. Damn it, if the girl is dying—"

Red washed through his vision. Not the red of fury, but one of blood spurting from a man's chest. Of seeing dark red on yellow damask walls. Of the smell that came not just from blood, but other bodily fluids as a man died.

"There will not be another death in this house," Max said.

"That's why the girl must be sent on."

"And what should I tell Prinny then? He ordered me to sort this out."

His father threw up his hands. "This is sorting it out!"

"It's sweeping it—and her—under the rug."

"That's where dead foreigners go. Good God, even a child can understand that."

"Maybe so, Father, but I am fresh out of brooms and rugs." They had all gone to wrapping up the mandarin.

His father pursed his lips, his sigh audible to the entire household. "Why do you persist in antagonizing me? I am trying to help! What you're doing is not how a duke—"

"Not how a duke acts." Max said the words at the same time his father did. "Then it is a good thing that you are not doing it."

"Maximillian—"

"Excuse me, Father. I need to consult with the doctor."

With that, he walked away from his very disapproving parent and straight up the stairs. He had no idea when exactly he set himself on an opposite path to his father. From his earliest memories, he recalled his father would issue a decree, and he as the heir was expected to follow it. There had never been any discussion or leniency in his father's commands but sometime around Max's sixteenth birthday, he decided that he would think for himself. He would choose his own actions regardless of what his father dictated.

That was a difficult position to take—refusing his father's dictates without also setting fire to the dukedom and all it represented. He'd walked that tightrope for years, but it was getting harder. He refused his father's demand that he take a position in the House of Commons but agreed to honor his betrothal to Lady Kimberly. But then he delayed that wedding by insinuating himself into Prinny's inner circle. And all of it was done while he tried to indulge his singular passion in all things oriental without leaving England. After all, the sole heir to a dukedom couldn't risk himself on foreign shores. But now that China had come to him in the guise of a frightened Chinese woman, he would not abandon her to the likes of Madame Sabate. Or allow her to die under his watch.

He simply would not allow it, and so he rushed upstairs to see if his will alone could ward off Death.

He mounted the stairs in quick steps and rushed to the hallway just outside Emmaline's bedroom where two very different medical men were bickering in front of a grim-faced Kimberly and a greenish-looking Chris. The one dressed in the finest attire—Dr. Morton—shook his head with a grave countenance even as he bowed to Max.

"My lord, sad news, I'm afraid. Very sad indeed."

Max waited, his entire body tightening as he glared at the man.

"Stop it, Max." Kimberly huffed. "It does no good to seek advice only to intimidate him into silence."

A fair point. He did his best to moderate his expression, but the truth was that nothing this day left him feeling particularly charitable toward anyone. Except Yihui, of course, who was the biggest victim in all of this.

"Kimberly, summarize it for me please. You have the best medical understanding of all of us."

His English fiancée winced. "Taking care of dogs is not the same—"

"But it is better than anything I've ever done." He looked at the woman he'd known since he was four years old. "Please, Kim."

She nodded. "The doctor believes amputation of both her feet is the only option."

The doctor nodded. "There is infection, my lord. And that will kill her for certain."

Lady Kimberly continued. "Mr. Torres... He's the surgeon. He agrees but feels that life without feet will be very bad for her. Very, very bad. He has seen several patients recover without amputation. The odds are slim, but survival is possible."

So it was exactly as he had guessed. Miss Wong wasn't expected to survive. He glanced into the darkened room. She appeared to be sleeping comfortably, but perhaps that was an illusion.

"How much laudanum did you give her?"

"None," the doctor said. "She refused it. I fear the fever has addled her wits."

"She said she'd had enough of that," Kim corrected, her tone curt. "Her English is awkward, but the meaning was clear."

"Just as well," Mr. Torres said. "She needs her strength to fight the infection. There's a balance to be found between pain and strength."

There was no balance in any of this and everyone was looking to him to make a decision. He looked at Chris who was, as usual, listening to everything but saying very little. "Chris—" he began, but the man held up his hands as if warding off an evil spell.

"Do not look to me for answers. I'm here in case the duchess peeks her head out of her bedroom. At this point, I'm the only one who can keep her calm."

That was true. His mother had a soft spot for Christopher, likely because he reminded her of her brother James. But that wasn't helpful right now.

"This is a gamble either way, yes?" he asked the four of them.

They each nodded, though the surgeon looked thoughtful.

"Yes?" he pressed. Mr. Torres was a little shabby, but there was intelligence in his eyes and not one whit of obsequious pandering, unlike Dr. Morton.

"We can wait through the night, I think," the surgeon said. "The morning will tell the tale."

"Unacceptable!" snapped Dr. Morton. "To put his lordship, not to mention the duchess, through a night of caring for a foreign woman—"

"I can care for a sick woman," Max snapped.

The doctor shook his head. "You do not know the kind of illness we are discussing, my lord. You have been shielded from the worst kinds of—"

Kim waved her hand. "I can stay."

"My lady! This is not something you should subject yourself to. It's very unpleasant, very—"

"I think," Max interrupted, "that my mother could use your attention, Dr. Morton. Something to calm her overwrought nerves."

"Yes, my lord, but—"

"Yes, yes, I understand your recommendation." Then he paused, the words choking him. "If it comes to it, will you be the one to do the amputations?"

The man's eyes bulged out in shock. "I should say not! That is…" He sniffed as he looked to the surgeon. "That is more properly something for a surgeon."

Which is why Kimberly had asked for him. "Thank you, Dr. Morton. Pray do see to my mother's nerves now."

The man knew he was dismissed, and so he bowed and left, moving with pompous care. Max turned his attention to Mr. Torres.

"What will be the signs if we wait too long?"

"The fever will be very bad. Red streaks climbing upward from bad blood. The rest will look very similar to what you see now."

Max nodded, his expression grim. "I'll stay with her. She has no one in this land except me, and I will not abandon her."

"Very well, my lord. I will return before nightfall to see if she has turned a corner in either direction."

"Thank you—" he began, but Kim touched his hand. It was a loud gesture for her since she rarely touched people. Her caresses were almost exclusively reserved for dogs.

"The odds are not good, Max," she said. "You need to prepare yourself."

"I know," he said grimly. "Go home. There's no need for you to stay."

She flashed him a wan smile. "Actually, I need to return to my cousin. She is doing a similar vigil tonight."

He frowned. "The black mastiff?"

She nodded.

"I'm sorry, Kim. This has been a hard day for you." He knew Kimberly loved that dog almost as much as her cousin did.

"It's his time," she said, her gaze going to the bedroom door.

She didn't have to say the words for him to know what she meant. She thought that he should allow Miss Wong to pass on as well. Life for a foreign woman with no feet was no life at all.

Unfortunately, he agreed, which made him feel sick.

He raised her hand to his mouth, giving her the most formal and devoted of kisses. "Thank you, Lady Kimberly," he said.

She tapped his arm before he released her. "It's not so awful being Ophelia, you know. Not when you are acting so kind to a complete stranger."

"I am not Hamlet," he grumbled. "Christopher, however—"

"I'm off!" his friend interrupted. "Prinny will want to know all the details and I have yet to shave." Then with a rakish grin, he headed for the stairs. Max would have thought him completely unaffected by the day's events, but he saw the man glance to the other bedroom door. Glance, flinch, then hunch away.

Chris wasn't nearly as sanguine as he appeared.

"Good luck," Kimberly said, drawing his attention back to her.

"Thank you," he said. Then he turned to the darkened bedroom. Was he really sitting vigil next to a foreign woman?

Apparently so. He prayed vehemently that this was not a death watch.

Chapter Nine

Yihui lay on a fiery cloud of softness. The cushions were suffocating, the blanket too light and yet too heavy at once. Where was she?

She turned her head and saw a man watching her.

"Baba?" she croaked, thinking it was her father. He had looked at her that way the morning he'd sold her to the Wong patriarch. But this was not the floor of her brother's bedroom, neither was she on the straw pallet that made up her bed.

"Yihui? Would you like some water?"

She frowned, not understanding his words. Nevertheless, the man came forward and gently lifted up her head. Cool water touched her parched lips, and she drank greedily. He was patient, keeping her head supported while she swallowed. And then, when the cup was empty, he gently set her back down on the finest pillow she had ever used.

This was definitely not her father nor was it her home. It took her some time to remember. In truth, the temptation to slip back into oblivion pulled at her, but she fought it. To sleep was to miss opportunities.

Her grandmother had taught her that. Indeed, her grandmother had taught her everything of value, including how to appear subservient while doing what was needed to create the life she wanted. At her father's home, that had meant quietly memorizing everything about making medicines. She'd learned his recipes and her grandmother's potions. And now she used that knowledge to survive.

But to do that, she had to fight the haze in her mind.

Her memories came back slowly. They'd broken her feet the night before she was to be given to the white ruler. That had been smart of them. She would have escaped the moment the ship docked otherwise. But with broken feet, she had no choice but to submit. She was dressed, carried, and presented to the English king only to have him reject her. She'd been given to a lesser man. He was the one who sat beside her now. And while she looked at him, she remembered the way he had burst into her room. His fists had seemed like hammers, slamming Weed and Pervert out of the way. And then when she thought Lao Gu would finally kill her, this white man had defended her with such force that an opportunity had appeared before her.

He was definitely not a "lesser man."

Still, she understood that he was not the king. He didn't look like someone Heaven favored. His face was rugged, not smooth, with angles that were not refined. The length of his earlobes was stingy, though the distance between nose and upper lip suggested favor in his middle years. As for his hands, his fingers were blunt. Indeed, he appeared to have broken two of them sometime in his youth.

And yet she found him appealing nonetheless.

"How do you feel?" he asked.

Damn him for speaking slowly. If he had rushed his words, she wouldn't be able to catch his foreign sounds. But he spoke clearly and gently, forcing her to work as she ferreted out his meaning.

He asked after her health. It was not a question she wanted to answer.

She already knew she was dying.

She could feel it in her fever, in the burning pain of her feet, and the swollen heaviness of her legs. But she could be wrong, she reasoned. It was possible she was just ill from a fever that had little to do with broken bones.

That was a false hope, but one she clung to even as she slowly maneuvered herself upright. He helped her, his hands large on her back. Such strength he had. Not in muscles, but in qi. Her captors had been physically strong, but their inner soul was weak. Not this man. His energy flowed like a golden river beneath her back. It pulsed with the life of a good man.

She dipped into it as much as she could, leaning back against his strength as he adjusted her pillows. She could not steal his energy. That was the work of a vampire, and she was not such a creature. Instead, she let it flow across her skin and in time, her own qi responded, giving her the wherewithal to finally look at her injury.

She pulled back the covers and peered at her feet.

It was bad.

Her feet were swollen to the size of melons and though there were no red streaks coming up from the infection, she knew they were there, just beneath the skin. She must have made a sound of distress because he squeezed her hand.

"Stay strong. You must fight for your life."

What did this rich foreigner know of fighting for anything?

She winced. That was the pain talking, even in her head. She was being surly. She'd spent her childhood learning about medicines for the sick, carrying tea packets to the ill, and offering hope to the dying. Now she was the one who needed medicine, and she was terrified.

She looked into the white man's eyes and tried to tell him what to do. She knew there was only one chance for her, and the sooner she took the medicine the better. But how would she explain it to him?

"I—" Her throat was very dry. "I—"

He gave her water, and she drank more. It was clean water, much fresher than anything she'd had on board.

"Thank you."

He nodded. "Can I get you some food? Broth?" He mimed drinking soup.

She shook her head. "Need medicine."

He nodded as his gaze ticked toward her feet. It was a slight flick of his eyes, but it told her that he knew the source of her illness.

"No one will hurt you here," he said.

Her lips curved in gratitude. Safety was something rare in her life. She felt it now as it shivered into her body through his chi.

"Need medicine," she repeated.

He shook his head. "You shouldn't take too much laudanum."

She frowned. Was he speaking of opium? "No opium. Medicine. Need…" She didn't know the English word. "Plant? Small plant."

His eyes widened. "What plant?"

She didn't know how to explain, which meant she would have to get it herself. Gritting her teeth, she swung her feet out. She would find it and make the tea herself. It was her only chance.

"Woah!" he cried out, obviously alarmed. "You can't walk!"

It was this or die horribly. She set her weight down on her right heel and nearly howled. The pain was excruciating, and he grabbed her as she swayed, gently laying her back on the bed.

"You can't," he repeated. "You must rest."

But she'd die without the plant. "Need medicine," she repeated.

He frowned, his gaze quickly scanning the messy room. "Can you draw it?" he asked, miming writing with his hand. Then, once he was sure she wasn't going to fall over, he crossed to a writing desk and pulled out paper and ink. He brought it over to her on a lap desk, setting it carefully across her body.

But what was she supposed to use? The hardened feather seemed very strange to her.

"Do you understand?" he asked. He dipped the quill in the ink and scratched it across the page.

Ah, of course. But when she reached for it, her hand was too unsteady, the weight of the quill too light, and the ink blobbed and botched. Her face heated with fever and embarrassment. How was she going to draw what she needed?

She set the quill down in disgust. "I go."

"You cannot walk."

"I go!"

"Where?"

An excellent question. She did not know this place where she was held, and she knew even less of London. If she walked around, she would likely be able to find it soon enough, but she couldn't manage it on her feet. Meanwhile, his gaze traveled from her to something across the room. His brows abruptly narrowed, and he got up.

Curious, she watched him cross to a messy bookshelf. He grabbed something rolled up in fabric and brought it over. And then he set it before her.

"Maybe this will help," he said as he untied the fabric.

Brushes appeared before her, set neatly in soft cotton. These she knew how to handle. She picked one up. It settled nicely in her hand, and she was unexpectedly grateful for something familiar in so strange a place. The ink was difficult to manage, but she figured it out soon enough.

But what was she to draw?

She started with a building. She didn't want to draw an out-house, but that was always a good place. Pigpen? There had to be places like that here, except the window out the other bedroom had shown her trees, cobblestone, and stately houses.

"Is that an apothecary shop?" he asked.

She had no idea what that word meant.

She drew pigs, but she was very bad at that. Then people. Little better.

"A stable? Is that supposed to be stable?"

Oh! Of course. Horses. That would have dark, dank corners. She hoped. Now how was she to draw mold? Her grandmother had taught her that when all else failed, a tea made from the mold that grew on the sides of buildings could save a life. Her father had disdained such wisdom, of course. He would not lower himself to go to such places. But the women knew, and they taught each other through the generations.

And now, Yihui prayed it would work for her.

She darkened a corner of the building she'd drawn.

"Is that mud?"

She knew that word and shook her head. She looked around and pointed at some colored paints on the same shelf as the brushes had been. He got them for her, and she carefully brushed dark green into the shadows.

"Medicine," she said.

"That's not medicine," he said, clearly appalled. "That's...that's dirt and..."

Yes, she knew what else was there. She'd been the one to gather it for her grandmother. They'd used it on the women who were sick after childbirth. It wasn't pleasant and it tasted terrible, but it worked.

She took the thinnest brush she could find and carefully drew the stages of growth for the mold from its earliest moments to its mature appearance. He would know that she had studied it under magnifying glasses to see that there were many different types of mold. Assuming, of course, that such things grew here as they did in China.

He stared at her, his mouth hanging open in shock. "You cannot know... You don't mean..."

She didn't need to know English to understand that he was refusing to go. That it was too demeaning a task for one such as him. Which meant it would have to be her.

She set aside paper and brush then made to stand again.

"No! No! You can't walk. I'll...I'll get it." He sounded appalled by the very words. "But what are you going to do with it?"

She mimed putting it in tea and drinking it. He shuddered in reaction.

"That's not medicine," he said firmly.

Any other time she would have pandered to his arrogance. No man liked to be shown as ignorant, especially not wealthy men, but she hadn't the strength to argue. The drawing had sapped her energy and she could feel her fever growing. She slammed her hand down on the paper, the sharp sound making him jump.

"I die," she said. Then she pointed to the paper. "Medicine." And her only hope.

"That can't be healthy. It can't—"

"Chinese medicine." She glared at him. "Women's medicine."

He stared at her. Her skin was damp, her feet throbbed, and her breath was coming fast, but she refused to waver. She needed that medicine.

Slowly, his gaze dropped to the paper. "You're a strange people," he said. Then he grunted. "I'll have to go to a public stable. Nerney would rather die that have mold anywhere near his tack."

She didn't understand his words. All she could do was repeat what she'd already said. "Medicine. Tea."

"Yes, yes. I'll get it." He ran a distracted hand through his hair.

"Quick. Please."

"Medicine. Tea. Yes, I'll go now."

He bowed politely to her before leaving. Such a sweet gesture to bow to her. In that simple movement, he gave her respect. Better yet, he listened to what she wanted even though he didn't understand why.

She leaned back and closed her eyes, replaying in her mind everything she knew of this man. She saw his fist connecting with Lao Gu's jaw. She heard again his kind voice when he sat beside her on the donkey cart. Then she lingered on the memory of him carrying her up the stairs to the yellow bedroom. He had such casual strength as he carried her. It matched his chi which flowed with such light.

Was he the man who owned her now? If she lived, would she

then surrender to this golden man and live her life in service to him?

The idea was tempting. Many would accept such a fate with gratitude. She let the idea of his hands on her body settle into her thoughts. That could be very nice. In fact, in her fevered state, the idea took root.

And yet, she knew that it was a dream. She would not surrender to him, no matter how he delighted her. When opportunity presented, she would run. She had skills and would use them to create her future. Surely the English people needed someone who knew medicine. They would pay her well for her teas and no man would interfere in her life.

Her future—if she had one—would be free of all men, including him.

"I vow it," she said as she bound her chi to her words.

Chapter Ten

MAX WAS RED-FACED and cursing long before he was interrupted. He'd thought to send his valet here—punishment for letting him out of the bedroom with a bleeding cut—but was too horrified by the task to give it to anyone else. And since he didn't dare check their stable where everyone knew him and would talk about what he was doing, he'd gone down the street with an empty jar and a chisel to sneak into a less exalted one. With luck, no one would recognize him in a dark cloak and thick scarf.

He found the mold in a corner with the water trough. Layers of it, thick enough to scrape easily into the jar, but he'd had to maneuver himself into an effective position to catch the stuff. Even with gloves on, he didn't relish rooting around on the ground for it after it had been scraped off.

"I thought I recognized that curse," drawled a man's voice from much too close.

Max jolted upright fast enough that he banged his head on a hanging bucket. It wasn't very painful, but it was loud as the thing clattered against the wall, and he had to scramble to keep it from falling.

Then finally, when everything was settled, he found the courage to see who had caught him grubbing about in a public stable.

"Lord Benedict," he said, dismay coloring his tone. "What are you doing here?"

The lanky man gave a lazy shrug. "I'm more interested in what you're doing right there."

Of course, he was. And given that Benedict was Max's unofficial superior at the Foreign Office, Max had to answer somehow. They'd also been friends since Max's first Season in London nearly a decade ago.

"I'd rather not say," he grumbled as he glanced at the jar. He had several inches of loosely dropped mold. Surely that was enough. He looked around as he stepped out from behind the water trough. "This isn't your usual haunt. Whyever would you stable your horse here?"

Benedict grinned. "I'd rather not say."

The two exchanged a long look, both assessing the other for mutually shared secrets. Max was excruciatingly aware that Benedict could deduce all sorts of wildly incorrect things about what he was doing and so the risk to telling the truth was small. But he could also see a burden of care around his friend's shoulders, a tightness in his movements that he could only discern because of their long companionship.

And while he was weighing all that, Benedict gave in. It wasn't a lack of fortitude. The man could outwait a stone. It probably had to do with the nature of his secret.

"My father insists I beget an heir."

Max groaned. Benedict would become an earl one day and was older than Max by six years Max knew the pressure his family set on his shoulders. The pressure upon Benedict would likely be a great deal worse because of his increased age.

"I was going to propose to Kimberly this season," Max said.

"That's what you said last season."

"I meant it this time."

"Ummm."

The two fell in step together as they left the stable. "Does your prospective bride live nearby?" Max asked.

"Not too far."

"Do I know her?"

"Perhaps, though she doesn't run with the Carlton House set."

"I should hope not."

Benedict smiled. "She does, however, have an unusual hobby. I was investigating it."

Max slowed as he turned to the man. "Now you have me intrigued. What's her name?"

"I won't tell you any more. Not until I know why you've put dirt in a jar."

"It's not dirt, it's mold. The Chinese princess asked for it, and I was too embarrassed to send my valet out for it."

"You don't say!"

He nodded. "I have studied some of their thoughts on medicine. It's very different from ours."

"Obviously."

"But it must work for them. Otherwise, why would they do it? For thousands of years and millions of people."

Benedict shook his head. "You have always admired them."

"How can you not be fascinated by people so different from our own? Their history, their medicine, their language is nothing like anything we have. Completely separate, completely different—"

"Completely exciting to you."

"Yes." No sense in denying it. Studying England would be like gazing at one's own naval. Max wanted to see what else was in the world.

Benedict picked up the jar of mold and stared at it. "I should not have asked you to babysit Prinny. I should have encouraged you to join the East India Company. At a minimum, you could have joined Staunton's diplomatic excursion. He hopes to speak with the emperor himself."

Yes, Max knew. And how it had burned when the expedition had set sail without him. But at the time, Prinny had been determined to involve himself personally in the war against Napoleon, and it took every resource at hand to keep him from making disastrous, ill-informed, amateur decisions with their troops. At the time, Max had been the only one able to convince Prinny to trust his own military leaders.

So Max had remained in London even when his heart had pulled him to China. And thanks to his efforts, Prinny had not commanded the military into doomed battles or ridiculous gambits.

Benedict handed back the jar. "Lord Castlereagh is well aware of your sacrifice. We know Carlton House is not where your heart lies."

Having the respect of England's lead diplomat was a balm to his bitterness, but he couldn't paint himself as so selfless a soul. "My parents would have fought tooth and nail to keep me in London, and I couldn't abandon Emmaline to their rancor." He sighed. "We both know the pressures of being the heir to an old title. Sometimes I think we are the most trapped souls in England, but then I recall that I have chosen to protect my people and my country. I serve where I am put to the best use. Even if it is at Carlton House where I am commanded to marry a Chinese princess."

Benedict nodded. This was a familiar discussion between the two of them as they both tried to navigate the responsibilities of their titles. Meanwhile, they walked easily back toward Max's home.

"Ben," Max began, "I need to know more about this Wong delegation."

His friend shook his head. "It was all very slap dash. We were notified the night of their arrival. I heard that they meant to see the king and was only barely able to divert them to Carlton House."

Max gaped at him. "You sent them there?"

"Of course, I did. Can't have them going to see the mad king, and I knew you were at Carlton House. What better place to send a Chinese delegation?"

Did the man understand nothing? "You should have said no!

They aren't a true delegation. They're from a merchant family, not the Chinese emperor—"

"And you were perfectly placed to figure that out."

"And perfectly placed to get saddled with a new wife!"

He could see Benedict try—and fail—to restrain his grin. The damned man found the situation amusing. "Truly, I am sorry about that. We had no idea about the girl."

"But you knew they weren't a real delegation."

"The country wants Chinese goods. Sometimes that means entertaining a bunch of merchants with a bribe." He slanted a look at Max. "Doesn't mean you have to do what they ask. Diplomacy is often about placating people while you do what you want." He paused as he turned to stare hard at Max. "You should already know that."

He did. But the whole thing had completely upended his life, and he didn't know what to do about it. "It's gotten too big to ignore."

"Has it?" Benedict challenged, and well he should. After all, everyone had been telling him the solution from the beginning. Get rid of the body and set Yihui in a home somewhere. He didn't have to give her to the likes of Madame Sabate. There were plenty of respectable places that would care for her for the right amount of money.

And yet he was planning on nursing her in his own home and was right now carrying mold for her medicine. His own actions did not make sense, but he could not abandon her.

"She's an innocent in all this."

"You know she's not a Chinese princess, right?

Max nodded. "She told me. She's the daughter of an apothecary, I think. She knows medicines." He looked dubiously at the jar he carried.

Typically, Benedict didn't argue. He asked for details. "Start at the beginning."

So Max did while Benedict listened without comment. And when Max was done, he realized how much his frustration had spilled into his words.

"I see now that Kimberly was right. This disaster was entirely predictable. I need a real posting. Surely, I can do something for the war effort."

"I'm sure you could," his friend responded. "But there are several men who could do as well, whereas you are the only one in a position to moderate the prince—"

"Prinny does as he wills," he interrupted. "I cannot control his whims."

"But you do moderate them. Just last month you stopped him from ordering the navy to South America to acquire pineapples."

"The navy would have refused."

"It would have required a great deal of time and effort on several people's part. Time that was better spent fighting Napoleon. You distracted him with a clever bit of Chinoiserie." He grinned. "How very prescient of you."

"It wasn't prescient. It was the only thing at hand."

"And you knew to do it."

"And now I'm engaged to a Chinese gel with shattered feet!"

"Yes." Benedict paused then gestured vaguely. "By the way, that's why I know she's not a noblewoman. Upper-class Chinese bind their daughter's feet. It's a practice that begins very young. It proves the girl has never labored and is thought to be the height of erotic beauty."

Max knew that already and still shuddered at the idea. "I can't imagine doing that to anyone, much less a little girl."

"The Romans did much worse, and we revere them." Benedict was well known for this one statement. He was famously nonjudgmental about all kinds of choices and predilections. He was never known to indulge himself, but he was the one Lord Castlereagh called upon to entertain sordid appetites. It was a dirty, despicable task, but necessity often required flexibility.

Max shook his head in disgust. "She said they broke her feet to prevent her escape."

"Undoubtably part of it." Benedict's voice was grim. "And

that explains why she killed him. Someone who is capable of smashing a woman's feet likely had other vices as well. I expect she did the world a favor."

Max shuddered. He couldn't help it. The sight and the smell of what she'd done haunted him. "I don't blame her, but it doesn't answer what I'm to do with her."

"See what Prinny thinks."

Max let out a snort of disgust. "And that is exactly the problem! I cannot allow Prinny to run my life."

Benedict's brows rose. "You are speaking of the Royal Prince and Regent. You are his loyal subject—"

"Don't quote patriotism to me. I am as loyal an Englishman as any. More so! But we are speaking about my wife. The mother of my children, one of whom will become a duke. You cannot think that such a decision..." His voice trailed off, seeing his defeat in his own words. If they believed Prinny was fit to command the country, then naturally, he was fit to make decisions on international affairs. Even ones that required a wedding. Especially those. "But this isn't a matter of international importance!"

"Are you sure?"

"Of course, I'm not sure. That's why I wanted to speak with you."

Benedict chuckled. "But I am not the expert on Chinese affairs. That's Sir Staunton's bailiwick."

"I know," Max said miserably. "But he's in Canton on his expedition and it will take months for any type of communication with him."

"A year most like. Six months, at least, until he receives your letter. And that long for a response."

"And what am I to do in the meantime?"

"Exactly what you are doing, I suppose."

"Making mold tea—"

"And seeing if she survives."

Max made a sound of fury, one that had been building for

longer than this one day. He'd passed his thirtieth birthday months ago. Much though he hated to admit it, his father was right. It was long past time for him to begin a useful adulthood. One that didn't involve drunken revelries with Prinny or murders in his guest bedroom. Unfortunately, he had no interest in following his father's ultraconservative political footsteps. He would inevitably enter the House of Lords, of course, but at the moment, he would rather drink himself to extinction than blindly follow his father's dictates.

Lord Benedict—a future earl—understood his frustration, probably better than anyone. The man was older and had fought his father for his unpalatable position in the Foreign Office. Which is why Max chose to listen when Benedict set a long-fingered hand on his arm.

"Diplomacy requires patience. If you wish to pursue such a thing without a foreign appointment—"

"I am the heir to a dukedom. I cannot risk myself abroad without risking the end of the entire title." Damn his forebearers for not giving him male cousins.

"Then you should have married earlier."

He knew that. He *knew* it, but somehow he'd never managed to do the deed.

"Perhaps you could take this opportunity to become our London expert on China."

"I'd rather help against Napoleon."

"And I'd rather not marry at all," Benedict returned. "Our titles exact a price. Did you imagine you would be exempt from that?"

No. But he never expected that doing his duty to king and country would involve marrying a Chinese girl. Trying to distract himself, he turned the discussion to Lord Benedict's problems. "Tell me about this gel you're going to marry. The one with the unusual hobby."

Benedict chuckled. "I believe you have enough burdens for today."

"What? But I have confessed all to you—"

"And I have not made my interest known to the woman. I doubt she even knows who I am."

Truly? "She must be a recluse."

"She is not, but neither is she a social creature. She is well occupied with her own interests, which makes her a perfect wife for me."

"Because she has no interest in you or your title?"

"Exactly. And now I must bid you goodnight. I have yet one more appointment before I can rest."

"Now? Good God, you do keep long hours."

Benedict shrugged. "Make sure to keep me informed. I find myself desperate to learn how this turns out."

"My life is not a circus sideshow," Max grumbled.

"Are you sure about that?"

"No," he reluctantly admitted. "Christopher is right now regaling Prinny with every sordid detail."

"And I was the lucky one to learn it directly from you." With that, Lord Benedict doffed his hat and turned a corner to head east. He walked with long, quick strides and a confident air that Max envied. He was likely on a mission of desperate importance for the Crown while Max went inside to boil water for moldy tea.

Good God, he was a sideshow freak!

Chapter Eleven

L ADY EMMALINE WRUNG out a rag then set it on their guest's forehead. It was a tedious task, but the woman's fever was climbing, and this was what one did when a fever grew too hot. She could have set a servant to the task, but the staff was frightened of the woman, and no wonder. No one wanted to soothe the fever of a murderess, no matter how justified.

Or at least, no one in their household.

Once Max had fled after uttering the mysterious words, "Finding medicine," it fell to Emmaline to care for the poor woman.

"What you must have suffered," she said as she stared at Miss Wong's features. She studied the golden skin tones that indicated time in the sun, now tinged with rose from fever. She noted the smooth, almost flat features of nose and forehead. The upward tilt of the eyes was interesting to her artist's eyes, and Emmaline thought about sketching the woman. She was unlikely to get a better chance to examine a Chinese subject at such length.

Strangely enough, her paints and brushes were close at hand. Why Max had suddenly decided to take up watercolors, she had no idea. And how annoying that he'd neglected to clean the brushes. Still, she supposed he could be forgiven such a lapse on today of all days.

She cleaned up the mess Max had left, changed the cloth on Miss Wong's forehead, and then settled down with her sketchpad, but the lines wouldn't form right. Truthfully, she wasn't in the mood to sketch, but she didn't know what else to do.

"You've brought chaos to my life, Miss Wong," she said conversationally. "I don't blame you in the least. Indeed, I'm grateful. I've lately wished for something—anything—to change the sameness of my days. I should be more careful with what I wish for."

She made a long line to indicate the sweep of brow, another for the curve of a high cheek.

"The staff is terrified of you, and Mama isn't much better, though she'll enjoy the attention from this for the rest of her life. Similarly, Father will remain mortified by the whole affair. I wish they would divorce themselves from the idea that everything Max and I do tarnishes them somehow. It's true, of course, but not to the degree that they bluster about it."

She paused to rewet the rag and set it back on Miss Wong's forehead.

"I have no idea what this is doing to Max," she said, her voice low. "He was there for the whole thing. The fight…"

She didn't want to relive rushing into the guest bedroom. She didn't want her mind to dwell on those first seconds. There was plenty to recall. She'd been the one to supervise the removal of the body. She'd been the first to speak to the Watch, and she'd be the one who would lie—eventually—and say that the room was completely cleaned such that no trace of blood or…

She shuddered as she mentally ticked off all the new things that would be needed for that room. She would completely refurbish it, including the paper on the wall, and still she would shudder every time she stepped inside it.

She looked down at her sketchpad, blank except for her first few strokes. "I'm going to have to marry," she declared. It was the only way she might never step into that bedroom again.

"I was thinking much the same thing," said a voice behind her.

Emma twisted to see Lady Kimberly entering the room. Her steps were quiet and her expression…well, her expression was what it always was when she was away from her beloved dogs. She was wary and tense. For all that she spoke carefully and moved with the refined elegance appropriate to a future duchess, Emmaline knew it covered a debilitating shyness that strained every aspect of the woman's life.

Emmaline couldn't understand why no one else saw it.

"Kim, you didn't have to come back here," she said.

"I promised Max I would." Her gaze went to Miss Wong. Her brows narrowed as she gestured to the foot of the bed. "May I?"

"Yes."

Emmaline helped her lift up the thin cover over Miss Wong's feet. Kimberly gently touched the flesh, her lips tightening at the level of swelling.

"Best keep the blanket off. I doubt it will help much, but it can't hurt."

Emmaline agreed, so they stripped the covers off the bed. Miss Wong wore one of Emma's nightrails, so there was no lack of modesty, but still it felt uncomfortable to have such hideously disfigured feet prominent in her vision. She didn't want to see such ugliness, and yet what was a sickroom for but to face an illness and fight for health as best as one could?

Kimberly, on the other hand, didn't appear to suffer the same affliction. She was careful not to disturb Miss Wong, but she spent a great deal of time studying the shape and character of the injury. In the end, she stood up with an audible sigh.

"The fever is a bad sign," she said.

Emmaline had guessed as much. "I don't know if it's better for her to recover or not. I can't imagine the life she will have if she survives."

Kimberly's brows rose. "You don't think Max will marry her? It was Prinny's express command."

"Prinny says a lot of things that Max ignores. He won't forget his promises to you."

"It's only one promise. And men are not known to be faithful creatures."

Emmaline heard Kimberly's unspoken words. *Unlike dogs,* men weren't faithful or loyal or remotely dependable. She couldn't argue that on a general basis, but she felt pressured to defend her brother.

"Max has neglected you, to be sure, but he's promised to marry you in a thousand different ways. He's never taken a mistress, never shown partiality to any woman above you. He's danced three times with you in an evening. Indeed, the *haut ton* regards you both as already wed."

Kimberly nodded, but her lips were pressed together in doubt. And what could Emma say to that? The truth was that the two were not actually wed, and Kimberly was already too old to step into the marriage mart.

Of course, that was nearly true for Emma, and she was not promised to a soul. "I begin to think the life of a spinster would not be so bad," she murmured, thinking of the eligible men this year. Unfortunately, her only other option was to wait hand and foot on her parents for the rest of her life. That sounded hideous. She wanted a household of her own. She wanted a smaller establishment with few servants constantly watching for gossip. And most of all, she wanted Christopher to notice her once and for all.

"Do you still long for Lord Christopher?"

Emmaline jolted, surprised and annoyed that Kimberly had remembered her youthful confession four seasons ago. She had always regarded the woman as her future sister-in-law, and so had been too forthcoming in her fantasies.

"He sees me as Max's scapegrace younger sister. I doubt he thinks of me as a woman grown." She had been a lonely girl, desperate for companionship when her paints could not distract her. It was only natural that she had spent her summers pestering her brother and his best friend. She rode after them when they went out, she intruded on their fishing during the day and billiards at night. She'd been a constant pest when she was young and a horrendous flirt when she was older.

She knew now that she'd merely been lonely. Her parents hadn't wanted her to play with the local children and only occasionally allowed her school friends to visit. The only reason Max had been allowed Christopher was because the boy had arrived on his own and refused to leave. And she, of course, had thought such casual defiance to be the height of masculine power.

She now knew it had been because of some violent altercation between him and his father. Violent enough, it seemed, that he had been forced to flee.

"What he thinks about," commented Kimberly as she wrung out the rag on Miss Wong's forehead, "is his empty coffers. He will not become a fortune hunter for your dowry."

"It's not so bad as that," Emma said, hoping it was true.

Kimberly shrugged. "I understand his brother wants to attend Oxford, but they haven't the coin to support him. And his sister has no dowry at all."

"She's too young to have a Season," she said, and thank God for that because the price of outfitting a girl was exorbitant.

Christopher's empty coffers were well known to her, but she didn't care. Of all the men she'd met, he still stood head and shoulders above the rest. He made her laugh when she thought she'd scream, and his smile always made her feel seen. As if he alone understood what she was feeling.

Fantasy, of course, but it would not leave her.

"Emma, you're smart, titled, and well-dowered. You know what to say and when to keep silent. If you want to marry, pick a man and crook your finger. He shall be at your feet within the moments."

"I know," she grumbled. "But they all seem so childish. I want someone to challenge me, to engage my mind and my heart." There was a summer, long ago, when she and Christopher had debated philosophy, religion, and even monetary policy. Neither of them had known what they were talking about, but it had sent her to study. They had a substantial library at their country estate. When he and Max had gone fishing, she had read.

And when they returned, she and Christopher debated.

No one else had ever challenged her mind as he did. It was the primary reason she loved him. Night after night, he would refuse to flirt, but he would discuss whatever erudite topic struck her fancy.

Compared to that, what could the fops and dandies of high society offer her? She looked at Kimberly.

"All they do is play and complain." That was rich coming from her. After all, what did she do with her life? She went to parties and complained about her mother's complaining. She dropped her chin on her head. "Good God, I've become one of them, haven't I?"

"No more than the rest of us. I, too, look for something more substantial to fill my days." Her expression grew sober. "I would appreciate it if you could visit my cousin Mary Ann."

"I'd heard that her dog is sick. Is he very ill?"

"It's Oscar's time. He's lived a long and happy life, but Mary Ann is inconsolable." Kimberly sighed. "With dogs, all one must do is hold them, love them, and when the time comes, let them know you are there for them. It's sad. It's hard, but it is natural." She lifted her hands in a gesture of helplessness. "I do not know what to do for people."

"It is much the same for people at the end, I think. It is the times when we are not dying that are harder to navigate."

"You will talk to her?"

Emmaline nodded. "I will visit. Only she can say if she will speak with me."

"I'm sure she will. You never fail to make people feel better. You're much like Oscar in that regard."

Emma laughed. Despite the awkwardness of the phrasing, she knew that was high praise from Kimberly. Unfortunately, the image stuck, and it did not help her mood. She pictured herself as a lap dog passed from one person to another. She soothed, she barked about the bad people, she performed tasks that pleased her companions, and then she went home feeling more disgusted with her life than ever before.

The thing that was both good and bad about dogs was that they gave complete love, absolute loyalty, and never, ever complained about how they were treated. They also never forced their masters to grow in any way, shape, or form. What good was soothing someone's irritation if they never changed what caused the irritation in the first place? She didn't want to be a lapdog. She wanted to be a scolding nanny to the most childish adults in the world.

Why didn't people want to change the things that made them miserable? Why didn't she want to leave her current life for something more fulfilling or at least different?

Her gaze returned to Miss Wong's face and found the lady inspiring. She couldn't imagine being torn from one's home, brought to another country where she didn't speak the language, and then offered as a plaything to a king. She'd clearly suffered terrible things and still had the strength to fight back. She'd killed one of her abusers. She'd learned to speak English. What had Emmaline ever done that compared to that?

She had no answer. Thankfully, she didn't need to because at that moment, Max came in with a jar of…was that dirt?

"Is she awake?" he asked as soon as he crossed the threshold.

"It's a fitful sleep at best," Emma responded. "What is that? I thought you went to get medicine."

He shrugged. "It's what she wanted, but I don't know if she's supposed to take it as hot tea or eat it straight."

"But what is it?" Lady Kimberly asked as she peered at the jar.

He blinked as he noticed the other lady in the room. "Oh. Hullo Kim. It's mold." He held up his hands to quiet her before she could ask. "I have no idea why, but she was very clear."

Kimberly nodded. "Add some honey to it."

"What?"

She shrugged. "Honey helps everything."

"I'll get it," Emmaline said as she pushed to her feet. "I hope it helps."

It could hardly hurt. She was quick to find a footman and ask for a pot of honey. Then as she returned to the bedroom, she heard Kimberly speak. Her words were formal, as usual, her tone matter of fact, but Emmaline heard how her words faded away in surprise.

"Wake her gently. We'll need to… lift…" She stopped speaking and Emmaline stepped into the bedroom to see what had silenced her longtime friend.

Max had settled on the bed, a place that was wholly inappropriate for an unmarried man. He was leaning forward while one finger gently stroked the lady's face.

"Yihui," he said. "I'm here with the medicine."

Emmaline had never heard her brother croon to anyone and a glance at Kimberly's face saw the same shock.

The Chinese woman's eyes fluttered open. Her skin was flushed pink, but her eyes appeared clear as she focused on the man above her. Her mouth curved into a soft smile even as her brows drew together.

"Medicine?" she rasped.

"I have it."

He supported her head and shoulders, easily lifting her up then holding her there while he looked to Lady Kimberly.

"Kim. The pillows, please?"

It took a moment for the lady to realize what he wanted. She rushed to do as he asked, fumbling a bit while he cradled Miss Wong.

Emma saw what her brother did not. She saw that Kimberly's cheeks had turned hot with embarrassment. That the lady served—as she always did—while damning herself for not seeing the need beforehand. And while Max gently lowered his charge, Kimberly stood by awkwardly, her gaze hopping between Max and Miss Wong.

"Tell me what I must do," Max said to the patient. His tone was soft, almost pleading, and Emma gaped at her normally brusque brother.

Miss Wong pointed at the jar of mold, gesturing for him to hand it over. He did, his movements rushed as he opened the jar for her. She sniffed, she nodded, then she looked to the sideboard.

"Tea?"

Max's head snapped up. "Bloody idiots," he muttered. "Where is—"

"Right here," Emma said in the same voice she used when her mother was on the verge of hysterics.

A footman entered carrying the tea tray. Max pointed with impatience at the bedside table.

"Damn it, Em, you've got too many fripperies here to fit the tray."

She had too many…? "Have you taken leave of your senses?" she snapped. And then she belatedly realized that she'd just been incredibly indiscrete in front of Kimberly and the footman. Good lord, what had happened to everyone today, herself included?

She hurried to clear a space and then personally moved the teapot, honey pot, and other items to the table. When it was done, she gestured the footman away. He disappeared quickly, no doubt eager to carry the tale of Max being besotted with the Chinese witch.

After all, there was no other explanation as to why her normally unflappable brother was suddenly gathering mold in jars and acting so solicitous of a woman he'd met not more than a few hours ago.

Meanwhile, Max was continuing his idiotic behavior. He held out the teacup, cradled in his enormous hands while Miss Wong pinched out a large amount of mold.

"Honey?" he asked as he passed the pot to her.

She sniffed it and nodded quickly. "Yes. Thank you."

You would have thought her brother had been gifted with the crown jewels, so wide was his smile as he dropped in several thick dollops of honey.

Emmaline stared at her brother. "It was Kimberly's idea," she said firmly.

He nodded absently. "Yes. Thank you, Kim."

Good lord, he didn't even look up. His eyes were on the Chinese woman as she took the cup from his hand and gestured for him to pour the water in. He did so, and Emmaline had to look away as the lady stirred it quickly, then gulped it down.

In her defense, she appeared to despise what she'd done as much as Emma would. Her nose was wrinkled, her face screwed up in disgust, but she did it. And that, apparently, was the depth of her strength as she collapsed back against the pillows.

Max set everything back on the side table, his expression solicitous. "Is there anything else? Water? Food?" He made gestures with his hands as he spoke, but the woman shook her head. Instead, she pointed down to her feet.

"Must see."

"There's no need…"

Max tried to deny her, but the woman was adamant. She took a moment to gather her courage. Emma could see it in the way she squared her shoulders and narrowed her brows. Such courage in this foreign woman! Then she pulled herself upright to see her feet.

Emma winced, as did everyone in the room. Her feet were a red, swollen mess and the lady gave a mew of distress.

"It'll get better," Max quickly assured her. "You need time." He quickly covered her back up.

Apparently, the woman had seen enough. She dropped back onto her pillows in misery, her gaze going back to Max. "Thank you," she said.

"I'll stay here with you tonight. You're safe here."

Again, Emma met Kimberly's shocked gaze. Max was going to sit vigil? Didn't he have to go entertain Prinny? Or perhaps discover a way out of this predicament? Apparently not because he settled his chair such that he could cradle the Chinese's woman's hand in his own.

"Are you feverish?" Emma blurted out. Good God, couldn't the man see that he was coddling a foreign woman right in front of Kimberly?

"What are you about, Em?"

She was about to knock him about the head. "Max," she said firmly, "your fiancée is over there!" She pointed to Kim who immediately straightened.

"I know where she is," Max said, abruptly removing his hand from beneath Miss Wong's. "Kimberly and I understand each other very well."

"Well, the servants don't. And I don't. Max—"

Kimberly abruptly interrupted. "No, no! Don't cut up at him."

"What?" Emma demanded.

"He's had a shock. You both have. Today has been incredibly difficult for all of us. He's concerned for his guest's health, and that is to the good. I, um… People tend to act very odd around death, you know, even a pet's death."

Max's tone was hard. "She's not dying."

"What? No, I meant the other one. The…um…violent one."

That silenced them all for a moment. The sight of the dead mandarin had not left her thoughts for one second. Perhaps cutting up at her brother was how she had distracted herself.

"Still, he cannot fawn over Miss Wong. It's not fair to you."

"I'm not fawning—"

"Of course, it's not fair," Kimberly retorted. "None of it ever is. But I have agreed to be Ophelia, you see. Not long, mind you, but for now."

Emma had no idea what that meant, but Max clearly did. He tucked his hands into his lap and frowned at Miss Wong. Her eyes were open, her expression neutral. She was clearly aware of the discussion around her, but Emma had no idea if she understood enough English to follow it. Hell, English was Emma's native language, and she wasn't sure what was going on.

Meanwhile, Kimberly continued. "I'm going to leave now, Max, unless you want me to stay."

"Good God no. There's no need for us both to lose a night's

sleep."

Emma huffed out a breath. "There's no need for either of you to do such. We do have servants."

"Who are terrified of her," Max said firmly.

Well, that was true.

"Figure it out, Max," Kimberly said as she gathered her things.

"What?"

"Figure out what you want to do. Everything waits upon you." She came around the bedside to look him in the eye. "I wait upon you."

His expression softened and he stood with awkward grace. His cheeks were tinged red as he gathered her hand in his. "A little bit longer, Kimberly. I swear." Then he pressed a reverent kiss to her hand.

"Very well, Hamlet."

"Stop that," he grumbled as he straightened.

She arched her brows at him while he rolled his eyes at her. Watching it, Emmaline could see the connections of long friendship, the bonds that allowed for mistreatment, forgiveness, and even an amiable future marriage.

But she also saw so many ways it could go wrong. Theirs was not a relationship built on mutual passion, thank goodness. Both were even tempered, rational people. But even rational people broke under extraordinary stress, and she did not like this sudden disruption of Chinese into their lives.

"Wait!" Emma said as she made her decision. "I shall go with you, if you don't mind."

"What?"

"Well, the patient is in my bedroom. I need somewhere to stay." And she wasn't going into the yellow bedroom ever again. "You and I can spend the evening together saying all kinds of nasty things about my brother."

"Emma, please," groaned Max.

"He's going to have a long, lonely night to consider his sins,"

Emma continued. "I say we do the same."

Kimberly grinned. "I shall love it beyond all else."

"Have at it," he harumphed as he dropped back into his chair. "I care very little about what either of you say."

"And that, brother dear, is exactly the problem."

Chapter Twelve

"THEY ARE ANGRY with you." Yihui waited to speak until the women had left. Even then, she kept her voice low, but he heard her.

"Yes," he said, his tone rueful. "Kimberly has a right. My sister, on the other hand, is always angry with me, so that doesn't count."

She nodded, pleased that she understood his English words. He spoke slowly, which helped. And there was a cleanness in the way he formed sounds that made him easier to understand. Each syllable was spoken clearly, and she liked watching the way his mouth moved. She discovered a wealth of meaning in the curve of his lips or the occasional pinch.

Right now, he was pinched, but the lift of his brows suggested humor.

"Do you have sisters?" he asked. "Brothers?"

"Two brothers which is why I was sold."

Now his mouth pinched even more. "What do you mean, you were sold?"

"I am not the true Wong daughter." She thought she'd told him that but wasn't sure now. "I am better than her. She is ugly with a mean temper and sick feet." Though she might also have sick feet now. "The Wong daughter's foot binding was done badly, and she suffers from them. I will make sure my feet are not so badly managed."

"It's true then," he said. "You bind every girl's feet?"

She shook her head. "Just the rich ones." Then she realized her mistake. If she wasn't the Wong daughter, he would have no reason to take care of her. Stupid! Stupid! She abruptly surged forward, grabbing his hand. "But I am better than they are. I make medicines. I can tend to your women. Their complaints will not bother you when I am around to heal them."

He caught her hands and held them firm. "I am sure you are prettier—"

"Not just pretty! Smart. Educated. I can teach your doctors Chinese medicine. Much better than your medicine."

His brows arched, and she could see she'd insulted him.

"I have seen your version of medicine—" he began, but she spoke over him.

"It is disgusting. Your doctors will not go to those places, but I will. I do. That is what I did for my father before…"

"Before he sold you?"

She winced as she dropped back onto the pillows. When she was taken, her fury had known no bounds. She had screamed until her voice was hoarse and woe to any who came near. That was when she perfected her curses, finding the words that made the staunchest men pale. But then she was set on the English ship, and the sailors had no understanding of her words and therefore no fear of her. She knew when the ship left dock that her old life was gone forever.

Her only hope was to learn English so that she could frighten them, too. Instead, she made friends with the rough English sailors.

"Why did he sell you?"

Because her father was a weak and stupid man. She'd come to realize that in the six months it had taken for her to get to England. "My father gambles and loses. The Wong patriarch worried that his daughter was too ill-tempered to entice the English king, so my father suggested me. He said that I was sweet and would make a better bribe." She lifted her chin wondering if it was ridiculous to be proud that she had been sold for a very high price. "My father's debts are all paid now."

"And you are in England with broken feet."

She was, but few girls got the opportunity to pay off their family debts so young. "I am free now. I have honored my father and my ancestors. Now I live for me."

He looked at her, his expression carefully blanked. His mouth did not shift, neither did his eyes. Then his head tilted, and his hair shifted across his forehead. Such a fascinating color. It did not seem to have the appearance of weight, and yet she knew he was an important man in his world. In China, any man in the emperor's palace would have heavy robes, a thick queue, and an air of weighty ostentation. This man simply looked at her with his bird-colored eyes and feathery light hair.

And yet, she knew he thought deeply.

Growing uncomfortable, she twisted her hands against her lap. "I am educated. I can help you."

"I will not cast you out, Yihui—"

How sweet to hear her name on his lips. He gave a strange musicality to her name so different than when her family spoke it. There was no command in his tone. He spoke as he might to a fellow scholar or personage in court. He spoke her name with respect, and she found she liked it best of all.

"Thank you, Max." She liked the hard, short sound of his name. "Do you have brothers, Max?"

"It is only me and my sister. We fight with each other, but we are very close."

She frowned, trying to sort through his words. He spoke with affection toward his sister, mentioning her though she had asked about brothers. She noted the warmth in his tone, and wondered if tenderness was common in English families. She knew many Chinese families where the children were not set in competition with one another, where brother and sister played happily together. That, however, was not her home or her family.

"I want to know more," she said. "The more I know, the better I can serve you."

He patted her hand. "You are not here to serve me."

"I am here to be your wife. Is that not service?"

His cheeks colored at that. She could see it clearly on his white skin, but his expression was too strange for her to read. That bothered her, especially as he shook his head.

"Get better first," he said. "Then we will talk about your future."

That was not reassuring. There were many ways she could have a good life as a concubine, but if the English did not take wives in that manner, what did they do with their extra women?

"I am very good at making medicines. You will see. Your doctors could not save me, but I saved myself." He wasn't listening to her. He was shaking his head and panic began to edge her tone. "You will see. I am important!"

"Of course, I see," he said, but it was in a tone reserved for a madwoman.

"Do not kill me! I will help you!"

He grabbed her hands again, steadying her frantic movements. She quieted because she knew speaking crazy would only make things worse.

"No one is going to kill you." He gently pushed her hair away from her face, taking the time to speak directly to her with clear, calm words. "You are safe."

The assurance of that slipped into her, and she found her breath eased. Still, she had to make him understand that she could be valuable to him.

"I will help you," she repeated. "I am—"

"You are important. I know."

Did he? Of course not.

"I will prove it to you. I will live. I will walk. I am—"

"Important. Yes."

Her strength was fading fast. She could not sort through his words to gain meaning, and she did not dare try to find the English words now. She would have to live and then convince him. Or at least get better enough to escape. Someone, somewhere would be interested in her skills. She was not worthless.

Chapter Thirteen

"GOOD GOD, YOU look awful."

Max sat down at the breakfast table and wondered why he'd bothered to shave before coming down. His father would make him out to be disreputable, no matter how dapper he appeared.

"It was a long night, Father."

"I don't doubt it." The man looked down at the newspaper. "Did she survive?"

"Yes, she did," Max said, his tone churlish. "In fact, the surgeon said he is hopeful."

"I heard him depart. And even if I hadn't, it's all the staff talks about."

Max looked up, startled. "Surely not with you. Chiverton wouldn't allow it."

"Gads, no. But I'm neither deaf nor blind. I see them casting fearful looks down the hall. I hear the maids whisper about you sitting vigil in her room. And the honey pot was missing this morning."

"It's not missing. It's upstairs to help her drink her medicine."

"Yes," his father drawled. "I heard all sorts of nonsense about that from my valet."

Max covered his reaction by drinking his tea. Then he nodded to the footman as eggs and toast were set before him. He was either desperately hungry or too tired to eat. Meanwhile, his father continued to needle him with difficult questions.

"Have you decided what to do with the gel? I'm sure a place for her could be found in Devonshire, especially if she has some trade. What did her father do?"

"He was a doctor of some kind."

"Well, that's no help. Heathen medicine will have filled her head with all sorts of superstitious nonsense."

Though Max had thought something similar yesterday—especially when he was collecting mold in the stable—this morning he found the sentiment narrowminded. "You don't think they could have stumbled upon something that we don't know? A plant, perhaps, or tincture that isn't available to us?"

"Of course, they did. Opium. But we've got it now, refined it, and sell it back to them at great profit. We have the scientific method of inquiry, and until the heathens adopt that, they've got nothing to teach us."

"What makes you think they don't have a scientific method of inquiry?"

"They didn't figure out opium, did they?"

"But maybe they figured out something else. We won't know until we ask."

His father arched a disdainful brow. "Then ask, if you wish to waste your time. Write letters to them, for all I care. But the girl is not going to help with any of that."

I am important!

Ylhui's words echoed in his thoughts. Indeed, they'd echoed throughout the night while he cooled her brow and wondered what he was going to do. He shouldn't be irritated with his father for voicing the exact same things that had tortured him through the night, but he was. Mostly because he knew the sentiment was wrong. He just couldn't prove it.

"She has value," he said firmly.

"How?"

"Because all people have value!"

His father leaned back in his chair and regarded Max with a quizzical air. "I begin to worry about you. Have you taken a religious turn?"

"What?"

"Sitting up all night next to a heathen, talking about her value as if a beggar at our door is important somehow."

"Even a beggar is a person."

"There!" he said pointing a finger at Max's face. "That's exactly what I mean. I don't deny that a beggar is a person, but they should be in the care of the priests and nuns. Unless you are about to take up vows, I cannot see why you would traipse about London collecting dirt or sit at her bedside through the night. And that is to say nothing of countenancing murder in our own home."

"I didn't countenance murder."

"Neither did you send her to Tyburn for committing it. No, you—"

"I sat vigil at her bedside. Yes, Father, I remember."

"Don't take that tone with me. You are my heir. Everything you do is noted and remarked upon by all of London." He tossed the newspaper at Max opened to the glaring headline, MURDER IN A DUCAL HOME.

He scanned the contents quickly, seeing that the reporter had gotten the substance essentially correct, though it was written in the most scandalized tone. He set it down with a sigh. "It was never going to be kept quiet."

"But it doesn't have to *linger*. Certainly not upstairs."

Max had no answer except the one his father would reject. "Prinny has not rescinded his order. I am commanded to marry her."

"Bollocks. Send her off to Devonshire to cook or something. Prinny will get around to it in time."

"She kept saying she was important. I don't know what she meant—"

"Well, of course she did! Everyone in our circle is desperate to be important. Otherwise, they can't be in our circle, can they? I'm a duke. You're my heir—"

"Can you not feel for the girl? Sold into slavery by her own father, dragged to the English court only to have a knife put her throat. Her feet were broken, she's wracked with fever, and she still had the wherewithal to tell me she could be useful. That I shouldn't kill her. Damn it, Father, can you not see the spirit in her?"

"What I see is my name in the papers, a bedroom that reeks of blood and worse, and my son lost in a romantic fantasy about a savage. Can you imagine Lady Kimberly acting in such a manner?"

"No," he said. "I cannot." He had a great deal of admiration for his childhood friend, but he doubted she would endure being sold to a foreign land, much less any of the other crimes Yihui had suffered.

"Of course not and thank God for that. Max, you must get a hold of yourself. She is a savage, and you can no more marry her than you would a tiger or a rampaging bull." In a rare moment of tenderness, his father reached out his hand. Not quite enough to touch Max, but the gesture was there. "Son, exotic fantasies are normal. Every man has them, but only a fool acts upon them. And he certainly doesn't bring them home to their mother."

"It was by Prinny's command."

"And how many of Prinny's commands have you disobeyed in the last month? How many of the man's drunken idiocies have you curtailed just this week?"

Max's eyes widened. He hadn't thought his father understood what he was doing at Carlton House.

"I have friends in the Foreign Office as well. I know what Lord Benedict has asked of you." He withdrew his hand to close up the paper, hiding the awful headline. "You have spent the last four years dancing rings around the prince. Why now, of all times, would you bow to royal decree?"

"It's not that simple. I cannot blatantly refuse a royal command."

"I'm sure it's devastatingly difficult. And yet, I know you

could do it. There's always a way to distract royalty. So why didn't you do it this time? Why did you spend the night praying by her bedside?"

"I wasn't praying," he said. He'd been thinking. The events of the day had forced him to take a hard look at his life and choices.

His title had kept him from the military or indeed any foreign travel for fear of contracting some disease or being shot by the French. He understood that his death would be the end of a very ancient title, and though he feared that less than his father did, he still chose to stay out of harm's way as much as possible. He did that out of respect for his forefathers.

He was not especially prone to scholarship and his father refused to let him manage the family finances, though he had tried dozens of different tactics to get their smallest estate under his control. That left him pursuing his only real interest—Chinoiserie—and serving as Prinny's court jester or secret brake if the situation called for it.

So many of his compatriots would relish this life. Money to burn with no responsibilities except for the getting of an heir. Max, however, found himself itching to make more of himself. Growing up, he hadn't just fantasized about being a pirate. He'd adored tales of King Arthur and had fancied himself a chivalrous knight. He wanted to punish evil, proclaim right over might, and rescue the princess. He still did. Only now, all he did was restrain Prinny from the worst of his excesses and tried to make restitution to Yihui.

That was not his job. He had not wronged her. And yet, he was in a position to help her. And so he would serve as her protector even if it meant defying his own father as he sought a solution. It also gave a purpose for this desire he felt for her. He had spent half the night in thought, and half the night in fantasy.

Even with broken feet, she was beautiful to him. The curve of her eyes, the shape of her face. Exotic, yes, and so very exciting. Her spirit enflamed him, her defiance against her captors made her into a warrior goddess. What man wouldn't want to claim that for his own? The two desires to protect her and claim her brought him to defy everyone around him.

"She is an innocent," he said. "I will not add to her pain."

His father didn't answer except to stand, choosing to tower over his son while tapping the newspaper against his thigh. It wasn't a hard whack, of course, but the sound was loud in the quiet house.

Slap, slap, slap.

Like the ticking of a clock or the drip of blood from a small wound.

"End this, Max," his father finally said. "Get the girl out of the house and our name out of the papers. If you need help with Prinny—"

"He hates you, Father."

"I was going to suggest you go to Lord Benedict for aid. You're right that Prinny and I will never see eye to eye on anything." He peered down at his son. "I rather thought that was what drew you two together."

"Not really, Father." He had chosen to entertain Prinny rather than openly defy his father's politics in the House of Commons. It helped that he agreed with some of Prinny's liberal ideas. The man was a great defender of the arts and could be extraordinarily generous to his people. He could also be flighty, selfish, and completely blind to deeper issues.

His father sighed. "Prinny's a prancing fool, not an idiot. He knows a duke cannot marry a merchant girl from China."

That was certainly true. "I'll have to speak with Christopher. He was with Prinny last night to tell the tale."

"Wonderful," his father drawled, heavy with sarcasm. "Trust Christopher to take an ember and make it into a conflagration. With him in Prinny's ear, we won't escape the tale for months."

"You've always been too hard on Chris."

"And you've always had a soft spot for broken creatures. Christopher is case in point with his disastrous father. They're sad things, to be sure. They're God's way of making us appreciate what we have. But that doesn't mean you need to marry them."

"I'm not going to marry her!"

"Then go to bed, Max. Get a decent night's sleep and some hearty food in your belly. Stop drinking all hours of the night and take a good look at your life. You're two and thirty now. It's time to take up your responsibilities."

Max lifted his chin to stare at his father. "And what responsibilities would those be? You won't allow me a hand in the running of the estate—"

"You spend too freely, Max—"

"I'm more likely to vote against your measures if you put me in the House of Commons."

"You wouldn't say that if you thought about the consequences of what those idiot Whigs are spouting on about."

"I cannot marry Lady Kimberly while commanded to wed Yihui."

"Is that her name? Sounds like a wheezing dog."

Max pushed to his feet to meet his father eye to eye. Or rather eye to forehead, as he topped his father's height by three inches. "It is her name," he repeated firmly.

"Fine, fine." His father stepped far enough back that he could look down his nose at Max. "I truly don't care."

"But you want me to take up my responsibilities. I ask again, what responsibilities are those? What meaningful use of my time would you like me to adopt?"

"I cannot pick your amusements, Max. Take up writing or the sciences. You were always good at mathematics."

"Why don't I take Yihui back to China? I could be England's special envoy—"

His father threw up his hands in disgust. "And now you are back to nonsense. England has people in China already. You're not just the heir to a dukedom, Max. You're the *only* heir. You're not going anywhere until you sire a few more. If you'd done your duty by Lady Kimberly, you wouldn't be in this mess now. So get rid of the broken Chinese creature and get on with your responsibilities as a man."

"Or what, Father?"

"Or remain as you are now, a jester in Prinny's court. A useful jester, to be sure, but a silly one nonetheless." His father sighed. "And a true embarrassment to the title we hold."

Chapter Fourteen

YIHUI WOKE QUICKLY, as was her habit. She had spent the last three days and nights in a fog of illness but was now alert and the feeling was startling.

"The fever is gone," she said. She spoke in Chinese as the words were for herself, but a woman to her right reacted.

"Good morning, Yihui. How do you feel today?"

She turned to see Max's sister, Emmaline. After that first night, she had not seen much of Max. His sister was the usual person beside the bed. Yihui pushed herself upright, taking the glass of water Emmaline offered.

She drank greedily, happy to find that she felt hunger. That was another good sign.

"My fever," she said in English. "Gone."

"Yes, it broke late yesterday. You finally got some good sleep."

"Good sleep," she echoed. "Yes." But she knew better than to stop the medicinal tea. She had seen many people grow sick again from quitting it too soon. She looked to the jar by the bedside. Someone had refilled it, most likely Max, and she flushed with pleasure at the kindness. She knew it was a disgusting task, and yet he had done it.

"I'll ring for more hot water," Emmaline said as she set down her sketchpad.

"Thank you."

"My maid will help with your toilette."

She nodded. What she really wanted was a bath, but that was too much to ask. And though her feet felt better, she knew she'd never be able to make it to a stream.

"And Max wanted to know when you woke—"

"No!"

Emmaline's eyes widened. "But—"

"I cannot see him. I need washing. Cleaning. Hair brush."

Her expression softened. "He has seen you every day that you have been here. He knows—"

"But I am better now." She pulled back the covers to show her feet. Still swollen but the heat was down and the pain less throbbing. "No red streaks. No fever. I am better—"

"That's good—"

She jerked the cover back over her feet. She did not like to see them so deformed. "There is a place between sick and well that men do not like. They expect very sick or nearly well." She gestured to the left and right with a wide distance between them. "The middle is very unpleasant for them."

The lady blinked, then leaned back in her chair. "That's very true," she said. "Of everyone, I think. No one enjoys the slow road to health." Then she shook her head. "But Max won't expect you to look your best."

Yihui shook her head firmly. How could this lady not understand? "Better he think I'm still very ill. It will give me a few more days to heal." She smiled even though she knew she would need weeks, not days. "It is the dance between men and women, yes? Men do not like to be troubled with women's pain. Best he not know the in-between steps."

Emmaline frowned, but her mood beyond that was unreadable. She didn't seem angry, but neither was she pleased. "What kind of life have you lived that you think men's pain and women's pains are different? We are all people. Patterns change, of course. People are different. But even men get sick and they wait as they gain strength slowly."

Yihui tried to sort through the woman's words. She understood the language for the most part, but it was the meaning that surprised her. "What world do you live in that have men and women so equal?" She glanced down at Emmaline's feet. They were set on an embroidered stool. Her feet were not large by a laborer's standard, but they were huge for a society woman. It was clear the woman walked easily. She could climb and jump without pain. Yihui knew of no highborn Chinese woman who could do the same.

As if guessing her thoughts, Emmaline stretched out her feet before her. "I love dancing," she said. "And in the country, I sometimes run as far as I can go. On the very best days, I run to a stream miles behind the house, and then I swim all the sweat away."

Yihui gaped at her. She could not imagine such freedom, even in the country. Women and girls were hidden away unless they worked. "Your brother, your father allow this?"

"Max used to go with me, but now he prefers to ride. Father doesn't care one way or another so long as I keep the servants doing what they're supposed to do."

Yihui shook her head, amazed. "You are not afraid?"

"Everyone knows me there. I am perfectly safe."

Was England truly so safe a place for women? The thought overcame her for a moment. The idea that a woman could feel protected outside, away from men, to walk—to run and swim—by herself. Such heaven.

The amazement must have been clear on her face because the lady leaned forward. "Were you never free in China?"

"I lived in Canton. It is a very large city. There are many dangers for a girl alone."

"I suppose there are here, too. For the men as well, but in a different way." She shrugged. "I do not go out alone in London."

"But you are allowed to dance, yes?"

"I love to dance."

"Are you taught to fight?"

Emmaline pulled back. "Not at all! Were you taught that in

China?"

She seemed to be intrigued by the idea, but Yihui had to shake her head. "Not usually," she confessed. "My grandmother taught me. My father often needed me to mix special medicines and bring them to him wherever he worked. Other doctors would send messages to the shop. I would mix them and carry the medicine to the patient."

"Was that dangerous?"

"Sometimes. My grandmother taught me where to hit or kick a man. And I can run very fast." Or she could before. She might never run again.

Emmaline understood the direction of her thoughts. "Why do you allow it? I couldn't imagine letting anyone break my feet."

"I did not allow it," Yihui said coldly.

"Oh. Yes, but…"

"Wealthy girls are bound when they are very little and cannot fight back. It is a hard process with many tears, but how else is the child to get a husband when she is grown?"

"Your feet were not bound. How were you to find a husband?"

She flushed and looked away. "I was a difficult daughter. I did not like the men who wanted me and so…" She shrugged.

"So you made them not want you?" Emmaline pressed. "If so, then we are alike."

"You have many men who wish marriage?"

The grimace on her face was comical. "Many stupid ones."

Yihui sighed. "Smart men are rare."

They both laughed as one might with a sister. Except that Emmaline's laugh was full and musical. She did not cover her mouth with her hand and titter but made full expression. Such freedom English woman had. The ability to run outside was miracle enough. It was clear Emmaline had very little fear, too, and Yihui admired the innocence of it. Her own childhood had been quickly bounded, not on her feet, but with rules and responsibilities. She had care of her younger brother when she was three. She began working in the shop soon after that. There was not much that a young child could do safely among such things, but in China, the whole family worked or the whole family starved. That applied double to the girls for they would be the first denied food if times were lean.

She did not fault Emmaline for her innocence. Instead, she longed to remain near it. As if staying in this woman's presence would somehow clean her of her constant worries. It was the dream of a child. This woman was a pampered daughter of England. Yihui could no more live in her shoes than she could sprout wings and fly. And yet, she wanted to share the lady's life until circumstances forced them apart.

"Tell me about your men of bad quality," Yihui asked.

"What?"

"And I will tell you about old Gao with the crooked teeth and clammy hands who would pay more if I let him whisper strange things into my ear."

"Strange things? Like what?"

That was not something for this lady to know. "I don't know. I never allowed it."

"Then how do you know they were strange? Maybe he was whispering a recipe for stew."

Was she truly that naïve? Yihui cast the lady a long look, and Emmaline relented. Her wide-eyed look changed to chagrin.

"I suppose it wasn't a recipe for stew."

"You do not have…uh…"

"Lechers? Yes, we do." Emmaline set aside her sketching. It was an awkward drawing of Yihui asleep, and there was no softness given to her wretched looks. Apparently, the lady was one who preferred accurate images to the sweeter, vaguer pictures of flowers. "You're probably uncomfortable. I'll ring for my maid."

She stood up just as a knock sounded. When the door opened, Yihui saw a maid who curtsied with nervous glances at Yihui, but behind her was Max, his expression cheerful as he stepped into the room.

"You're looking much better now."

Oh no. The clock on her recovery was now ticking. She dropped her gaze immediately, but not before she noticed that he looked exquisite in the English way. His face was clean shaven, and his hair curled in wet disarray. His clothing was dark and gave particular attention to his broad shoulders and trim waist. The Chinese style was different, with elegant sweeps of robes, but she found this trim style more appealing. Or at least more appealing on him.

"Good morning, my lord," she said awkwardly, using a hand to smooth down her hair. It didn't help. It was a tangled mess. Fortunately, he was kind enough not to remark upon it.

"Your fever broke. That's excellent."

"It's the beginning," Yihui said, trying to balance not being a burden on the household with the truth of her recovery. "I will not be fully strong for a week," she lied. "Maybe more."

"Maybe?" he said with a laugh. "I should think you will need months, not weeks."

"I won't be a burden—" she rushed to say, but he waved it away with a flick of his hand.

"You're mending now, that's all that matters. You said you would, and here you are."

"I can help your house, my lord. I can help if anyone else grows ill."

The maid squeaked in alarm at that. She'd been busy arranging water and cloth, but her fear was palpable. Neither Emmaline nor Max seemed to understand why, but Yihui had seen it before. Many feared illnesses they did not understand.

"I don't bring illness!" she rushed to say. "I heal it. I swear!"

Max held up his hands. "Of course, you don't bring it. Were you some kind of doctor in China?"

"I made the medicine. I helped with the women." She added this last bit to see if the maid felt better with that news.

She did not.

"Max," began Emmaline, "Yihui said she'd like to bathe, but I cannot carry her to a tub."

His eyes widened. Apparently, what his sister suggested was startling. "I've just now finished mine. I'll carry her into my room. No sense in bringing up water twice."

"Are you sure—"

"She is our guest, and she needs our help." He flashed an awkward smile. "I'll put on a blindfold or something."

Something was going on, and that usually meant trouble. "No, no!" Yihui exclaimed. "I can manage—"

He turned and caught her with his blue eyes. His gaze was feather soft, but his words were clear and hard. "It is no trouble, Yihui. And it is the least I can do."

There were layers to his words she did not understand. Did she sense guilt? Was she about to be thrown away? Alarm shot through her at his words, but even as her breath tightened and her hands clutched the coverlet, he knelt down before her such that they were eye to eye, she on the bed and he squatting before her.

"Yihui, you are safe here."

Her heartbeat eased, her breath slowed. She didn't believe him. She was a wounded foreigner. There were many dangers for her, and yet, looking into his eyes, she felt safe. Indeed, the warmth in his eyes echoed how people looked on their riches, be it gold, a child who performs well, or... their most cherished concubines.

When Max looked at her, she felt cherished and that was such an exquisite feeling that it robbed her of all thought. Her breath stopped, her sight narrowed to him, and her body began to tingle. Suddenly, everything, everywhere was Max.

Chapter Fifteen

I F THERE WERE an award for the biggest idiot, then he would win it hands down. Max couldn't believe how stupid he was being, and yet, he was doing it anyway.

"Max, are you sure?" Emmaline pressed. "Perhaps—"

"Don't be silly. The bath is prepared." They always used bathwater for three people at least. It was too cumbersome to heat and carry that much for separate baths. "I'll just tell Moore to bring up more hot water." He turned to Yihui and mimed cleaning one's body. "Fifteen minutes."

"Max—" his sister chided.

"I'll wear a blindfold. Everything will be very proper."

It was not proper. And no blindfold would prevent what he'd feel when he picked up her naked body wrapped badly in robe of some kind. He wouldn't look while he carried her to his bedroom, but he would feel every inch of her body when he set her in a tub filled with steaming water. Then he'd wait nearby listening to the sounds of her toilette. He would hear the water splash, imagine the soap bubbles as they slicked down her skin, and dream what she looked like as every inch of her was cleansed and oiled. Would her black hair spill about her like ink? Was her skin truly as flawless as it seemed? Were her breasts as high and tight as he imagined?

These questions would torture him as he created answers in his imagination. And then he would be called back when she was done. He would crouch down beside the cool water, he would slip his hands under her thighs and back, and he'd lift her up. He would feel the heat of her body and listen to the cascade of the water. And his cock would throb, just like it was now.

He ducked out of the bedroom and headed to his own. Giving instructions to his valet took thirty seconds, then he had to sit and wait the next fourteen minutes. Fortunately, he wasn't able to linger in his fantasies as his sister stomped right up to him. She had her hands on her hips and her expression fixed in disapproval. He took one look at her and spoke up before she could draw breath.

"You used to smile more. I distinctly remember you laughing when you were younger. And I cannot think of one time when you scowled at me."

"I worshipped you. Now I'm an adult and see the truth clearly."

He cocked his brow, bracing himself for yet one more family member who thought she could tell him what to do. "And what is that truth?"

"You need something more to do than carry injured women to their baths."

"Do you think there is an occupation for that? Just lifting and carrying women? Upstairs and downstairs in their nightgowns." He mimicked an old nursery rhyme.

"I'm serious, Max. Things between you and Father have never been worse. Mama won't come out of her room until *that woman* is gone. And all you've done for the last three days is—"

"Try to find a solution," he interrupted. And when she arched a brow at him, he decided to enlighten her. "I've been learning everything I can about England's relationship with China."

"You already know everything."

He snorted. "I have been a hobbyist, asking questions of my friends. In the last three days, I've been to the offices of East India Company and knocked on the door of anyone who might know something helpful."

"And?" she prompted when he fell silent.

"And they find my situation highly amusing."

Her lips twitched but she didn't smile. That was unfortunate because his sister had a really beautiful smile, and he wondered why it had been so absent of late.

"That's all?" she pressed.

"They agree that the mandarin wasn't a representative from the Chinese government. There's little worry there will be repercussions from his death. At least no official repercussions."

"That's good news."

"Yes." No international incident, thank God. England had enough on its hands fighting Napoleon.

"Did you learn anything else?"

He shrugged. "General stuff, much of which I already knew. The East India Company has verified that there's a hubbub about the cohongs and the Hoppo."

"The what?"

He waved his hand. "It doesn't matter. The entire thing could already be resolved. They're on the opposite side of the world. Letters go very slowly between there and here."

"Then why would they send her like that? Why bother at all?"

That was a question Max had been asking for days now. "She's not really the Wong's daughter. She's some girl sold by her father to cover his gambling debts."

"That's awful!" she exclaimed. But true to her quick intellect, she understood the implications. "But that also means you don't have to marry her. After all, she's not who she claims to be—"

"*She* didn't claim anything."

Emmaline waved her hand. "Yes, but you know what I mean. You don't have to marry her. The bribe was a false one."

"Yes, I will make that case to Prinny. Given what happened, he'll let the thing drop."

She nodded slowly. "But that doesn't really answer the question, does it?"

"What question?"

"What are you to do with her? She's terrified you're going to toss her out of the house before she can even stand."

"I'm not going to do that," he growled.

"I know you're not, but…" She lifted her hands. "Maybe you should. Not throw her into the streets, obviously, but there must be work she can do. In Devonshire, perhaps? At a minimum, she could convalesce there without…um…you know, all the bother here."

He knew what his sister meant, and to her credit, she flushed at his hard stare. Send the woman away and go on with their normal lives. Which would be well and good for them, but what kind of life would she have? "Do you mean for her to be one of our pensioners for the rest of her life?"

She shrugged. "Better than your wife."

"Not for her," he snapped, unaccountably irritated. It wasn't as though he wanted to marry her. Bed her, yes. Marry her? Perhaps in his fantasies, but it would never work in reality. She'd never be accepted by society, and that was a miserable way for any person to live. In any event, he disliked how everyone— including her own father—disposed of her as if she were of no account. "She's a person, not an old pair of shoes."

"We're all people, Max. The world is full of them in all sorts of wretched situations." She shook her head. "You've always had a soft spot for strays. You dance with wallflowers, employ handicapped veterans, and do you remember that stinky ferret when we were children? No one adopts a ferret with a broken back, except you!"

"It didn't live long."

"But you still tried, and you cried when it passed. But you cannot take care of everyone." She set her hand on his arm. "Can you not see it? She is one more sad soul who wants to live off our fortune. She is beautiful and in trouble, and so you wish to save her. But you cannot marry her."

"Now you sound like Father. He'd shortchange his tailor if I didn't make sure he paid his shot."

"I'm not saying discard her. Just set her aside quietly. Pay someone to care for her—make it months if that will ease your conscience—then let her find her own place and purpose." Her gaze skipped for a moment down the hallway to the once-yellow bedroom. "This whole thing is wretched. I can't manage it much longer."

He winced. While he'd been out knocking on diplomatic doors, she'd been here, trapped in the sickroom because the staff was too frightened to do it themselves. But that was the way of things, wasn't it? Men handled the world's affairs while the women managed the household. Except in this case, the world had intruded on the house, and Emma had shouldered the brunt of it.

"I'll speak with Prinny tomorrow. Mayhap I can convince him that the Crown should shoulder her expense."

Emma's brows rose. "Is that likely?"

No. But that was something he'd face tomorrow. In the meantime, it was time to help Yihui with her bath. So with an apology to his sister, he pulled off his jacket, grabbed yesterday's cravat, and sauntered down the hallway to Yihui's bedroom.

"I'm tying a cravat over my eyes. I shan't see a thing," he said.

He did exactly as he promised, wrapping the silk fabric around his head tightly. It reminded him of childhood games, and yet his blood was already thrumming at the idea of being able to touch Yihui. Was it exoticism or true attraction? He didn't know and didn't care. She would be in his arms soon.

"All done," he declared.

His sister's voice drawled in his ears. "You are not fooling anyone. You just want to handle her."

"I'm trying to help," he said in a harsh undertone. "Did you want someone else to carry her? A ham-handed footman or three?"

"Maybe," she retorted. "At least they wouldn't give her ideas above her station."

"But that's the problem, isn't it? We don't know what her station is, do we? I'm still under—"

"Royal command. Yes, I know." He heard her open the bedroom door. "Come on, Max. I'll guide you."

He grinned. That was his sister's way of giving in. "Yihui? Are you ready?"

"I am," she said. The voice was directly before him, the words so sweetly spoken that his entire body tightened at the sound.

He stepped toward her, his hands already outstretched.

Emmaline spoke from his right. "She's sitting on the bed. Careful of her feet."

"You'll need to guide me."

"I am here," Yihui said, and he felt her small hand grip his wrist, gently urging him closer.

He found her.

She wore a silk robe, thin enough that he could feel the shift of her bones, the expansion and contraction of her ribs, and the solid control of her muscles. She moved her hand up his arm, gripping him as he knelt before her. His right arm settled behind her back. She was forced to let go of his arm then and instead, pull herself up to wrap an arm around his shoulders.

She was so slight that he could support her easily. Even better, she had strength in her arm as she lifted herself against him, and he felt the ripple of her back muscles. More delightful was the press of her breasts against him.

The best came to his left hand as he found her hip, then slid down her thigh to the bend in her knee. She was so compact compared to him. He often felt like his arms and legs were awkward things too long to manage smoothly. She, however, was a shifting bundle of energy. It was only her feet that kept her from running circles around everyone.

He slid his hand under her knees and straightened up. As she settled, he was able to wrap his right hand along her thigh while erotic images flooded his mind.

"This way," his sister said, her voice an irritating distraction.

"You'll have to guide me better than that," he said as he twisted his body to lead with Yihui's feet. He didn't want to accidentally bang them on the doorframe.

"Take three steps forward," Emmaline directed, though he probably could have managed it on his own. But it allowed him to focus on Yihui and how she felt against him as he walked down the hall.

Once in his room, he moved even faster. He knew the proportions of his bedroom and exactly where the tub had been placed.

"I'm going to set you down now."

"I cannot take weight on my feet," Yihui murmured against him. "Eventually I will walk on my heels, but for now, you must set me down in the water."

"Your robe will get wet," he said. "But I am sure we can find you another."

She nodded against his shoulder as he began to squat down. It was awkward for him, and he was excruciatingly aware of her injury, but he finally managed it.

He hadn't thought about how it would wet his own clothing. He would have to change his shirt now, but that was nothing compared to the feel of her skin as he withdrew from the water. Silky smooth, beautifully strong, and the most perfect size for a woman.

"Thank you, Max," she whispered just as he pulled his hands away.

Lust slammed through him at her hoarse whisper. He had been aroused before, but now there was a need in him that pounded through him. He was not a man to be overcome by lusts. And yet her modest whisper had him longing to banish everyone else from his room.

But that was wrong. In truth, it was rather depraved.

Or so he told himself as he forced himself back. "I'll wait...um..." He cleared his throat. "Notify me when all is done. I'll—"

"Your shirt is wet," Yihui said.

What? Oh yes. His shirtsleeves were dripping on the floor.

"Right. Um, I'll have a maid set up the divider," he said as he backed toward his bed. "I'll change on this side."

The two of them in dishabille and only a thin paper screen between them. As fantasies went, it was rather paltry, and yet his body was taut with hunger and nothing—not even his sister—could get him to leave now.

Chapter Sixteen

W HITE MEN SMELLED different than Chinese. They ate different foods, they bathed with different soaps, and they often shaved off their beards. Yihui had hated the scent of them on the boat, but the sailors were coarse men who lived rough. Thankfully, the sun and wind had eased the shock of such unfamiliar smells, and in time she had come to accept the different scents.

Then Max carried her into his bath. He had been fresh from his own toilette and so she knew the scent of him as it mixed with orange flower and rosemary.

She pulled herself higher on his body and pressed her face into his neck. She felt the strength in his arms as he carried her, and the caution in his step as he maneuvered blindfolded to the bath. Thankfully, there was a maid there to direct him and help her. Still, she felt like a precious vase in his arms where any misstep would shatter her into a thousand pieces. And yet he held her securely.

Once at the bath, she was reluctant to let him go, but so very grateful to sink into the water. It had been months since she could wash from head to toe, and the luxury of it left her speechless with gratitude.

The tub was sized for a large man which allowed her to stretch out her legs. Any other time she would wiggle her toes as she luxuriated in the water, but she knew better than to test her broken feet. Instead, she inhaled the scent of the water—Max's scent—as he backed away. A maid hastily moved the screen to block his view of her, but it did not stop her from looking at the details of his bedroom.

It was not very masculine in décor. The wallpaper was soft blue, and matching pillows were set in two wood chairs by the fire. The rug was thick enough that she could see the wet imprint of his two feet and a pair of slippers that had been discarded near a wardrobe. But what struck her was that everywhere she looked had something with words upon it. Several newspapers were scattered about, all turned to different pages. She saw sheets with neat rows and books bound in leather.

Someone had tried to neaten the piles, but just as clearly, someone else—Max—had been careless with where he set them. That spoke to her of untold wealth. So many books littered the room as if they were the easiest thing to come by. And even more startling, papers with scribbles on them, notes and thoughts, perhaps.

Max was a man of learning, and she could not help but stare in frustration. It was all in English. She could learn so much about what he wanted if only she could understand what he read. Meanwhile, Max seemed loath to leave her alone. Rather than depart, it sounded like he dropped onto his bed and wanted to chat.

"I'm very impressed by your command of English. How did you learn it?"

Was this usual? To talk to a woman as she bathed? She looked at the maid who was there to help her. The woman didn't appear upset by Max's presence.

"Oh, um, do you mind if we chat?" he asked, as if sensing her awkwardness. "I thought we could get to know one another better."

"I am happy to speak," she said. It wasn't a lie. Awkward as this might be, she wanted to know more about him. "Canton is a city of many languages. I learned as much as I could. It was a way to help my father."

"He was a doctor?"

"He made medicines in tea. Customers explained their pain. He made the right tea."

"An apothecary then."

She didn't know this word, so she repeated it as a way to learn. "Apothecary."

"Yes. Someone who makes medicines. So you learned English from your customers."

"My father did not have many English customers, but he always wanted to expand. So I learned as much as I could. I thought I would be a help to him always, even after I married." She'd never guessed that her ability to speak some English would be the reason the Wong patriarch wanted her. "I learned the most English on the boat."

"Did you speak to the crew? The sailors?"

"The other girl became sick with a fever. I spoke with the surgeon. I told him the medicine to give us." As she spoke, she grabbed hold of the soap. It would not be prudent to linger in the water just because he remained nearby chatting with her. She lathered the soap between her hands, smiling as she inhaled his orange flower and rosemary scent. Then she was handed a washcloth and began to clean herself.

"There were other girls?" he asked.

"One other. Also a bribe."

"What happened to her?"

"She died," she said. Then because she did not want to remember, she flattened herself in the tub, pulling her head under water. She scrubbed her scalp and ignored everything for as long as she could hold her breath. Or almost that long because she wanted to talk with him some more.

She pushed herself upright, her thoughts on him. And because of her inattention, she accidentally banged her foot. The sharp stab of pain made her cry out. *Idiot!* She clenched her knee tight to her chest, letting her foot dangle free as it throbbed. She shut her eyes and her mouth, and in so doing, she trapped the anguish inside her chest. But he must have heard her. He must have known because a moment later, she could hear his sharp demand.

"What happened? Are you hurt?"

Her feet were broken. Of course, she was hurt.

"I was clumsy," she said. And she'd been thinking about him.

"You need help. Should I call someone? Who is there with you?"

"I am well," Yihui said, but her words were covered by the maid.

"It's Millie, my lord. I…um…she looks well enough."

"She doesn't sound well, Millie," he snapped. "You are there to help her. Do I need to find someone more capable?"

"No, my lord!"

No, no! She would need to make friends with the servants. She could already see the girl's face had gone white with fear.

"I am well," she repeated, and this time she didn't lie. Her foot had stopped the worst of its throbbing. "I was trying to wash my hair and…" She didn't have the words to explain. She smiled at the servant. "Is that pitcher used to pour water over me?"

"Y-yes, miss."

"I will ask for it soon."

"Yes, miss."

She lathered up the soap and applied it to her hair. Normally, she would be busy thinking so many things while she did this. Today, she only thought of him on the other side of the screen. Of why he would linger to speak with her. Did he not have other tasks? The piles of books would suggest he had studies to complete, but perhaps he was tired of them.

"What are the books you read?" she asked.

"This and that," he answered. "Whatever strikes my fancy. A great many historical accounts. Prinny loves it when I compare something he does to some figure from the past. A great emperor or explorer or scientist. I am constantly looking for little bits of their lives to use to flatter him."

"You do not sound happy with the task." She was fishing for information. The more she understood who he was, the better she could fit herself to his needs. Long enough for her feet to heal. Now that the fever was gone, she would need to bind her feet so that the bones set correctly. Not in the way of a Chinese princess, but in the way of Emmaline, who was allowed to dance and run.

"I like the subject matter well enough. It's the constant flattery that wears on me. Prinny has great vision, but I fear his vanity needs too much attention." She heard the rustle of cloth as he moved on the bed. "I am speaking out of turn. I have utmost faith in the prince."

She didn't understand his last words, but she could tell from his tone that he was not speaking his true thoughts.

Meanwhile, her eyes were beginning to sting from the soap, so she gestured to the maid. "Millie? Will you pour?"

"Yes, miss."

The stream of water was pure delight. She fanned out her hair to let the water run through. She must have made a sound. A murmur, perhaps, of appreciation because Max spoke a moment later.

"You sound better."

"Millie is helping me."

"Good, good."

There was a moment of silence, then a creak of bedding, perhaps, or clothing. He was restless, moving about his side of the room.

"I know so little about life in your country," he said. "Do you bathe like this?"

What a question to ask. Did the Chinese bathe? But then, she had not expected such luxury here in the land of the white ape, for that is what the English were called by those who did not like them.

"A bath is required of all citizens every five days. Many go more often."

"Required?" There was shock in his voice. "By the government?"

"Yes. Every fifth day government workers are excused. It is their bathing day."

"That's extraordinary. And do you use big tubs like mine?"

"There are bath houses with great pools in Canton. In every city."

"Roman baths, then. Extraordinary."

"Is there nothing like that here?"

"Of course, there are a few, and the city of Bath is famous for it."

She looked at the large tub and again recognized the wealth that supported him. "Then I am grateful for the water."

He chuckled, a sweet mellow sound. "Fear not. In this house, we also require regular bathing."

She said nothing, her thoughts turning. She knew so little of the English people. She had not seen any sailors bathing and had assumed that none of the English did. Obviously, that wasn't true. She would need to learn as much as possible before she left here. And since Max was in a talkative mood, she would do well to ask her questions. But she wasn't exactly sure where to begin.

"What do you do?" she asked, her ability with English failing her. She didn't know if her question was insulting or not. "What is the… What eats your time?"

"A great deal of nonsense," he said with a chuckle. "I'm a courtier to the prince. I am his companion in whatever he chooses to do."

"A worthy task," she said because that is what she would say at home. But his answer was not nearly as assured.

"Worthy or not, it is how I spend my days. Or rather my nights. Prinny's fascinated with China these days, and since I've always been equally fascinated, he's pulled me into his circle to entertain him with tales. I've run out of things to say, so I hope you will talk to me about China."

"I will answer whatever I can."

He clapped his hands with clear glee. "Excellent! And in return, I will show you as much of London as you care to see. And if you are up to it, perhaps we can even visit Bath."

He sounded delighted with the idea, and she gaped at the screen in response. What man relished showing a servant around his city? But of course, that was old thinking. She was no longer the lowly daughter of an apothecary. She was a concubine and—if appearances held true—a favored one.

What a change in fortune for her! A concubine had luxuries and sometimes her own wealth. But often, her freedoms were severely restricted, and her behavior was scrutinized by everyone. Better to be a servant, someone no one cared about so long as the work was done. Much easier for a servant to disappear when it was time to strike out on her own.

But she could not regret her connection to Max. If she were to be his wife, then she would consider that role. Indeed, part of her was very excited by it. But she knew that men could be fickle in their favors. Best to act as a dutiful concubine, and then, when ready, she would disappear. Pretend, pretend, pretend with Max, and then escape.

Now that she had done her duty to her family, she was determined to have no obligations to anyone except herself. That was a future that no man, not even Max, could take away.

Chapter Seventeen

"**S**HE'S STILL ALIVE!" gasped Prinny.

Christopher winced. He'd been trying to divert the prince's attention since the moment he'd arrived that afternoon, but he'd used up all his tiny diversions. Max had begged him to keep Prinny distracted while Max figured out exactly what he was going to do with his Chinese fiancée. Christopher had agreed because they'd been brothers to each other since their first days at Eton. But the Chinese bribe was the talk of the *ton*. Everyone wanted to know what was going on, including Prinny, and there was a definite limit to the prince's patience.

Max's time was up.

Which put Chris on his heels as he considered his priorities. First and foremost, he needed to remain relevant to the aristocracy. The only way he ate in London was by invitation to other people's parties. It was also the only way he managed a complex system of favors and kindnesses that translated into his family's survival. He cared for an aging dowager's cantankerous dogs and thereby received a trunkful of old gowns that his mother could remake into dresses for his sister. He saved a naïve young lord from card sharks and turned that into several bags of free seed for his tenants plus a litter of pigs.

Favor after favor was parlayed into his family's survival, but only if he remained here playing entertainer to society's richest patrons. And few were as rich as the prince regent.

"Come on," Prinny whined. "What news have you of Max's

fiancée?"

Chris leaned back in his chair, surreptitiously surveying his audience. If he had to give up the goods on Max, then he needed to wring some benefit from the betrayal beyond dinner at Prinny's table. Lord Henderson was here—Ernie to his pals—and Chris had long been working on getting the man's cooperation on a matter.

"She survives," he said. "Everyone is agog. Doctors and surgeons alike are flabbergasted."

Prinny narrowed his eyes. "You said that she was infected. That her fever would kill a normal gel."

Chris nodded. "She was very ill for several days. But before she passed out that first night, she gave Max instructions for some Chinese medicine."

Ernie leaned forward, his bushy brows contracted. "Chinese medicine?"

Excellent. He had the man's attention.

"That's a secret, Lord Henderson. But I can tell you that finding the ingredients sent Max all over London. It's why he hasn't been here these last days." That was a lie. Max had been combing through London trying to talk to anyone who knew anything about China. The man had even visited the docks to talk to several ship's captains.

Ernie rolled his eyes. "If her fever has broken, I can assure you it wasn't because of some Chinese medicine. She either wasn't that infected or she recovered as a matter of course."

Damnation, he was losing the man, not to mention the prince who had just called for more wine. Christopher needed them fully entranced by his words, not thinking of their stomachs.

"I believe Doctor Morton is known to you." He treated half the aristocracy or at least the ones who could afford him. Ernie was status conscious enough that he would surely use the pompous man. "He swore to me that the lady would not live through the night."

Ernie pursed his thick lips. "He treated my mother. I always thought him a competent man. But even the best can be wrong."

Prinny looked about the room. "Do I know this doctor?"

No one answered because no one had any idea.

"Have him brought here. I want to talk to him about this Chinese medicine."

"I doubt he knows much. The surgeon Mr. Torres might know more." He didn't say the obvious. Out of everyone, Max would know the most. But he was trying to give his friend as much time as he could.

"Bring them both here. I want to question them."

Two footmen were immediately dispatched on the errand.

"Very clever of you," Chris intoned. "Asking them to come here before they know she's still alive. This way you can quiz them and get their true opinion of her health."

"My very thought!" Prinny exclaimed. "And you were very clever to work that out."

Christopher smiled in a vague way while his peripheral vision kept track of Lord Henderson. The man was frowning into his drink, his thoughts obviously churning. A moment later, he smiled in a way that was meant to be friendly if one ignored the meaning underneath.

"I'll bet you know more about this Chinese medicine than you're letting on."

"Hmmm?" Christopher answered. "It was Max who had to find it."

"But you've been to the house every day, haven't you? You've kept us all apprised as to the lady's health."

It was the only way to keep Prinny from showing up on Max's doorstep and upsetting the entire household. "I have done my best to be of assistance to my friend. That hardly means—"

"You know something." The words were as much accusation as interest. Which meant Chris had caught the man. Now all it required was to reel in the fat bastard.

"Of course, I know things." He leaned forward under the guise of extending his glass for more wine. And as the footman poured his drink, he whispered to Ernie. "Perhaps, I would be willing to trade you."

The man flopped backwards, clearly pretending to disinterest. "It's not worth that much to me."

A lie. Chris had seen how he gripped his leg, how he winced when he walked. Gout, most likely. What if the Chinese woman had a remedy that had eluded the English?

"Probably not," Chris agreed. "After all, heathen medicine is rarely what one hopes. But they do, on occasion, discover something unusual. Something from a plant or animal that is not known to us in England."

"What could they possibly know that our scientists do not? Haphazard mumbo jumbo from witch doctors."

"True. But even a heathen can get lucky. And a girl can learn a recipe from her father. Especially if he is a respected medical man in his own country."

The man frowned. "I thought he was a merchant. Wong Hippo or something."

"Ah, I see you are behind on the gossip. I'm told the lady is not actually the Wong daughter, but a woman kidnapped to be used as a bribe. You don't think a man would give up his own daughter, do you? Even heathens have feelings."

"If she's not the Wong daughter, then who is she?"

"No one, I'm sure," Chris said with a sly grin. "No one at all."

The man grunted with clear disgust. "Probably some poor street urchin."

"Who speaks English? I'm sure all street beggars in China are so well taught." The sarcasm was thick in his tone.

Ernie straightened even further in his seat, his bushy brows drawing tighter as he thought through the possibilities. Even Chris wasn't sure about the truth of Miss Wong's parentage, but the mystery served him better than the truth, whatever it might be. He expected to dine at many tables this Season as speculation turned to outright fantasy.

"Why would anyone risk abducting a woman of consequence?"

"I'm sure it wasn't the intention. And once in the hands of her captor, what's the poor gel to do? She was told she'd marry the King of England, after all."

"You think she's educated then. Not like our women, of course, but in…" He waved his hand in the air. "In heathen things."

"Oh goodness," Chris said with a matching wave. "What do I know except what everyone does? She speaks English, was expected to die, but has miraculously survived after sending Max all over London in search of ingredients for a mysterious brew."

Ernie's eyes narrowed. "You must tell me these ingredients."

"No, I must not. Max is my dearest friend. I cannot speak out of turn about his private affairs."

"Of course you can't," Ernie agreed even as he sidled closer to Chris. "But you might be induced to share a secret, couldn't you? With a very discreet friend. One who was in a position to do you a favor?"

Caught. The man was caught as surely as a wriggling fish on a hook.

"What favor?"

"Don't be coy. Your brother has been writing me for months now, desperate to curry my favor."

Chris pretended to shock. "Yours? Whatever for?"

"You know he wants to study at Oxford, but we both know that he hasn't the pocket to live there."

"Study should be about merit, not money."

"And girls should be virgins before they marry. They are not."

"My brother is brilliant and would be a boon to Oxford."

"Oh, no doubt, no doubt, but he needs my vote to gain admission. And he needs coin to do so without starving."

What a pig! The only reason Jonathan hadn't been admitted yet was because he hadn't the coin to bribe his way into school. And Ernie was the hold out. "Oh, I'm sure he'll find a way. He's clever that way." Actually, his brother was too puritanical or too ignorant to be clever. Which was why Chris had to help.

"Not without my vote, he won't."

Come on, come on. Out with it.

Chris didn't have to wait long. Eventually Ernie gestured for a footman to refill Chris's wineglass, then he waited while Chris took an obliging sip.

"Tell me what this Chinese medicine is," he said, "and I will vote for your brother's admission into Oxford."

Chris appeared to think about it. Indeed, he did consider it closely and from every conceivable angle. In the end, he decided he could milk this bastard a little longer.

"I do not sell my friends' secrets," he said stiffly. "Not even for my brother." It was a lie. He would do it for his brother, if it were the only way. And so far, this was the only way. "Oh look," he drawled. "The doctor is here. Let us listen to see if the lady's recovery is as miraculous as Max has said."

It was. Of course, it was. Chris had been there when Dr. Morton had predicted the girl's grizzly demise. He had relished his dire predictions and would likely repeat as much to his royal audience. Especially since he had not been apprised of the lady's survival.

At least Chris hoped he hadn't.

And so everyone listened with rapt attention as Prinny quizzed the man on Miss Wong's health. The responses were eloquent, graphic, and absolutely clear.

"She will not survive, Your Highness. And I believe that is a kindness."

"You are sure?" Ernie pressed.

"Completely. I stake my reputation on that."

Chris grinned. "And what if she had some mysterious Chinese brew? Something that allowed her fever to break. Indeed, what if that medicine not only broke her fever but allowed her feet to heal such that she might one day walk again?"

"Preposterous. The Chinese are godless barbarians. They do

not have such a thing."

Chris nearly laughed, amused by the arrogance of a man who could condemn an entire people without knowing the least thing about them. Fortunately, it served his purpose as Ernie once again sidled over.

"The girl is completely recovered?"

Chris did not know. The signs were hopeful, of course, but there was a long way between "not dying" and "completely recovered."

"Ernie," Chris drawled, "you want the secret Chinese brew. I want my brother to thrive at Oxford."

"Get me the medicine and I will vote for him. I swear it."

"I require his admission, not just your vote."

"I hold sway—"

"Then it shall be easy for you."

The man grimaced. He appeared to think about it for a long while, but the end was inevitable.

"Very well—"

"And he needs free lodging at a place that shall provide meals. I believe your cousin owns such an establishment."

"What?"

"The Magdalen Arms, is it not? A central spot for the Oxford elite. He has a few rooms to let?"

"For dignitaries, intelligentsia, and dons! For the prince if he ever wished to travel to Oxford!"

"My brother deserves no less than such a place."

"But—"

Chris gave the man an arch look. "If you want this miracle Chinese brew, then I want my brother studying in the lap of luxury. It is the smallest of what the boy deserves." That wasn't a lie. His brother, for all his naivete, was the best of the family. If Jonathan wanted to fill his prodigious mind in Oxford, then Chris would make sure he did it in style.

"I cannot do such a thing! The cost alone—"

"Then I will not betray my oldest friend's confidence." And as he spoke, he "accidentally" knocked Ernie's foot, causing the man to howl in pain. "Goodness, Ernie," he drawled. "Is something the matter?"

"Yes," the man snapped. "A greedy earl has taken unfair advantage of me."

"Hmmm. I wonder what a priest would think of a man who required coin to vote for a student's admission into Oxford? Would that be taking unfair advantage?" It was a risk to poke Ernie so hard. People who accepted bribes didn't like their sins spoken aloud, and in the prince's presence no less. But Chris was tired of fencing with idiots all day, dancing about their vanities, all while trying to carve out a place for himself and his family. It was men like Ernie who kept even the most deserving down.

"Shut up!" Ernie hissed as if his extortion of prospective students wasn't known to everyone here. "Very well. If she dances, then I will see to your brother's comforts."

"And then I will give you her recipe."

Now all he had to do was see that the girl survived.

Chapter Eighteen

"LADY EMMALINE, THIS cannot continue. We all think so."

"Indeed, we do. I've had three maids threaten to leave just last night."

"I couldn't agree more, my lady. The duchess's stomach is so upset that there is nothing I can cook to please her. I've tried everything, but it is *her* presence that is the problem. Not my cooking."

Emmaline took a breath as she faced off against butler, housekeeper, and cook. All three of them coming into her parlor during her first quiet minute of the day.

"I see," she said, keeping her voice calm. "And by *her*, I assume you mean Miss Wong."

"It's not her fault, my lady. We all know that."

"She's had a bad go of it, and that's a fact. But you see—"

"If I could explain plainly, my lady, the hubbub is simply not appropriate for a ducal home. Not when there are other places she could go—"

"To rest and recover."

"In safety."

"Away from your mother."

Goodness, they were tripping over each other in their haste to make their point.

She tilted her head. "And you all feel this way?"

"Absolutely."

"Yes."

"With regret, my lady."

"And all three of you believe that you can't manage your duties while Miss Wong is in residence. Because why exactly? Does she make demands on the kitchen? Yell at the maids? Throw things at the footmen?"

"My lady!" Chiverton said with a hard sniff. "It's because she's a murderer."

Mrs. Pizzi visibly shuddered. "No one will go into the room. I've brought on extra people—like you said—to clean up the mess—"

"They were a rough lot, milady," inserted Chiverton, "but they did their job. I saw to it."

"Yes," Mrs. Pizzi cut in, her voice hard. "But even so, no one will go in the room. I've had to shut it up."

And Emmaline was still staying with Lady Kimberly while Yihui used her bedroom. "The new wallpaper was put on yesterday," she said. "The linens and rug should have arrived by now."

"But that's not the point!" Mrs. Pizzi cried. "I've had one girl leave already and more threatening. They won't go upstairs. They fear for their lives."

Emmaline huffed. "Then they are remarkably silly girls. You've seen Miss Wong's feet. She can't walk. She can't hurt anyone."

Chiverton took up the argument. "My lady, you are a Christian example to us all, sitting day and night with the...the foreigner. But I've seen you turn away from the bedroom. Even you can't go into it."

She couldn't deny it. She still flinched from the memory. The room itself brought everything back in a way she couldn't deny. "But what has that to do with Miss Wong's presence? The room will still be the room, even with her gone."

"Once she departs," Chiverton said clearly, "we can all put this wretched thing behind us."

The cook agreed. "Without the reminder, your mother will

rest better and eat again."

"My mother is not in danger of fading away," she snapped. "Neither do we allow silly maids and timid footmen to decide who resides as our guest. Especially one commanded by Prinny himself!" She set aside her embroidery. It was hideous anyway. "And if you cannot control your staff—"

"My lady!" Chiverton huffed, his tone matching hers for indignation. "No one is more cognizant of the responsibilities of this family to the Crown than I am. I fear, however, that you forget how the rest of the country scrutinizes everything you do. I've had to chase away reporters climbing on the ivy. Even the smallest gossip gets recorded and printed for everyone to read. Just imagine what is being said about this family!" He sniffed. "It cannot be allowed. It cannot!"

What was outrageous was that a member of the household staff spoke to her in such a way. Worse, instead of coming to speak to her directly, Chiverton had stirred up the rest of the staff to force her hand. *He* wanted Yihui out of the house, and he wasn't above fostering open rebellion as a way to get what he wanted.

But such was the privilege of a butler who had been with their family for generations. From father to son, the Chivertons had served the dukedom for a hundred years. As much as she hated it, he had the right of age and ancestry to speak so boldly to her. Then before she could frame a suitable reply, Mrs. Pizzi took up the cause.

"There are places she could go, my lady. Good houses where she could recover. You wouldn't have to exhaust yourself staying in the sickroom with her. Your father could come home instead of sleeping at his club."

"Mrs. Pizzi, of all people, you know how she was hurt."

"Our hearts bleed for her," their chef, Mr. Gaudreau, said firmly. "But you must see that this upset is not good for anyone. It's terrible, just terrible."

There she had it. Every reasonable, logical excuse to send

Yihui packing. She even had the name of a boarding house that would treat the girl well. And if getting the foreigner out of here quieted not only their home but the entire neighborhood, then really it was for the best, right? They couldn't have their family name bandied about in the papers. That wasn't how a duke's family behaved.

But such casual cruelty was not how she behaved.

She stood up from her chair, being sure to face them squarely. "What I find terrible is that the three of you can go to church every Sunday, recite words of charity and understanding, and then be so callous at home. Do you fear that we will die, Mr. Gaudreau, if we don't consume your food every day? Do you think a few articles in the paper will destroy the dukedom, Mr. Chiverton? And Mrs. Pizzi, it wasn't so long since your own family came to these shores. Indeed, I believe I had a few girls threaten to leave when you were hired. Shall I bow to their demands now?"

"My lady!"

"Such a thing to say!"

Housekeeper and cook stiffened at her harsh tone. They both exclaimed their outrage but didn't say more because they waited for the ringleader—Mr. Chiverton—to express their opinions in a more formal way. He was Emmaline's true adversary, and so he spoke with pompous righteousness.

"Articles in the paper—even a few—cause damage. It is our duty to bring these matters to your attention."

"You are right, Chiverton," she said. "Pulling journalists off the ivy is too much for a man of your years. I shall speak with Papa directly about lightening your duties."

The gasp of shock was audible, not from Chiverton but the other two. Threatening a change in butler was akin to declaring war on the entire staff. A war, incidentally, that Emmaline could not win. Chiverton was only echoing her father's position and in a battle between herself and her father—well, in this household, the women always lost.

"My lady," Chiverton said coldly. "You are overwrought. Might I suggest a lie down? I shall have Mrs. Pizzi bring you some tea."

She smiled. Time to show them her mettle. "An excellent idea. Mrs. Pizzi, I shall be residing in the yellow—er, green bedroom for now. The workmen are done. I understand that the maids are being silly about going in there, but I'm sure you aren't made hysterical so easily. I expect that you—personally—can see the room prepared for me?"

That last question was more of a statement, one that implied obedience or immediate dismissal. And as an Italian foreigner, Mrs. Pizzi knew it would be impossible for her to get another position without a reference from Emmaline.

The lady's eyes widened in shock, then she dipped her head. "Of course, my lady. Right away." She turned to depart, but Emmaline didn't miss the venomous look she shot Chiverton.

"It's really cruel," Emmaline said to the woman's retreating back. "Men stir up trouble, but it's always the women who pay."

She saw the comment land on the housekeeper, causing her steps to pause and her shoulders to twitch. Given the woman's earlier compassion for Yihui, Emmaline guessed that the butler and chef had stirred her to outrage. Hopefully, she wouldn't be as quick to rebel in the future.

Which left Emmaline to confront the other two. Or rather one, since Mr. Gaudreau quickly bowed out.

"I shall finish the tarts, my lady. They are perfection and will be delicious with your tea."

She barely acknowledged his departure because she was still eye to chin with the butler, a man who had once cleaned her scraped knees and retied her hair ribbons. Indeed, as a father figure, he had been warmer than her own. But now they stood as if a frozen ocean churned between them.

"Chiverton, this quarrel does neither of us any good—" she began. He didn't let her finish.

"I do hope you choose a husband soon, my lady. You have as

much responsibility as your brother to carry on the title and the longer you wait, the fewer children you'll be able to bear. Indeed, that number may already be frighteningly small."

Emmaline gasped, the barb finding its mark with a sharp pain. Chiverton knew how much she wanted children. And they both knew that the lack of heirs was a constant worry for her parents. To throw that in her face now was the kind of petty cruelty that was, well, it was just the kind of thing her father would do if she dared question his behavior. And because Chiverton had been cruel, she returned the statement in kind. It wasn't a normal action on her part, but sometimes wounded souls lashed out.

"Be sure to air out the green bedroom. I shall be looking to you to see that the air is clear in there, the furniture dusted, and everything in its place. Assuming that's not too hard for one of your advanced years."

If he poked at her age, then she would return the favor. Of course, she immediately regretted it. When all was said and done, she was the mistress and he the servant. It was cruel of her to punch down at him, even as he arched a mocking brow at her and sketched a very shallow bow.

Stupid, stupid, stupid to fight with her own butler. Perhaps they were right. Yihui was upsetting her more than she thought. And now her pride had made it so that she'd have to sleep in that room. How was she going to close her eyes and not have nightmares?

Best do it now. She'd always been one to face her fears, so she squared her shoulders and purposefully left the parlor to head to the newly christened green room. And since there was a maid in the hallway, she couldn't flinch from her task now.

The room was closed because neither Chiverton nor Mrs. Pizzi would open the room themselves. Or at least not alone. So it was left to her to twist the knob and push the door back. For the briefest of moments, she saw the soft green paper that she herself had selected. She noted the stripped bedframe without even a mattress and the equally bare floor.

And then the memories overcame her.

Chapter Nineteen

"Oh my God. What now?"

Max and Lord Benedict were walking toward the ducal residence when a long line of carriages passed them, all headed into Grosvenor Square. Beside him, Lord Benedict chuckled as they watched the entourage.

"I believe you're about to receive a royal visit. Your father will kick himself for not being here to bend the regent's ear, but I daresay your mother will appreciate not having contentious political discourse in her drawing room."

Max sent him a reproachful glare. "Damn you for enjoying this. You and Chris are a pair."

"On the contrary, Lord Christopher uses humor to distract from his desperate circumstances. I, on the other hand, am pleased as punch that you are the focal point of royal attention. It allows me to finish off Napoleon without interference. Pray continue to be as fascinating a diversion as possible. It makes my life much more manageable."

"So happy to serve," Max drawled, his tone heavy with sarcasm.

"I know you are," Benedict said quietly, "but you need to expand your understanding of where and how you serve. London is as much a battlefield as France."

There was a message here. An obvious one, to be honest, but Max couldn't accept it. "I could make a difference on a battlefield."

"Of course, you could, but you are being asked to serve here. And now I should make myself scarce." They had reached the edge of Max's property quickly, having used the servants' path up to the back door.

"What? You can't abandon me with Prinny. He's here to demand answers I don't have. The London office of the East India Company was barely helpful, and there hasn't been enough time to hear from their offices in China."

"Excellent!" Lord Benedict clapped his hands. "That's good diplomatic training. You cannot imagine the number of times I've had to appease important people before I've any of the proper information."

"But—"

"Best hurry. Prinny's carriage has nearly arrived."

Indeed yes, the Prince Regent's ornate conveyance was nearly at Max's front door. Christopher, on the other hand, had apparently leaped off early and was rushing up the walkway with a harried look on his face. Damn man ought to be panicked bringing a royal visit to his home without the slightest word of warning.

"Please," Max begged Benedict. "Distract him for a moment while I get…" Max looked around. Damn it, where had Benedict gone? A hurried scan of the back path showed the man well out of earshot, his long stride covering the distance faster than some horses.

"Bloody perfect," Max groaned, then he rushed up to the house and shouldered his way into the kitchen.

It was a madhouse. Obviously, the staff had seen their royal visitor coming, but no one had taken charge.

"Where's Emmaline?" he asked the nearest footman.

"My lord! We d-didn't know… How'd y-you…"

"Where's Chiverton?"

"Right here, my lord," came a voice from the cellar as the man in question topped the stairs. He looked harried and annoyed.

"Who is there to greet the prince? Under no circumstances is he to be allowed above stairs."

"Er, well, as to that, my lord, I'm not exactly sure."

Max gaped as his normally unflappable butler. "About what?"

"Thomas is above stairs. I'm afraid I was in the wine cellar at the time."

"You weren't at your post for a royal visit?" Good God, what was happening? Not only his life but his entire staff was falling apart. Chiverton started to answer, but Max held up his hand. "Never mind. Who's home? Has Mama been informed? Is she even here?" He thought she was going on calls today, but he couldn't remember.

"I'm afraid I'm not sure, my lord." For all that his tone was even, the man was clearly sweating. "I was below stairs for—"

"A very long time, apparently. Very well, get upstairs. Serve the prince some good wine and tarts." He pointed to a tray cooling in the corner. "Give me fifteen minutes. I can't greet the prince dressed like this."

He'd been tromping around London asking after some midwife that was of interest to Lord Benedict. The man often gave him strange tasks that had diplomatic implications. Max had once been sent to discover the parentage of a servant girl only to discover that she was a Russian spy. He was never told the true reason until afterwards, and this was no different. Fortunately, midwife Betty Gill did not appear to be a foreign spy, though she did have a mysterious past.

In any event, he couldn't think about that now. He needed to change out of his tromping-about-London clothes and into something more appropriate to a royal visit.

"Right away, my lord," Chiverton said before snapping his fingers at the stammering footman. The servants disappeared up the front stairs while Max climbed up the back. But in this he was stopped. The moment he stepped into the hallway, he came face to face with the prince regent.

"Your Majesty!" he cried, startled. Damnation the man was

already upstairs! He must have bowled past the young footman and headed straight upstairs. Behind him, Chris was babbling as he clearly tried to slow down the royal.

"Oh good," Christopher cried. "Max is here. What are you wearing? I'd like a glass of good wine. You must want one too, Your Majesty. It was a long drive from Carlton House. And I hear that Max's chef is a wonder with tea cakes—"

"Tarts," Max corrected.

"Tea tarts! What a capital idea! Let's go back downstairs."

It might be, but the prince was having none of it. "Lord Christopher has been keeping us apprised," the prince intoned. "Now we should like to see the lady's feet."

Two steps behind the royal, Chris threw up his hands. "I informed his majesty that the lady is feeling better."

Prinny huffed as he pointed at Christopher. "And created a discussion regarding the strength of her medicine. Dr. Morton claimed she was at death's door. We should like to see the condition of her feet and judge for ourselves." So saying, he boldly opened the door to the yellow—er, now green—bedroom. Yihui was not in there, of course. She was down the hall. But when the prince threw open the door, they found a different woman there.

Emma sat on the bare floor. Her head jerked up when the door was flung open, and though there appeared to be nothing wrong with her, there also was no explanation as to why she was sitting on the floor. And while everyone stared at her, she slowly recognized that the prince regent stood before her.

She scrambled to her feet. "Y-your Royal Highness?"

Chris took a step forward. "Emma?" he said but was stopped by the prince's ample bulk in the doorway as he tried to back out of the room.

"Lady Emmaline," Prinny said. "My apologies. Are you quite well?"

"Yes, Your Highness," she said. "I, um, twisted my ankle and was merely resting it." A lie if there ever was one. "It's quite well now."

"Hmmm," Prinny said.

"May I assist you? Brandy perhaps? I believe there are fresh tarts." She gestured down the stairs, and for a moment, Max hoped that the ploy worked. Unfortunately, Prinny was determined.

"Thank you, Lady Emmaline," he said. "But we are here to see the Chinese woman's feet."

Emma blinked in confusion. "Her feet? But your highness, that is not appropriate!"

And that was not the right thing to say to a royal. Prinny stiffened. "What is not appropriate is to declare a miracle Chinese medicine and offer no proof. We are here—"

"Your Majesty," Max intervened. "You must understand. The Chinese believe a woman's feet are as private—as sacred—as we think of a woman's, um, breasts or other intimate areas. No man except her husband may view a lady's feet."

"If it is so sacred, then why do they deform them? That makes no sense, and we begin to suspect that we have been lied to." He turned to glare at Lord Christopher.

"Your Majesty!" Chris objected. "You have two worthy men of medicine who have testified to the brutality of the lady's injury!"

"She was hurt!" Emma snapped. "Most dreadfully. But that does not change the private nature of her situation." For Emma to stand so boldly and chastise the prince shocked Max to his core. His sister was normally the most rational person in any room, but today her temper was clearly overruling her sense of decorum.

And it was no surprise that the prince did not take well to the chastisement. "We do not need to see her ankles," Prinny huffed. "Just her feet."

Before Emma could respond, Max stepped straight in front of her. "Of course, I understand your interest. Chinese medicine is a fascinating subject. But to ask to inspect something of such intimate nature is—"

"It's her feet!"

"Which is the same as asking about her breasts! Or her..." He dropped his voice. "Or her cunny. You asked me to understand her details. I have spent the last week studying everything I can about China. This foot binding business is very strange to us, but it is their custom."

This was a very precarious position for Max. The prince had clearly come here with a mission—one no doubt triggered by Chris's ability to create dramatic tales out of the most trivial nonsense—and now he was angry at being denied. Max might keep the prince away, but he would pay a cost.

He smiled as gently as he could. "This standing about in hallways is exhausting. Shall we go downstairs and discuss—"

"Your Majesty?" a low voice squeaked from Yihui's bedroom. A moment later, the words were repeated louder by a voice he recognized. "Your Majesty!"

"Lady Kimberly, what are you doing here?"

A good question. Max hadn't seen her for several days now and felt extraordinarily anxious at the idea of her becoming the subject of the prince's ire.

"I brought Lady Emmaline home. She has been staying with me while the bedroom was being repapered."

"Repapered?" the royal asked. "Whyever would you..." He glanced past Max's shoulder into the room, then his eyes abruptly widened as he remembered. "Oh yes, the murder. Christopher said it was very grizzly." He continued to peer into the room. "Looks respectable now."

"We hired excellent workmen," Max inserted. "Ones I expressly hired because of their work on Carlton House—"

"Yes, yes," Prinny said, waving to silence Max as he stepped down the hallway. "Is that Miss Wong's sickroom?"

"It is, Your Highness." Lady Kimberly dipped into a curtsy—a little late, but Prinny didn't seem to care. "And Miss Yihui has expressed a desire to meet you, if you would like."

Oh good God no! This was no doubt a generous gesture on Yihui's part, but she had no idea what kind of a ham-handed brute Prinny could be. He'd treat her like a pig at a county fair. Or a back-alley whore. Neither was acceptable, even from a royal, and so Max rushed forward to forestall the coming disaster.

"This isn't…" Max's voice trailed away as he looked into the bedroom. It had been a week since her bath. He'd certainly gotten reports of Yihui's health multiple times a day. He'd even checked in when he could, making sure not to disturb her sleep. But he'd never seen her like this.

She was seated upright on her bed with pillows behind her back, but she didn't seem to need them. She sat with her chin lifted, her lips curved in a polite smile, and her hands clasped before her. She dipped her head and pushed her hands forward in a kind of Chinese greeting, and when she straightened, she kept her head lowered but her eyes raised.

The position emphasized the beauty of her dark eyes, even as her head tilt showed her humility. A deferential woman with hauntingly exotic eyes. She was stunning, and for a moment, he was knocked silent.

Not so for Prinny, who blustered forward with a large smile. "My lady, a pleasure to meet you under less formal circumstances. I am so sorry you have been feeling ill."

"I am honored to greet you," she said, her English clear enough that Max was strangely proud, as if he had something to do with her language ability.

"How are you feeling?" Prinny continued, his gaze going quite clearly to the lumps beneath the cover that were her feet.

"The duke and his family have treated me well. I am grateful."

"Max is a good man. His father is a bit more prickly, but Max and I are great friends."

"We are," Max inserted. "But perhaps you would be more comfortable downstairs?" He already knew the ploy wouldn't work, but he had to do something to save Yihui. But apparently, the lady didn't need rescuing.

"I will show them to you," she said, her gaze demurely downcast. "But then you must speak to the emperor about how it is wrong."

Prinny took a moment to fully hear her words, then pulled back with a frown. "Speak to the emperor? The Chinese emperor?"

Yihui dipped her head. "Yes, Your Majesty."

The prince pulled a chair close and settled himself upon it. "My lady, you cannot think I can command the Chinese emperor what to do in his own country."

"You are the leader of this country, yes?"

"Of course, I am, but—"

"You can speak big man to big man. You can say this thing of binding a woman's feet is wrong."

The prince shifted uncomfortably in his chair. "That would be like me coming into another man's home and demanding that he do things differently. I have no right to tell him what to do."

A long silence ensued as everyone—including the prince—realized that he had done exactly that in this house. He had entered and demanded to see a lady in her boudoir. And in the awkward silence, Prinny shot an annoyed look at Max.

"Your home is different. You are my loyal subject."

"Yes, Your Majesty—"

"I can demand anything I like here," he kept saying. "But I cannot do such a thing in China."

Yihui bowed again. "I understand."

"Of course, you do—" he began.

"And so I cannot show you my country's shame. If you will not help end it, then I will keep the ugliness from your eyes."

The prince did not like that answer. He had come all the way here just to see her deformity, and now he straightened as if he were the one insulted.

"But the others have seen it. Max has seen it!"

"Max is to be my husband, yes? He has the right."

Max nodded. "And the others were doctors plus my sister and Lady Kimberly who has helped with her care. Please, this is most irregular." He was choosing his words, softening them as a good diplomat would. But inside, he wanted to scream at his leader. The man was here to gawk, nothing more, and a royal should know better than to treat a woman like a cripple at a bearbaiting.

Unfortunately, Prinny did not take the admonition well. He stood upright with an angry glare. "I only wished to learn of her Chinese medicines. How can I know if they work if I do not see the damage firsthand?"

"You know," Max said curtly, "because she is alive. You know because the doctor said she would not last the night and yet here she is, growing stronger every second. You know because myself and my family have been tending her, watching as the fever left her screaming in delirium until her medicine turned the tide. You know, Your Majesty, because I have said so and I have never lied to you."

Max's patience was at an end. He had never spoken so harshly to the prince and Prinny's face reflected the fury of his reaction. Too bad. Max held out his hand and gestured down the hallway.

"Now perhaps, we shall leave Miss Wong to her recovery."

There was nothing the royal could do now short of throwing a tantrum, and that was something he rarely did unless in his cups. But he wasn't above getting back at Max. He turned to Yihui with a hard look.

"Max has seen your feet because you are to be married, yes?"

"Yes."

"Then I look forward to attending the happy event." He turned back to Max. "Three weeks to call the banns. I shall see that the cathedral is at your disposal."

And there it was. The royal decree repeated that he and Yihui would wed. Forget that Lady Kimberly stood nearby. Forget that Yihui would never be accepted in society, much less able to fulfill her duties as duchess. Forget that his descendants would be forever tainted by Chinese blood. Prinny had been insulted, and so he forced shame upon Max and his heirs for generations.

It was a cruel punch, and one that Max had to accept simply because he had lost his temper and demanded that the royal behave like a compassionate adult.

"I shall expect an invitation forthwith," Prinny commanded, and then he swept out of the room leaving Max—as usual—to pick up the pieces.

Chapter Twenty

Like everyone else in the hallway, Emma heard Prinny's conversation. She heard the royal command that he marry and saw not only the stiffness in her brother's back but the dismay on Lady Kimberly's face.

Unlike everyone else in the hallway, though, she knew exactly who to blame for this disaster. It wasn't Prinny. The royal was like a force of nature, showing up and wreaking havoc wherever he went. That was the nature of royal pomp and circumstance. But nature only went where the wind blew. And if one knew how to work royal desires, then one could encourage or prevent one's best friend from being forced to marry a woman he didn't want.

Someone like Lord Christopher. Indeed, he was wholly to blame for this disaster, and so she intended to tell him in no uncertain terms.

She waited for her moment. Prinny burst past her, headed for the front door. Max waited long enough to see that Yihui was all right, then bustled after the royal. He wouldn't make any headway now. Prinny was too embarrassed by his own actions to forgive Max for pointing it out, but she supposed her brother had to try. Lady Kimberly looked down at her feet, then trailed behind, no doubt heading for a dog to chase away her tears.

Last came Christopher. He was being polite as he let the ladies go first. She smiled at his wan face, linked her hands around his elbow, and then swung him into the newly papered bedroom.

And shut the door.

"Emma! What are you—"

"How dare you!" she growled. "You and Max have been friends since you were in leading strings! How could you do this to him?"

"Me?" he gasped. "Prinny—"

"Don't give me that. Prinny wouldn't be here if you hadn't dangled some tale about Yihui."

"I didn't dangle—"

"What did you get, Chris?"

"I didn't get anything!"

"Don't lie to me. I've known you my entire life. You are clever, subtle, and always in the thick of things." He could also be kind and ridiculously honorable when it came to her. He'd never so much as kissed her when she'd thrown herself at him as a teenager, and now…now he'd ruined everything. "What did you get for betraying my brother?"

Chris opened his mouth, but then shut it with a snap. His gaze lifted to the ceiling as he clenched his hands into fists. "Emma, I didn't mean to…" He gestured toward Yihui's bedroom. "I didn't know he'd come here like that."

"And now Max has to marry a Chinese woman he's just met. He was being kind! He saved her from dying—"

"I know!"

"And now he'll have to marry her! Do you know what my father's going to say? After my mother takes to her bed for a week weeping and wailing?"

"It's not Max's fault—"

"Doesn't matter, does it? Father's going to bemoan the disaster of the dukedom. We can trace our heritage back to William the Conqueror, but we'll never live down the shame of marrying a Chinese."

"The king is married to a mulatto—"

"And the queen has never lived it down. Everything she does is about her race. She can't just be a queen. Everything she does, everything she says relates to her race, as if she alone represents every mixed-race soul in England."

"She does. She's the queen—"

"And now everything Max does will be about his Chinese wife. If he makes a mistake, it will be her fault. If he succeeds, he will have overcome being saddled with her."

"You're overreacting."

She might be. There were worse things that could happen to Max. And definitely worse things could happen to Yihui. But Emma knew the strain of fitting into a ducal household. Not everyone was cut out to weather the demands of society. And honestly, she had wanted her brother to have a better time of it than her parents.

"It's hard, Chris, really hard being married to someone who won't help you, who doesn't understand you. My parents are a daily disaster. Yours—"

He held up his hand. "Do not bring my parents into this. They were ten thousand times worse than yours. It was a blessing when my father died, and I am daily trying to recover from the mess he left."

She knew it. Hadn't Kimberly mentioned that he didn't have the money to send his brother to Oxford? But how did any of that lead to this afternoon's disaster? "Fine," she snapped. "Answer the question, then. What did you get for bringing Prinny here? For forcing my brother into a marriage without love?"

He sighed. "What does it matter? You will damn me either way."

True. Especially since he'd just confirmed that he had bartered away her brother's happiness. He could have gotten money, a horse, or a whole damned estate for it, and she would still hate him.

She slumped back against the bedroom door, her heart breaking. "I thought you loved us."

"Us?" he challenged. "Or you?"

Of course, she meant her. She'd been in love with him since he helped her onto her first pony. "I wanted better for my brother."

"What?" he mocked. "Love? Max has never looked for that. He knows better." He stepped close enough to tower over her. "You, on the other hand, have always coddled such ridiculous fantasies about it."

"Ridiculous? To have parents who don't hate the sight of one another?"

He put his hands on the doorway, one on either side of her head. "Don't make this about them. They hated each other before they ever married. This is about you and your ridiculous fantasies."

Damn him for towering over her like this and hating her as he did it. And damn herself for smelling his scent and feeling lightheaded at the spiced heat of him. She slammed her hands against his chest, but she didn't have the leverage. He didn't move an inch, so she fought him with words.

"Love is possible!" she cried. "Unless you bargain his choices away!"

He dropped his head down until they were nose to nose. Her heart began to thunder in her ears, and she struggled to catch her breath. He was so close. How many nights had she dreamed of him like this? Whisper close but saying very different things.

"You don't know anything about love, Emma," he said, his voice low enough that it seemed to shiver down her spine. "My parents were in love, you know, and look how that turned out."

"Not everyone is like that!" she said as she shoved again. It didn't work. And truthfully, she wasn't sure she wanted it too. He pressed his nose along her cheek, sliding his mouth so close to hers.

"Love doesn't exist, Emma. It's only passion."

"No," she said. She knew there was a difference. And yet, at this moment, she couldn't think of it. All she could do was feel him there caging her in the circle of his arms as his breath heated her skin.

"You have wanted me for years, Emma. Do you think I didn't know?"

She whimpered. Of course, he'd known, but he'd never thrown it back at her like this. He'd never sneered the words even as his lips nibbled at the curve of her jaw. She closed her eyes, she willed her body not to react, but it was a losing game. She wanted this. Never had she felt anything so exquisite.

"You know my situation, Emma. You know I have nothing I can give you. My family—we are impoverished."

"My dowry—"

He slammed his mouth over hers. He invaded her mouth with a swoop of his tongue, thrusting inside and out until she was dizzy with the feel of it. And when he pulled back, he kept whispering.

"Your dowry is not enough. I would have taken it if it were. I would have wed and bed you when you were sixteen and first growing breasts."

To her shock, his hand cupped her left breast. No soul had ever touched her like this, not even herself in the bath. His hand was large as it held her, his thumb heavy where he stroked across her nipple.

"You have the most glorious breasts," he said against her neck. "I have wanted to suck them since I first understood what they were."

Behind her back, her gown loosened. He'd pulled apart the ribbons without her being aware. She still wore a shift beneath, but it was old and soft, and his fingers were very clever. He scooped out her breast and squeezed her bare nipple. And while lightning fired through her blood, he did the same on the other side.

Two breasts lifted free, and his hands molding her flesh until she shook from the feel of it.

"I'm going to teach you, Emma."

"What?" she gaped.

He dropped onto his knees before her and pressed his mouth to her breast. She cried out in shock as his tongue lathed her nipple.

"Press your arm against your mouth, sweetheart. Do it now or I won't continue."

She could stop him. He was on his knees before her, and she could refuse him. She could step away and never feel his glorious touch again. She could, but she didn't.

So while she looked at him there before her, she slowly pressed the back of her hand against her mouth. It would stifle any sounds she could not.

He grinned.

"This is what you want, Emma," he said. He went back to teasing her nipples. He nipped at them, he rolled his tongue over them, and he suckled until her knees were weak and the door was the only thing keeping her upright.

And then, while he gave attention to her other breast, she felt his free hand beneath her skirts. His clever fingers, his large palm, skidded up her calf, behind her knee, and then to the top of her stocking. And then his fingers swept into her most private place.

"So wet. I knew you would be."

Oh! His fingers were so large, so…everywhere. He pushed into her, and she pressed up onto her toes. He leaned in and forced her knees apart. She squeezed them together but met his shoulders and arms instead. No way to close and no desire to as he stroked her. In and out. Up and down. She had no knowledge of what he was doing, only that she was breathless. Her body was on fire. And she wanted more.

"Have you ever felt this?" he asked against her belly. And when she didn't answer, he stopped what he was doing to look up. His brows were drawn together. "Emma! Have you?"

"No," she said, dropping her hand from her mouth. "Never!"

"Good," he said, satisfaction in his tone. Then he took her hand and guided it to where he still teased her. Except she resisted.

"What are you doing?"

He grinned at her. "I'm teaching you about love." He pulled her hand to her own body and shaped his to cover hers.

"This isn't…love," she gasped. She had enough awareness to say that, but it was fast departing.

"You'll see," he said as he pushed her middle finger inside herself. He was right. She was wet and slick, but with his hand guiding her, she felt not only the slip of her finger but the thickness of his thumb. Both together, deep inside her.

"That's where I want to be," he said. "But you'll prefer it here."

He moved her hand. With one hand, he held her open and with the other, he showed her where to touch.

She gasped at the explosion of sensation. She would have cried out, but she was holding her breath. Such feelings. Such wonderful feelings!

He taught her how to stroke herself. He showed her how to press and swirl. He knew the tempo she wanted. He pressed her fingers down in steady pulses. So much variety. So much delight. Her belly tightened, her knees squeezed.

"Cover your mouth," he said. And when she didn't move, he used one of his hands to push at her free arm.

Oh God, she didn't want him to stop. She wanted to let her own hand fall away and let him do as he willed with her—to her—but he refused. With every gasping breath, he forced her to touch herself.

Here. Again. Again!

"Yes," he said.

The tide took her.

It washed over her in a roar of sensation.

She couldn't breathe, couldn't scream, couldn't do anything but feel and fly. Such pleasure!

He held her throughout. He kept her upright while her body pulsed and writhed. And when she was merely floating, he picked up her up and carried her to her bed.

"There," he said as he set her down on the pillow. "The glow should last a while because it's your first time. Enjoy it."

He straightened and she languidly grabbed his arm. "You're leaving?"

"I am," he said as he stepped back and gave her a little bow.

"But—" She'd thought… Well, she didn't know what she'd thought, but it wasn't this.

"You can now love yourself, Emma. Men find this out young. They discover ways to pleasure themselves. No need for marriage or anything but one's own hand."

She looked at her hand as if she'd never seen it before. Damnation, her mind was scattered.

"Now you can love yourself, Emma, and cease looking to me for it."

"But that's not what I want from you," she said as she levered up on her elbows. He was nearly at the door. "I mean, this is not love."

"Yes, it is," he countered. "And it's all I have to give."

YIHUI COULDN'T SLEEP. This was the longest she'd been inactive in her entire life. Her fever was gone, her bones were knitting, and her mind was filled with Max, Max, Max. How many times had he saved her? Once when she was presented to his king, again when he saved her from Lao Gu, and now again against his own ruler. How had she not realized he was a Dragon King?

How was this possible? How could a foreign man possess the strength of a dragon? But that was ignorance. Dragon power was too strong to be contained in China alone. Only vanity made her think such a thing.

And now she knew that Max was a dragon, and she was left in awe. Better yet, she would marry him. The royal had declared it, and Max had bowed his head in agreement. Such was the way of heaven, she supposed, to have her own father sell her to a foreign king, only for her to find a man who...

Who must love her. That was the only explanation! She had not believed in love at first sight or that beauty could turn a man's heart, but she had no other explanation for the way he treated her. Kindness, respect, honor. These were the actions of a man in love.

She had to sit with the thought for many long minutes. She knew people who loved. Couples who adored one another throughout the years. Those who still gazed warmly at each other even in their old age. And of course, there were fables of great souls who loved. Gods and goddesses, powerful men and the women they wanted. It wasn't always about the woman's beauty. Sometimes she possessed extraordinary skill.

Yihui knew her strengths. She was not a great beauty in China, but perhaps she was enough here in England. She also knew she survived when others failed, plus she understood great medicines from China. She would be an asset to any man. Why couldn't an English dragon see her worth? And why wouldn't he fall in love with her?

The excitement of this thought shivered through her. It was possible! And if it were true, then she vowed here and now that she would honor him as truly as any wife could. She thought about their children, wondering how dragon strength would filter into a half-Chinese child. She'd been taught that the English were too pale, too shallow to sustain elemental power, but obviously, that was wrong. Which meant her children would have the power of a dragon and the cunning of a rat, which was her zodiac sign.

What a joy that combination would be. So she spun dreams around a foreign man who would take her as his own. She was deep in a dream of presenting him with their son when a soft knock interrupted her fantasy.

"Come in," she said, expecting it was the maid here to take away her evening tray.

The door opened, and it was no maid. It was Max, his shoulders broad enough to block the light. Yihui immediately straightened, being sure to keep her head bowed respectfully even as she tried to peer surreptitiously up at him.

"My lord, you are welcome."

He smiled and pointed at the book on her lap. It was a child's primer on English that Emmaline had given her. "Are you learning to read?"

"An educated woman must read and write." It would be a necessity for her as his wife.

"That's true." He frowned as he stepped into the room. "Is it hard? I can't imagine trying to learn a new language now. I had the devil of a time with Latin and Greek, and I've forgotten most of it."

"I have always been clever with languages. It was my best asset to my father."

He nodded. "I imagine that's true."

He stood there a moment, long enough for her to be daring enough to lift her head. Only a wife could do such a thing, and she was thrilled that he seemed to like it. Then he pulled up the chair and sat near enough to kiss.

She didn't lean forward, though. That would be too bold. But she felt his presence like the heat of the sun. So close. So attentive. A man in love with her.

For a woman used to being dismissed, the idea was like opium in her blood. She was dazed by the very possibility. Meanwhile, he continued to talk as if she weren't reeling from the clash of hope and cynical experience inside her.

"I have been very busy lately trying to learn everything I can about your country. I'm afraid we don't know much, and so I will listen closely to everything you say."

She flushed, delighted that she had a purpose in his life. "What do you wish to know?" She touched the book. "I could teach you Chinese."

"A worthy goal," he admitted, but then shook his head. "But I have something else to discuss with you first."

Their marriage, perhaps? She knew all the customs of a Chinese wedding, but nothing of his traditions. She would have to learn quickly if she was not to shame him.

"You heard what Prinny said," he began. "You know he commanded us to marry."

"I know." Should she say how happy she was at the idea? That she would make a very good wife to him? In China, she had been taught that a lady kept her expression opaque and her hopes hidden.

"The thought must terrify you," he continued, oblivious to

her thoughts. "You've left everything behind."

"I am not afraid."

His lips curved into a warm smile. "You amaze me. I don't think I would fare half as well."

"It would not have happened to you." No Dragon King would be sold as she had been.

"There is always someone stronger. Or several someones who band together." He shook his head. "But that's not important. The thing is, I cannot contradict the prince. He has declared that we wed, and I must honor that."

It was true then. She would be his. She would lay in his bed, bear his children, serve his people, she—

"At least," he said slowly, "I must appear to honor that."

It took a moment for his words to penetrate her fog of hope. But the lurch in her chest told her that she should have remained cynical. Hope was a painful trap.

"You look upset."

"I do not understand, but I will learn. I swear I—"

"Don't be so afraid of me, Yihui. I will find a way to make us both happy."

"Yes, yes," she said, trying to stall for time. "Happy is a good thing."

"Yes," he agreed. "In England, a man cannot cry off. Once engaged, he cannot refuse to wed." He paused, his gaze steady. "But a woman can."

"A woman can refuse to wed?" The idea shocked her.

"Yes. Exactly. She can refuse a man who is not suitable."

"But you suit me. The king said so."

"Prinny said we must marry, and so we will pretend to do so. The banns will be read. The invitations sent out. Everything will look like a wedding."

"But we will not marry?"

"The night before, you will cry off. You will say that you cannot marry someone so different from you. Say we do not suit."

Panic had her heart beating very fast. "But then what will I do?"

He caught her hand, trapping it easily between his two much larger palms. "I shall give you an annuity. That's a yearly amount of money to live on. I can give you a home in the country if you like. Or if you want to stay in London, then it will be enough to live well if you are careful."

"An annuity," she repeated, testing out the word.

"Yes. Say five hundred pounds a year. Something like that."

She had no idea how much money it took to survive alone, but she had bargained all her life. She knew better than to accept the first offer from anyone. "Five hundred is much too little," she said firmly.

He cocked his head. "Is it? And how do you know that?"

"I know many things," she countered. "Double that would not even be enough."

"Five hundred pounds is very generous."

"Do you live on so little? No, you do not. I think your boots are worth five hundred pounds. I am an apothecary. I am worth very much more than a pair of boots."

He chuckled. "Yes, I guess you are. But an annuity is paid every year until you die."

"You get new boots every year."

"I do not!"

"You get new clothes then. Boots one year, shirts and…" She pointed to the silk cloth about his neck.

"Cravat."

"Cravat. New, every year. Am I not worth more than a cravat?"

He was silent as if considering. When he spoke, he showed that he was not as easy a mark as she hoped. But then what Dragon King would be?

"If I gave you a thousand pounds per annum, what would you do with such a fortune?"

"I would buy good boots for winter. And a warm coat."

"I shall purchase those things for you."

"I must have a home, yes?" Her hand tightened in the heavy coverlet. She had thought she would live here with him in the riches that surrounded her.

"I will see that you have a good home. A safe one with enough coal in the winter."

She shook her head. "A Dragon King does not do such a thing. Not for a discarded woman."

"A Dragon King?" he said. "Is that what you think of me?"

Had she called him that aloud? She should not have revealed so much, but he spoke so gently with her, even as he dashed her dreams. She found it easy to speak honestly with him. "I think that discarded women starve."

He touched her face. A gentle stroke of his large hand across her brow first, to pull her hair away. Then his palm cupped her chin and his thumb caressed along her jaw. And he steadily pressed her face upward until she looked him in the eye.

"You are not a discarded woman, Yihui. Indeed, I think I shall be paying an exorbitant amount for your livelihood."

"How much?" she asked as tears filled her eyes. The Dragon King did not want her.

"Fifteen hundred, and not a penny more."

"Seventeen."

He pulled back a bit, clearly shocked that she fought even as tears slipped past her lashes.

"Sixteen."

She shook her head. "Seventeen or we wed."

His thumb continued to stroke her jaw, back and forth until she was nearly mad with the sensation. She wanted to feel that over her entire body, but all she had of him was this single caress. And his money.

"Seventeen," he said softly. "Most daughters are not dowered so well."

"You must write it down. Seal it with your chop."

He frowned. "My chop?"

She touched the signet ring on his finger. "Your chop. Your—"

"Ah. My seal. Yes. I will have the papers written up. Every-thing will be proper, Yihui. But first you must agree to pretend we are engaged. We must make a good show of it for the prince."

"And then I am to cry."

"Cry off. Yes. The prince cannot force you. You are not Eng-lish."

"And if I do not?"

His hand dropped away. "Then I will say that you have, and no one will contradict me."

He would force it. Of course, he would. No dragon wanted her. She should have known better than to create fantasies about something that could never be. She could fight this, but to what end? They held all the power. If she could manage money from this pretense—money enough to keep her clothed and fed—then she could ply her trade. She would open an apothecary shop. She would treat those who needed medicine. And if they did not want such things from a woman, then they could die.

It was what she'd planned, anyway, before she thought he loved her. Before she'd realized he was a Dragon King, and she would be pleased to be his bride.

"I will pretend," she said. "And then I will set you free." She shrugged, pretending every word didn't hurt. "I will put on a good show for everyone as I throw you away."

He smiled. "I look forward to it." He straightened up, pulling his hands and body away from her. "I have errands to do tomorrow, and a surprise for you. But it won't come until the afternoon."

"A surprise?"

"Tomorrow," he said. Then he winked at her. It was such a delightful gesture, one done between people who care. It was not done with lechery in mind, but as a friend might to another. And it was so startling that Yihui once again felt lost in the fantasy of love. It was an illusion, but when he smiled at her, she forgot.

A moment later, he bid her good night and was gone.

Chapter Twenty-Two

MAX WAS LOATH to step out of Yihui's room, but he had to go before he touched her again. Something about her clung to his thoughts and would not be dislodged no matter how inappropriate his desire. How ironic that honor demanded he not touch his own fiancée. It would be no hardship to give her longing looks or public caresses. He would act the besotted fool and show Prinny that he wanted to marry Yihui.

He did not, of course. He knew his duty to the Crown. It did not include marrying a stolen Chinese woman. But such was the twisted motivations when dealing with the prince. The royal wanted to punish Max for stopping him from leering at Yihui's feet. If Max appeared to enjoy his punishment—his upcoming marriage—then Prinny would be irked. When Yihui eventually jilted him, Max would appear devastated. At that point, the prince would be very pleased and allow the nuptials to end.

It was a convoluted process, but Prinny could be petty. This was the best way to handle his royal moods.

Satisfied with this day's work, Max headed for his bedroom. Lord, his cock throbbed as he imagined her coy eyes as she wrapped her lips around—

He stepped quickly into his bedroom. No one would know what he was about to do. He'd already dismissed his valet for the night and—

His nose wrinkled at an unexpected scent in his room. It wasn't unpleasant, per se, but it was a scent he connected with

Kimberly, the liniment she used on elderly dogs to ease their pains, not quite covered by her perfume.

He quickly lit the candelabra and turned to see, to his shock, Lady Kimberly sitting by his fire. Her feet were stretched out before her, and her head was tucked against the chair wing. She looked asleep, but as he took a step closer, he saw her green eyes open to regard him with her usual quiet calm.

The sight was unnerving.

"Kimberly? You shouldn't be in here!"

"You'd be surprised what can be ignored in a long-time family friend. Especially one who should have married you by now."

He winced. "I'm doing everything—"

"Papa has commanded me to seduce you."

He gaped at her, sure that he had misheard. Her father was more conservative than his own.

"That cannot be true."

"I assure you it is. Mama suggested I wait until we are sure to conceive a child."

He blinked. "You can determine that?"

She shrugged. "She mentioned several old wives tales that will guarantee conception."

He had no idea what to say to that. And then, while he was still gathering his wits, she straightened off the chair. Some women coil out of their seat. Some women seemed to flow upwards. Kimberly simply thrust out her feet until she stood squarely before him. And then she set her hands to her bodice.

"What are you doing?" he gasped, shocked that she would be so bold.

She pulled apart the ribbon. "Haven't I just told you?"

Good lord, where was his valet? "Don't be daft. Moore could come in any moment!"

"I have bribed him to stay away." She smiled. "He believes you have treated me poorly and promised to scream like a stuck pig when he discovers us in the morning."

The bloody traitor. "Kim, we cannot begin like this.

"I don't care how we begin, Max, so long as we do."

What was he to say to that? She was right. She was *always* right. But the truth was, he had no lust for her. No desire beyond duty. Especially since she usually acted as an older sister rather than a future wife.

Worse, having come from Yihui's room, Kimberly suddenly seemed overly large with blunt features and no artifice. It was unfair. She was a lovely Englishwoman of statuesque proportions. Unfortunately, his imagination was caught by an injured Chinese woman with soft features and exotic eyes. It was nobody's fault, but his erection had shrunk the moment he realized Kimberly was in his bedroom.

"This isn't going to work."

"That's what I'm here to find out." She stepped forward, facing him squarely. "Kiss me," she said.

"What?"

"A single kiss. You owe me that much. Surely that's not a hardship."

"Of course not, but—"

"Make it a good one. I want passion in my marriage. I want to be swept away, and I want you to do it."

"Since when?" She'd never said such a thing before.

"Since now, I suppose," she said, apparently as surprised as him by the statement.

Then she spread her arms wide. She offered him her plump breasts, her bodice already loosened for his ease. And she looked at him with a kind of desperation he didn't know how to refuse.

He still tried.

"Listen, Kim, I have a plan."

"So do I." She put her hand around his neck and pulled him forward. He could have stopped her, but she was right. She was the woman he planned to marry.

But he couldn't do it.

He untangled her hand from his body. "I will not seduce you, Kim. Nor you me. I have worked out an arrangement with Yihui.

We are to pretend to be enamored of one another. Long enough for Prinny to become annoyed that I am not suffering under his supposed punishment."

"What punishment?"

He waved his hand in a gesture meant to convey stupidity. "You know how Prinny is. He's forcing our wedding because he thinks I'm completely against it."

"You are completely against it?"

Maybe yes. For the most part. "I will pretend to enjoy my punishment, then become devastated when Yihui cries off. Prinny will see me despondent, believe me adequately punished, and so will allow this wedding nonsense to end. Then I can marry you."

Her mouth dropped open. "After appearing despondent over losing Yihui?"

"Yes, but you will remind me of your charms, and I shall tumble head over heels in love with you."

"With me? You won't even kiss me. You've *never* kissed me."

It was true, and now he saw how deeply that hurt her. For all the years he had known her, she'd seemed happy to live apart from him, to care for her dogs, and speak of their engagement in "whenever" terms. It was only lately that she had begun to press him. And only tonight that she spoke about passion.

"Kim," he rasped, suddenly overwhelmed by how deeply he'd hurt her. "I'm so sorry."

She pressed the palm of her hand against his chest. It was the warmest gesture he'd ever received from her. Her hand lay flat there, her fingers long, and he covered it with his own.

"I am crying off, Max."

"But—"

"Neither of us want to wed. I could have brought you up to scratch years ago, but I let you delay and delay."

"Prinny prefers bachelors as his confidents. It's what Lord Benedict asked me to do. It's how I serve—"

"I know. And I allowed it because I don't want to marry you."

He sighed. Just like an older sister, she made him admit things he didn't want to acknowledge. "We've never really suited, have we?"

"Of course, we do," she said. "As friends. As brother and sister, perhaps, but we'd make terrible lovers."

"And you want passion in your marriage bed."

"Don't you?"

Yes. But he knew better than to expect it. "What will you do?" he pressed.

"I don't know. I'll have to make the social rounds."

She was going to hate that.

He squeezed her hand. "I'll help however I can. Do you want me to stay away from you? Shall I act piqued? Shall I—"

"Pine for me?"

"I will do it if you want."

She snorted. "I think you are doing altogether too much playacting, Max. I think you should act exactly as you would with a good friend. We shall dance together occasionally. We will laugh with one another rather more than usual, I think. And we will show the world that neither of us ever cared for the other."

"You know that's not true."

"You know what I mean."

He did. She wanted his friendship, not his passion. And that suited him just fine. "You have always been my true friend."

"And you mine." She smiled. "I haven't forgotten all the times you danced with me to help me relax. You told me terrible jokes and—"

"Made fun of your ugly dogs."

"As if you understand what is beautiful in a dog."

"Maybe not a dog," he said as he gathered her fingers. Lifting them up, he pressed a kiss to the back of her hand and gave her the most courtly of bows. "You are a beautiful woman, Lady Kimberly. I would be sore aggrieved if I have destroyed our friendship."

"You have not," she said. "But your sister will never forgive you."

He groaned. That was true.

"I'll handle her," he said.

"You'll try," she said with a laugh. "But I'll explain it to her. You can figure out what to tell Moore tomorrow morning when he bursts in on nothing."

He chuckled. "May I walk you home?"

"Just to the stable, I think."

"You cannot walk home alone."

"Oh I shan't be alone. I brought Rufus and Brown Dog with me. They're right now terrorizing your stable hands."

"Good God. The boys will quit, every one!"

"Just tell them that we will never wed. That will soothe their nerves."

And so he extended his elbow to her, and she set her fingertips upon his forearm. They descended the stairs together as he had always assumed they would one day as duke and duchess.

He ended up walking her home though her two mastiffs intimidated him. He knew that at a word from her, those animals would tear him to pieces. It wasn't until his return walk home that he realized he was whistling. It was a happy, jaunty tune that filled the night air with joy.

Good lord, when was the last time he had ever felt so free?

Chapter Twenty-Three

Y IHUE STARED AT the missive in her hand. She was very slow at reading English, but was able to sound out the large, dark letters. Usually, Emma would help her, but the lady had been absent since yesterday afternoon. And the maid who brought the paper had been unable to read, so that left Yihui to sort through Max's handwriting like a child exploring a favorite toy.

Please put on these clothes and be ready by 11 o'clock.

MAX

She did not know what the word *clothes* meant but guessed when that same maid delivered a pair of breeches made of blue silk.

"He wants me to wear this?" she asked the girl whose name was Millie.

"Coo, but isn't it soft? But why give you boy's clothes?"

"This is for a boy?" Yihui had been wearing pants since her earliest days. Gowns were for ladies who did not work.

"Yes, but yer a foreigner. Everybody expects you to act odd."

Apparently, Max did. She looked at the fancy clock on the mantle. One of the first things Emma had taught her was how to tell time. She had very little of it left before she was supposed to be ready.

"Millie, will you help me? It will take the hour."

The girl hesitated. She'd been the only servant bold enough

to dare help the foreign killer. Yihui had tried to reward her with things, but she had nothing of her own to give. So she gave the girl time to rest from her labors. She invented excuses for Millie to sit with her. And in that time, the two had discovered something else in common.

They both wanted to learn to read, so they practiced together.

"Aye," Millie said as she pulled over the primer. Together they sorted out words until it was time to pull on the pants as if she were a boy. And though Yihui tried to hide it, they both knew she was nearly bouncing with excitement over Max's gift. What kind of surprise would it be?

The clock had just struck the hour when Max knocked on the door. Millie opened it, and he stepped in, his eyes bright as he looked at her sitting with her hands clasped before her.

"Aren't you looking lovely, Miss Wong? Are you tired of these four walls? If so, I've come to take you for a walk."

"My lord," she began, wondering exactly how to express her confusion. "I cannot walk yet."

"I know. That's where my surprise comes in."

He didn't leave her time to object. Within moments he had surrounded her with his arms and lifted her up. She had no choice but to wrap her arms around him, to revel in the feel of his hands on her body, and sigh as he effortlessly carried her out of her room, down the stairs, and out the front door.

He moved so quickly and with such happy enthusiasm that she was still deep in his warmth when he stopped—outside—as he held her above a small horse.

A small horse?

"Spread your legs," he said. "Careful. I don't want to knock your feet. I'm sure breeches feel strange, but it is the safest way."

"I have often worn my brother's clothing," she murmured as she stared down at the creature.

"Truly? I see we have a topic of conversation." Then he tried to set her down, but she gripped him too tightly. "Come, come," he chided. "You're healthy enough now that this will work. Won't be confined to your bedroom so much."

"But I have never ridden a horse."

"Never?" He seemed startled. "Surely someone put you on one as a child."

"I ran when I needed to go somewhere. And twice, I have ridden in a rickshaw." She shook her head. "I don't know anything about horses."

"You must tell me about rickshaws. Perhaps as we begin our walk."

"Uh…" She clung to him, refusing to leave the strength of his body. But he was firm as he gently settled her on the creature.

"Grip here," he instructed. "You can steer the pony with your legs and with the reins. No need to use… Oh my. What did you do to your feet?"

Too much to understand so fast. Or maybe not because as she sat there, things began to get a little easier. She could balance and breathe. That was the first step. Then she began to notice things.

First, he and the creature were dressed to match herself. His waistcoat was the same robin's-egg blue of her dress which she wore above her pants. The animal, too, had a fresh straw hat with bright blue flowers on it.

Max patted the horse's neck. "She's named Blue for her hat. I had to order her special from the country, and she arrived yesterday. And now she's here for you." He beamed at her, clearly pleased with himself, but she could only stare. How was she supposed to manage a horse? "Don't you have ponies in China?"

"We have horses in China." She didn't know the word *pony*.

"Blue is of a very small breed. Small enough that she can maneuver inside a house. She can go through doors and up and down stairs."

"You want me to ride her inside?" She couldn't imagine that.

"Only if I'm not around to carry you. This way you don't

have to stay cooped up in your room. You can see visitors. The entire *ton* wants to meet you."

"On a horse?" she gasped. "Inside?"

"Not if you don't want to. For today, let us just take a walk, yes?"

What could she say to that? It was glorious to be outside again. And wonderful to be by his side. And so she smiled and tried not to fall off the creature.

"Excellent," he cried. And then he frowned as he looked down at the stirrups. She hadn't put her feet in them, but the raised skirt showed the bindings on her feet.

"They are wrapped," she answered. "Not bound as they do in China, but for proper healing. Mr. Torres helped me."

In China, the bindings were tightened as hard as possible to make the foot smaller than a man's fist. With Mr. Torres's help, Yihui had set boards around her feet. One beneath with a rag for the arch, and two on either side, to hold the shape of a proper foot. Then she'd wrapped all of it in cloth and stiffened it with plaster.

It took a very long time to dry—nearly two days—but the fabric had been given shape by the wood boards and now would serve to keep her safe from the normal bumps of moving about in the world. Eventually, she hoped to take off the bindings and walk again. But for now, she could totter a little on her heels without rebreaking the bones.

"Looks fragile," Max said. "Did it hurt?"

"Not once it was done." The maneuvering of it had been difficult, but in the end, she was pleased with the result.

"Very good then," he said with a nod. "Shall we go?"

She looked at him, her heart beating in her throat. She felt incredibly precarious up here. She had no idea what to do. And worse, he was clearly surprised by her lack of understanding.

"Don't worry," he said as he took hold of the reins. "I shall lead. You just stay seated."

She cast her eyes down, unable to find the right words to

voice her discomfort.

"Yihui," he said quietly, gently lifting her chin. "Trust me?"

"I am frightened," she finally confessed.

"Blue is as gentle as a spring rain."

She wasn't nervous about the horse. Well, not completely about the horse.

He took her clenched fingers into his own. "Be honest with me. This is meant to divert you. I thought it a grand plan."

She knew that, and usually she would be excited for her first ride upon a pony. But this wasn't just a ride. He was taking her out in public in boy's clothes and on a tiny horse.

"You are showing me to the world in a way that everyone will notice."

He nodded, his expression serious. "You are a Chinese woman engaged to a future duke. Everyone will take note of you regardless. I thought it best to show them that you are delightful."

She bit her lip, trying to find the right words to explain. "I have lived by being small, by doing my work. I did not upset anyone."

"I have done the same, you know. Not in the way you have, I expect, but I have done everything everyone else wanted as much as possible. It made me a good son and good lord, but I have recently discovered something shocking."

"What?"

"Everyone gets upset anyway. I cannot please them. So I shall please myself. That means—if you will agree—that you ride a pony while I ask about rickshaws and Chinese clothing. It is a fine day and be damned to anyone who talks. They mean nothing to us."

She heard a sharp kind of freedom in his words and saw a defiant lift to his chin. It pleased her.

"You will keep me safe?" she asked.

"Always."

She looked down at the creature who stood placidly in front

of the door. Blue did not seem overly large between her thighs. She could manage the pony, couldn't she?

"Teach me how to ride this beast," she said.

He laughed. "It's a pony, Yihui. Barely larger than a big dog."

"To a woman who cannot walk, a dog, a pony, or a horse are all the same."

He was silent for a moment, then agreed with a gentle smile. "Of course, you're right." He took the reins from her hand. "Hold the pommel with your hands, grip Blue with your thighs, and smile, Yihui. This will be fun."

Chapter Twenty-Four

I T WAS NOT fun. It was wonderful.

At first, all Yihui wanted was to remain seated upon this strange creature. She was a child who had run the streets of Canton, bringing medicines to one customer or another. But never had she sat atop a large animal and tried to match her movement to it.

Just going down the front steps had her terrified, but with Max holding her steady, she managed without tumbling headfirst down the stairs.

"See? Easy as dancing a jig."

She had no idea what a jig was. Neither would she be dancing anytime soon. But she didn't argue. He was too happy with his gift for her to dash his excitement. Plus, it felt good to have the sun on her face though she had to tilt her head back to a ridiculous degree to feel it beneath her bonnet.

Unfortunately, she didn't have time to relax into the situation. They already had drawn attention from servant and dignitary alike.

"We'll walk down the lane a ways. Let you get the hang of sitting astride."

She nodded as if she understood. She did not. Instead, she focused on the sun in his hair, the light in his eyes, and the grin on his face. The man was excited to be walking with her.

"Tell me about this rickshaw thing. Do people really run in front of carriages like a mule?"

She spoke slowly, working for the English words.

"Horses are costly. Rich men pay for people to pull them in a chair."

She started to explain more about the lives of wealthy men, but he seemed more interested in the runners. He was fascinated by the idea of old men run to exhaustion. He grinned when she spoke about young men strutting in their strength.

"I should love to see it one day."

She would enjoy showing it to him, but that would never be. She would not return to China. By now her father would have figured out that her brothers did not know nearly as much as they pretended. He would know, to his shame, that he had traded away the one child who could run his business.

If she returned to China, he would find a way to capture her again. And as much as she missed her mother and her younger brothers, her duty to her ancestors was done. When she was sold to the Wong patriarch, she had cleared her father's debts. No child could be expected to do more. She would not return and risk falling under her father's thumb again.

"I hope you get there one day," she said.

"You will not show it to me?"

"I will never return."

"But why?" he gestured about him. "Don't you long for home?"

She looked at his bright eyes and happy smile. He truly did not understand his fortune.

"Not every home is as pleasant as yours."

His expression sobered. "I am sorry."

His statement took her by surprise. His words were said with a good heart and a kind face, but the disparity between them had never been larger. He was a leader among his people, a man who was respected simply for breathing. Even now, people all around them were angling for a way to speak to him. She could see their intrigued looks and their prancing about to get his attention.

She was nobody. Even her own father had no idea of her

worth. And yet, looking into his gentle eyes, she felt some of her fury fade. It was like looking at the sun and being annoyed that he did not understand she was a shadow.

She wanted to be in his light forever.

Then she lost the chance to respond. A couple walked up to them with bright words and false smiles. Max greeted them with matching brightness, bowing over the lady's hand and saying things like, "What ho" to the man.

What did "What ho" mean?

She was introduced next and with Max's help, she returned the welcome much as the other lady had. Her hand was kissed and when she turned to the woman, she said what he had said to the man.

"What ho, my lady?"

Laughter greeted her words. Clearly, she had made a mistake. She looked nervously at Max, but he patted her hand.

"What ho, indeed."

There was more conversation which she could not completely follow. Something about the weather, she thought. And a party? There were several surreptitious glances at her feet, but Max had made sure that her gown covered them.

Then it was over. He nodded politely to them and walked on, bringing her with him.

"You handled that very well," he said when they were out of earshot.

"They laughed at me."

"They laughed because you are delightful. They are kind people or I would not have allowed them to approach."

She fell silent. She did not like being the center of so much attention, even with his protection. She had no idea how to function in his world, and this felt very difficult. And yet he was smiling at her as if she had passed a great exam.

"Tell me more about your country," he pressed. "You come from a working family, yes? Apothecaries. Did your brothers learn as well? Or did they choose something different?"

"Something different?"

"Well, yes. Perhaps the law or doctoring."

"They will become apothecaries if they can, carrying on my father's work. Neither of them seemed fit to take the government exam."

"The government exam? That sounds fascinating."

She thought of all the medicines she had brought to young men whose entire life would be determined by how they performed on one exam.

"It is a difficult test given to young men who study their entire lives for their moment. Those who pass will serve in the government. Their families will have honor, their life assured."

"For government jobs? You mean like a barrister or a minister?"

She did not know those words. "It is a system that brings the smartest minds to serve the emperor."

He gaped at her. "That's extraordinary."

"Even a shopkeeper can sire a brilliant child."

He nodded slowly. "And all are given the opportunity?"

"Yes. Though only the wealthy can afford to teach their children what is required to pass the exam."

"No doubt. No doubt." He frowned at her. "But everyone may take the exam? Even a servant's child?"

She was silent a moment, trying to judge his interest. "Doesn't England have a way for the poor to advance? If the child is very, very smart?"

"Of course, we do. I mean, there are all sorts of ways for a child to have a better life than his parents."

She watched his face carefully. She was in too precarious a position to argue with the man who controlled every aspect of her life. And yet, as a daughter of China, she had seen so much that she had not been allowed to say. She had slipped into sickrooms, hidden in the back counting houses, addressed the poor who could not afford a man's services.

Her father had not wanted to spend his time on such people,

so he had sent his daughter to get them away from the shop door. And she had gone to them and learned to listen. Like them, she'd had no power to change her circumstances, but they taught her how to listen.

"Tell me what you are thinking," he commanded.

"Only that I am grateful—"

"No, don't do that. Yihui, if I wanted flattery, I would be surrounded by very different people."

Very well. If he wanted honesty, then she would give it to him. And if he did not like what she said, then she would judge him harsher for it. And perhaps, love him a little less.

"Why do you not teach your people to read?"

"What? We read and write."

"Your servants do not."

"Well, they can if they want. I don't stop them from learning."

She didn't speak, but she was very well aware that she had to lie to the housekeeper to give Millie time to read with her. Millie wanted to better herself but had been given no time or opportunity.

Fortunately, he was thinking ahead, his mind already guessing her thoughts.

"I suppose there is little time for most of them. And who would teach them? Tutors are expensive."

She nodded, not daring to speak.

"You know, Mother speaks of how I hated doing my lessons as a boy. Ran like the devil himself was on my tail. But a gentleman must know his letters." He cut a hard glance at her. "Do you say that everyone reads in China?"

"No. But even the poorest know a few words. Our language is done in pictures. Everyone recognizes a few words."

"It's the same here. Most know their name. A few letters here and there. Numbers are more common."

"But you value it, yes? Reading and writing is the basis of advancement, yes?"

He didn't answer. They were distracted as another couple came to greet them. Yihui did better this time. She didn't say anything but the barest hello and though the newcomers seemed disappointed by this, no one laughed at her.

They moved on a moment later and Max went straight back to their discussion. "There was a boy in my village who was very smart. Mother allowed him to sit with me when the tutor came." He gave a self-conscious shrug. "It was the only way I would sit for instruction." He sighed. "It worked for months until Father stopped it. I was furious that I had to stay in and study when I didn't want to, and my friend got to play when he wanted to study."

"What happened to the child?"

"He farms pigs just like his father. Does a good job of it. He's very smart."

"Can he read and write?"

"Some, I think."

"You don't know?"

He shrugged. "He's one boy out of dozens on an estate we lived at for a few summers. I have not kept track of them all." And that thought troubled him. She could tell by his tight expression. "I should find out. He was clever. Moreso than I." He glanced at her. "In China, he could have taken an exam, then? And gotten a government job?"

"If someone sponsored his education, yes. He would not be limited by his father's occupation."

"Yes, yes. We do that as well. If the boy catches our attention."

There were more people on the street, more interruptions as they greeted every well-dressed soul who came by. She remained silent most of the time. So many words came too fast for her, but she was getting better.

And then, when it was time to return home, he demonstrated that he was still thinking on her words.

"You believe my servants want to read and write?"

Did she tell him about Millie? Did she risk—

"There must be someone," he continued. "You would not bring this up if you didn't know."

It was the truth, and it was proof that he was clever in his own right.

"Who is it?"

"Max…" She didn't know if it would get the girl in trouble.

"No, no, let me think." A moment later he snapped his fingers. "What's that maid's name?"

"Millie."

"She wants to learn?"

"She has been very helpful to me. We have been learning together."

"Hmmm. Then I should get you both a proper tutor."

She looked at him in surprise. A real teacher would make a world of difference. There were so many things she could not learn just by listening hard.

"I would be—"

"Very grateful. Yes, you say that a lot."

"I am grateful."

"And I am getting an education alongside you. Very well, any other servant who wants to read will be tutored as well." He sighed. "Even if it means that the food is not always hot and my boots are not always black."

She stared at him, her heart beating in her throat. How could she not love a man who listened? One who thought about his actions and changed them because of her words?

She had spoken her mind honestly and expected him to disappoint her. And yet now, she was deeper in love than ever before.

"Don't look at me like that," he grumbled. "It's just a tutor. It's nothing of import."

"Millie will think it is a very great deal."

He smiled, apparently pleased by her words. His step was jaunty as they climbed the stairs back to the house. He was jolly as they waited by the door and a stable hand held the pony. Then he scooped her up, but the moment they stepped into the house, his expression tightened into chagrin.

There, just coming down the stairs, was his mother with a furious expression on her powdered face.

"Have you taken leave of your senses?" the lady demanded.

Max sighed. "I'm mad as a hatter, Mother." If his levity was meant to disarm her, he missed the mark badly. The lady pointed one long finger at the parlor.

"You will explain yourself right now!"

Yihui had so enjoyed her time with Max that his mother's fury was very jarring. It was not customary for her to say anything in these situations. She had been trained since birth to hide in shadows. But this short walk on a pony had changed her in some fundamental way. She did not like to see the cloud come over Max's face. And though she did not know his mother well enough to understand how to divert her rage, she still took the risk.

She squeezed Max's shoulder such that he looked directly at her.

"Are you mad," she asked, "like the king is mad?" Millie had explained that the prince regent led the country because the king was very ill in his mind. "If so, you cannot be questioned. Everything you do is as if done by the Emperor of Heaven?"

She knew it wasn't true, but it was the best joke she could come up with. Fortunately, it worked. Max grinned back at her, and his eyes seemed to dance with delight.

"Absolutely," he said. "That's exactly what it means."

Chapter Twenty-Five

MAX CARRIED YIHUI into the parlor, well aware that his mother would follow.

"Shall I set you in a chair?" he asked Yihui. "Or would you prefer to stay—"

"Whom did you meet out there?" his mother interrupted. She crossed to stand right before him with her hands on her hips. "What did you say? What did *she* say?"

He gave Yihui a wistful smile. "I think I'll take you upstairs. My mother and I will be in conversation for—"

"Of course, she needs to stay!" his mother exclaimed. "If we're to see her transformed into a duchess, I need every moment with her."

Max paused, stopping himself before he said that it was all a ruse. His mother was not known for her discretion. She wasn't a terrible gossip, but she did enjoy the attention garnered from a tall tale. And Yihui was as great a tale as they could get.

"Mother, I think her instruction can wait. She can't even walk yet."

"As if a duchess needs to walk!" she huffed. "And you're the one who began this by taking her outside. If you had consulted me, I would have told you to wait until after the Season was done."

"She cannot be cooped up in a bedroom for that long." Giving in to the inevitable, he set Yihui down in the nearest chair.

"I am trying to help you," his mother huffed. "I've spent the last week thinking exactly how it should be handled. I have asked you to come speak with me, but you have refused. And now we are in a pickle."

"Mother, I am managing things. The prince has demanded—"

"I know what Prinny said." His mother peered through the curtains to see the great many people promenading out front. "Why didn't you consult with me before you took her out in daylight? You know better than that."

"And you know better than to lie to Prinny. He saw her yesterday, remember? He knows she is not—"

His mother rounded back on him. "And if her health takes a disastrous *turn?*"

A lie? "Prinny would see through that in a second." Though, if enough time passed, the man might choose to ignore it. It was hard to say. Either way, Max much preferred to act rather than hide, and so he had taken Yihui out to face the world.

His mother obviously understood that. She pursed her lips with dismay. "Well, it's done now. What did she say and to whom?"

Max smiled, his amusement getting the best of him. "She said 'What ho' to Lady Marsh. We all thought it very funny."

If he thought to distract his mother with this anecdote, he was sorely mistaken. The lady looked like she would have an apoplexy on the spot. But since his mother often looked like that, he wasn't concerned. He'd lost count of the number of times he'd been sent for her smelling salts only for her to recline dramatically on a settee for an hour with no visible injury.

This time was no different. She set her hand on the side table, leaning over as she gasped for breath. She could breathe just fine, but she enjoyed the drama of it. Even Emmaline gave no credence to the way Mama waved her hand in front of her face and glared at whomever was in the room.

"Mother—" he began, but Yihui interrupted him.

"Help me!" she cried as she tugged on her sleeve. "Get me to her!"

Oh dear. Clearly, Yihui did not understand about his mother's preference for drama. "Please, don't upset yourself. Mama's spells—"

"Bring me to her!" the woman commanded.

He gave in. There was no need explain that Mama was exaggerating. She'd figure it out soon enough. So at her direction, he carried Yihui to the chair nearest his mother. Yihui immediately leaned over toward his mother.

"Please. Her..." She pointed to her wrist. "Give me her arm." Then she looked at his mother. "Lady, please sit down."

He groaned. His mother was very prickly when not addressed correctly. "Your Grace," he said softly to Yihui. "She is properly addressed as 'Your Grace.'"

Yihui nodded and then pointed to a chair. "Your Grace, please sit down!"

His mother's face was already regaining color, her breath slowing though not yet returned to normal. He supposed she had decided she'd had enough attention.

"See? She is better," he said as he helped guide his mother to the chair next to Yihui.

"Give me her arm!" Yihui commanded again and in a moment, he set his mother's limp arm in her grasp.

"What are you doing?" his mother said weakly. She didn't appear angry so much as curious. More attention, he supposed.

Yihui didn't answer, but her expression was one of concentration as she apparently counted his mother's heartbeat.

"I have seen this before," she finally said.

"So have we," he said. Then he tried to give his mother the benefit of the doubt. "She has spells. They never last long. She's perfectly fine afterwards."

Yihui shook her head. "Your Grace," she said carefully, "I know a tea to make your heart better."

Max all but rolled his eyes. His mother's heart was fine. She'd been suffering from a lack of attention all her life, and this was her way of getting it. He must have made a sound or perhaps Yihui was merely observant, but she turned to him with a dark look.

"You think she lies."

"They all do," his mother cried.

"Of course not," he lied. "I believe she gets overwrought when people disagree with her." That was as polite a statement as he could make in front of his mercurial parent.

"They say that in China, as well," Yihui said. "Women never get help from my father. But if a man clutches his heart as you do, there are seven doctors to give him medicine."

"Really?" his mother asked, clearly hanging on every word.

"She is just overwrought," Max repeated.

"Yes, she is." Yihui turned to his mother. "I will make you the tea. It will calm you for a time, but you cannot allow yourself to become so upset. No matter what people do, you must keep yourself calm. Your life depends upon it."

"My life!" the lady gasped.

Oh good heavens. He should have warned Yihui about his mother's dramatics.

"I will show you," Yihui continued. "Do you feel your heart?" She tapped her neck. "It beats very hard?"

"Yes! Yes, it does!"

"You must learn to control that."

"What? But it's my heart! How can I—"

"I can teach you if you want to learn, but you cannot expect them to understand."

By them, she clearly meant Max, which was deeply insulting. He cared for his mother. He loved her, but he also understood her faults.

Nevertheless, Yihui continued. "You have had this most of your life?"

"Since Max was first born."

Yihui nodded. "So he has seen you like this his whole life. He does not believe."

"None of them do. Not even Emmaline, and she sometimes has fits of her own."

Max frowned. "She does not."

His mother sniffed. "She does! But she doesn't tell you because of how you react. And your father, too."

He folded his arms, irritation getting the better of him. "But there is nothing wrong! You will be up and railing at me again in five minutes as if nothing happened."

"But something did happen!" his mother shot back. "And no one listens!" She was dabbing at her face with a handkerchief as if she cried. It was all playacting, and it irritated him that Yihui was falling for his mother's lies. Especially when she patted his mother's hand.

"Men do not listen to women's complaints," Yihui said. "That is why there must be women doctors, women who give medicine."

"But are there any of them?"

Yihui straightened up. "I am an apothecary." She struggled to form the English word, but it was clear enough. "If you will let me, there is a tea. But you must remember, it will only ease the pain for a little while. You must learn to control yourself."

"But is that truly possible? I have no control over my heart."

Yihui tsked loudly, her expression as fierce as he had ever seen it. "What do they teach girls in this country? Why do they say you cannot learn?" She looked to him. "Girls can read. Women can control themselves."

He opened his mouth to argue, but what could he say? He'd wanted his mother to control herself from his earliest memories. And he wanted her on Yihui's side instead of railing at them both. He just hadn't expected that they would bond together in this way.

Meanwhile, Yihui looked about the room. "Take me to your place of medicines. I will find you what is needed for the tea."

She'd had his mother complete cooperation until that point. The woman had reveled in the attention but fell short the moment it involved a strange Chinese tea.

"Oh, I don't know," she said. "The duke says they aren't real fits."

Yihui nodded. "And your son believes his father. Even his daughter. But what do you feel? When you are very angry?"

His mother tapped her chest. "Tight. It's very tight."

"And your eyes? Black spots?"

"Yes! Sometimes."

"And afterwards, you are very tired, yes?"

"Yes!"

Yihui nodded. "I have seen many cases of this, but only you can decide if you will take the medicine."

"You think it will help?"

"Yes."

His mother dabbed at her eyes. "Very well, Max. Take her on that ridiculous pony and get me her medicine." She sniffed. "Don't talk to anyone along the way. Don't think I've forgotten how impossible it will be to train her correctly before the wedding. Or that I shall be working very hard on your behalf."

Of course, he wouldn't forget. She wouldn't let him.

"Yihui is doing very well," he intoned.

"As if you know what it takes to be a duchess."

He winced. It was an old argument between them. She believed she managed a thousand things which he and his father never appreciated. That might have been true once, but Emma was the one handling things nowadays. And yet, his walk with Yihui had made him question a few things. She had pointed out something he had never considered, and he wondered now what else he didn't understand.

Could his mother truly be ill?

"I shall ring for Emma. She should sit with you."

"No, no!" his mother cried. "Don't do that!" Yet more proof that she wasn't truly sick. If she were, she'd be begging for help.

"Why don't you want Emma here?"

"She's painting." His mother rolled her eyes. "You know how she gets when she's painting. If we interrupt her, she'll only be cross and make me more upset."

Yihui touched Max's arm. "Trust your mother to manage her own body. She can decide if she needs help."

Max nodded. He supposed that was the only sensible solution. But he didn't like that Emma had suddenly resorted to painting. She only did that when she was very upset.

"Do you know why—" He cut off his words. If his mother knew why Emma had locked herself away with her paints, she surely would have said. Besides, that was a problem for another time. Apparently, he had to take Yihui to an apothecary now.

"Very well, Mama," he said giving the lady a deep bow. "Yihui, you are not too tired? It is a long way."

"I want to help your mother as soon as possible."

Another walk then, and a long one. "I'll call for Blue." Then after he had sent the order, he remembered the one thing he'd meant to ask his mother.

"Mother, do you know of a good tutor for reading and writing?"

The lady frowned at him. "I know of several who have excellent recommendations. Why?"

"I should like to hire one for Yihui." He glanced at her, making sure she understood this next bit was for her benefit. "And for whatever servant should wish to better themselves."

"Better themselves? Whatever do you mean?"

"With reading and writing."

His mother gaped at him "You *have* taken leave of your senses. The servants have plenty to do without adding learning on top."

"Nevertheless, I should like to. Could you send out a query to the tutors? Or shall I apply at the employment office?"

"Oh good God, don't go there. Never mind, I shall do it for you. Just one more task among the hundred others."

He barely held himself back from rolling his eyes. "Thank you, Mother."

"Just get me this Chinese tea. I shall write your letters while I wait."

He nodded as he carried Yihui outside. Blue was brought back soon enough, and she settled into the saddle with ease. But just before he left, Chiverton caught his attention.

"Yes?"

"Her Grace wishes to ask you something before you depart." The butler glanced disdainfully at Yihui and Blue. "The stable hand can hold the pony while you speak with her."

Max nodded, disliking his own butler's attitude, but choosing not to make an issue of it. After all, Chiverton had been their butler as long as Max had been alive. As such, he was given a little latitude. Though he was determined not to abandon Yihui for long.

"I'll be right back," he said before he headed in to see his mother. He crossed quickly into the parlor where his mother was already at her writing desk. "Did you need something else, Mother?"

"I did," she said as she looked up from the desk. "Have you written to the church yet? To post the banns?"

He winced. For all that his mother was dramatically inclined, she was not stupid.

"Er, no. I have not."

"Do you think the regent will forget to check the papers?"

He shook her head. "No."

"Do you think to delay him then? Say you had forgotten about this?"

Perhaps.

"Most wise," she said with a nod. "You mean for her to cry off, yes?"

Since she'd already worked it out, he might as well admit it.

"Yes. I've explained it to her."

"Good. I'll shall support your charade in every way I can."

He frowned at her. "But you just said that she was the only one who understood you. You were getting along famously with her."

"Well of course I did. She's going to get me that tea. Doesn't mean I should accept her into the family. Good lord, imagine what your children would look like." The lady gave a delicate shudder.

And that had him stiffening in anger. "She's a smart woman, Mother. Worthy of respect."

"Then she'll have no problem landing on her feet—so to speak—once this dreadful situation is over." She set her hands together on her lap. "Now go on. Get me this Chinese tea. I mean to try it and pray it doesn't kill me."

Chapter Twenty-Six

"DO YOU REALLY think she's ill? Or are you just making up to her?"

Yihui looked at Max. She didn't understand the words, exactly, but she comprehended the meaning. He thought his mother exaggerated, and maybe she did. But her illness was real.

"Her channel moves badly. My tea will help, but she must do the rest."

They were walking outside again, moving quicker than their earlier stroll. She could already tell she would be sore from sitting atop this pony for so long, but it was worth it to finally do something that she was trained to do.

Meanwhile, Max glanced at her, his expression troubled. "I will be sure to take care of you. You need not worry—"

"I am not lying. Neither is your mother."

She was not insulted by his attitude. Well, not insulted very much. Men never took women seriously until it was too late. It was to his credit that he was considering her words.

They walked in silence until interrupted. Twice they were stopped by couples curious about her, but he kept the encounters brief.

"Those four are obnoxious people," he grumbled. "Steer clear of them. Toadies to anyone who has money. They'll bleed you dry with a smile, then move on the moment the tap is cut off."

Then after another interruption, he visibly shuddered. "Terrible lech that one. Don't ever be cornered by him."

He commented on the people they encountered, but in so doing, he revealed a great deal about himself. Regarding the lecher—a word he had to explain—he said he'd tried to get the man banned from the highest levels of society, but that there were too many such men for his protests to make any difference.

Still, he made sure any women under his care was aware of the man's proclivities.

Then he went on about the toadies. "They don't protect the people who rely on them. They don't think of anything but their own pleasure." He shook his head. "It's a reprehensible abuse of their position."

She let him ramble. It was a good opportunity to practice English. And she liked hearing his voice. But after another five minutes, she turned to him.

"Why are you telling me this?"

"Because you will meet these people soon enough. You should know their tricks."

She shrugged. "I always look for tricks."

"I suppose you do."

They walked on a bit more, long enough for her to think deeper about their conversation.

"You are telling me how to behave," she suddenly realized.

"What?"

"You are telling me the kind of people you approve and those you do not."

He shrugged. "Perhaps. Or perhaps I was showing you that I am not completely blind to those around me."

"But you see faults, not illnesses."

"And you see illnesses, not faults."

She would say that they were arguing about tiny things, but the difference was significant when one addressed treatment. An illness implied that the victim wanted to change, that they longed for health. He was suggesting that his mother enjoyed her illness too much to let it go.

That, too, was a possibility.

"I will listen to your guidance," she said.

"Be careful," he admonished with a chuckle. "My thoughts often differ from other people's."

"That makes you intelligent."

He looked at her. Because she was on the pony, they were of a level together. Eye to eye and nearly nose to nose. She saw the interest in his eyes. How could she not? She had learned to read a man's lusts when very young.

What a surprise to return the interest a hundredfold. She had thought these emotions long since destroyed. Her father had made it clear when she was very young that she would not sully herself with anyone or he would kill her. So she had kept herself away from interesting men…until now.

"English men do not take concubines?" she asked.

His brows rose. "Not as such. But mistresses are common among those who can pay for them."

"Are they well treated?" How odd that she could ask these questions so openly.

"Mistresses have a difficult life, subject to the whims of their consort. How they are treated depends upon the man and on the situation."

She already knew Max would be kind. He would treat his woman well. But before she could do more than imagine such a fate, his brows drew together with a frown.

"You do not need to think of such things," he said firmly. "I will see to your needs. You will not need to sell yourself."

She had not thought about the money aspect. Only about his mouth on hers, his body entwined with hers. She knew the specifics, of course. She had helped her grandmother bring medicine to the whores in Canton. Indeed, her grandmother ran a lively business in cursing men who hurt women. By the time Yihui was ten, she had heard details that left her with no illusions about love or tenderness.

And yet, somehow her fantasies lingered whenever she looked at Max.

So they stood close to one another, walking slowly and focused only upon each other. Until he was jostled from behind. They were in a market area, and even he could not take up so much space and not be touched.

"Right," he said, as he cleared his throat. "The apothecary is through there."

"I will be fast. Your mother's needs are small—"

"No," he interrupted as he set his hand upon her knee. "You have caught the prince's attention with your medicines. I'd like you to buy what you need to treat many ailments."

That could be a very long list indeed. "What illnesses?"

He shrugged. "Many. I should like to see you work."

Was this a test? To see if she was able to do as she said? "Will you report to the prince? If you think it is nonsense?"

"Yes."

"And how will you know if it is false teaching?"

"The same way everyone does. Do those you treat get better?"

That was a tall order for even the best healers. Many patients never improved. "I have studied this all my life, but even the best cannot guarantee a body heals. Surely your own medicine men can do no better?"

"You already expect to fail?"

No, she expected to be judged unfairly. But if she believed in her training, then she would need to stand by it.

"I understand," she said quietly, though her belly quivered in fear. It was so easy to blame the medicine for whatever ill occurred.

"Yihui, I need to know if it's a lie. Prinny likes to chase new things. Chinoiserie is his newest hobby."

"Then I am to teach him?"

His denial was swift. "No. You will teach me."

If it were possible, she would willingly share everything she knew. She wanted to prove herself to everyone around. How else was she to gain customers? But not everyone was capable of learning these medicines. Her own brothers were thickheaded when it came to the subtleties of their profession.

"Max, is your mind open enough to learn?"

"I should think so," he said as they crossed the street to the apothecary's door. "You've already spent the day schooling me."

He thought that was schooling? "I have not even begun."

And so her task was set before her. She would fail miserably, of course. She could not imagine any powerful man who would stoop to learn from a foreign woman. But Max had proved himself surprising in so many ways already. Perhaps white men were different.

She entered the shop with hope, but the apothecary inside was not different. He was exactly as obnoxious, insulted, and pompous as she feared. Indeed, he matched her own father for arrogance. Fortunately, she knew he'd be well paid for whatever herbs she took from him, whole jars of ingredients some badly stored, some prepared too coarse, but serviceable nonetheless.

Then she saw a book on the table, one clearly meant as a recipe guide. She couldn't read it yet, but she could figure it out. If she had a copy.

She pointed to it and asked, "How much?"

The proprietor was outraged. She didn't understand all his words, but his meaning was clear. This was his livelihood, and he would not give such important knowledge into the hands of...

Whatever he said was insulting. She could tell from the tightening of Max's jaw and the flash of fury in his eyes. As if knowledge should be hoarded to the few who could profit from it. Medicine was for all, or so her grandmother had taught her.

Yihui held up her hand in a placating gesture. She would learn if he were a true healer by his response to her next words.

"I will trade what I know from China for the knowledge of England."

As expected, the man blustered with arrogance. She had expected no less. But she was watching the old woman in black clothes huddled near the fire. That woman looked up with interest and indeed, she reminded Yihui of her grandmother. Immediately her heart softened to the woman. It was to her she addressed her next words.

"When I am free, I will come back," she said. "We will teach one another."

The woman nodded but the man huffed.

"As if I have anything to learn from a Chinese woman."

She ignored him, already seeing in him all the faults of her father. For Max's benefit, she swept a hand over the large pile of supplies.

"I do not know what this should cost in England."

"What quality is it?"

"Medium. I believe the grandmother has skill."

"Then he shall get a medium payment."

While Yihui supervised the packaging of her supplies, she watched in awe as Max pulled out coins and set them on the counter. The amount looked hefty to Yihui, but she had little understanding of English money. She did see the proprietor's eyes light with greed, though he was in a precarious position. He could not barter with a man of Max's status. He could also not allow anyone to think his wares were anything less than perfect.

That left him both protesting and obsequious at the same time. It was tedious, which was why Max didn't engage. He ignored the coins the moment they left his hands, helped with collecting the wrapped packages, and then gathered Blue's reins as they departed.

She was very impressed.

Max used simple expedience without pompous display.

She sighed. She didn't need more reasons to be attracted to him.

They spoke little as they returned, being interrupted every few feet. She was introduced to a dozen people who all merged into a formless mass in her mind. Max was cordial to them but moved on as soon as possible.

When they finally returned to the house, she discovered he'd had a table in the library set for her use. Apparently, he meant to watch everything she did.

"This is not the best place to mix teas," she told him.

"I'm aware, but it is where you will work for now. I cannot crowd into the kitchen with you, upsetting all the servants there. At least here, I can listen and learn."

He was serious. He meant to attempt an education.

"Very well," she said. "First I will prepare your mother's tea."

She began to speak about a body's winds, about chi energy, and where the channels flowed. It was the most basic instructions she had given to her brothers, day after day. But her English words were not adequate, and he had no understanding of life force. It should have been a frustrating, miserable experience.

And yet, somehow, it was not.

Chapter Twenty-Seven

MAX HAD NEVER seen Yihui so happy. He'd thought her a fiercely aloof beauty before. An exotic princess who could turn into an avenging angel. Never had he seen her nearly giddy with delight.

She whistled while she sorted through the herbs. Not a jaunty tune, as Max sometimes did when he was bored. Neither was it tuneless. Her sounds were commentary on what she inspected, punctuation as she approved or disapproved of her supplies.

It was delightful to listen to, though there were no words. Every click of her tongue meant something, every angry exhale or satisfied sniff conveyed information. And it was all the more revealing because she had no idea she was making noise.

They were in the library where he had set up a table for her use. He'd given Blue to the stable hands and carried her to the stool set there for her use. She'd smelled of the herbs they'd bought, and he set her down quickly rather than give in to the desire to inhale such alluring perfume.

The first thing she did as she settled was explain the tea she made for his mother. It was difficult for her to express what she wanted in English, but he could see her passion for the topic. He also realized there was a great deal more to understand than the simple humors every boy learned in school, though there did seem to be some similarities. If only he'd been more interested in medicine than in King Arthur and his knights.

Given his lack of medical education, he couldn't follow what she said, especially when she started labeling body channels in Chinese. But he loved watching her work. There was a joy in her skills, the way a master musician enjoyed his instruments.

And when she was ready, she called for his mother to drink the tea.

It was ridiculous really, all three of them staring in anxious anticipation. Was there an effect? Did his mother suddenly change into a serene lady of relaxed countenance?

Of course not. But she did enjoy the attention. Mother always enjoyed attention.

"Please, Your Grace," Yihui said, "write down your feelings every day this week. What made you angry. What made you happy. Everything."

"Goodness, that's a lot of writing. Whatever for?"

"So we may see! If you take the tea, are you happier? Sadder? Better or worse?"

"But I can feel it, if it happens."

"Better to write it down. Keep paper always at hand. We will read it together."

"Together? You and me?"

"To see patterns."

His mother nodded, her expression half confused, half thrilled. "I will get some paper right away." And so she left with an excited purpose to her step.

"That cannot be real," he said. "She just wants attention."

"And she will get it while the tea settles her chi. It takes time for the herbs to take effect. Now she will give it that time."

He could see how that would be effective. "But what happens when you stop giving the tea?"

"Why stop?" She dropped her hands on her hips. "Either she learns to moderate her moods or not. Either way, she becomes a wonderful customer."

"Only if you listen to her."

She nodded with a smile. "Yes."

"But you can't spend all your day listening to—"

"Silly old women?"

He didn't want to say that, but then again, that was what he was thinking.

"As a girl, I was assigned to listen. My father was too important to hear the complaints of old women, but my grandmother told me there were women things to learn. So I sat, and I heard. Such things I learned!"

He leaned back to perch on his desk as he watched her. "Like what?"

She winked at him. "I learned how to sell things to old ladies. And young ladies. And all the ones in between."

Well, that was very clever, but it had nothing to do with medicine and everything to do with commerce. His parents would decry such knowledge as baseborn, but he found it interesting. All of his time with Prinny, the work of the Benedict in the Foreign Office, and even his future as a duke had him dealing with the plans of men and the movement of nations. He'd been too busy to bother with the life of women.

Until Yihui. Now he had all sorts of questions. What exactly could one learn from the fairer sex that was hidden from men like him? Meanwhile, she was grinding leaves with a pestle as she spoke, her words taking on the rhythm of a storyteller.

"Every man has people who listen to him. Women, if no one else. But who listens to the women? Who knows what the women know?"

"You do?"

She looked up from her work and gave him a brilliant smile. "Yes, I do. I listen. It was the best thing my grandmother ever taught me. Some of it is silliness, so we got the ladies to talk to one another over tea. Some of it is important and so there is always a girl there who pays attention." She picked up her pestle again. "Always someone."

"You." It wasn't a question. He said it as he tried to imagine a small Yihui grinding away with mortar and pestle while listening to a chattering group of old women. The thought was delightful.

"When I was young, yes," she said. "Then I grew older and had other responsibilities, so I taught the next girl what to do and what to see." She smiled at him. "Seeing is just as important as listening."

"That is very clever."

She chuckled. "Now you have listened and learned."

There was a sparkle in her eyes, a glint that had nothing to do with sexuality and everything to do with who she was when she was not afraid. She challenged him, teased him, and was genuinely happy to be there with him without extra demands. Indeed, she was the one proving her medical skills to him, and yet all he could think was that she was the most amazing woman he'd ever known.

He was standing beside her before he realized his plan. And once he smelled her scent, he was lost to the need to possess her. But he was not a man to simply grab what he wanted. He touched her face first, trailing his fingers across her brow so that he could see her eyes. Too often she kept her head down, feigning a timidity that was not in her nature. He wanted to see her boldly, and so he swept her hair aside and watched as surprise flashed across her face.

"Have you been kissed before?" he asked, startled by how raspy his voice was.

"A few times," she answered. "But only twice by my own choice."

"And what happened?" he asked as he let his fingers slide across the smooth silk of her neck. "With the boy you said yes to?"

"Two boys," she corrected. "One was a bad choice. I was fortunate my brother caught us."

"And the other?"

Her lips ticked up in a smile. "He was sweet, and I was young. My grandmother caught us."

"She didn't approve?"

"She thought I could do better." She shrugged. "She told me

the boy was smart, which he was. He saw my worth but underneath, he was not kind."

"Kindness is important to her?"

"She said it is the most important thing in a husband."

"Not love?"

She shook her head, and the movement brushed his thumb across her lips. "Not love," she said.

"Not passion either."

"Never that."

He curled his fingertips beneath her chin, tilting her head up such that they were nearly kissing—he leaning down, she stretching up. It was his favorite time in a seduction, that moment that teetered between no and yes.

He felt her breath on his lips and ached to taste what he could only feel.

She closed the distance between them. She stretched that last fraction of an inch until their lips touched, their teeth clashed, and his tongue could finally delve inside her.

Lust coursed through him, but he kept it in check. He knew the pound of his heart, the hot swell of his cock. But this time, he also learned the shape of her mouth, the rapid dart of her tongue, and the near panicky catch of her breath. She did not know whether to be frightened or aroused, and he was determined to wait until she decided one way or another.

He continued to tease her lips, gently brushing across them as he darted into her mouth. He was tempting her to do more, to open herself up to him, and to surrender to what he wanted. And all the while, he kept his thumb stroking along the sweep of her neck.

It took a delightfully long time. Yihui was not a woman to surrender easily, but he won her over. She swayed against him as she gripped his arms. Her mouth fell open to his plunder. And her breath stretched into sighs as his hand slid down her neck to cup her breast.

She made a mew sound, high and sweet. He paused to see if

that meant he had gone too far, but she clutched him. Her nipple was a tight nub, and he brushed it with the edge of his nail, back and forth while she trembled.

He licked her top lip then, a daring little stroke as he pulled back to look at her. He watched her eyes flutter open above cheeks that were flushed a dark pink. And still he played with her breast, letting it fill his hand while he squeezed it.

"Is this new?" he whispered.

"Everything is new with you."

He grinned, loving the breathiness in her words. He used his free hand to press her head to the side so that he could kiss down her neck. She arched into him, letting him tease along her jaw and throat. He nipped at her, timed with a squeeze of her nipple.

She gasped in surprise, and he pressed her backward to give him better access.

Damn it, why had he sent her a dress that buttoned down the back? He wanted to taste her breasts, to suck on her nipples, and to feel that moment when her legs spread for him. Already he was tonguing across the line of her bodice. She was trembling beneath him, her hands clutching him in a rhythmic pulse that echoed his own.

He could bring her to climax right here, right now. All he need do was slip his fingers inside her quim. He began to do just that only to realize she wore pants. Damn it, clothing everywhere.

She was almost prone on the table, his left arm supporting her shoulders as he stepped between her thighs. He wanted to rip her attire apart and thrust himself inside. If he had leverage, he might have, but she lay on his arm, and he had a shred of honor left to him.

So he focused on her pleasure. He set the heel of his hand to the junction of her thighs. She was already gripping him with her knees. It was easy to press in to where she wanted. To thrust as he would with his hips, to circle over her nub while she gasped. And to listen to her sounds as she climbed the heights of arousal.

He wanted her naked. He wanted to see her breasts bob as she gasped, to feel her wetness covering his cock. But he had to content himself with her gasps of surprise, and her mews of desire.

Her hips began pulsing into him, her back arching as her eyes fluttered. God, his cock throbbed, but he took delight in watching her.

He pulled his hand out from under her. He shaped her breast as best he could through the fabric. And he squeezed her nipple when he found it.

"Feel it," she rasped. "Feel me!"

He dug his thumb between her folds. God, the fabric was soaking wet. Her belly quivered, her mouth parted. He pulsed against her mound, thrusting hard and circling. Once more. Once…

She cried out. The sound wasn't loud, thank God. But the sight was as explosive as if she had screamed. Her body undulated beneath him, her breasts pushing against his hand while the tremors burst through her.

He watched while his cock screamed its own demands. He nearly scooped her up to carry her straight to his bed.

He didn't. Instead, he watched the magnificent pulses roll through her body. He reveled in the length of them and marked the slow dying pulse as they eased. He watched her eyes flutter as she came back to herself. And he felt her knees tighten against his thighs as awareness of her position returned.

He stepped back slowly. Then he eased her upright and resettled her clothing.

She was quiet and her gaze wouldn't settle. She looked down at herself then at his hands, then darted up to his face before dashing away again. She opened her mouth a few times as if she wanted to speak, but no words came.

Just as well. He didn't know what to say either.

So he touched her face, bringing it up until her gaze settled on him.

What was he to say? That she'd just given him the most erotic experience of his life? That only the thinnest shred of honor was keeping him from taking her right here, right now? Her lips were so red and her chest was still flushed rosy above her bodice. Such beauty and so many things he could teach her.

Unable to stop himself, he kissed her again. He angled her head and thrust into her mouth with all the need that burned through him. And then he forced himself to back away.

Only a base roue took pleasure from a woman in his own household. He was not such a man, and yet need burned him.

"That," he rasped, "is passion."

She blinked at him. Her mouth parted, but what was she to say to that? He didn't even know what he meant by those words.

He took another step backwards, the motion jerky as he forced himself to move away.

"I'll be upstairs for a bit now," he said. "I need to change before going to my club."

What the hell was he talking about?

"It should take about an hour."

What should? Reliving every exquisite moment of what they'd just done? That would likely linger in his thoughts for the rest of his life.

"If you are well occupied here for now," he said, "I can carry you back to your room later. In…in an hour or so."

She frowned as she sorted through his words. And then she looked back at the jars on the table. "I am…" She swallowed.

Beautiful? Exotic? Clever? Wonderful?

"I am well occupied."

"Then I'll bid you good afternoon."

He bowed to her, his body still fighting itself. Then he spun on his heel and rushed away.

Chapter Twenty-Eight

EMMALINE SAT BACK, thoroughly disgusted with herself and the canvases she had created. That was a sure sign that she had painted enough. She'd done a record number this time—six landscapes filled with dark clouds and bright-purple lightning. Part of her knew that lightning wasn't purple, but for some perverse reason, she had painted it thus anyway. And that was another reason for what she was about to do.

"The usual, Nora, please."

Her maid dipped her chin in agreement or acknowledgment, it was hard to tell which. Then she passed over a rag. Together the two of them set the room to rights, cleaning brushes and pulling the canvases off their frames. Emma tried to wash the paint from her fingers to little effect. She would have to be extra careful to wear gloves for the next few days to hide the stains.

Then she turned to where Nora had built up the fire. "Tell me all the gossip while I've been hidden away up here."

The girl did, talking about ponies and apothecary powders set up in the library. Her father would have a fit when he found out, and Emma wondered if she should make herself scarce until the storm blew over. That all depended on whether her father had been drinking heavily or not.

Meanwhile, she stood and watched as Nora fed her canvases to the fire. Such perverse satisfaction she felt in watching her work turn to smoke. Hours of labor gone and thank God for that. She painted for herself and no one else. Even she wasn't sure why.

So the canvases burned while she cleaned and heard all about her brother getting a pony for Yihui.

"Perhaps I shall go see how she's doing." It couldn't hurt as she was heartily sick of her own company. All she'd done for the last three days was think about Chris and what they'd done. About how it felt and what she wanted. About what they'd both said and not said. And every bit of it wrapped in questions and useless, wonderful fantasies that would never come to pass.

But now she was done.

She would think no more of him and herself together.

She'd washed her hands, she'd burned her creations, and now she was ready to find out what nonsense her brother had visited upon their home. Indeed, she was spoiling for someone to rail at other than Christopher.

But Max was locked in his room and unavailable to anyone, according to Nora. So Emma went in search of Yihui.

She found the woman inspecting a dozen or more jars in the library. Yihui sat on a stool, leaning forward and back as she rearranged the jars, but what she accomplished was a mystery to Emma.

"Do you need anything, Yihui?"

The woman startled, spinning around on her stool so fast that she had to catch herself or fall over. Unfortunately, she caught her foot on the stool—as any normal person would—except that her feet were broken. She cried out in shock and alarm while Emma rushed to catch her.

"Oh dear! I'm so sorry! Oh no."

Emma's words were useless, of course, but they spilled out anyway as Yihui clutched her. Fortunately, the pain passed quickly, apparently muted by the plaster bandages.

"I'm so sorry," Emma repeated. "Let me call for Max. He can carry you—"

"No! No Max."

"Oh." Clearly her brother had done something reprehensible.

"Would you like to sit down somewhere more comfortable?"

Yihui shook her head as she released her grip on Emmaline. "I am fine here." She gestured at the table. "I enjoy setting this in order."

It already looked in order, but Emmaline wasn't one to argue. Instead, she sat down near to their guest and searched the woman's face. "You seem unsettled."

Yihui didn't answer with words. Instead, her expression slowly tightened until every part of her seemed to frown.

"Has my brother been awful to you?" Emma pressed. She would welcome a chance to vent righteous indignation.

But Yihui shook her head. When she spoke, her words came carefully. "In China, my life was not happy. I wanted to escape. But there, I knew my place. I knew what to do and how to get what I wanted in small things." She looked down at her hands. "Here, I am grateful and confused."

No doubt. Emmaline couldn't imagine what it would be like to leave everything she knew. Not even the language was the same. "Does Max want you to do something you don't want?"

Yihui's eyes widened, and it seemed like she would deny it, but in the end, she said, "Prinny wishes us to wed."

Yes, she'd heard that command, but she'd forgotten it beneath the weight of her other…experiences. At least she could put Yihui's mind at ease on that matter. She patted the woman's hand.

"Don't worry. Prinny doesn't really mean it. Everyone knows Max can't marry you. He will be a duke one day, and he won't be allowed to marry a foreigner. Even a Chinese princess." Emma tried to smile reassuringly at Yihui, but the woman looked even sadder than before. "He's being confusing, isn't it?"

"He has told me what he wants."

"Yes?"

"We are to pretend great love—"

"And then you'll cry off." She threw up her hands. "I hate all this nonsense. You should not be forced to wed by royal command. He should not have to go through an elaborate pretense just to soothe Prinny's temper. And you should be able to have a life free of the demands of ridiculous men."

Emma knew she was speaking of herself more than Yihui. She was so sick of having her life defined by men. Her father's moods had always dominated the household, even when she was a child. Then, in her adolescence, her mother made every moment about how Emmaline should catch a husband. And now, she'd just come to terms with how many years she'd wasted waiting for Christopher to look her way. Well, now she knew the truth. He would never offer for her, and she had best see to her own amusements.

She had Yihui to thank for that decision. The woman was a model of strength and courage. Characteristics that Emmaline sorely lacked while she pined for a man who'd made his position clear a decade ago. She'd just refused to see it. Honestly, it was embarrassing how weak she was compared to Yihui, and she resolved to be more like their foreign guest.

So she leaned forward until she and Yihui were eye to eye. She wanted both of them to hear her question loud and clear. And give an equally bold answer.

"What do you want?" she asked.

Yihui bit her lip. "He will not marry me?"

"No. You are free of that, but he will see you established however you want."

She watched as Yihui absorbed the information. If she collapsed a little as she thought, then that was to be expected, wasn't it? Forging one's own path was difficult, even for a man. But in the end, her gaze found the jars of herbs.

"I will make medicines for your mother and others like her. I will be an apothecary." Her words grew stronger as she spoke. "I always thought I'd do it in my father's shop."

"And now it will be your own shop." She smiled as she gripped Yihui's fingers. "Hold on to that dream, Yihui. If you're to go through this elaborate charade for Max's sake, then make sure every moment of your time is paid for with a step toward your own dream."

"What do you mean?"

She wasn't exactly sure, but the plan formed in her mind even as she spoke it aloud. "You will have to go to parties soon. You have been seen in public, yes? My maid said you went out on your pony."

Yihui nodded. "We spoke with several people."

"That means you'll be invited to parties. I expect the invitations are already arriving. Everyone will want to meet you. That means gowns, polite conversation, and, well, you won't be dancing but can you sing or play an instrument?"

Yihui shook her head. "No. Not even Chinese ones."

Right. She hadn't thought that the Chinese would have different kinds of instruments than they did, but she supposed that made sense.

"Can you paint? I know you can use a brush."

"All I have ever done is work in my father's shop and help my brothers with their studies." She looked at Emma with a kind of panic in her eyes. "Must all English women sing and dance? Or paint?"

"In our set, yes. Those are the outward graces. Everyone expects you to excel at one or another." She rolled her eyes. "The hidden graces are the ones that manage a household and know how to hostess a party. We're to support our husbands in their endeavors and the height of talent is to appear as if you did nothing at all." She clenched her hands together. "How I wish I had something to claim as my own! Something that I'm good at."

Which was to say she was a disappointment in all the feminine graces. Certainly, she danced without tripping, and she spoke French in the usual way of polite conversation, but all the great talents had escaped her. She looked longingly at the array of jars.

"You have a skill, Yihui. Something that is yours alone, and I envy that. I say that if Max is to parade you about the *ton* as his fiancée, then you should get a place of business out of the charade. And customers, too. I think every hostess who puts you on display must, I don't know, try a headache powder or something."

"You want me to use your brother to find customers?"

"He is using you to appease the prince. Why not get something out of it for yourself?" She lifted her chin. "That is what I plan to do."

"How?"

"I believe I shall start asking for payment from my father. I manage the meals and the servants, plus whatever entertaining is to happen." She looked down at her hands where they were clenched in her lap. "I shall take control of the household accounts. I will pay the bills, manage what is spent, and save what is not. Better yet, if I am to attend a party as mother's companion, then I should be paid for that as well. I am worth at least that much, am I not?"

It was clear that Yihui didn't understand what she was saying, and no wonder. Emma already knew that her father would hate every radical idea in her head. He would call it preposterous. Both her parents had lived in dread of the possibility of her becoming a spinster. The shame of it had haunted her earliest days. They would be revolted by the idea of her declaring herself on the shelf, but that was what she meant to do.

"What will you do with the money?" Yihui asked, proving that she was smart enough to see to the heart of the matter.

Emmaline deflated. "I don't know. I have spent my life fitting into the roles I've been commanded to fulfill. I wasn't given a passion like Kimberly nor a skill like you." She lifted her palms in an open gesture. "Surely God has given me a talent of some kind. I simply haven't found it yet." Her gaze brightened. "Perhaps you could teach me about medicines!"

Yihui released a small sigh. "Everyone wants to learn about my medicines when all I want is to be a good woman for Max."

Emma shook her head. "No, Yihui. Believe me, you are much

better as you are. A woman with a skill, a woman of substance."

"What if I want to learn how to dance?"

Emmaline looked for a moment—truly looked—at the woman before her. Stripping away the myths around her, Yihui was a shop girl who had been thrust into the world of high society in a foreign country. Of course, she wanted the glittering world of the *ton*. Because she didn't see the darker side of it. She didn't know how women tore at each other all for the chance to subjugate themselves to a husband who might or might not care for them.

It was not a world that treated those born to it with any sort of kindness. It would be disastrous for a foreigner.

"Even if your feet were not broken, Yihui, there is no way to succeed here. It speaks well of you that you want to repay Max's kindness, but there is nothing you can give him that the world will value. You are Chinese. He is a future duke. Best you turn to your own happiness and leave him to his games with Prinny. You are nothing but a pawn here and equally powerless."

She looked at Yihui's face, realizing belatedly that the woman could not understand everything she'd said. What did a Chinese shopgirl know of playing chess? Or of the power games among the elite?

"Trust me," Emma said. "Your best option is to barter for your apothecary shop. And I shall be your very first customer."

Chapter Twenty-Nine

YIHUI THOUGHT FOR a long time about what Emmaline had said. Sitting in the library with her herbs, she mulled over the words like a woman grinding seeds into paste. It was clear that no one could imagine her as Max's wife. She shouldn't be disappointed. As far as she could tell, England had the same social levels that China did. As a merchant's daughter, she might bring medicines to the elite, but she could never marry one of them. Which meant she could no more marry Max than she could step into the Forbidden City and kiss the emperor himself.

It was an extraordinary twist of fate that she had come to Max's attention at all, but that was a temporary thing. And if she were smart, she would make the most of this opportunity and be grateful for whatever she could get.

She had to put aside her feelings. It shouldn't be hard. After all, she'd been trained from birth to be content with whatever meager portion she managed to grab.

So that's what she did. She put away her fantasies, shored up the walls around her heart, and—most important—put away the memory of his hands on her body. By the time Max came down to carry her back to her bedroom, she had her plan in place. But that was immediately undone by the sight of him.

He was dressed exquisitely. She was used to large robes with elaborate embroidery in a riot of colors. Not so for Max. He wore black in tight-fitting attire that showed his form to perfection. Broad shoulders, trim waist, and powerful legs. His waistcoat and cravat were a silky dove gray and his shirt snowy white. Hand-some, but austere. As if he couldn't afford decoration, which she knew was not the case.

"You should have a jewel," she blurted when she saw him. "And embroidery." Even in her short time in London she had seen waistcoats with decoration.

He stopped and looked down at himself. "Truly? I've never found it necessary. But I suppose you prefer my father's sense of style?"

She narrowed her eyes, trying to remember his father from the one time she'd seen him glare into her bedroom. She couldn't recall except in the vaguest ways. "Was his waistcoat...?"

"Dizzying. He's nothing like Chris, of course, who never found a color he didn't want to splash all over the place. But Father enjoys the ornate in his waistcoat. Patterns too complicated for the eye to follow. He hides it beneath his coats, of course, but I have seen him in his shirtsleeves. Never fails to give me a headache."

He was teasing. She knew it by the twinkle in his eye and the curve of his mouth. In China, it would be unheard of to so disrespect one's father. Or more accurately, her father would punish her severely if she did such a thing. But she found it endearing that Max could make jokes about his parent without fear of reprisal.

"You have gone too far to distance yourself from your father. Your dress is too plain for a man of status."

"You think so?"

She nodded. "One decoration would be enough. One jewel, one pattern—"

"Not a pattern!"

"A colored..." She touched her chest, forgetting the right word.

"Cravat? Gray isn't enough?"

She narrowed her eyes at him. Was he teasing her? He didn't seem to be and so she spoke her mind. "Red is the color of celebration."

He wrinkled his nose as he stepped to see his reflection in the window. "I'd feel like a man trying to be a flower. A rose or something."

"Try a gem."

"A ruby? Perhaps." He waggled his brows at her. "I don't want to be a dandy, you know."

Whatever a dandy was, she guessed he was far from it. "You must follow your own heart."

His expression sobered as he turned to look at her. The look was entirely at odds with his words. As if he were apologizing with his face even as he spoke words of flattery. "What if I wish to please you?"

How was she to answer that? She stared at him without voice. What did he want from her?

She must have made a sound of distress. Or perhaps he could read the confusion on her face. He crossed immediately to her side but stopped short of dropping down on one knee to speak to her. Instead, he pulled over an embroidered footstool and perched on it like an awkwardly large frog. One in impeccable dress, which made it even more comical.

"Yihui, I must beg your forgiveness. I behaved abominably." He reached out as if to touch her face but stopped halfway between them. "No true gentleman does...what I did. It was without honor, and I swear it will not happen again."

She swallowed. She had already steeled herself to that possibility, and yet the reality still cut. She fought it by studying his face, by thinking about his mannerisms, and finally seeing what was the truth of him.

He was a man who had desires but was forced to suppress them. She didn't understand the reasons for his control, but guessed they were significant. Either way, he denied his needs until they came spilling out in an unguarded moment.

At such a time, he would act. He would kiss her and touch her in ways that set her body soaring. But once it was done, he would leave in shame. He would disappear only to come back and apologize for his actions.

Her father was one such man. The main difference was that his outbursts were violent. His needs screamed so loud sometimes that nothing else could be heard and no one was safe.

Max was of a different sort. His needs were for pleasure. His desires were to give happiness, but something about his life kept him in austere colors as he danced attendance upon a mercurial ruler. Every moment they had been together he had tried to give her what he could—protection, healing, and physical delight.

What was wrong with the others in his life that they could not take such a thing from him? That they rebuffed his need to make others happy? She already knew his mother was perpetually sour. Perhaps it was because of her physical pain, but the lady was sour even when she wasn't in pain. Yihui knew little of his father except that he made demands of everyone. Emmaline had said as much. As for his sister, she adored her brother and yet never ceased picking at him. It was often as a tease, but the rejection remained the same.

"You wish to see me happy?" she asked as she felt her way through her revelation.

"Of course."

She almost smiled at that. No man said, of course he wanted to make a woman happy. Men usually wanted to make themselves happy and their wives needed to stay out of their way.

She nearly demanded that they wed. No other woman would see him as clearly as she did. With this knowledge, she could be the perfect woman for him. She would be faithful as he gave her whatever would make her happiest. Who wouldn't want a husband like that?

But she knew there were restrictions. He would become very powerful when his father passed. She understood that much of English society. And she could not fit into that mold. Therefore, she would take what she could, even if it was less than she wanted.

"I want to have an apothecary shop. Can you find me a place to work?"

He frowned. "You don't have to worry about that right now."

"You do not have to worry about it, but I am a woman with nothing. If I do not look to my future, then who will?"

He nodded. "Very well, if that's what you want. I shall find a place for you and help you establish it. But first—"

"I will learn whatever your mother wishes to teach me. I will act the perfect bride for you. I swear, I will become everything you need me to be."

His breath eased out of him, not as a release of tension but an acceptance of a burden. "She will not be easy on you."

Yihui nodded. "It is necessary. This is what you have asked of me, yes?"

"Yes." Then he touched her hands. He wrapped his fingers around hers as if he wanted to shield her from this very task. "But you will tell me if my mother demands too much."

"Yes," she said. "I will tell you when you fulfill your other promise." He had not made any other promises, but she was going to hold him to it nonetheless.

He frowned. "I don't remember another promise—"

"I will be your perfect bride. And I will change my mind before we speak any vows."

"I hate that you're caught up in this nonsense."

"I will do it because you want it." She smiled. "And because every night…" She lifted her chin, forcing herself to be bold enough to grab what she wanted. Or at least a little part of it.

"Every night?" He stroked a finger across her brow, pushing the hair away from her eyes as he searched her face.

"You will come to me, and you will kiss me again."

"Yihui—"

"I insist. I want a kiss from you. One a night."

"Why?" His word was spoken low, the vibration of it sliding through her energy channels until her whole body tingled.

"Because I want it," she said. Because she already knew her life would be difficult. She intended to make medicines for women and live independent of all men. That meant he would not be in her life. No man would be. And if she wanted to feel the excitement of his mouth upon hers, if she wanted to experience the frantic beat of her heart as they dueled tongue against tongue, then it would need to be now. Here. Once a night, every night until she was established on her own and saw him no more.

"Because I will not be your wife."

"You cannot—"

"And I will not become a whore."

He reared back. "Absolutely not."

"Then I will have your kisses. One a night." She bit her lip, trying not to let her nervousness show. "That is your second promise to me."

He squeezed her hands, his thumb pressing a long stroke from her wrist to her knuckle. "And what if I want more? What if I cannot stop myself?"

She looked him in the eyes. "Would that be wrong?"

"Very."

"It would dishonor you?"

"Yes. And ruin you for an honorable marriage later."

Honor was of supreme importance to him, as it was with all good men.

"Then I will trust in your goodness."

He groaned as he dropped his forehead to hers. "That is not a wise decision."

"I know," she confessed. "But it is what I want." Then she pulled one of her hands out from beneath his. She touched his cheek and gently lifted his gaze to meet hers. "Will you do this for me? Will you accept this bargain?"

She knew the answer before he said it. She saw it in the softening in his eyes and the yearning in his whisper.

"I rather think it will be for me," he said. And then he leaned forward. She thought he was going to kiss her now. She stretched her mouth for his, but he avoided it. Instead, he slid his hands beneath her and picked her up. He scooped her up and balanced her in his arms as she squeaked in surprise and then gripped his shoulders for balance.

Would it always be this way with him? Would he always surprise and unbalance her?

Heavenly Kwan Yin, she prayed to the Goddess of Mercy, *please let it be so. If not forever, then at least for a time.*

"I shall be away most of the evening," he said as he settled her tighter against his chest. "So if you are done here…?"

It took her a moment to realize he waited for her answer.

"Oh yes. The herbs are set as needed."

"Good. Then I shall take you to your bedroom now."

"And…" She didn't want to say it again.

He glanced down at her face, his smile growing as she realized his intention.

"Yes," he said. "I think we should begin our bargain immediately."

Chapter Thirty

MAX LOVED KISSING Yihui. And it didn't even bother him that it left him hard and achy all through the evening. Well, it didn't bother him enough to regret the exquisite press of her lips and the sounds she made when he teased her mouth open and pressed her back in her bed.

He didn't follow through to a full seduction, though his body had burned with the need to possess her. Instead, he'd taken his time as he thrust with his tongue, took delight in the taste of her mouth, and reveled in the sweet pressure of her hands gripping him as if he were her only lifeline.

He lingered in Yihui's bedroom until the throb in his cock threatened to overpower his reason. Then he'd forced himself back and bowed deeply to her.

"I'll begin looking for your apothecary shop tomorrow," he promised. It was the least he could do because he was sure his mother was going to start Yihui's instruction in the morning. Yihui was going to be a miserable, henpecked woman by the end of the day, to say nothing of the week. But there was nothing he could do about it. The banns had gone in this morning and would be read first thing on Sunday. This path was already set.

He was getting off cheap by setting her up with a business of her own. Which was what he was explaining to Lord Benedict over a brandy at their favorite club. Old Gold was located in a tiny corner of London, hidden away from the elite and political people alike. Truly, it was more of a drawing room for those who wanted absolute privacy and Lord Benedict sponsored Max's membership provided he never gave the location to anyone.

He hadn't, but someone else had and the constant flow of souls through the doors never failed to surprise him. Merchants, elites, even someone who looked like a wizard from a fairy tale slipped in and out of the doors in cloaked silence. It was quite intriguing, but Max knew better than to ask anyone's name. In truth, he was perhaps the best-known man here simply because he was dressed in his usual attire without any attempt to hide his identity.

It made up for the fact that the brandy was of middling value.

"An apothecary shop? Really?" Lord Benedict was intrigued. "With Chinese herbs?"

"Their medical theories are very interesting. Different names, but the basis is similar to our idea of humors. They've taken it far beyond anything I understand."

"But does it work?"

"She's alive, and no one expected her to survive."

Lord Benedict nodded, his long fingers tracing the sides of his brandy glass with a thoughtful gaze. "I should like to speak with her sometime."

"You and everyone else. I was stopped by no less than seven people today as I walked here."

Benedict's eyes widened. "You didn't tell them—"

"I said I was headed to Bond Street, as usual, then came here through the tobacconist." There were actually several secret entrances to this building and the guarded staircase that led up to this floor. Even Max didn't know what happened in the two floors above this. He had enough difficulties to manage without delving into secrets best left alone. That Benedict was a frequent visitor upstairs was enough to tell Max that it was an area the government chose to utilize rather than expose.

"Once you have rid yourself of an unwanted fiancée, what will you do?"

"I'm out of Prinny's good graces, so it's a good time to explore other options."

"You can't go to war, Max. Napoleon might be on his heels, but his army kills rich and poor alike. Worse, as a peer, you'd be a target and you haven't the training to be more useful than the cost of your protection."

Max winced at the blunt phrasing. Fortunately, he'd already given up that idea. His parents would lose their minds if he stepped into battle, to say nothing of the worry that would descend upon Emmaline's already overburdened shoulders.

"It's a large world, Benedict. I don't have to go to the continent."

"You're thinking of China."

"We understand so little of such a large part of the world."

"They don't want us to know them. We had to force them to allow us into Canton."

Max grimaced. "I'm aware." Then his gaze lifted to his friend's. "What if they have medicines, treatments, ways to combat things we don't understand?"

"I'm sure they do. The world is too large for England to have discovered everything first."

"Why not bring that information back to us?"

"How?"

"With a Chinese apothecary shop in London. With Chinese doctors who will teach us."

Benedict snorted. "Where will you find English doctors willing to learn from heathens?"

"There has to be a few whose pride will not get in the way. Young women, if no one else."

"Women!"

"Why not? Lady Kimberly's knowledge far surpasses many doctors. Surely you don't believe that only men can learn such things."

Benedict chuckled. "Oh, I have a great deal of faith in the intelligence of women." He abruptly leaned forward. "Very well, I shall support you in this endeavor."

Elated, Max grinned. "Really? How?"

Benedict shrugged. "I know of several people open to new elixirs, special teas, all sorts of cures. Provided she doesn't kill anyone, I can nudge them her way."

"An excellent idea." And one that he'd already had. It was the reason he'd brought up the topic in the first place.

"But I have a condition."

"Yes?"

At this, his friend looked decidedly uncomfortable. He took refuge in his brandy and then looked at a point somewhere over Max's left shoulder. "I can no longer refuse to wed. My parents are aging, and…" He sighed. "Like you, I cannot in good conscience leave England until I have an heir."

Max nodded. It was the same problem he faced every day. "How can I help?"

"I have found a woman perfect to my needs. I respect who she is and believe she will make me an excellent wife."

"I cannot wait to meet this paragon of virtue."

"She is a midwife."

Max nearly choked on his brandy. He had nothing against midwives, in general. Indeed, he thought them important women providing a vital service to those who could not afford a proper doctor. But the idea of a peer of the realm marrying one shocked him to the core.

"You mean to marry her?"

"Yes."

"Your father will never allow it. Your mother—"

"They will have no say in this. The lady has an adequate pedigree."

"Then she cannot really be a midwife."

"And yet, she is." His gaze fixed on Max. "I need your help in hiding her activities."

"You want her to continue?"

"I want her occupied with something other than gossip, parties, and mucking about in my affairs."

"Then get her a charity!" Max leaned forward. "You understand, Benedict, that a wife can be a significant boon to a man's career. Especially in politics."

"I do not need help. I need heirs and a wife who allows me my freedom."

Max snorted. "There are any number of society women who will do that. Hell, Kimberly might even do that if it meant she could skip the folderol of stepping into the Marriage Mart."

"I have made my decision. If I am to steer people to your lady's apothecary, then you can help me in—"

"What? Bringing your lady customers?"

Benedict shook his head. "I should like you to introduce her to Yihui. I believe they could aid one another. Provided, of course, that the shop remains above reproach."

Max huffed. "You just said she need not kill anyone. Now you want her to be above reproach?"

"It would not benefit my wife to associate with a shop filled with charlatans."

The idea was preposterous. Benedict could not marry a working woman. And yet, he had never seen his friend more determined.

"You are mad."

"Just be sure that the apothecary is of good quality. Leave the handling of my wife to me."

Max stared at his friend. The man was crazy. He was adept at many things. Indeed, as a diplomat, he had successfully balanced the demands of warring nations, greedy tyrants, and bizarre customs. But this was not something he could do. He could not marry a working woman without setting the entire *ton* on its ear.

"It won't work. You know it won't."

"It will never work until someone makes it so." And with that, Benedict relaxed back in his chair and lifted his drink will all appearance of calm. Except Max had known him for years now. He knew Benedict wasn't nearly as confident as he pretended.

"You're heading for a disaster," Max said. "But if you want, I shall stand by the side of the road and watch you destroy yourself." He said the words. Indeed, he meant them, but as he spoke, he thought about the joy he had seen in Yihui's face as she inspected her herbs. She'd been happy at her task, blissfully so. Why had he been taught to disdain such a joyous occupation in a woman? Why was the wife of a peer disallowed from productive occupation?

"You will do more than watch me, Max," Benedict said, his voice hard. "You will help me hide her passion from those who would destroy her."

Max nodded. That was indeed the promise he had given Benedict. He truly did believe it would be a disaster, but he could not fault a man for pursuing the woman of his dreams.

"You must love her very much."

Benedict's eyes jerked back to him in shock. "Love? Good God, I'm not so idiotic as that."

"But—"

"She suits my needs perfectly, Max. That is all."

And that is where he intended to end the conversation, but Max couldn't keep himself from poking one last time. "I look forward to your coming courtship." Benedict had already told him that he hadn't yet made his intentions known to the lady in question. "When do you plan to begin?"

"Soon. As in diplomacy, timing is everything."

After that, the conversation drifted to the movements of armies and the diplomatic negotiations behind the scenes. It was a pleasant discussion, one that allowed him to focus purely on the affairs of nations without the anxiety of personal problems. And yet, even as the talk continued, his mind wandered back to the sight of Yihui at her table, Yihui in his arms, Yihui as she writhed in pleasure.

How she fascinated him! He knew he needed to set her aside, and yet, every part of him rebelled at the idea.

He was still struggling with this idea when they were interrupted by pounding feet as Christopher burst into the room.

"Good God!" he uttered, the words half curse, half gasp. "I've been looking all over town for you." The man grabbed a chair and plunked it down right beside them. Worse, he lifted the brandy snifter right out of Max's hand and took a healthy swig.

"How the hell did you get in here?" Max asked. Of all his friends, it had caused him the most guilt to not share this most secret of havens with Chris. And yet here he was, plunking himself down as if he were a founding member.

Chris rolled his eyes. "I followed you here years ago."

"Followed me!"

"And once I'd discovered it," he grinned, "I found a way to become useful to the owner."

"Useful? Owner?" Max didn't know who owned this club. His dues went through Benedict who—

"Never mind that," Benedict interrupted. "What is it that you've learned?"

Christopher rolled his eyes. "I haven't learned anything except that royalty is damned hard to entertain." He looked at Max. "I've delayed Prinny as long as I could. I even told him your mother's sick."

"Mama? How did you know—"

"She's always ill when worldly things get upsetting. You're the one who told me that if she can't manage it with a tea party, then she's useless."

True enough. "What exactly does Prinny want?"

"What he always wants. Entertainment! He expected you to be at Miss Kaur's come-out ball."

Max frowned. "Whyever would I be there?"

"Because Miss Kaur and her sister were great friends of Emmaline at school. I guessed that Emmaline would be there and require you as escort."

"She didn't feel up to it and sent our apologies."

"So I gathered!" Christopher huffed. "I was just there *with Prinny* who made a surprise visit at the girl's come-out just so he could find you."

"Why not simply send round a note commanding me to visit him?"

"Because he thought this would be *funnier*."

Which naturally meant that Christopher had created an elaborate fiction about how it would be a delightful diversion. But that only worked if Max had been there. He sighed.

"How irritated is he?"

Christopher snorted. "I'm here, aren't I? Prinny was threatening to throw me in the Tower."

Ah. Max gestured for another brandy and then began to make plans. He hadn't intended to spend an evening in debauchery with Prinny. The very idea made him ill. But he could delay facing the royal only so long—

"My God, of course you're here," a voice interrupted them.

Max's blood froze. It couldn't be. One of the prime attractions of Old Gold was that it was unknown to his father. Except obviously, the duke knew exactly where it was as he stomped through the parlor door like an angry golem.

Max looked at Lord Benedict. "I thought this was a private—"

His mentor waved a negligent hand. "I am not in charge of membership."

Meanwhile, Max watched as Christopher settled into his customary bored sneer. It was the expression he always wore when confronted by someone of the older generation who was rabidly political. It didn't matter which party, Christopher made sure to appear completely bored by the nation's future. Something that was sure to infuriate whoever dared approach.

Which, naturally, was the point. One could learn a lot from infuriated people.

"Father. I didn't realize you were a member here," Max said. "Pray, pull up a chair."

"I'm not a member, you damned idiot. God, I'm choking on the shame that my son frequents a Molly house." The man visibly shuddered as his gaze swept the room in contempt.

"You're mistaken, Father." This was a private club that had

nothing to do with homosexual activities. There were no men getting debauched with unnatural acts. Indeed, there weren't even the usual courtesans hanging about. It was all very proper, at least on these floors.

But his father never gave him the chance to point out the obvious.

"I'm finished," the man continued to rant. "Absolutely finished with your nonsense. It's bad enough that you're here, but this idiocy at home must end. I'm tired of sleeping at my club." He frowned as his gaze hopped over Chris to land on Lord Benedict. "Bloody hell, Benedict, I thought you had more sense."

The man shrugged, sublimely unaffected. "Apparently not."

"You'll do as you must, I suppose," his father said. "I don't pretend to understand the Foreign Office."

And thank God for that. If his father knew half of what went on in diplomatic circles, he'd be shocked and appalled into an early grave. At least, if Benedict's stories were true.

"Come along, Max. We'll discuss an end to your madness in the carriage. I will not stay here another instant."

Lord, he was so tired of everyone railing at him. Christopher had the right, given their many years of friendship. Obviously, the prince regent could command whatever he chose from his subjects. But his father was treading too heavy tonight, and Max was done with it.

"What madness, exactly?" he drawled as he was served another brandy.

The color in his father's cheeks and neck darkened noticeably, but the man had generations of breeding inside him that refused to make a scene in public. Even in a place as secretive as this.

So despite his demand for an immediate departure, the duke gestured for the footman to bring over another chair. The man did so with speed, and much to Max's dismay, his father sat down with spread legs, flushed countenance, and a cane that thumped hard on the floor as he settled.

"You're to marry Lady Kimberly in the morning. I've already

obtained the special license. She is right now being informed of the matter by her own father. You'll come home with me now where I shall set a guard on your door until you do what is right by that gel."

"You would have me commit high treason? I am under royal command to marry Miss Wong."

"That's a ridiculous command and you know it. And Prinny cannot set aside a marriage once it is done."

Christopher snorted. "He can still throw him in the Tower."

The duke's gaze flicked to Christopher and away. "Like your title, your thoughts are impoverished."

"Father!" Max snapped, but Chris was ahead of him.

"Good thing Prinny enjoys frivolous people." Chris rose to his full height. "Well, Max? What do I tell His Royal Highness?"

The message was clear. If Max were about to be put under house guard, Chris could slip that threat into Prinny's ear and stop the wedding forthwith. Assuming, of course, that Prinny was of a mind to interfere. For all that he'd made a show of demanding Max marry Yihui, he knew as well as anyone that the dukedom did not want to pull in Chinese blood.

"That I shall visit him forthwith and we can discuss when Miss Wong shall be presented at court. She is most anxious to meet His Royal Highness in better circumstances."

"Excell—"

"Miss Wong is right now being settled in a location better suited to her social standing," his father interrupted. "I have told you that I would not tolerate this murderous disaster for long, Max. My patience has reached its end."

Max bolted upright in his seat. "What have you done? Damn it, Father, she can't even walk. Where have you put her?"

"Be thankful it's not Tyburne."

"Be thankful the prince doesn't clap you in irons!" Max cried as he jumped to his feet. Damn it, the places where his father might have put her were endless.

"I must agree, Your Grace," Lord Benedict inserted in his

low, diplomatic voice. "Max has been threading a very difficult needle with the prince. To insert yourself in the middle of this—"

"Insert myself!" his father all but shrieked. "That woman"—he spat the word at Chris's feet—"sleeps in my home, lives at my tolerance, and is completely *unwelcome at my table.*" He used his cane to thrust himself upright. Max could see the bulge at the man's temple and the white-knuckled grip he had on his cane. If ever a man were about to have an apoplexy, it would be now. And at the moment, Max was furious enough to not care.

But he knew better than to match his father fury for fury. Screaming back was not the way to get through, though it had taken him most of his adolescence to understand that. Instead, he took a page from Benedict's book.

He rocked back on his heels and pulled up a calm façade. His face and his voice gave no room for disagreement.

"You have two choices, Your Grace," he said coldly. "Either tell me where Yihui is or Chris will see that Prinny claps you in irons."

"As if—"

"Oh, he would," Chris interrupted with a vicious grin. "I shall be sure he knows how much you despise him. I shall spin a tale of your political ambitions, your desire to topple the monarchy—"

"Ridiculous!"

"Is it?" Max asked. "How many times have you publicly voiced your disgust of the prince?"

Again, the duke's cane slammed down on the floor. There weren't any other people in this room beyond the footman at the door. That was the beauty of Old Gold. Many rooms led to better privacy. But more than one person had slowed as they passed by the door. Max's father was certainly aware of that.

"You will marry Lady Kimberly!" the duke bellowed.

"She has foresworn me." That statement shouldn't give him satisfaction, but it did.

"You need a bride."

"And I have—"

"You will—You—obey—"

Max had thought the word "apoplexy," but he hadn't expected it. His father grew excited over a great many things. He bellowed, he blustered, he spoke in heated, explosive terms in the House of Lords. And that was nothing compared to the outright bullying he did when his choler was up.

But he did not gasp like a dying fish while he banged his cane down. He did not clutch his chest while his eyes bulged out. And he didn't stiffen as if his whole body had turned to stone.

He did now.

And then his father, the Duke of Fernbury and leader of the Tory party, toppled like a great tree felled by a very sharp axe.

Chapter Thirty-One

EMMALINE KICKED OFF her shoes and tucked her feet up under her bottom. She settled leaning sideways onto the wing of the large chair. This was the most hideously improper position in which to read a book. Not a single line of her body was straight and if she had a kitten curled up on her lap, she would be in heaven.

No kitten. No puppy even. But she had a good book on this balmy spring evening and enough light to read. The men in the family were out pursuing their interests. Her mother was attending the theater after imbibing another cup of Chinese tea. And Yihui was practicing English with Millie. Emmaline was supposed to go to her friend's come-out ball, but she'd sent her apologies. All she wanted tonight was to read in quiet in whatever twisted way she chose to sit. Why, if she wanted, she could even throw her knees over the armrest and stretch her head back until she was upside down. She'd done that several times as a child and wasn't averse to doing it again just because she could.

She'd finally gotten to the good part of her book—the salaciously silly part where the heroine is rescued from her own idiocy by a very handsome man—when someone banged loudly on the front door.

She jolted upright, annoyed on multiple levels by the interruption. She looked at the time. It was much too late for callers and too early for any of her family. Besides, even father didn't pound that loud.

She stood up, marking her place in her book and then smoothing down her dress. She refused to put on her slippers. She would stay in her stocking feet because, well, sometimes a lady wanted to feel comfortable while at home.

Chiverton took his time answering the door. He had no more interest in indulging whoever was banging either. She wished she could peek out the window, but she'd been in the back of the house, not the front parlor. All she could do now was stand in the hall and wait to see if she was needed.

Maybe she should put on her shoes?

Too late. Chiverton opened the door with his customary, "Good evening, sir—"

"Good evening, Chiverton. The duke has asked us to move Miss Wong to a new home. If you could show us to her bedroom, we'll get this finished quickly."

"I beg your pardon, sir—"

"My name's Mr. Pearson, and as you can see"—he pulled a piece of paper out of his pocket—"I've got the duke's seal on his instructions. I'd prefer not to upset things overmuch. If you would—"

Emmaline charged out of the back room. "Now just a moment here. Yihui is not going anywhere—"

"Lady Emmaline! Good to see you again." A very handsome man stepped into the light. His blue eyes sparkled, his broad face showed even white teeth in a face used to smiling. His skin was rugged, his shoulders broad, and his fit body was attired as nicely as any gentleman, albeit in not quite the first stare of fashion. And if she didn't mistake her guess, there was a stain on the cuff and a tear near the shoulder.

She saw it only because he bowed before her in the most exquisite manner despite his lack of fresh tailoring.

"Do I know you sir?"

"Mr. Noah Pearson, my lady. We met in your first season. I don't attend many parties, as a rule, but it was my sister's come-out."

Memories tumbled into place. Good lord, was this the third son of Baron Trottham? He'd matured into quite a handsome devil, and the glint in his eyes told her he knew how to use his charm.

"Mr. Pearson," she said, refusing to give him her hand. "Why have you disturbed my evening?"

"Apologies, my lady. As I was explaining to Chiverton—"

"How do you know his name?"

"Your father told it to me when he wrote his letter." He gestured to where Chiverton was holding out a note that clearly showed her father's wax seal.

The butler handed it over to her with a slight frown. "It says Miss Wong is to be moved."

"Moved to where?"

Mr. Pearson gave a teasing kind of shrug. "I'm not allowed to say, I'm afraid. His Grace wished to keep the woman's destination private."

"Private! You can't simply take a woman out of our home."

"Of course not. But His Grace can have one removed at his direction." So saying he gestured to the men behind him. While he'd been talking, three other burly men had crowded into the hallway, and he now pointed them up the stairs.

"You cannot go up there!" Emmaline cried as she dashed forward. She meant to stand in front of them, but she hadn't expected Mr. Pearson's speed. Or strength.

She'd taken no more than one step when he caught her about the waist and swung her back around. "I can't let you interfere, my lady. You might get hurt."

His arms were like rope, thick and unforgiving. And they were a shock to her mind and body. No man had ever handled her as such, picking her up and setting her aside like a sack of potatoes.

"Don't touch me!" she cried as she slapped him as hard as she could manage.

Or she tried. He caught her wrist as easily as some caught a tossed ball, and he held her arm aloft, well away from scratching his eyes out. She twisted as viciously as she could, but to no avail. His hand was heavy, his grip bruisingly strong. And when she went to kick him, he rapidly spun her around, flattening her back to his front.

"Go on, boys. Find her quick."

He didn't have to encourage his men. They were already halfway up the stairs, but at his words, they quickened their pace.

"Let me go!" Emmaline screamed, but it made no difference. Even Chiverton appeared lost as he waved his hands in distress.

"Unhand her immediately!" he bellowed, but Mr. Pearson spoke right over him.

"I know this is upsetting. It's not my intention at all."

She slammed her feet down as hard as possible, cursing her lack of shoes. Damn it, his boots were thick. His arms were tight across her belly in the most horrible way.

"Stop it!" she cried, and she wasn't the only one.

One of his men appeared at the top of the stairs with Yihui casually tossed over his shoulder. She was fighting, but they had her pinned. Then Emmaline watched in horror as the man banged one of her feet against the wall. Everyone could hear her howl of pain and Emma's captor jerked sideways.

"You're not to hurt her."

"Then she shouldn't scratch, damned foreign cat."

"Let her go!" Emmaline screamed. So did Millie who was hitting one of the other men with a book. Down the hall, a pair of footmen came running, but they were young men against hardened brutes—easily shoved backwards and out of the way.

"Please, please," Mr. Pearson kept saying. "This is only making things harder."

Emmaline jerked her head back as hard as she could. She was held tight to Mr. Pearson's front, and she desperately hoped to crack the man's jaw.

She didn't. Her head thunked heavily into his muscled chest and made no apparent impact. The others went less easy on the staff. One slammed Chiverton into the wall. The other punched their hardiest footman hard enough to knock him off his feet. And in very short order, the man carrying Yihui swept out the door.

"Where are you taking her?" Emmaline screamed. "You can't do this!"

But of course, they could. They did. They were gone in less than three minutes while the ducal household was left in shambles. Last to leave was Mr. Pearson. He set her down and dashed toward the door in one fluid motion.

She was quick, too, rushing after him, but what could she do except grab his coat? It tore in her grasp, and she heard him curse, but he didn't slow. Within a few breaths, he leaped into the carriage as it barreled down the street.

Emmaline might have been impressed by his athleticism. Instead, she was revolted, sick to her stomach as she watched the carriage escape. Her skin crawled with the memory of his arms around hers. She'd been completely helpless.

They'd taken Yihui like robbers holding up a carriage, except it had been in London in her *home*. The violation of it made her furious, sick, and so shaken she could barely stand.

"Are you all right, my lady?" Chiverton asked, his voice wavering.

No! She'd never be all right again.

What was going to happen to Yihui?

Oh God!

She wasn't accomplishing anything by standing in the doorway. She turned, seeing her aged butler looking older than she'd ever seen the man. He was pale, his hair askew, and his hands were shaking.

"Are you all right?" Her gaze skipped past her butler to where the footmen were regaining their feet. One was holding his arm as if it might be broken. The other had a hand pressed to his head.

"Just rattled, my lady," Chiverton answered.

She stepped back into the house, absurdly furious that her stockings were now wet. She should have been wearing shoes.

The men were straightening, their injuries looking less serious by the second. Indeed, Millie looked the most injured and that was because she was cupping her wrist while still holding a broken book.

"The bloody cheek!" the maid cursed.

Emmaline heartily agreed. "Thomas, Henry, do you need a doctor?"

Both men shook their heads. "No, my lady."

"Naw, my lady. But I've punched softer walls."

She understood the sentiment. "Get some ice pressed to your head, Thomas. Millie, how bad is your wrist?"

"Just a sprain, my lady. Nothing that won't heal in a few days."

Emmaline nodded, coming into the center of the foyer. She had her arms wrapped tight around her belly as she tried to erase the feel of a stranger holding her helpless. She had to will herself not to vomit. Thank God her mother wasn't here.

"It's my fault, my lady," Chiverton said as he smoothed down his hair. "My deepest apologies."

"It's not your fault that ruffians attacked—"

"No, my lady. No!" He straightened his coat, clearly using the gesture to pull his thoughts back in order.

"Chiverton, don't fret—"

"My lady, it was the duke's command." He picked up the letter where it had fallen to the floor. He smoothed out the creases and set it carefully on the side table. "We shouldn't have interfered."

Emmaline spun on her heel, at last finding a target for her fury. "What?"

"I should have just allowed them in."

"You did allow them in!"

"They wouldn't have hurt anyone if I'd just let them do as they wish."

"They did do as they wish!"

"Yes, yes, but with so much hubbub. It was unseemly and

completely my fault."

She took a breath, thinking it would calm her. Instead, it set the fire inside her belly to white hot. Damn it, how long had she tolerated his insolence? He'd been campaigning to get rid of Yihui from the very beginning, despite what Max planned and what Emma explicitly ordered. Hell, even her mother had thrown herself into training Yihui to be a lady, but Chiverton had his own ideas, and he regularly demonstrated his attitude.

"Chiverton, they abducted our guest."

The man looked awkward, his expression apologetic. "His Grace mentioned several days ago that she had overstayed her welcome."

"And so you let anyone burst inside—"

"He had a letter!" Chiverton squeaked as he pointed at the thing.

That was it. She was done getting disrespected in her own home.

"You won't."

Everyone stared at her as the cold finality in her tone cut off all the noise in the house. Eventually, Chiverton gathered enough dignity to question her words.

"I beg your pardon, my lady?"

"You're sacked without reference."

"My lady!"

"Get out." Then she turned to the room at large. "And if any of you want to stay employed, you will find my brother and bring him home!"

Chapter Thirty-Two

MAX HAD ALWAYS been considered athletic. He was light on his feet and his hands were quick. All in all, he had the reflexes to catch his father as the man fell. It was his mind that was slow. Throughout his life, he'd seen his father rage until spittle was flying as fast as the crockery. He'd watched the duke punch straight into a wall, leaving a hole that remained to this day. This fury wasn't even in the top ten of his father's rages, and yet when the man clutched his chest and began gaping like a dying fish, all Max could do was stare.

His father was not one who fell. His father made other people fall.

He watched as the duke's knees bent. He saw the slow descent of his father's torso as he pitched forward. If it were not for Lord Benedict, Max would have watched his father land face first at his own feet while he did nothing but stare.

"Don't try to talk," Benedict said. "Just take a moment."

With Christopher's help, they turned his father over, settling him on his back with a cushion under his head. His father's eyes were wild, and his mouth kept opening and closing. He was breathing in a choppy, ragged way and making grunting sounds that shook Max to the core. He couldn't grasp that this gasping man at his feet was his father.

Lord Benedict looked up at the footman, speaking in low urgent tones. "I believe Dr. Carter is upstairs. Please tell him that

Lord Benedict requests his immediate attention on a medical matter."

The footman nodded and dashed away. Meanwhile, Christopher was loosening the duke's cravat. But what caught everyone's attention was the way the man was waving his left hand. The fingers were curled as if cramped, but he seemed to be gesturing at Max.

And so Max went down on his knees beside his father. He grasped the duke's hand, letting the fingers curl around his own, but feeling for the first time the lack of muscles in the hand. It was as though his father's hand was just bone and skin, skeletal without sinew. Or perhaps it had been that long since he'd touched his father in any way at all.

"Don't try to talk," Lord Benedict was saying, but his father wasn't listening. Of course not. The man never listened to anyone.

"Take a slow breath," Max said. "A doctor is coming."

The duke was still trying to say something. As his breath lengthened, the wild look in his eyes shifted to a glower. Then he worked hard to form one word.

"Home."

Lord Benedict shook his head. "It isn't wise to move you that far, Your Grace. There are beds upstairs—"

"Home."

Max set his jaw. "If you cannot be moved, then you will have to stay here."

The duke's jaw clenched, and his brows drew down in a glower. "Home!" he repeated, and no wonder. Staying at a place he thought was a Molly house would be adding insult to injury. And now that Max was watching his father carefully, he saw the extent of that injury. One side of the duke's face didn't move as well as the other.

"Oh dear…" A high male voice filled the room. Max looked up to see a dandy strut into the room. His expression was warm and his smile compassionate as he set his medical bag on the floor. Christopher stepped back to give him room. Good God, the duke was going to hate being treated by a dandy, but if Benedict recommended him, then the man knew what he was about.

And with a doctor here to attend to his father, Max's mind clicked back into focus.

"Chris, could you please go to the house. Yihui—"

"I'll stop whatever idiocy is afoot." Chris glanced down at the duke. "And prepare Emmaline."

"Thank you."

Chris gave his shoulder a squeeze before heading out at a run. Max relaxed a bit. He desperately wanted to rush home and find out what had happened to Yihui, but he knew his duty to his title and his father. His place was right here for all that he still wanted to rage at the duke for causing this disaster in the first place. Instead, he watched with a grim expression as Dr. Carter completed his business.

In the end, the doctor rocked back on his heels. "If I could have a word, my lord?" he said to Max.

Max shook his head. His father was awake and calmer now. He would want to hear the diagnosis himself. "Speak to the patient, please. I will listen as well."

"Very well. Your Grace, I'm sure you have guessed the truth. You have suffered an apoplexy. Fortunately, it has not compromised your breathing nor your heart. I believe whatever hope of recovery you have will be in complete rest." He glanced at the nearest footman. "A room shall be made for you here, and a litter can carry—"

"No." The duke's one word was clear to all of them.

Max sighed. As far as he could tell, his father's faculties were not impaired. The duke had guessed what had happened from the very beginning and stated his desire to rest at home. Certainly, he could override his father, but he saw no reason to do so out of spite.

"We will take him home. Dr. Carter, if you would accompany us and see to my father's well-being, I would very much appreciate your efforts."

The man flashed a warm grin. "Of course, my lord. I am at your service."

He saw his father's grimace but didn't care. Max had lost faith in Dr. Morton's skills a long time ago.

The business of transferring his father took time. The duke was warned against any type of movement and so he lay on the floor and tried to glower everyone into doing his bidding. And for the first time in both their lives, people turned to Max for direction instead of his father. Certainly, they smiled at the duke, they expressed their condolences and hope for a speedy recovery, but they treated him as a lesser man in all aspects, deferring to Max for any decision.

It was jarring to go from second place to first all in the matter of minutes. And though Max managed to get everything arranged, he couldn't shake the feeling that his life had just changed irrevocably for the worse.

Unless his father made a full recovery—and he had never heard of a man who did so after an apoplexy—then Max would very rapidly have to take over the running of things. Any dream of going to China was at an end, not to mention diplomatic trips, once the war was over. He would have to take the reins of their vast ducal lands. He'd been begging for this responsibility for years, but his father had been unwilling to relinquish the tiniest amount of control. Now he would have to do it completely.

The idea should have filled Max with satisfaction. Instead, his spirits dropped lower with every moment that he sat beside his father and worried.

Chapter Thirty-Three

CHRISTOPHER RAN DOWN the street, grateful for something useful to do. His own father had been a drunken wastrel who did the world a favor when he passed out in a ditch, caught an ague, and conveniently expired soon after he was discovered the next day. Max's father had been a towering pillar of conservative values and rigid authority. He never bent, never compromised, and never released control once it was in his iron grip.

To see the duke topple like that, cut off mid-rant, was like seeing a foundational part of his world falter. To be sure, he and Max both had railed against the man, despised and defamed him as often as possible. But somehow, they'd never grappled with the reality of their archnemesis crumpling into himself.

It shook Christopher in ways he couldn't measure. And the thought of what it must be doing to Max horrified him.

So Chris was grateful to be sent on a useful task. He didn't bother with a hackney in the usual way. Waiting for one to come around would be a waste of time. Instead, he ran in the right direction then hopped gingerly onto the back of the nearest one already going toward Grosvenor Square. He was too large a man to do this without getting noticed. Normally, such a thing was for boys who had no coin for travel. But he kept his head down and leapt off the moment the coachman thought to object.

He was fortunate in his choice of hackneys and so was able to rush with relative speed straight up the steps of Max's home. He banged the knocker as hard as he could, steadying his breath to appear at least partially in control. And then was confused when no one answered.

What the devil? The house was lit with candles in the front parlor and the upper bedrooms. He noted that Emmaline's bedroom was dark, so she was probably in the back room reading. Still, someone should have answered the door by now. Chiverton was a prig, but he knew his job.

Christopher banged again and was relieved when a muffled voice responded.

"Coming. Jes' a moment."

He waited, anxious at the time. Finally, the door was pulled open by... the cook? "Mr. Gaudreau?" He looked over the man's shoulder to the empty foyer. "Someone is coming for Miss Wong and—"

"Yes, yes! We know!"

Oh bloody hell. He was too late. "What happened? Where's Chiverton?"

"Chiverton has been sent packing and everyone else is looking for his lordship. I've made tea for Lady Emmaline, but..." He shook his head. "It was very bad, my lord. Very bad indeed."

"His lordship is on his way here. Both of them."

Mr. Gaudreau's expression brightened. "Oh good. You have found him—"

"Not good. The duke has taken ill. His room must be made ready. Someone must send for his valet who has been at his club." He frowned. "Where is Chiverton?"

"Sacked."

"What?" Good lord, he could barely wrap his head around anything this man was saying. He needed to speak to the one person who always and forever knew how to manage things. "Never mind. Where is Lady Emmaline?" He didn't wait for an answer nor even an invitation. He sidestepped Mr. Gaudreau, entered the house, and quickly looked about. He noted a new dent in the wall and a side table pushed out of place. He also realized the house seemed deadly quiet.

That was not good.

He headed straight to the back parlor with Mr. Gaudreau mincing along behind him. What he saw shocked him on a night full of shocks.

Emmaline stood in the middle of the room as if she were heading to her favorite spot for reading, but she wasn't moving. She had wrapped her arms around her belly and was staring into the fire. He'd known her for much of his life, and in that time, he'd seen her in many moods. This was a new one.

She wasn't listening, didn't appear to be thinking, and possibly wasn't even breathing. It was as though the very essence of Emmaline wasn't even there.

"I brought the tea…" Mr. Gaudreau said. "But—"

"Thank you. I'll handle it from here."

"That'd be good, sir." He paused a moment. "I'll direct the maids to get the duke's chamber ready. There's one that stayed behind who isn't hurt."

Chris's head snapped around. "Hurt? You've got injured?"

"Nothing too serious. We've sent for Mr. Torres."

The surgeon. "Broken bones, then?"

"Sprains, I think."

That was something. He turned his attention back to Emmaline. She didn't appear physically injured, but she certainly wasn't herself. "Thank you, Mr. Gaudreau," he said. Then he waited a moment while the cook withdrew before he entered the room.

"Emma? It's Chris."

Damn it. He wasn't exactly sure how to approach her. Certainly, he'd dreamed nightly about their last encounter. Dreamed, fantasized, and tormented himself with it, but in all that time, he hadn't figured out how best to approach her in the aftermath. He shouldn't be the one to be here with her, but there was no one else. And he, at least, could take whatever she fury she threw at his feet. He deserved it.

But she didn't move. Didn't even seem to recognize his presence.

"Emma?"

"I heard you."

Oh good. She was cognizant, but she wasn't looking at him.

"Things seem to be a bit upset here. Can you tell me what happened?"

"Why are you here?"

"Max sent me. Your father was planning something regarding Miss Wong. I was supposed to stop it."

"You're too late."

Yes, he'd gathered that. "We only just found out."

"You're never here when I want you."

He winced. There were too many layers to that statement for him to address it directly. "Tell me what happened."

"Men came. Chiverton let them in. They took Yihui away and wouldn't say where." She shuddered. "I tried to stop them."

He reached out a hand to touch her but stopped short. He didn't have the right to comfort her. "Did they hurt you?"

"They hurt her. She screamed. They banged her foot. Why would they do that? Why would they—" She squeezed her eyes tight.

"We'll deal with that in a moment. And there's more after that. But first..." He let his hand settle gently, warmly on her arm. "Emma, what happened to you?"

She whipped around, her total stillness abruptly tossed aside as her eyes blazed in fury. "What happened to me? Nothing. Absolutely nothing, Chris. I wasn't hurt. I wasn't injured. Millie's wrist might be broken. Henry might have a concussion. I'm not even bruised."

"But—"

"I told them to stop. I told them to get out. They didn't listen. I tried to stop them, but he grabbed me. He held me back as if I were a toddler and nothing I did made the least difference. When they were done—when they had Yihui—they left. They just left. I did *nothing*."

"You did something, Emma. You fought them. You tried—"

"Nothing!" She screeched the word straight in his face. "*Nothing!*"

And then he understood. She was the privileged daughter of a duke. The world had always deferred to her, respected her, treated her with reverence. Indeed, he knew the only reason she was so fixated on him was because he was the only one to never bow to her wishes. That wasn't completely true, of course. Certainly, there'd been a nanny somewhere who had said no to her. But in general, the world moved in a predictable, deferential pattern for her.

Until tonight.

She'd been powerless, and she'd probably never felt so helpless in her entire life. Unlike him, who fought daily against impossible forces, she'd always been protected and supported.

"Oh Emma," he said softly. "I'm so sorry."

He gently pulled her into his embrace. She didn't want to go, and he did not force her. But the longer he stood there with his arm on her shoulder, the more she leaned toward him. In time, she surrendered. She pressed her fists to his chest not to press him away but because she didn't know who she should punch or how. She was tight with fury and pain. He held her and murmured the only words he had.

"I'm so sorry. How can I help?"

She didn't answer. He didn't expect her to since, truthfully, there was nothing he could do to fix what had broken. Her sense of personal power was gone now, and there was no way for him to give it back.

Worse, he couldn't even let her grieve. There were things she had to do.

And yet he couldn't force himself to end this moment. She was rigid in his arms, her body shaking from her emotions, and all he wanted to do was hold her safe. He would kill the men who had done this to her. He would find them and rip them apart.

"How many men?" he asked.

"Four. I only knew Mr. Pearson."

He jolted, pulling back with shock. "You knew them?"

"The leader. Mr. Noah Pearson. He's the third son of Baron—"

"Trottham. Yes, I know."

She frowned. "You know him?"

"Only by reputation." It wasn't a savory one. On the other hand, it wasn't especially dark either. "He works for... for..."

"My father." Those two words were filled with defeat. If there was one person the privileged daughter of a wealthy duke could not defy, it was the duke himself.

She peeled out of his arms and wandered listlessly to the settee where she sat down with a dull thud. "I cannot blame men who were working on my father's orders."

But he could. He absolutely could.

"Emma, there's something else."

She looked up and the sheen of pain in her eyes nearly defeated him. Of all the people in the world, he was the last person who should be delivering this news. His animosity to her father was well known, and the reverse. But the task had fallen to him, and he would not shirk it.

He dropped down beside her and gathered her listless hands in his. "Emma, I'll find Miss Wong. You have that promise." He didn't know how, but he had resources. He'd figure it out.

"Thank you—"

"But right now, you must send word to your mother. You must get her home."

"I don't remember which ball she's at. Besides, she never wanted Yihui here, either."

He shook his head. "Your father's collapsed. Max is with him. They've got a doctor there, but the duke is demanding he come home."

Her eyes widened as shock rolled through her body. "Collapsed?"

"He and Max were arguing about Miss Wong. It was heated and..."

"The duke collapsed?"

He nodded. "Apoplexy, I think. He's aware. Making his demands known. You need to get the house ready for him."

"I fired Chiverton."

"Yes. Um, why did—"

"He undermined me one too many times." She pushed herself to her feet and he matched her movement. "How long until they come?"

"I don't know. I rushed here to try and stop them from taking Miss Wong."

"You didn't make it in time."

He winced. To be fair, she wasn't attacking him, merely stating the fact of yet another instance when he could not measure up. "I will find her—" he began.

"Yes. Yes. Good. You go do that. You find her and bring her back. I'm going to…" She squared her shoulders. "I'm going to prepare Father's bedroom. It hasn't been aired since…"

Since Yihui arrived and upset everything.

"Emma—"

Her gaze to his. "Go save Yihui. I'll handle things here."

She was on solid footing now. At least she appeared to have pulled herself together, but even so, he was reluctant to leave. She was shaken to her core, and yet there was no softness in her anymore. Not toward him or anyone. Her eyes glittered with a deep resolve.

"Emma, perhaps I should—"

"Shut up, Chris. I've told you what I need. Find Miss Wong. Can you do it?"

He wasn't sure, but he'd be damned if he admitted that without trying. "I will."

"Then go." There was such hatred in her tone that he barely recognized her. This was Emmaline, the lovelorn adolescent who adored him…no longer.

He waited a moment, studying her face for a hint of the girl who once cared for him. Or maybe the woman he had brought to completion a few days ago.

She was not there. In her stead stood an angry woman who dripped with disdain.

"Can. You. Do. It?"

"Yes."

He sketched a deep bow and withdrew. Time to find Noah Pearson and beat the man to a bloody pulp.

Chapter Thirty-Four

YIHUI KNEW SHE was in a whorehouse even before they carried her upstairs and chained her to a bed. Whether in England or China, the sounds and smells of a place like this remained the same. At least her room was cleaner than some places, and she heard no sounds of violence. That was a comfort.

A very small one.

"I don't need chains," she said. "I can't walk."

It was a lie. The wood and plaster around her feet had kept her from the worst of the damage the bastard had tried to inflict. She could hobble on her heels if she had to. She wouldn't be fast or fierce, but it would be better than being chained like a dog.

Neither of her captors responded. It took two of them to chain her down. She didn't fight them. It would be too easy for them to rebreak her feet, but she didn't make it easy on them either. And she memorized their faces so she could get revenge on them soon. A good curse if nothing else.

Then she was left alone.

After nearly two weeks living in luxury, this was a shock. She kept trying to tell herself it wasn't. She had slept on bare floors before, and this room had a cot. She had fought with rats for her food, and so far, she had not seen any vermin. All in all, this was not so bad. She had survived worse. Certainly, it was better than the ship that had brought her to England.

It was horrible.

She was alone again, completely lost again. She knew what

happened to girls chained in brothels. She wanted to believe that Max would come for her. Emmaline had said as much, but in her heart, she knew that Emma had as little power as she did. If Max's father declared that she be tossed in a whorehouse, then that was where she would stay. It was the nature of powerful men to destroy women.

What an idiot she was for thinking Max would keep her safe. He was not the family patriarch. His father was the one with real power. The son might be kind, and the son could make promises, but it was the father who made the decision.

She curled in on herself, as miserable as she had ever been. Why had Heaven given her two weeks of kindness? Two weeks of good food and a man's gentle touch, not to mention friends and hope for a future? Why give her those just to snatch them away? Better to have never felt such things, never known a soft caress than to have a taste and lose it.

Those were her most coherent thoughts and even they were sharp needles scattered between sobs. She was a survivor. She was a woman who made her own chances and created her own fortune. Except now she felt utterly broken. How pitiful she was, she mocked herself. Where was fierce Yihui? Could she be destroyed simply because Max was lost to her?

Yes.

Yihui had been raised under her father's casual disregard, had accepted being sold, and had survived the ugliness on the ship. She had cursed her abusers and even killed one. But give her two weeks of kindness, fill her with hope for a future in a beautiful man's arms, and suddenly, her spirit was broken when it was snatched away.

She should have expected this. She should have had a weapon ready. But she had grown soft and stupid because she loved a beautiful man who made promises he could not keep.

She was a fool.

She lay on her pallet and cried. And when there were no more tears, she stewed in her stupidity. She deserved whatever fate came. She knew eventually she would gather herself together and figure out a solution. She knew in time she would develop a plan for survival. But for right now, she damned her own stupidity.

Max was lost to her, and she grieved.

It was hours before anyone disturbed her misery.

She heard the door scrape open and bolted upright. She'd long since learned to protect her feet when moving, so they remained immobile, the heavy iron chain glinting dully in the growing candlelight. She wondered if there was any way to protect herself, any weapon at hand. She cursed herself for crying like a child instead of planning for this moment, but that was all the energy she had for recrimination.

She would face whatever came with a cold, hard heart.

And then was momentarily crushed when the person who entered her room wasn't Max.

She hadn't been expecting him, and yet she was still wrapped in her dreams as two women walked into the room. The first strode in calmly. She was the madame, dressed in elegant but functional clothes. Sturdy fabrics stitched well. Her face was calm, her expression one of calculation.

Yihui pushed the hair out of her face and squared her shoulders. She would not face what was coming as a victimized child. But before she could speak, her attention was absorbed by the second woman.

That lady swept in wearing silk, powder, and a canny expression. Her eyes were alight with interest, and she looked positively ecstatic by the sight of Yihui.

"You poor thing!" she exclaimed. "Chained and broken. How awful."

Yihui extended her chained foot. "I cannot run. The chain is unnecessary."

"And cruel!" the lady gasped. She waved at the madame. "Please get rid of that."

"Are you sure?" the other asked, her expression still mostly blank.

"Absolutely!"

With a nod, the madame glided forward and released the shackle. Meanwhile, the lady shook her head and audibly tsked.

"What do you need to heal your feet? Potions? Plasters?" She again gestured at the madame. "Make sure she has anything she could want."

"Yes, ma'am."

Yihui leaned back against the wall, pleasantly surprised that it wasn't damp. She wasn't fooled by the display in front of her. Though the lady appeared very sympathetic, she was the one who had likely ordered the shackles in the first place. She was the one in power here with the madame pretending to be the harsh one.

Either way, Yihui would accept new bandages for her feet. She needed them to heal as quickly as possible, so she listed what she required. The madame nodded and glided out, presumably to get what was needed. Which left the lady here to discuss the future.

"I've already asked them to bring up tea. Are you hungry? I can ask for something more than biscuits."

"Food is always welcome," she said. Though she would have to be very careful of any drugs in it.

"Naturally."

So saying, the woman settled down at the base of the cot. She arranged her skirts around her, moving with a sensual grace. She was likely a courtesan of the very expensive kind, and Yihiu couldn't help but admire her beauty. This woman knew how to seduce in the most subtle of ways.

"Pray let me introduce myself. I am Triana Sabate, and I am very interested in you."

Yihui dipped her chin as Emma had taught her. "Very lovely to meet you, Lady Triana."

The woman trilled a beautiful laugh. "I am no lady, I'm afraid, but I like the way you see me. You may call me Madame Sabate."

Yihui dipped her head in a pretense of overwhelm. As she guessed, Madame Sabate pinked beautifully at the sight. Obviously, she was a woman who enjoyed flattery.

"Please, lady," Yihui said, "what is to happen to me?" She kept her voice tremulous and even shuddered a bit in terror. It wasn't all pretense. She was frightened and if this woman chose to help her, then she would be grateful.

"Of course, you must be terrified," the woman said. She dropped her hands into her lap in a show of decisiveness. "It's these horrible men. We women are forever at their mercy. Some man declares that you are to be wed to a foreign prince, then another prince declares that you must wed someone else. No one asks your thoughts. No one cares. They break your feet, lock you in chains, toss you away like bad rubbish." She touched Yihui's hands. "That is not a good life."

Of course, it wasn't, but what did this woman think she could do about it?

"Tell me about your Chinese medicine. Does it work?"

Everyone asked that, even in China. Will the medicine work? Will my health come back? Why don't I feel like I did when I was young?

"Some work very well, some only a little. You know this is true of all medicine."

The woman nodded, her expression tightening. "Do you know where you are?"

"I can guess what is done in this building."

"Good. Is that something you wish to do?"

Whore? "No."

"What about a woman like me? Do you know what a courtesan is?"

She did. "Do you have one master? Or many?"

"When I was younger, I went from man to man, giving them such exquisite experiences that I was sought after by the king himself. Now, I have enough money to do as I will." She gestured to the building around them. "I own this. Madame Florina runs it, but I am the owner."

That made sense, and Yihui appreciated such independence. A woman who had forged her own path was always to be admired.

"I will make a very poor courtesan. I make medicines. I do not flatter men."

The lady smiled. "Which is why you find yourself in your current situation."

Yihui couldn't disagree. But how could she have flattered the duke when she'd had only had the barest glimpse of him? He wouldn't even stay in his home while she was there. Women like her had no access to the ones with true power.

"I can see that you are railing at the unfairness of it all. Men make decisions, and we women live and die by them. It's a terrible way to live."

This conversation was depressing her. Yihui was keeping control of herself through sheer determination. She had no hope, no idea of how to save herself, and precious little strength left with which to fight.

"What do you want from me?" she asked, her voice heavy with defeat.

It was the question the lady was waiting for. Also, the sad attitude. "I want to know if your medicines work."

Yihui huffed out a breath. "They work for some, sometimes very well." She didn't like answering things twice.

"And if I told you that your life depended on good medicine working well?"

"I would tell you that I will do my best. I cannot promise how your body will answer to my efforts." She lifted her gaze, searching the lady for signs of illness and not finding any. "What is your complaint?"

The woman laughed. "I have so many, but I am not ill if that's what you mean."

"Then why—"

"Because I am owner here. Because the women here need

medicines. Can you stop a pregnancy?"

"Most times, yes."

"Can you prevent one?"

"Many times, yes." She winced. "If I have the right plants. I do not know if thunder god root is grown here." She spoke the English translation for the Chinese words. All her plant knowledge was from China. She did not know if there were English equivalents.

The woman nodded as if she had expected that. Then, before she could speak, a polite knock sounded on the door.

"Enter."

The door opened as two very large footmen carried in a table and set it down. A moment later, chairs followed, linens and a lovely tea service. Yihui's stomach grumbled as the lid was pulled off of a very nice roasted duck. The duke's men had grabbed her before she'd received her evening tray, so she had not eaten yet this night. Odd how quickly she had become used to regular meals.

"Excellent timing, Madame Florina. Please, will you join us?"

The madame nodded even as a footman held out a seat for Madame Sabate. Meanwhile, Yihui noted the distance between the table and her cot. How was she to hobble over there to eat?

She wasn't. She didn't even have to say a word as Madame Florina spoke for the first time.

"Shall we bring the table to you, Miss Wong? Or would you prefer to be carried to a chair?"

The less she moved, the better. "If I could eat from the bed?"

It was no sooner mentioned than done. She was even given a cushion to lift her higher on the bed so that she sat at a better height to the table.

There was a great business of serving the food, pouring the tea, and generally making the meal a very elegant one. Yihui's mouth watered at the abundance of food, and she wondered if she were about to be poisoned. She also wondered if she cared. Whatever was to come would happen whether or not she was well fed. They had no need to go to such elaborate measures to drug her. Tainted water would be enough.

Still, she waited until the others had drunk and eaten at least a bite. If there was poison in the food, then they would be dosed as well. She tried to eat daintily, as they did. Emmaline and Millie had taught her the use English cutlery, and she felt her skills adequate to that. So, too, was she able to answer the questions that came with the food.

"What is thunder root? How does it prevent pregnancy?"

"How did you survive your fever? Did you brew the tea yourself?"

"Will you ever be able to walk again?"

She answered them honestly, trying to learn as much from their reactions as they were learning from her. She was not disappointed. These two women were of uncommon intelligence. Indeed, with them, she found a matching fury at the domination of men. Both of them had been cut, beaten, and ridiculed. Both had found a way to band together to take money and power from the men.

Or perhaps not *from* the men but *for* themselves. To her shock, they did not wish to destroy the men who had hurt them. They wished to use them, milk them for money, and then turn all their gold into something else.

"Medicine for women. Treatment for us. No men, no interference."

Yihui lifted her chin, intrigued. "How can you do this without men?"

Madame Sabate smiled. "I own property, Miss Wong. Several buildings, in fact, with a garden in the middle." She shrugged. "Or rather, an overrun pile of dirt in the middle, but it can become a garden. You can grow plants there. You can grow this thunder root."

Madame Florina spoke up. "You will physic us and the women we send you."

"But what of the doctors who already treat you? What will

they think of me?"

Both women looked at her, their expression telling her all she needed to know. The capable doctors did not treat whores. Those who did were inferior and cruel.

She leaned forward, her intellect well and truly caught now. Could there be a place in London for her? One where she did everything she wanted, and no man could interfere? She didn't think it was possible, and yet here were two women bold enough to see that dream and make it a reality.

There had to be traps. Nothing came so easily.

"What will I owe you?"

"Rent, of course," Madame Sabate said, her voice airy.

She knew this trick. China had plenty of cruel landlords. "I cannot pay rent for a shop that has no customers."

"Of course not!" the lady trilled. "That is why I shall loan you the money. I'll have to charge a modest interest rate. It's only fair. Once the shop is established, you'll have no problem repaying me."

Yihui snorted. China had loan sharks, too.

And yet, for the first time since coming to London, Yihui could see Heaven's design. This was everything she wanted—a shop of her own, customers who didn't discount her because she was a woman, and a life that couldn't be snatched away by a bitter man. She'd just never expected it to happen in England and without the protection of a good husband.

But that made it all the more exciting.

Yihui leaned forward. "Tell me more."

Chapter Thirty-Five

THREE NIGHTS. THREE days. No news.

Max nearly put his fist through a wall. He would have enjoyed throwing a bottle of wine at someone or smashing the teapot into smithereens. Instead, he sat at his father's desk staring at stacks of correspondence that had been completely ignored and wishing he could set fire to the entire room. Unfortunately, Westminster was not a location that could be set alight without significant pain to the country.

He bloody well didn't care what pain it gave his father.

Three nights ago, his father had collapsed before Max could beg, barter, or beat the man for information on what he'd done to Yihui. He'd do so now if the man weren't a furious lump of man trapped in his bed. Indeed, Max had tried, but the duke spread hatred around with equal measure these days. And that included refusing to do anything useful out of spite.

The duke was a powerful man frozen in a body that only responded to partial commands. His entire right side was sluggish at best. But what he did with his left was villainous. He threw food at people, he cursed them in incoherent screams, and he refused to interact with anyone but his valet. And that man was on the verge of quitting, despite years of faithful service.

Meanwhile, Max had scoured London looking for a Chinese woman secreted away somewhere. Anywhere. He had all his contacts looking, called in all his favors, and even paid a Bow Street runner for leads. They'd come up with nothing and he'd been furious enough to contemplate patricide.

Unable to stomach one minute more with doctors or his fretful mother, Max had gone to his father's office in Westminster. There was a great deal of business here or so his father claimed. Papers regarding the management of the country. Treaties on the proper commerce of corn or cotton or slaves. All of it bore his father's characteristic hard slash of commentary.

Max had come here to find any information he could about where Yihui had been taken. What he found instead lit the last flame that burned down any respect he had for his own father.

He found a haphazard pile of unopened mail shoved into a drawer. Closer inspection revealed them as reports, questions, and demands all regarding the family's properties. Most were from their stewards, some were from solicitors regarding a legal requirement, and a few were unpaid bills that had gone neglected for months.

Max thought of all the times he had begged his father to turn over the management of the estate to him. How he'd worked to prove his intelligence, to show that he'd studied the latest farming techniques or land management theories. His father had steadfastly refused to consider turning over any management because Max was too immature to be capable, too lazy to do the hard work, or just plain wrongheaded in his ideas.

That was what his father had said. Now Max knew his father had been shoving reports into a desk drawer to gather dust. The duke had chosen to do nothing rather than allow his son any scrap of control.

A quiet knock sounded at the door. Max rounded on it with a snarl but held back the bulk of his fury. Whoever was on the other side of the door didn't deserve what was boiling inside of him. He took a moment to compose himself, then bid whomever to enter. And if God was smiling on him, it would be Chris with news of Yihui.

God was not smiling. Neither was the man who opened the door.

Major Gabriel Michael Lance was the bastard son of the Duke of Torbay and famous courtesan Triana Sabate. He had a blunt nose and full mouth beneath his light blond hair. And though his dark-blue eyes were always deferential, no other aspect of his body gave quarter to anyone. Except to Lord Benedict.

He was Lord Benedict's right-hand man. If anyone could find an answer, it would be him. And since he would not normally be here, knocking on the duke's office door at Westminster, Max felt a surge of hope.

Max immediately snapped to attention, though it was the other man who hailed from the military. "Good afternoon, Major. Have you come with news? Or does Lord Benedict require—"

"Nothing, my lord. I'm here with news."

Thank God! "Please, come in."

Typically, the man never overstepped, never went where he wasn't invited. At least not when being observed. What the major did unofficially was another matter entirely, but Max knew better than to ask about that. There were darker sides to diplomacy, and the major was the man Benedict turned to whenever that was needed.

If anyone could find Yihui, it was Major Lance. But getting the man to speak was always a problem. Max restrained his impatience while the major shut the office door and settled into a parade rest.

"Have you found her, Major?"

"Yes."

Max leaped up from his chair, ready to dash away. He only needed the address. But before he could demand it, the major held up his hand.

"You cannot go to her, my lord. This information is for your peace of mind only."

"The devil you say! Tell me where she is!"

"I will not, my lord."

Rare was the soul who could stand in apparent ease before an angry peer of the realm. Max gathered all of his consequence about him and tried to intimidate the major with the force of his next words.

"You will tell me everything, Major. I am not in the mood to give quarter."

"Even if it is expressly against her wishes? You have her best interest at heart, do you not? You wish for her safety? Her happiness?"

It was the word *safety* that stalled him. And that left room for the question of her happiness to truly penetrate his thoughts. First things first, though.

"Is she in danger?"

"No."

Always short and to the point, but Max wanted details. That meant making sure the major was comfortable enough to share them. So he gestured at the seat across from the desk and then reached into the back depths of the lowest desk drawer. "Please take a seat, Major. Care for some Scots whisky?"

The man visibly brightened. "Thank you, my lord."

"It's the best thing that comes out of our northern estate." He poured them both a healthy measure. Whisky wasn't his favorite drink, but he appreciated its hard burn.

The major, on the other hand, didn't seem to savor the alcohol, but slammed it back with unusual speed. Max felt his brows rise in surprise. The normally unflappable major appeared to be…flapped.

"I think you'd best tell me what is going on."

"Miss Wong is safe and well. Indeed, I've spoken with her, and she said she's content. And that she doesn't want to see you."

Max shook his head. She must be confused. "It was my father who abducted her. I didn't do it."

"She knows."

"I've been spending the last several days trying to find her. I still haven't heard from Chris, and he went out that very night."

The major nodded but didn't respond.

"Doesn't she know I tried to stop it?"

"Yes. I told her all of that."

Max stared down at his drink, then emptied it. The burn didn't ease any of his confusion, but it certainly focused his attention—momentarily—on something other than feeling completely betrayed.

"I've been trying to find her." That was why he'd come to his father's office. He'd wanted to search for information on Noah Pearson. His father had to have some record of how he'd found the man, how he'd used him to grab Yihui. "Is she well?"

"Better than well, my lord. She's healing and seemingly happy."

"Happy?" She was happy? When he was steeped in misery and frustration?

"She sends her regards, my lord. She is very aware that you saved her life in more ways than one. She knows that you had nothing to do with her abduction, but she has found her feet...so to speak. She is well and..." His voice trailed away.

"And what?"

"And she wants no more to do with men of any kind."

"I'm not any kind!" he snapped. "I'm... I'm..." What was he to say? He was the one who touched her in ways that had thrilled them both. He was the one who planned to set up her apothecary shop. And he was the one who alternated between nightmares of what might be happening to her and memories of what they had shared. "I'm her fiancé."

"She believes—rightly, I think—that with her disappearance, the prince will not hold you to any engagement. You are free, my lord, to marry whom you wish." The major frowned at Max. "She gave me the impression that was exactly what you wanted."

"What?"

"To marry someone else. Lady Kimberly, I believe."

"Kim has thrown me over."

"My condolences."

Max dismissed that with a sloppy jerk of his hand. "She was

right. We don't suit." But he and Yihui always had.

Logically, he knew that was a ridiculous thought. He'd only known Yihui for two weeks, probably the most difficult weeks of both their lives. It had certainly been an impossible one for him. Together, they'd found a rhythm. He'd always been able to talk with her. She made him smile and he thought he'd brought some lightness to her.

Though, damn it, the truth was that she'd been in an impossible situation. Any man who didn't hurt her was an improvement on her situation. So whereas he'd found her to be a delight, she had probably been grateful to survive until the next day.

"I have to speak to her," he said. He had to see if what he felt for her was a reflection of his unsettled life or if there was genuine feeling between them. "She's still my fiancée."

The major's face tightened. "My lord," he began, then he softened. "Max, what are you about? She's a foreigner, and you're a duke's son. There can be nothing between you. I came to tell you that she is safe and happy. You can ask for no more than that."

"How did you find her?"

"How is your father?"

"The same. By which I mean he is debilitated and furious. As far as I can tell, his mind is whole which makes it all the worse. He can think, he can want, but he cannot express himself well. The only mercy is that he tires easily."

The major nodded even as his gaze swept across the disaster that was his father's desk. "Do you need help with this lot?"

"This?" he asked and pointed at the piles of treaties, proclamations, and whatnot. All of his father's most important political maneuvering. "It can go to the devil, for all I care." He'd never enjoyed his father's politics and couldn't care less about them now. "But this lot..." He pulled up one stack of unopened mail from their various properties. "This shall require a man with a steady hand, clear head, and a mind for figures." Unfortunately, he seriously doubted he was such a man. He understood it, could eventually sort through it, but the sheer volume of work defeated him.

He poured himself another glass.

"You need help with it, my lord."

"Do you know anyone?" He knew the major was too busy with his work for Lord Benedict to spare the time.

"I might—"

"The person you find can't be political. The last thing I want is one of my father's cronies pressuring me or anyone who works for me—"

"I know of a man. He's common but brilliant with numbers. Don't know anything about his education, but he was damned brilliant in the army."

"What did he do?"

"Quartermaster, mostly, but not in the usual way."

"What does that mean?"

"He found things that weren't there, stopped things from going astray, and never failed to have another plan with things went bollocks."

Max's brows went up. Such a man would have found employment in any of a thousand of different places. "What is wrong with him?"

"He's Irish. And mouthy."

Max chuckled. "But he can handle numbers?" He looked at the mound of papers. "Lots of numbers."

"He prefers them to people."

"Excellent. Send him to me at the house." He finished his whisky and capped the bottle. Then he began gathering the papers into a satchel. He might as well get started on them tonight. The major took his cue, straightening up as well. He still looked apologetic, but definitely more at ease. Which made it the perfect opportunity for Max to strike.

"She's at the Rose Garden, isn't she? That's how you know. Your mother owns that brothel."

The major covered his reaction well, but Max had timed it perfectly. He saw the flash of shock in the man's eyes quickly covered by a flat expression.

"I will not let this rest," Max continued. Indeed, he was going there right now.

The man abruptly reached across the desk. His hand was large and calloused where it landed on Max's arm, but it was not harsh. Indeed, it was almost kind.

"To what end?" he asked. "Think! It is best for both of you to let it be. She can move on with her life, and you certainly have plenty to settle in yours."

Max shook off the man. "She's in a brothel!"

"Not exactly!" The major huffed. "She's not servicing customers. She's doctoring the whores. She's even getting an apothecary shop apart from the Rose Garden." He looked hard at Max. "That's everything she's ever wanted, isn't it? That's what she told me."

"Everything she's ever wanted." It wasn't a question. He was echoing it to make sure the words sunk into his soul. He'd seen her mixing her teas. She'd been so happy then, likely in heaven right now if the major's words were to be believed.

He swallowed. The logical part of his mind argued sternly that he should face the problems that had landed on his plate and not the woman who seemed to be happily settled.

He couldn't do it. "I must see for myself."

"And if you see her content?"

What would he do? Could he leave her to enjoy the rest of her life?

"She will hear no more from me."

The major nodded, though the expression seemed resigned. "Then I will take you." His gaze sharpened. "And once you have seen the truth of my words—"

"We will go home and drink the rest of my father's whisky."

Chapter Thirty-Six

THREE DAYS—AND MORE important—three nights without Max had torn Yihui apart. She missed him with an ache that was completely nonsensical. She knew they could never marry. Hadn't he said so? But the speed with which he had been ripped from her life left her reeling.

Once again, everything in her life had changed. First, it had been the morning her father had sold her to the Wong patriarch. She'd been on board the ship by evening and headed to England. The next time had been when she'd been brought before the English king. She'd longed for death that day. Instead, she'd killed Lao Gu and ended up protected inside Max's home. She'd lived in luxury then, been cared for as the fever took hold, and made friends.

She'd been kissed by Max, and a great deal more. She began to dream again.

Until it had all been ripped away. Now she slept in an old building across from a whorehouse. Her thoughts were filled with plans for the garden, not wishes about marriage. She was in every way freer and safer here, away from the machinations of men.

She was content now, or so she told herself. Unless it was at night, when she ached for Max. Then she let silly tears slip down her cheeks as she wished, prayed, and wanted a man who could not be hers.

At those times, she forgot how hard she had fought for this

opportunity. She discounted the bargain she'd struck with Madame Sebata. And she pretended she was too broken in mind and body to escape the lady's traps.

But by morning, she rose and went to work again.

The bargain was simple. She lived and worked in the building across from the Rose Garden. She would till the garden, manage customers, tend the whores, and pay rent plus interest on the monies forwarded to her to set up shop. If she failed to pay, they would own more and more of her business until she had nothing left.

If they betrayed her, she would poison them.

They had moved her into the new building the very next day. At her request, they had also recruited the old woman at the other apothecary shop. Mrs. Druina Parise arrived the very next day carrying a satchel filled with seeds and the recipe book that Yihui had seen in the other shop.

The one thing not under Yihui's control was the name of the shop. Madame Sabate declared it would be My Lady's Apothecary. Medicine for women by women who would never be beholden to a man again.

So it was done, and Yihui began to work.

Her feet were still aching despite the bandages, and so Madame Florina offered her a solution. A taciturn Irish woman named Olivia would act as her servant. The woman was thick shouldered and scarred but had a smile that warmed Yihui's heart. She easily carried Yihui wherever she needed to go.

And so it was done. Nights were filled with aching loss. Mornings had no time for tears as she steadily worked through mental lists of what needed to be done.

The major had found her around noon on the fourth day. Their conversation had been brief, but to the point. She had no time for Max. No desire to see the man. No need to bring the aching sadness of her nights into the day when she had a great deal of work to do.

That didn't stop her from listening for a man's heavy footsteps throughout the rest of the day. He came after dark when she sat at the primary worktable studying Druina's recipe book. She knew it was Max by the way her heart leapt into her throat. She recognized the weight of his step and the cadence of his breath. Or perhaps, she merely knew it was a man and hoped it was him.

Either way, her desperate wish was rewarded. First, the major stepped into the room and then, quick on his heels, Max filled the doorway. He quickly surveyed the large dimensions of the room, and then he stared at her hungrily, even as he pulled off his hat and stripped away his gloves.

She didn't move. She couldn't. For all that she had shoved him from her mind, the sight of him filled her with a churning kind of delight both nauseating and wholly wonderful.

"Yihui," he whispered.

"Max," she echoed, equally breathless.

And then neither said a word more.

It was the major who spoke, his shrewd gaze hopping between the two of them. "He would not leave it alone until he heard directly from you." The major straightened to his full height. "You are safe to say whatever you wish. I will not leave you alone with him."

Max jerked as if slapped. "I wouldn't hurt her!"

The major clenched his jaw. "Doesn't have to be blows to hurt."

"And just what do you think—"

"Thank you, major," Yihui interrupted, effectively silencing Max. "I should have guessed he would insist."

Max immediately turned his focus to her. "Are you so afraid of me?" His voice held shock and hurt.

She wasn't afraid of him, per se, but dreaded this horrible desire that filled her whenever he was near. She'd barely started to shove down all the things he stirred inside her. Now she would have to start that all over again.

Even as she resigned herself to such a sad task, she drank in the size and feel of him. The hard edge of his jaw and the bold slash of his nose were sweetly familiar. The shadow in his gaze and the slump to his shoulders, though, were more pronounced.

"Not afraid," she finally said. "I wished to save us both pain."

He stepped forward, his gaze searching as much of her body as he could see. She wore an old gown, borrowed from the brothel. It hung on her loosely and covered her feet.

"How badly did they hurt you?"

She smiled and twisted in her seat, pulling aside her skirt to show him the bandages. "Very little damage. The wood and plaster saved me."

He exhaled in relief. "So you will heal?"

As much as it was possible. But then they had already discussed this. "I am better every day."

She saw the genuine concern on his face and her heart swelled.

"How is your father?" she asked.

His eyes widened at her question. "How can you ask after his health? I would think you want to curse him to the devil."

Her expression turned rueful. "Perhaps I want to know that he is very ill." She already knew from Madame Sabate that the duke had suffered an apoplexy. She knew the symptoms and feared that if the man had not died quickly, the rest of his life would be extremely difficult. But then her expression softened. "And perhaps I want to know how you fare after his fit."

Max lifted his hands in surrender. "He is very angry. The right half of his body works sluggishly if at all." He looked about the room. "Do you know of a brew to help him?" Then he ducked his head. "If you want to, that is. I cannot forgive him for what he did to you."

"I can," she said honestly. "If I were not stolen from you, I would never have met Madame Sabate. I have an opportunity now that I will not squander."

Max nodded slowly, his gaze coming back to her. "And what, exactly, is this opportunity? Madame Sabate is not known for her generosity."

"Neither am I," Yihui countered. "I have bargained for advantage all my life."

There was silence between them. A settling, of sorts, as they began to speak together as they had once done in her bedroom each evening. It was familiar and so sweet, and yet it brought with it a longing that she knew would tear her apart the moment he left.

"My lord," she began, "we cannot—"

"We can," he interrupted. "We can speak together as friends. We can talk to each other about our days. For example, I can see that this is something momentous. I want to learn what is happening here. And…" He swallowed. "And I have learned some things about my father that burn like acid in my gut." He looked at the stove pressed against the far wall. "Surely we can have tea together and talk about our day. That would not be so very bad, would it?"

"Of course not." She spoke quickly, not allowing herself to think about the choice she was making. Or perhaps it was no choice at all since it was already done. The feelings he stirred already flooded her body.

"Thank you, major, for bringing him here," she said. "I should not have asked you to keep him away."

The man nodded, his expression polite. "I've got work to see to nearby. I can return—"

"No need," she said. "Olivia will see to my needs." At the mention of her name, the Irish woman stepped fully into the room. She had been nearby this whole time, standing right outside in the future garden. Her expression was fierce, and Yihui could not help but cheer the woman's transformation. Yihui knew Olivia to be as kind and careful a person as it was possible to be. Unless she felt threatened.

And while Olivia stood with her brows raised in challenge, Yihui watched Max for his reaction. Rather than affront, Max seemed pleased.

"Shall I set the pot for three then?" he asked.

Yihui burst out laughing. "Do you honestly know how to 'set the pot' in any way?"

"Yes, I do!" he retorted. "I did it all the time at school. I just…" He frowned as he looked at the stove. "I don't recognize how…"

"I'll do it," came a fourth voice as Druina pushed her way in from the garden. "Olivia won't take any tea. She's a coffee drinker, but—"

The woman shook her head and shrank back outside. Probably too many people in the room for her. She'd be inside in a flash if there were trouble, but for the most part, Olivia preferred fresh air. Even if it was dust-choked London air.

"Good afternoon," Max said, his eyes narrowing. He was probably trying to remember how he knew her.

So Yihui performed the introductions while the major took his leave. Then within a few minutes, all three of them sat around the worktable discussing their plans for the shop. Yihui didn't hold back. She told him everything she planned while Max listened with an increasingly alarmed expression.

She didn't notice at first. Excitement overran her and once begun, she could not stop. But in time, she saw his face and her words abruptly stopped.

"You don't think it will work," she said, anger in her tone.

"On the contrary, I think it will make Madame Sabate a great deal of money," he said. "But it is your work, yours and Mrs. Parise's. It will take time for the plants to grow, time for the shop to be made habitable, and time again for the customers to come."

"Workers from the Rose Garden already come."

"And how much do they pay?"

Not enough. Madame Florina had negotiated to pay a very small price for all the workers at the Rose Garden. Unfortunately, Yihui had underestimated the number of people who worked there and the extent of their illnesses. She had spent much of the last few days tending to one ailment or another without the right herbs to do much for anyone.

Max must have read the problem off her face. He tapped the table with a heavy hand. "May I see the paper you signed? I fear your rent to Madame Sabate is reasonable for an established business, but it is not manageable for one that is just beginning. How will you pay this winter?"

"The customers will come," she said. She voiced it with assurance because she had no choice. She had raised all those questions to Madame Sabate before, but the woman had remained adamant. So Yihui had been left to either take the risk with a bad deal or choose a different life, possibly as a whore.

She chose the risk and prayed that an answer would come.

And perhaps he had. Perhaps he could convince his mother to speak of the miracle of Yihui's teas to her friends.

"Max—" she began, but he held up his hand.

"I only want to help. If you recall, I had promised to set you up in a shop like this."

"I did not know if I would ever see you again," she said. "I made the best bargain I could."

He nodded his understanding. Meanwhile, she glanced at Druina who had been silent the whole time. Without needing Yihui to ask, Druina crossed to the side table where her book sat in what would become a protected corner. She carefully opened the pages and drew out the written page on which Yihui had affixed her name.

He scanned it quickly, his lips tightening. "You will never make this rent," he said grimly. "And then you will need to borrow money from her to delay payment, but she will charge interest. Very soon every penny you make will go to her and you will have nothing left on which to live." He looked up at her. "You have been tricked."

She winced, her gaze locking for a moment with Druina before she looked down at her hands.

"I had little choice." It was a lie. She could have waited for him. Hadn't Emmaline promised that they would find her? Didn't she know that he would try? At a minimum, he would have tried to protect her.

"There is a way out," he said. "This paper is not legal. Women cannot sign contracts. As your fiancé, she needed my signature."

Her gaze rose up to his, and once again her emotions churned in fury. "I do not need a man to make my promises!"

"You were duped!"

"I agreed." She pointed at the paper. "Even if it was a bad choice, I agreed. Madame Sabate, too! She had no man there to sign."

"Which makes it even less legal."

If she could, she would have shot to her feet and stormed out of the room. But she couldn't, so she leaned forward as far as she could. "We know what we promised."

He frowned. "Do you think she will honor it?"

Yihui pursed her lips. "It is a trap for me. Of course, she will honor it. And as you say, the rent is reasonable for a thriving business, yes?"

He nodded. "Yes, I believe so."

"Then I must thrive."

"It is not possible," he said. "Not without borrowing the money from someone."

Yihui threw up her hands. "Max, I am the girl daughter of a gambler in Canton. It was not possible for me to come to England to be engaged to a prince, but I was."

"I'm not a prince," he said. "And that was Prinny being—"

"Nothing that has happened to me is possible. And yet I am here."

"Just because you have experienced a miracle doesn't mean you should rely on them."

"I rely on my skills. I rely on my intelligence. I jump however I must to survive."

His lips curved but it wasn't a happy smile. The expression held frustration and dismay. "Come back home with me Yihui. I will set you up in a new shop. One without Madame Sabate dogging your heels every time you turn around."

"I have already promised myself here," she said.

"And this is a trick."

"If I go back on my word, then I am nothing. Trick or not, I promised."

He nodded slowly, his lips pressed tightly together. She didn't want to anger him. She already knew that he was her only hope of escaping the trap. But he had to know that she would not put herself in his care. For all that he had done nothing to harm her, he was not a god. He answered to the prince, to his father, to any number of other responsibilities. She needed to stand on her own, even with broken feet and a woman as her taskmaster.

"There is an obvious answer," he said finally said. "I can loan you the money you need. Enough to survive until the shop is established."

"I would welcome that," she said. "Thank you."

And she was enormously grateful despite becoming beholden to a man. Her declaration of independence had lasted four days.

"Consider it my payment for your continued pretense."

"What pretense?"

He caught her hand and slowly pulled it up to his lips. "The banns are being read in church. The prince has declared his intention to meet you."

"But I have disappeared. No one need—"

"You are setting up a shop in the middle of London. I cannot claim to have lost you when you are right here."

That made sense. "So the original plan remains? I am to act as your fiancée."

"And meet the prince."

"And then end our engagement—"

"The night before our wedding." His smile was wistful. "A little under three weeks now. Surely that is fair repayment for the money I will loan you."

"But it is a loan! I will repay it."

"I will not charge you interest. You can repay it as you need." He shrugged. "Or not at all, Yihui. You will be doing me a great favor to pose as my fiancée. My mother will pick at you incessantly and all the *ton* will declare you unworthy, no matter what you do."

"But I will see Emmaline again. And Millie."

"Yes."

And him. Always him. Dressed in his finery as he escorted her to meet the prince. What a dream come true!

She smiled. "Yes, I will be your fiancée."

And so began the most difficult, delightful, and absurdly funny week of her life.

Chapter Thirty-Seven

"YOU CANNOT SIT like that. You look like a sack of grain. Straighten up or I shall be forced to put knives in the back of the chair. Really, you're worse than a child."

Max groaned as he came around the corner and entered the parlor. He saw what he expected to see. His mother sat perched on the edge of the settee like a bird teetering on the edge of a vase. Yihui, on the other hand, sat fully in her chair, using the furniture as it was intended. At his mother's admonishment, she straightened up her back and he quickly grabbed a small pillow to shove into the space she'd created.

"Max! She cannot depend on pillows. That's not how a lady sits."

"She's been working night and day at her shop—"

"For God's sake, don't mention that!"

He glanced ruefully at Yihui and felt his lips quirk at her angelic expression. She'd already told him that she intended to mention her apothecary shop often. It was the best way to get aristocratic customers. And if she didn't let the information drop, he absolutely intended to. He'd already talked to his friends about how her miracle tea had eased his mother's spells.

In truth, he had no idea if it were the tea or the fact that his mother was the center of a great deal of attention. She always thrived when she was busy, but Emmaline had remarked that their mother was also more even-tempered lately. No hysterical outbursts or unexplained tears. And not a single chest-clutching episode of interrupted breath.

If any of that was due to the tea, then he was pleased to share that information with everyone. Meanwhile, he smiled at his mother.

"I'm pleased that you're here this evening and not out at a ball. Did you have any special afternoon callers?"

His mother gasped in shock. "Absolutely not! She's not remotely ready to be seen by anyone."

"Oh," he said. "That's unfortunate because I've invited a friend to join us at supper." He glanced at his pocket watch. "Indeed, I believe he should be arriving any minute now."

His mother leaped up, her expression downright furious. "How could you invite someone to dine without mentioning this to me? Do you think this is a game, preparing your fiancée to be presented at *court?* Everything she does shall reflect upon our name. *Everything!*"

"Your Grace," Yihui interrupted just when his mother was drawing breath. "I am mindful of your work, even if your son is not. The strain upon you is significant. Do you wish to send for more tea? I have added a touch of orangery as you requested. Perhaps you could tell me if that improves the taste."

His mother turned to glare at Yihui, but her expression slowly eased as Yihui visibly inhaled and exhaled. The duchess did the same. And as the woman continued to ease her breath, Yihui rang a small silver bell that was set near her hand.

To his delight, Olivia stepped forward in her new ducal livery. It looked very good on her, he thought, especially when she smiled which is what she was doing now. Sadly, her curtsy was a tad rough, but he was sure it would get smoother with time.

"Her Grace needs a taste of the new tea. Can you bring it for us please?"

Olivia didn't speak her answer, but she did curtsy again and disappear.

"I see that the new gowns have arrived," he commented as he finally remembered the proprieties. He clasped Yihui's hand and bent over it as he might for the queen. He gave her every respect in word and form, but he reserved a special moment when their eyes connected to tease a finger along the underside of her wrist.

It was scandalous flirtation, but she seemed to delight in it as much as he did. Her cheeks flushed, and her eyes took on a dreamy quality he couldn't resist. She wore a gown of the brightest-yellow silk embroidered with a pair of playful goldfishes dancing along the skirt. It was a whimsical dress and one that surprised him. Of all the qualities he had witnessed in Yihui, whimsy had never appeared.

Until now.

When given the safety to indulge her tastes, Yihui had a playful side that delighted him.

"And have you no greeting for your mother?" the duchess asked tartly. She was right. As the highest-ranking woman in the room, she should have been acknowledged first. But how could he defer any interaction with Yihui? She drew him like the sun. Or more accurately, as a flower just beginning to blossom. She was coming alive despite the hours his mother picked at her and the tedious work of fixing up the apothecary shop.

"Max?" His mother's tone was exhausted, not irritated.

"Hmm?" Damn it, he'd lost himself in looking at Yihui. "I have waited because I have a surprise for you," he covered quickly.

"A surprise?" the duchess asked, her tone skeptical as she offered him her hand.

He bowed over her as was appropriate, but when he stood, he pulled out a gilt-edged letter with a royal seal upon it. He handed it to her.

"It is our invitation to the palace, Mother. We have an official date for Yihui's presentation to the king."

The lady gasped as she tore open the letter. And then she dropped it into her lap with a horrified cry. "Tuesday next?" she squeaked. "Tuesday next!"

"Yes, it's an informal gathering, or as informal as these things go. The prince is aware that Yihui cannot dance, but she will be expected to sit with his majesty for a bit, perhaps share some wine. The queen will be there, as well as several dozen courtiers." He grimaced as he looked back at his fiancée. "I'm afraid we were not officially invited to dine, though that may come if you do well during the first part." He truly was disappointed with that lack, though he supposed it would come eventually after they married.

Or rather, it wouldn't come at all because they wouldn't actually marry.

"What does Christopher think of the situation?" Yihui asked. "Does he have any ideas?"

Max's jaw tightened as fear burned beneath his skin. "No one has heard or seen Chris since the night…" He didn't finish. He didn't need to. Yihui was well aware of his worries for his best friend.

"You have not found him?"

He shook his head. "I am at my wit's end. He has disappeared, and I am alarmed. The Bow Street Runner I hired has learned nothing."

His mother looked up. "Oh, I hardly think that was necessary. That boy was always wandering off somewhere. He'd turn up a day or a month later with a cheeky grin and a tale of adventure."

That was true, and certainly Chris was an adult and therefore able to disappear to wherever he wanted. But the last thing he'd done was rush off to confront Noah Pearson, a man Max now knew led a gang of thugs. According to the runner, Mr. Pearson hired himself out to wealthy people who needed someone to perform unpleasant tasks. That was, after all, exactly what he'd done for the duke. He'd been paid to abduct Yihui and deliver her to the Rose Garden.

So what would the man do if Chris confronted him in a hotheaded rant? Christopher could hold his own in a fight one on one, but one on six? Especially if all six were trained fighters? No man was that skilled.

Naturally, Mr. Pearson claimed he never saw Chris and knew

nothing about the man, but Max had the horrible fear that Chris had landed at the bottom of the Thames. And the worst thing was that there was absolutely nothing he could do about it. He kept the runner searching, Chris's friends and family were commanded to write the moment they heard word of the man, and he watched for news of bodies.

Yihui caught Max's eyes, and he knew she shared his worry. She said nothing, and yet he still felt comforted. Waiting without news was horrible.

Meanwhile, a roar and a loud clatter sounded from upstairs. Everyone looked up as if they could see through the ceiling, and maybe they could because his mother brushed the invitation irritably through her fingers.

"I see your father has woken from his afternoon rest," she drawled. "He will want to speak with you directly."

Max frowned. "About what?"

"As if I know. His secretary was here this morning to report on political matters which naturally put him in a foul mood. And now…" She shrugged. "I don't suppose you have happy news for him?"

"What shall I tell him, Mother? That I have increased all our servants' pay first to bring them in line with everyone else in London, and then again to counter his outbursts?"

"No, I don't believe that will make him happy."

"Or shall I tell him that he has sorely neglected the Irish estate to the point that I am afraid I shall have to visit it myself and see to repairs?"

"Good lord, he'll despise that. Said he wants the Irish to—"

"Yes, I know what he wants done with the Irish," he interrupted.

Meanwhile, Yihui pulled a small clay pot from her pocket and offered it to him. "It is the best Druina could find. I have mixed it to the proper amounts according to a recipe my father used with several of his patients."

"How successfully?"

She grimaced. "There is no cure for what he suffers. Only an easement of pain. He must learn to adapt or he will be miserable for the rest of his life."

Max grimaced. "I believe he has chosen to be miserable. And to make everyone else so, as well." He'd had to double the pay for his father's valet just to keep him on for another month.

"You must talk to him, Max," his mother implored. "We cannot live this way."

"Anything I tell him will likely enrage him further."

"Then lie to him. Tell him that he is still the most important person in the Tory party. That Prinny himself will come to get his advice. Something. Anything!"

"And what do I say when Prinny refuses to visit?"

"We'll tell him Prinny did, and he just forgot."

"Father? Forget a visit from the prince?"

She shrugged. "He's angry at his ailment anyway. Might as well blame everything on it."

"Mother, even in his weakened condition…" His voice trailed away. His mother didn't care. She and the duke had always survived by staying out of each other's lives as much as possible. She ran the social whirl. He occupied his time with politics. Twice a week they shared a morning breakfast, and that was more than enough for everyone.

To have him in the house this much was an impossible situation for everyone.

Max grimaced. "Perhaps it is time for some plain speaking."

"Oh good God, no!" his mother gasped. "Never that!"

He smiled. "Mother, you have your way of dealing with Father, and I have mine." He looked at Yihui. They had discussed different methods of handling his father last night when he had escorted her to her home. He'd found her advice to be sound in that she didn't offer him any. She listened attentively, helped him clarify his own thoughts, and finally kissed him sweetly on the cheek. A kiss that he rapidly changed to something a great deal more intimate.

In short, she gave him support for whatever he chose to do. She had no understanding of English norms of behavior, and so left it to him to choose. And in her steady presence, he found his way through the fog.

It was time now to speak plainly with his father. Though, he wished his surprise guest would arrive before he had to head upstairs. None of his family had ever met his old schoolmate before. They'd heard his tales, of course, because Reggie was the friend who had gone to Canton with the East India Company. Max spent as much time as possible with him whenever the man was in town. His family, however, would not know what to do with him. And Max really wanted to see the look on Yihui's face when she met him.

His wish wasn't granted. The knocker remained stubbornly silent, and so he finally bowed to both ladies and withdrew.

It was time to give the full truth to his father.

Chapter Thirty-Eight

MAX ENTERED HIS father's bedroom after a polite knock. He didn't wait for any response but walked in with the assurance of a man resigned to a firing squad. What he was about to do was unforgiveable, according to English tenets of appropriate behavior. A son never laid down the law to his father, and most certainly not when the man was ill.

Oddly enough, it was harder to do in the cold light of day than it was in the heat of a half-inebriated argument. But that didn't change his plan at all.

"Good afternoon, Father," he said. His father was settled near the window. He was dressed in a bed jacket that had stains on it. The nearby table was empty, but Max noted the smear of some kind of sauce had stained the wallpaper. There was a wet spot beneath it as well that he guessed was tea. And no one, not even his father's valet, was cleaning up the mess.

That had been Max's latest order. If his father wished to throw tantrums, then he could damn well suffer the stench of bad food in his room until someone felt like cleaning it up.

"I see you have been throwing your food again. I believe Nanny's response was to make us clean it ourselves until we learned how to control our temper."

His father called him a cruel name. The word was slurred, but Max understood the meaning. He also saw that the right side of his father's face was slack and that his right arm rested in his lap with the same animation as one might find in a doll.

"Mother said that Doyle has come by. I'm sure you were very interested in the political news, such as it is. You know, you could continue to hold enormous sway over the party if you would stop acting like a child. Throwing your food and grunting in fury only convinces everyone that your mind has suffered an enormous blow."

As expected, his father's breath increased to a furious growl. In and out like an angry bull. And his left hand was clenched in a fist.

"I'm sure you'd like to hit me," Max continued. He'd certainly done so throughout Max's childhood. "But you have limitations right now, and so I will exploit them."

He dropped his hands on his hips as he regarded his father. It was an arrogant pose, one that his father used to adopt when Max was a boy. One that allowed him to glare down like God himself delivering the Ten Commandments.

Good lord, what an obnoxious position.

Max dropped his hands to his sides, feeling small for even attempting such a petty action. Instead, he pulled over a chair. The nearest one was wet from whatever his father had thrown, so he dragged another from the far side of the bed. Then he sat down and faced a man who had shrunk so much in the last week, and yet still had the ferocity of a gentleman half his age.

"I shall be brief. You have a problem, and I will let you decide how you will handle it. Continue to throw food, torture the servants, and frighten Mother, and I shall ship you off to Ireland and the tender mercies of the people there who have no cause to love you."

He paused while his father threw invectives at him. His left fist pounded on his leg, and he leaned forward as if to grapple with his son.

"I shan't catch you if you tumble. Indeed, I will leave you there until…well, until someone chooses to help you. It will not be me or Mother. Or even Emmaline. I heard what you said to her yesterday. She has been selfless in running your home seamlessly for many years." He leaned forward. "By the way, I've hired a new butler. I expect he will work better with Mrs. Pizzi and relieve the burden from Emmaline. My sister needs some fun and is certainly not going to find it here. I believe she plans on a long summer of painting in Cornwall, once the Season is done."

That would also keep her busy until they had definite news on Christopher. If they ever got it.

His father grunted something obscene about Emma. It sufficed to harden Max's heart for the next step in this disagreeable task.

"But back to my original purpose. If you choose to stop acting like a toddler having a temper tantrum, then I shall arrange for Doyle to have an office nearby. He can write your letters for you, appraise you of the party shenanigans, and generally be your proxy in the political realm."

"He's Irish," his father growled.

"Yes, he is. Which makes him the only one stubborn enough to stick around."

"No. You."

Max smiled. "Never." He knew his father had long planned for Max to step into his role as de facto leader of the conservatives. Though he understood many of their beliefs, he disagreed with a great deal more. And most of all, he had no interest in devoting his life to arguing domestic policies ad nauseum. His interest had always been in other cultures, other nations, which meant he would continue to aid the work of the Foreign Office. But until he produced an heir, his focus would be on maintaining his future son's inheritance.

Especially since he'd gotten a real look at what his father had ignored all these years.

All these thoughts filtered through his brain as he waited for his father to find control of his temper. It took a long time, and he considered leaving in the middle of it. Fortunately, his father realized that whatever he was trying to say was not getting through to his son.

The problem wasn't the man's failing body. The problem was that Max no longer felt the need to please his father. The man had finally gone too far when he ordered Yihui's abduction. And in so doing, freed Max of any filial obligation.

"Now, let's assume that you find some peace with Doyle and continue to exert political influence according to your wants. There will be no more tantrums, no more threats, no more childishness." He waved vaguely at the set stain on the floor. "Here are the things you will have to accept." He smiled as he ticked them off on his fingers.

"First, I have taken control over all financial matters. You were miserable at it, and I cannot believe I allowed you to be so disastrously bad without stepping in."

Ridiculous how much satisfaction he had with saying those words. The deeper he pushed into all the things his father had neglected, the more furious he became.

"Second, we will have to economize as we put money back into the estates. Really, Father, did you think roofs would repair themselves? That our tenants could continue to deplete the land to no effect? While you scream about supporting the English industries, you have systematically impoverished our own estate."

His father had stopped bellowing. Instead, he poured all of his fury into his glare. It was enough to chill Max's blood. It did not, however, stop him.

"That means that the next servant you mistreat will be your last. I have already had to double their pay. They will no longer tolerate your abuse. Nor would I ask them to. Not when there is an Irish estate ready and willing to equally mistreat you."

His father's response was a dark, angry growl.

"Third, you will be happy to note that repairing the estate will keep me out of Prinny's circle. He's lost interest in me, I think, without Christopher regaling him with made up tales of my…" He made another vague gesture with his hand. "Whatever came to mind."

It had been one of Chris's most ridiculous quirks. The man had told tale after tale—most of them fiction—of Max's exploits as a child. It had kept Prinny endlessly entertained even after Max explained the truth behind whatever exaggerated detail had been embellished. But without Christopher at court, Max was suddenly much less entertaining.

His father huffed his approval.

Max struggled to keep his thoughts away from Chris's possible demise.

"And now for the last. Father, you will have no say whatsoever in the woman I marry. Lady Kimberly has thrown me over and thank God for her intelligence. I shall choose my duchess as suits my fancy. And again, if you make my lady the least bit uncomfortable, you shall be the one shipped off to…" He grinned, loving the strength of this threat. "Yes, the Irish estate."

Silence greeted this pronouncement. Good. He and his father had come to an understanding. The shift in power was natural and normal, given the situation. And though Max had true sympathy for his father's difficulties, he had begun to take the long view of matters.

In his prime, his father had been a mean, domineering bully. Now that he was injured, the duke was suffering the effects of a life spent without respect for his fellow man. Max would see to his comforts as best he could, but he would not give much kindness back. Not until his father found a way to appreciate the people who cared for him.

"Well," he said as he slapped his hands onto his thighs. "I believe we understand each other. And now, if you excuse me, I believe I heard the knocker. That's my present for my fiancée, and I shan't like to miss it." He stood up and gave his father a cheeky bow. "Good afternoon, Father. I'll have someone bring you some towels to clean up your spill. You still have use of one half of your body. That's plenty to clean up your own mess. Though, I suppose if you ask nicely, your valet may help you."

Then with a jaunty wave, Max departed, feeling both lighter

and heavier at the same time. True, this was exactly what his father deserved. But he wasn't sure that he wanted to be a man who meted out just desserts. After all, exactly what kind of mercy would he receive then? He'd spent the last half decade carousing with Prinny.

Chapter Thirty-Nine

YIHUI HEARD THE noise upstairs and worried for Max. In the week that she'd been coming here to be taught how to behave, she and Max had often discussed his father's illness. She knew he struggled to balance respect for his elder, duty to his title, and his own personal honor. For Yihui as a female child, her responsibilities had been so much less. She was to do what her father commanded, even to the point of being sent to marry a foreign king to pay his gambling debts. Blind obedience was terrible, but she didn't have to daily question her path the way Max did.

So when he headed upstairs to speak with his father, she worried about what would come. Even if Max won this battle, how would it hurt his spirit to discipline a parent that he had once respected?

Though she didn't say it, the duchess worried as well. They heard the sounds coming from upstairs and exchanged worried glances. And neither said a word as they waited in taut silence.

Then it went quiet. No outbursts, no thrown dishes, no thuds, thunks, nor raised voices. Whatever was going on upstairs, it had reached a balance point. And that, apparently, was enough to recall the duchess to her task.

"Now then," she said, "from the beginning. Whom did William the Conqueror marry and who were his children?"

Yihui tried to remember, but the foreign names were so much nonsense to her. The duchess couldn't understand why she could barely pronounce Plantagenet, much less remember who begat whom. By the time the knocker sounded, they were both relieved by the distraction.

The duchess looked up with a frown when an unfamiliar voice introduced himself as Mr. Reginald Karr. Yihui could see the woman struggle to place the name somewhere, anywhere in her prodigious memory. In the end, she put on a bland expression as the man was announced in the parlor.

Mr. Reginald Karr had a broad face, a placid smile, and a stiff bow. Yihui thought him a harmless kind of man who might or might not be a good customer one day, depending upon his female relations. Then he turned to greet her and spoke in Cantonese.

Her jaw dropped open in shock. How wonderful to hear her native language again, even when spoken in an English accent. It was so delightful, it took her a moment to answer while she blinked back tears of surprise.

"Greetings," she finally managed in the same language. The word fell across her tongue like an old nail. "How are you?" Those words came a bit faster.

"I am doing well. Lord Maximus said you would be kind enough to speak to me in Chinese. I am so grateful to be able to practice."

"We are speaking Cantonese," she corrected. She switched to the emperor's dialect. "This is Mandarin," she said. "It is for all formal conversations with Peking."

"I am not well versed in that," he said, continuing in Cantonese.

"No matter," she said honestly, switching back. Her words were speeding up now and she had to consciously remember to speak slowly for him. "This is the language of commerce from Canton, and it is wonderful to hear it again."

They exchanged a few more pleasantries until the duchess cleared her throat in obvious irritation. "It is impolite," the lady said, "to exclude one member from a conversation."

Mr. Karr immediately turned to her, his expression contrite. "I do apologize, Your Grace. My excitement over being able to practice Chinese has overwhelmed my good sense."

"Very well, sir. Can you explain the reason for your visit—"

"Reggie! You made it!" Max strode into the room like a returning prince. His expression was filled with good cheer, and though Yihui studied him closely for signs of distress, she could detect nothing but an impish delight in seeing his friend.

Or perhaps it was delight in introducing Mr. Kerr to her because he very quickly turned that devastating grin her way.

"This was my surprise," he said. "I thought about how I might feel thrust into a country that was in every way different from my own. I thought I might long for even the smallest thing from home." He gestured for Mr. Kerr to sit down even as he settled on the chair closest to her. "Was I right?" he pressed.

Yihui nodded, her eyes brimming with silly tears of delight. How could something so small fill her with so much joy that she was literally overflowing with it?

"Thank you," she whispered.

"Reggie and I met in school, though he was a few years ahead of me. Then off he went to Canton with the East India company, and I've only recently renewed our friendship."

"I only got back a year ago."

"I found him thanks to my inquiries at the company office after you entered my life." He smiled as if her appearance hadn't disrupted every aspect of his life, and she lost herself in a rush of wishful feelings. What if they had met as equals, as suitor and maiden, at one the *ton* balls? What if she didn't have to cry off in two weeks' time? What if...

"Now, don't be shy," he said, oblivious to her thoughts. "Talk in Chinese as long as you like. Mother and I will be content to listen. Maybe we can learn something, eh?"

"Max!" his mother admonished, but he would not allow her to diminish his gift.

"Nonsense, Mama. Yihui has had to listen to us speak in English without stop. The least we can do is enjoy a bit of her beautiful language."

"But I don't understand a word of it!" his mother exclaimed.

"Then perhaps we could learn."

Max was firm with his mother. And Yihui was sure to switch to English to include Max, his mother, and Emmaline when she joined them at dinner. But even when the talk was in English, the discussion often centered on China. Mr. Kerr had lived for a short time in Canton and knew a great deal about the city, but even he had questions about life inside the Middle Kingdom. Given his interest and Max's encouragement, Yihui had the most enjoyable evening of her entire life.

Her thoughts and opinions were respected. The stories from Mr. Kerr were entertaining. And she listened to thoughtful comments on the differences between their two countries. For the first time, she saw a place for herself not just as a foreigner selling Chinese medicines, but as a woman who had something to share with the world. And as a person who was learning about a new way of life—the English way of doing things.

Or perhaps it was Max's way of doing things, because in every moment she felt his presence. He was the one who had arranged this dinner. He was the one who kept his mother from dominating the conversation to her narrow area of interest. And he was the one who pressed for more details, more thought, more exposure to the way she'd once lived.

Best of all, he was genuinely fascinated. She could see it in the sparkle of his eyes and the laughter that so often filled the room. He saw her and she, in turn, saw a place for him in her life.

They couldn't marry. She knew that. But they could be something together. Friends, of course. Temporary support for her business, definitely. But she wanted more. For tonight, at least, she wanted a great deal more.

Eventually, Mr. Kerr had to take his leave. Emmaline and the duchess departed for the theater, escorted by someone too exalted for Yihui to meet. And Max did her the favor of offering to escort her home.

She agreed, of course, and he helped her onto Blue all while looking around for Olivia. "Where is that girl? I can't have her walking through London in the dark—"

"I sent her back earlier," Yihui said. "She's been working very hard for me and deserved an early night back in her own bed at the Rose Garden."

He frowned. "I thought she had her own room at the apothecary."

"Not yet. The furniture has not all arrived. Soon though." She smiled at him. "Thanks to your loan, everything is coming together."

"And the tutor? Has he been difficult?"

Yihui smiled. "He is perfect. He was excited to teach Millie arithmetic." The man was young and too hungry to object to teaching a Chinese foreigner and a maid. "Thank you for letting Millie come every day to help." The girl still lived in the ducal home, but came at first light to work for Yihui and often stayed till dark.

"Millie's learning arithmetic?" She heard surprise in his voice.

"She wants to master bookkeeping. I already taught her how to use an abacas. She is very smart and wasted as a maid, I think."

"I think you are right." He shook his head. "How many other bright people surround me but are lost for lack of opportunity?"

She glanced at him. "Do you think to provide teachers for all your servants?"

"I believe so. There are smart children throughout our estate. We have been remiss in not educating them before now." Then he sighed. "In truth, my father has been remiss in a great many things. I have spent day and night in shock at what he and I have allowed."

"You didn't know."

"I should have."

She heard the weight of disgust in his voice. Here was something of his character that she was only now beginning to appreciate. He felt a personal responsibility for the people who worked his lands and served his meals. Whereas her father cared only for money and the status he gained from serving elevated clients, Max tried to care for those around him.

She hadn't realized until now, however, how that responsibility weighed upon him. Especially when he felt he had failed them.

"You are an honorable man," she said. "Whatever is wrong was your father's failure."

"It will not be mine."

She smiled. They had reached the entrance to the apothecary shop. Every night for the last week he had escorted her here then taken his leave after a single, scorching kiss. Olivia had carried her to her bedroom then. And Olivia had helped her undress while she dreamed of what Max might have done if her servant wasn't around.

So tonight, she had arranged for Olivia to sleep elsewhere. Druina, too, was gone, having traveled north to a relation who had seeds they needed. Recipes too, if all went well.

Which left her alone with Max.

"I hope you enjoyed tonight," Max said. "I thought it wonderful."

In China, refined women never made the first move. Even the whores pretended to an innocence they did not possess. But she had long since learned that women who waited on men often waited forever.

So with an anxiety that surprised her, she looked to Max and spoke words that she had never said to anyone.

"Come to my bed tonight, Max."

His eyes widened and his breath caught. She saw hunger surge in his expression, before he shut it down and stepped back from her.

"You cannot praise me for my honor and then ask for such a thing." He stroked her face, and she felt his fingers tremble.

"We have kissed before."

"I should not have." His lips quirked. "But I could not resist you." His thumb trailed across her bottom lip. "You fascinate me, Yihui. And the more I learn, the more I want."

"Then why deny—"

"Because I cannot. I will not treat you as my whore." His words were crude, and though her blood was burning hot from his caress, she felt the violence in his rejection. Not of her, but at the way she might think.

"I know I am not your whore," she said.

"Yihui—"

"I love you. And for once in my life, I would experience that with you."

Chapter Forty

MAX FELT THE blood roar in his ears. It wasn't from lust. He'd felt overwhelming desire for Yihui for weeks now. But this was the first time he had heard her say the word, love. And more importantly, that was the first time he'd heard a woman say such a thing to him and really mean it.

The word was overused by the younger set, never used once past the blush of youth in the older set, and roundly scoffed at by those inside his own circle. And yet, when she said it, he felt it all the way to his soul.

And once felt, he could not stop himself. He kissed her. He drew her mouth to his and then thrust inside. He licked her, he tasted her, and he thoroughly enjoyed possessing this one part of her body.

When he pulled back, her eyes were dazed. He couldn't stop touching her, so even as he pulled back, he kept a hand on her cheek before letting it slide down her neck. A small shift would have him cupping her breast, but he held back.

"Yihui—" he groaned. An honorable man would leave her. He would not take what he did not intend to marry.

"I will not beg," she said. "I am a free woman, and I can give what I want to whomever I want."

And she chose him. The magnitude of that humbled him. How could he not give her what she wanted?

Suddenly decided, he turned to the neighborhood at large and released a loud whistle. Shadows moved around them. Street boys were always around, especially in this area of town.

"A quid to the one who takes the pony—"

A shadow resolved into a dirty freckled boy. "Where's it belong, guv?" the child asked.

He gave directions, tossed the boy a coin, then added, "They'll give you supper, too, if you ask nice."

Then he scooped Yihui off Blue and started carrying her inside. She'd always felt tiny to him with small bones and small breasts, but holding her like this stirred his senses to a fever pitch. Every part of her was exquisite and he was going to enjoy learning every hill and valley of her body.

"You're never going to see that pony again," she said against his ear. "He's going to sell it—"

"He won't. Ponies are harder to sell than you think, and the boys know the value of a generous benefactor."

He slowed as he turned a corner and began climbing the stairs, but he couldn't wait until he got to the top. He leaned back against the wall to steady himself and her in his arms, then he proceeded to kiss her. Her arms were wrapped around his shoulder. She could have pushed away at any moment, but she didn't.

She tightened her hold on him, she pressed her breasts against his chest. And she took him as thoroughly as he took her. It made no logical sense. His tongue was inside her mouth. But the way she played with him made him feel like both the conqueror and the conquered. And if his footing wasn't in question, he might have taken her right here against the wall.

Instead, he carried her to her bedroom.

It was a simple room, especially by his standards. She had a bed, a stool, and a table for a wash basin. Not even a wardrobe for her clothing. As he slowly lowered her to the bed, he couldn't help but imagine her in his bed, in his home, as his duchess.

"You deserve so much more," he said as he looked around.

She pulled his face back to hers. "And what would I do with more? I would need to hire a servant to care for my clothing and clean the furniture." She nipped at his nose. "You are spoiled with so much."

He couldn't disagree. "Not enough of what I need," he said as he kissed along her jaw. She lifted her chin and whispered her delight.

He was still trying to convince himself to leave when he unbuttoned her dress. Part of his mind told him this was the last kiss. Or this one. Or that one. He could still keep his honor if he stopped now.

He did not stop. Not with her shivering at his every caress. Or with the way she gripped his shoulders and ran her knee up along his flank. Her dress was yellow silk that he did not want to rip, but the buttons frustrated him. They were on her back while his tongue was drawing circles along her front.

Still, he managed it. He pulled her upright, then kissed her neck as he undid her buttons. And as her bodice loosened and fell away, he was stymied by the most serviceable stays he had ever seen. Rough linen bound tight. He had seen horses with looser harnesses.

"What is this?" he asked as he stared at the hard fabric.

She chuckled. "Proof that no one goes where I do not wish them to."

"How do you breathe?"

"How do you?" She tugged at his cravat until the knot all but choked him.

He pulled it off, shedding his coat and waistcoat in very quick order. She watched him, her eyes bright in the dusky moonlight. But he wanted to see all of her, so he lit the candle by her bedside and despaired that she had so little in her tiny room.

"Come back to the house," he said. "You will be more comfortable."

"This is where I work, this is where I will live after I have thrown you over. Why get me used to luxuries that I cannot have?"

He winced. He could tell by her tone that she missed what he could offer. Soft sheets, servants at every turn, and light. Candlelight on her skin, moonlight in her hair, starlight in her eyes. He wasn't making sense, even in his own mind, but she took his breath away.

Her expression softened. "I cannot stand. Can you help me undress? I don't want to crush the silk."

The dress had gathered around her waist, a pool of yellow in which goldfish swam. He crossed to her and wrapped an arm around her ribs above the gown. She held on to him and let him lift. With wriggles—and a few giggles—they managed to set the silk aside. He folded it carefully as he placed it on the stool. She had so little, he did not want to damage anything of hers.

"Millie will come tomorrow," she said. "She will bring me whatever gown your mother wants me to wear and take this one back. I think Emmaline will still be able to wear it, if she wants."

"The gowns are yours," he said. It was the least he could give her.

"And what would an apothecary do with a silk gown except get it stained?"

He had no answer. He hated the idea that soon she would be out of his life, that she would have no need for fine things. And while he stood there, thinking that he had to find a way to change that, she carefully untied her very serviceable stays and set them aside.

There was a tiny bow holding her shift together. It sat low between her two breasts. And as he stood there, she pulled at the ribbons and let the fabric part all the way to her belly.

His throat went dry looking at her. Such ripe perfection. She no longer seemed small to him but exquisitely formed and lusciously female. He walked to her, his mind and body filled with the sight of her. She reached up, the shift in the fabric teasing his sight with the full swell of her breasts, but it denied him a view of her nipple.

"Won't you take this off as well?" she asked, tugging at his shirt.

He stripped it off without thinking. Then he knelt on the hard floor before her. Slowly he tugged the shift down her arms, watching with hunger as the fabric caught for a moment on the points of her breasts, and then fell free.

"You are beautiful," he murmured.

"As are you," she answered. She touched his chest and stroked her fingers through the hair. Then with a quick twist of her fingers, she pinched his nipple.

Fire shot through his already throbbing body, and he caught her wrist with a surprised gasp. "Someone taught you that," he said.

"I brought medicines to whores." She smiled. "You think I never asked questions?"

"I think I should never be surprised by you, and yet I constantly am."

She frowned. "Does that upset you?"

He chuckled. "That delights me." He caught her chin and pulled her close for a kiss. "And now, perhaps we shall see if I can find something you don't know."

She laughed as he pressed her down, and he was surprised at how wonderful the sound was. He had heard it so little before, but like the whimsy on her gown, Yihui was rediscovering her joy. And with her laughter came his. He chuckled as he nipped at her shoulder. He smiled as he ran his teeth across her collarbone. And then he reveled in the shape and feel of her breasts. He kissed them, he kneaded them, and he returned her pinch a dozen times over while she gasped and arched.

She was not a silent lover. No need to be in the empty building. And he liked listening to her as he teased her breasts and kissed down her belly. He could smell her scent here, strong and earthy. An alluring brew he could not refuse.

Easy to slip her shift past her bottom and away. She wore no stockings. They wouldn't fit over the plaster that surrounded her feet. And so now she was naked except for her casts, and he was at last able to do one of the things he had dreamed about.

He spread her legs.

"Max."

He spread her honey with his fingers.

"Max!"

His name wasn't a command or even a call for attention. It was shock as she experienced something new.

He grinned. "There is more," he said. Then he tasted her. He stroked his tongue into her curls, he pushed it into her deepest recess, and then he began the long exploration to her nub.

Her legs were on his shoulders as he lifted her up for his feast. Her cries were no longer words. And as he stretched her with his fingers, thrusting deep inside, his tongue danced faster and faster.

Her body went tight beneath him.

Soon…

Now.

Her body bucked. She cried out, the sound pure delight. And best of all, he was able to watch her fly into bliss.

Chapter Forty-One

YIHUI HAD NEVER guessed sex was this much fun. At least not for the woman.

Max clearly enjoyed himself because he was grinning as he eased up the bed alongside her. He still wore his breeches, blunting the hot thrust of his cock against her thigh. But he did not rush her while she lay basking.

"Thank you," she said as she raised her hand to touch his lips.

He pressed kisses to her fingertips. "I enjoyed that as much you," he said.

"I do not believe you."

He chuckled. "Well, maybe not quite as much."

She lay there thinking she should adjust on the bed to give him enough room. Good lord, he hadn't even taken off his boots.

She sighed as he pressed kisses onto her shoulder. Then she did her best to imitate his mother's most officious tone.

"It is rude to reject a gift freely given."

He jolted hard enough to jerk the bed. Then she watched in delight as his face shifted into the most gloriously insulted frown she had ever seen.

"I have never met a woman more determined to be debauched!"

She rolled her eyes. "No man is this virtuous. Not even the monks. There must be a reason." Then she winced as he moved, and his boot accidentally kicked her shin.

He saw it, and all but leaped off the bed.

"I am sorry! How badly did I hurt you?"

She sat up, not bothering to cover herself. "If a man squeezing my toes cannot destroy my feet, then the scrape of your boot can do nothing. Take the things off. You are getting mud in my bed."

He immediately pulled his feet off the bed then peered at the linen. Was he looking for stains? "Max, what is the matter with you?" Then her gaze suddenly widened as she thought of an explanation. "Is it that you do not… Do you desire… women?"

He jolted at her words and started laughing. "I want you, Yihui." He caught her fingers and pressed them to his cock. Even through layers of fabric, she felt its heat. She squeezed it, measuring the length and girth while he hissed in reaction and his hips jerked.

"You want me," she said softly. "And I have said yes. Why do you deny yourself?"

He trailed his hand down her thigh. She shivered at the caress, her blood heating in the wake of his touch. But she didn't move except to rest her hand on his thigh. She didn't creep upwards to his cock. Neither did she take it away. She wanted to touch him as he was touching her.

"Yihui, I am a large man. Even without these…" he lightly tapped the plaster and wood that splinted her feet, "I fear I would hurt you. In the depths of…" He winced. "During passion, I often forget myself."

She shook her head. "Do all Englishmen think so hard about simple things? Or is it just you?"

He laughed. "Just me."

"Emmaline said you spent the last five years whoring around with Prinny."

He shrugged. "I drank more than whored."

"That may be the only reason your head did not explode. So much worry. So much concern. Who thinks of you? Not your mother. I have seen how she worries about you until something more interesting catches her attention. Not your father, who wants a copy of himself without regard to you. Emmaline, certainly, but she is as exasperated with you as I am."

He was not taking her words well. He flinched as she spoke. "Perhaps I should go home—"

"You will take off your boots," she said tartly. Then when he gave her an arch look, she lifted her chin. "I will wait on your clothes."

"Yihui," he said with a heavy sigh. "I have explained—"

"And now you will listen to me. *After*—"

"Yes, yes. All right. My boots."

It was not easy to take them off. She had not realized how ridiculous those beautiful hessians were when trying to disrobe. She had to help him without bracing her feet, and that made for a very silly time. By the time the second boot clattered to the floor, they were both gasping for breath between the laughter.

It was healing, this laughter. In all her life, she had not spent a more joyous time than whenever she was with him. He had a wry way of looking at himself, both too serious and quietly arrogant. He was a man raised to be a leader, so much so that he thought only of his responsibilities and nothing of how truly fallible even the best man could be.

She knew that all souls were weak. She'd been raised around illness and frailty. And so she now saw how much he needed her to bring him back to life. Pleasure for him without thought to anything else.

"There," she said as she flopped back on the bed. "Isn't that better?"

He chuckled as he stretched out again, this time wiggling his bare feet. His stockings had come off during their tussle with his boots.

"Much better."

"Good. Now tell me why do you think women are weak?"

He frowned. He didn't need to answer. She knew that his own mother sometimes reveled in her weakness. She enjoyed it when people waited upon her. And Emmaline herself had never been encouraged to find independence.

It was much the same in China for the upper class. Moreso since those women had bound feet and were forced to teeter or be carried everywhere they went. But in the lower classes where she had been raised, many girls had to fend for themselves or die. She had learned to be practical above all other things.

"I know you have stren—" His words ended on a cry of alarm as she rolled herself on top of him and straddled his hips. Between her thighs, he responded on instinct, thrusting upward despite the separation of clothing. "Yihui!" he rasped.

"You think me weak because I am a woman, because I am a Chinese girl in a foreign world." She leaned forward and nipped at his nose just as he had done to her. "I am stronger than you know. I will not break."

He touched her arms, caressing up and down in long strokes. In his eyes, she saw indecision and desire. He wanted her, she knew, but he was still holding back.

Why?

She thought over this evening. She thought about how he had nearly stripped her naked by the door. And how he had kissed her with such need that she thought she would melt from his desire. And then, at the very last, she remembered what had triggered his passion.

"You think I am using you," she said softly. "You think I am no better than a whore or a woman seeking money."

His eyes shot wide. "What? No! Of course, I don't think—"

"I am not using you, Max," she said. "I love you. I want to share this love with you."

His nostrils flared and his hands tightened on her arms. But he didn't do more. It was as if he feared what would happen if he took that love inside.

"You don't believe me," she said softly.

"I…I don't know," he finally confessed. "It is not a word I use."

"Neither do I. Until tonight."

"But—"

"Tonight, I love you. Tonight, Max, will you love me?"

His expression turned tortured. His breath rasped. And he managed one word. "Yes." Then he pulled her down to kiss him.

Here again was the passion from the doorway. Here was the kiss that unlocked all her hunger. It was a kiss that desired her as much as breath. And she returned it a thousandfold.

Their mouths fused, their tongues danced, and when she pulled back to unbutton his clothing, he was there before her. While she twisted sideways, he pulled off everything, wrenching them away enough that he jerked against her.

"Wait!" she gasped, though she hated saying the word. "Wait!"

He froze as she pointed at envelopes set behind the washbasin.

"Do you know what those are?" she asked.

He grabbed one and opened it, his choked laugh filling the room. "French letters," he said as he drew out a condom. "How did you get them?" Then he shook his head before she could answer. "Madame Florina, of course."

"Yes."

"I am glad you remembered."

"Let me put it on you."

Silently, he held out the envelope. She took it, her belly thrumming with excitement. She had never been able to touch a man before. Not like this. So she took her time. She held the length of him, she felt the softness of the flesh, and the hard throbbing pound of it when she squeezed. And she licked her lips, thinking of what he had done for her.

"No," he said, his voice choked. "I won't last."

She looked at him and smiled. "Maybe tomorrow then."

He groaned as he captured his mouth with hers. And as he pressed her backward onto the bed, she lost hold of the condom, his cock, and even her reason. She wanted him inside her. She wanted to know this. She wanted his love in its most carnal form.

He was quick with the condom.

He was slow with his kisses.

And when she was frantic for him, he was strong as he pressed her thighs apart.

She gripped him with her knees, and she pressed her slick center up around him. He held himself back so she could only strain.

"Please, Max."

"Say it again."

"I love you."

"I love you," he echoed.

For tonight.

He thrust.

She welcomed him in.

And then she felt the pain.

Shock made her cry out. He froze, his face tight with horror.

She remembered, belatedly, what this was. As a rule, whores did not talk about the pain of the first time. Only of faking such a thing. And so she had forgotten about it or perhaps chose not to remember. And the dismay on Max's face was enough to erase the physical discomfort.

"I am fine," she said, her breath shallow. "You are…large."

"You are a virgin?" he asked.

She did not know the English word, but she guessed. "I am new." Or she had been.

He dropped his forehead to hers. Then he pressed a kiss to her cheek and neck. "I didn't know," he said. "I didn't think it was possible. You were a prisoner."

"I was a gift to the king. No one could touch me."

"I should have known," he said. "I should have asked."

Now his worry for her made sense. Now his care to not hurt her became clearer. He thought she'd been brutalized, but she had been pure.

Meanwhile, her body adjusted. As he pressed kisses to her face, she felt less shock, more fullness. The tiny movements he made soon felt good rather than too much. And as her breath returned, so did her desire.

She lifted her knees, drawing her thighs up along his.

He groaned as he arched, drawing out by the slowest degrees.

"No," she said. "Don't go!"

She tried to grip him, to keep him with her.

"I can't stop," he said as he tilted his hips, pushing inside her again. It was the tiniest of movements, but she felt it. She wanted it.

"Yes. Again."

Whether because of her words or because he must, he drew back again. A little farther this time before his thrust. Her back arched, her legs widened, and she opened herself completely to his penetration.

"Yihui," he said. There was no meaning behind the word. No command. Just her name as he thrust into her again.

"Max," she echoed as she learned his tempo.

He thrust again. She arched into the impact.

Together and apart.

Together again.

Harder.

Faster.

Yes!

Pleasure swept her away. Then once the rush of it eased, happiness remained. Happiness that she knew was love.

Love for tonight. For now.

It was more than enough.

Chapter Forty-Two

MAX DID NOT stay the night, though he clearly wanted to. "There are things I must do tomorrow morning," he said. "This morning."

Her body was sore, her feet aching, but she was loath to let him go. She held him as long as she could, but in the end, he left her. She pressed her nose to the blanket that still held his scent, and she dreamed about what they had done.

Tonight, she'd been loved.

Maybe tomorrow night she could feel it all again.

HE STAYED EVERY night afterwards, sometimes for a short while, sometimes until just before dawn. Yihui's heart had never been so full. Her days were busy, and her nights were a delight.

For two weeks she prepared the shop to open. With luck, the customers would find them out of curiosity. And then, when her feet were better, she would go to the docks to buy what she lacked. It might take a year or longer before she had enough supplies, but she would work with Druina to find new recipes with English plants.

She always spent afternoons with the duchess, learning everything possible to become presentable at court. It was tedious, horrendous work, but she was making progress. Occasionally, the lady would give her a satisfied smile.

And then, at night, Max would reward her for her diligence. Together they found such bliss that she could not believe her luck. How had she found such perfection? Every day brought new challenges and every night had new joys.

Too bad it could not last. Every moment ticked her life closer to the day she would have to cry off her engagement to Max. And if she forgot that their time together was nearly at an end, the duchess made sure to remind her. It was the day before she was to be presented at court, and she did it in the apothecary shop, the one place Yihui thought herself powerful.

"Yihui, I must speak with you."

So many people had said that to her over the last weeks. So many people had come to her asking for brews for every ailment. But never once had she heard the duchess's voice in her place of business.

So Yihui looked up with wary eyes and a heavy heart. The only reason the lady would come to her here was because she wanted to bargain. And the only thing the lady wanted was her son's freedom.

"Welcome to My Lady's Apothecary," Yihui said with a smile. She was in the back mixing room, trying to understand Madame Druina's recipe book. The plants here were so different from the ones at home. She was not sure she could make the transition to English medicines while she waited for seeds from China. "Please sit down, Your Grace."

She would have leaped off her stool, but she still had to be careful of her feet. Though she could totter about on her heels, Mr. Torres had told her it was best if she waited another month before trying to walk again.

"Would you like some tea?"

"No, I would not," the lady said tartly. "Really Yihui, you are to meet the prince tomorrow night. Do you really think you should spend your morning working?"

Yihui smiled. "I am not working, Your Grace. I am learning

and that is always a lady's pleasure, is it not?" Those were the exact words the duchess had said to her when she demanded Yihui memorize generations of English kings.

"Don't be churlish," the lady returned. "I've come to you to discuss something we both care about." It was clear she thought it an insult that she had to travel to see Yihui.

Rather than argue, Yihui folded her hands and adopted a listening attitude. The duchess was often pleased by this posture. "I am eager to understand."

"I should hope so." The duchess looked at her hard, and then she abruptly sighed. She waved imperiously at her maid to leave them alone. Yihui jolted. She hadn't even seen the girl there, but of course, a duchess never went anywhere alone.

The maid disappeared, the duchess pulled out the near stool, and then settled herself with much shifting of skirt, shawl, and reticule. It took forever, and Yihui found that she hadn't the patience for it. Not today. Not when she already guessed what was coming.

"Your Grace," she said, "please let me set your fears to rest. I shall cry off as promised. I will not marry Max."

The duchess looked up, her regard heavy. "I know he has shared your bed. I'm sure you dream of marrying him."

"You do not know my dreams," Yihui returned tartly, even though the lady was absolutely correct.

"Every girl wants to marry a duke, and my son is the best of the lot," the lady retorted.

Yihui could not argue that point. Instead, she repeated her early statement. "I will cry off. As I have promised."

"Good." The lady straightened. "You must do it tomorrow night."

"What?" At first Yihui didn't understand the words. But when she did, her entire body rebelled. She would not give up one second of her time with Max. "No! We agreed on the night before the wedding. That was Max's plan."

The duchess snorted. "Max's idiotic plans are what created

this disaster in the first place. It was his plan to rescue you, his plan to keep you at the house. And his plan—"

"Your Grace!" Yihui snapped. "You may say what you want about your son in your home. But in mine, I will not disrespect him. It was his plan, and I will honor my bargain with him."

The lady glared at her, but she could not contradict Yihui's words. After all, she had been speaking poorly of her own family and that was something that no good woman should ever do, whether Chinese or English.

"Be that as it may," the lady finally ground out. "Max does not understand the *haut ton*. He cannot simply declare you have cried off the night before the wedding. No one will believe it. They will think you are being forced."

"I am being forced!" A month ago, she would not have had the fortitude to speak so plainly. Not without great fear. But she was an independent woman now. She was not beholden to anyone, least of all this privileged woman who had no compassion. If she lost a customer from it, then so be it. She would not hold her tongue any longer. "I was forced by my father, who sold me, by the Wongs, who gifted me like a prized goat to the prince. I was forced to kill my attacker because no one else would. And now I am forced to play a game for your benefit, not mine. If I had my way, I would be done with it now."

It was a lie. She did not want to be done with Max, merely with the games that society played. She despised the rules that said she could not have the husband she wanted, that Max would suffer from his association with her, and that she must learn all the rules of being English in order to survive here where she had been taken against her will.

Most of the time, she thought little of the ill path that had brought her here. It did no good to dwell on it. But sometimes, resentment boiled up and she could not contain her fury.

"Just like the Wongs, you want to dress me up like a prize pig," she continued, her voice modulating as she gained control of her emotions. "You want to present me to the prince. I have agreed because it is what I promised Max. Do not seek to change it unless you mean to end it."

"That is exactly what I mean to do," the duchess said.

The cold finality in the woman's voice hardened Yihui's fury. It was bad enough to be a toy to powerful men. It was worse when women did it to each other. For all that the duchess had softened toward her, it was clear she still thought Yihui an ugly problem to be solved. She might drink Yihui's teas, but she would never give her respect.

"What do you want?" Yihui asked.

"Exactly what you do. To end this charade as quickly as possible." She leaned forward. "Tomorrow night in front of everyone, you will throw over my son in front of the prince himself. He cannot force Max to marry if you do such a thing publicly." The duchess leaned back, her expression smug. "Then you will be free several days early."

"I am supposed to cry off the night before the wedding. That is several days further along." Four extra days and nights, to be exact.

"I thought you wanted it ended," the woman taunted.

"I will honor my bargain with Max," she countered. "If I am to change it, then what will you give me in return?" It was a stupid response. There was nothing the lady could offer that she wanted. But when cornered, Yihui resorted to bargaining. She would not discuss her feelings for Max, certainly not with this woman. What was left then, except commerce?

But it brought everything down to the measures of gain and loss, and the duchess was clearly disgusted by that. "I knew you wouldn't cry off," she spat. "I knew you would need more."

Yihui had just confirmed all of the duchess's worst opinions about her. With a self-satisfied grunt, the duchess withdrew a large stack of notes from her reticule. The lady threw it down on the worktable, the weight of the impact blowing tea leaves onto the floor.

"Is that enough?" she asked.

"No." The answer was automatic. Yihui had no idea how much money was on the table. She guessed it was a great deal. But the amount didn't matter. She would not end her time with Max one second earlier. She had found too much pleasure in his touch, too much peace in his arms.

"That is enough to keep your shop alive for years," the lady retorted. Then she added to the weight of her offer. "Don't you understand? This is for Max! He needs to be free of you. It must be done in front of the prince, and there must be no doubt that you are the one demanding an end. It must be a spectacle in front of everyone."

"Or what? What will happen if I remain devoted to your son?"

"Then you will be a weight around his neck. Whatever his political ambitions, you will thwart them. And he will never choose a wife while still lusting after you."

Yihui jolted at those words. She knew that Max lusted for her, but the duchess made it sound filthy and wrong.

"He cannot marry you!" the lady cried. "Have the decency to set him free to find a suitable wife."

Yihui didn't look at the stack of notes. She watched the duchess's face, saw the throb in her throat, and the panic in the lady's eyes. The woman believed that Max would never fulfill his potential with Yihui as his wife. Worse, she knew her son would not look for another woman as long as he graced Yihui's bed.

The belief was so strong that the duchess's heart raced, and her eyes bulged. She looked on the verge of her own apoplexy, and so Yihui made tea for the lady. She had to get off her stool to do so, and winced as she tottered on her heels, using her arms to support herself when the weight became too much. Fortunately, the hot water and the leaves were close at hand. Even better, the ache was not so bad. Her feet were healing.

Small comfort.

She said nothing as she worked. Yihui needed the time to let her mind steadily pound down the anguish in her heart. What did it matter, said her mind, if she set Max free early? Especially if she gained enough money to cover her debts? And the duchess was likely correct. Without a very public display, Prinny might not believe she had cried off. He might yet be a problem for Max. Without a very clear end to their relationship, Max might struggle to attach himself to a new woman, an appropriate English woman suitable to his status.

The duchess might be a bitter, arrogant shrew, but she was protecting her son. And if Yihui wanted the best for Max, then she would do well to listen to his mother.

Once the tea had steeped enough, Yihui passed the cup to the duchess.

"If I do this, you must buy my teas. You must tell your friends to buy their medicines from me. You must make sure they know this."

The duchess reached out an unsteady hand. She took her time before answering. She sipped her tea then stared into the swirling depths of the liquid. And she smiled because she knew she had won.

"I will tell them all to visit you. And you must swear to never see my son again."

Yihui slowly grabbed the stack of notes. She drew them close though the feel of the paper made her skin crawl.

"I will cry off in front of the prince. In front of everyone."

"And you will not see my son again."

She couldn't force those words through her throat. She couldn't make herself say what she knew deep down must happen for both their sakes. Could she stand by and watch him marry another? No. Could he climb in her bed after courting another? No. If they were to end, then it must end.

So she tucked the pound notes into the pocket of her work dress and felt filthy from it. Then she looked the duchess in the eye.

"I agree."

"Excellent. Now I will tell you exactly what to say."

Chapter Forty-Three

IF SHE THOUGHT the duchess would go easy on her lessons, Yihui was sorely mistaken. The lady became even more taxing that afternoon. The woman's disgust of Yihui rose and fed into a new level of torture as Yihui was quizzed on everything from the appropriate way to dab at her mouth to which battle had won a war she couldn't remember. It didn't help that Yihui had little desire to perform well.

Thankfully, Emmaline chose that afternoon to emerge from the attic. Her eyes were rimmed red, her face was sallow, but she stood tall and spoke as if she hadn't spent the last weeks grieving.

Lord Christopher was still missing.

Even though there was no body, it was clear that Emmaline believed him dead. Yihui gave what comfort she could, which was to say that she offered Emma a special mixture of teas and then said little more. There was nothing more that could be done.

For her part, Emmaline promised to be with her during the presentation and did her best to distract her mother when the inquisition became too strident. Fortunately, Yihui's training was almost done. Tomorrow night, everyone including Lady Kimberly, would be beside her at court. Except the duke, of course, who refused to be seen in public until he was well.

He would never be well, but he was improving. According to Max, the duke could use the left side of his body with growing skill. And even the right side showed some small improvement. But the best news was that the duke had kept his rages down to once every other day and even those were less violent than before.

On this last night together, Max escorted her home as had become his custom. Some nights he went on to an evening's amusements, but not tonight. There was a quiet around him tonight, an increasing tension that she didn't understand.

He carried her into her bedroom and commented with approval on the new linens on the bed. Olivia and Millie knew their work, especially since her liaison with Max was an open secret.

"I must change my bandages before tomorrow," she said when he set her down on the bed. "Will you help?"

"Of course." He had already stripped off his jacket and cravat. And tonight, thank God, he had chosen to wear shoes, not boots.

"What do I do?" he asked.

"Bring the basin with soap and water and set in on the floor. I need to wash."

He did as she bid and then looked at the pair of scissors, she handed him as if they were instruments of torture.

"You want me to cut them?"

She chuckled. "It's easier for you to reach than me."

"But what if—"

"You're cutting away old, dirty bandages. I am much better now. I won't break if you are gentle."

He nodded. "I'll be careful."

She took a few moments to strip out of her dress. Another fine gown, this one blue silk with tiny yellow butterflies on it. She would miss this finery when they were done.

While he folded the dress and set it aside, she unbound her stays and lifted up her shift, though she didn't remove it. This was not a seduction. She needed new bandages before meeting the prince tomorrow.

"Ready?" he asked needlessly. He was seated on the floor with scissors in one hand. She said nothing, merely smiled as gratitude filled her.

Here was a future duke, a great mandarin of his people, about to tend to her abused feet. How had she found such fortune?

He cut away the bandages, carefully pulling them off her skin. She'd splinted her feet on three sides with flat pieces of wood which were now soft from her sweat and the world. He pulled those away gently, and she gasped at the sensation.

After so long wrapped, it was a wonder to feel something new. The heat of his hand, the brush of the air, and most especially the caress of his fingers. The sensations were exquisite, both too much and not enough.

"Is it painful?" he asked, worry in his tone.

"No," she whispered as she bit her lip. "It's wonderful."

He understood then. They had explored each other's bodies enough to know what was loved, what was too much, and what was sweet torture.

He cut away the bandages on her other foot and pulled away the wood. Then he gently set her feet into the basin of water. She had thought he would just watch them soak. That was all she meant to do. The gentle lap of the water was delightful enough. But sitting there on the floor, he washed her feet.

Gentle brushes with a cloth set her heart pounding. Then he scooped up water and sluiced it down her ankle all the way to her toes while she grew breathless with desire. But it was the way he watched her as he worked that made her intimate places throb. He looked up at her from the floor, and his eyes shone with delight every time she gasped.

He was teasing her on purpose, his fingers sensuous as they stroked along the arch of her foot. He even pinched her toes just to hear her cry out in hunger.

She had heard from some of the old women talk about this in China. This thing, this very erotic touch on their toes, was something she'd never understood until now.

"Max," she finally said. "Please."

He grinned as he gently dried her feet. "Should we bandage them first?"

She couldn't wait. She pulled him down on top of her. She

freed him of his clothing as he lifted up her shift. He didn't take her like she wanted: in heat and need. He was too careful of her to do that without her feet being splinted. But he thrust deep while he held her knees up high. She was as open as she could ever be, and the feeling was perfection.

She climaxed quickly, but he drew it out. She writhed beneath him, and he remained strong. She was the wild thing, gloriously alive, while he was the man who kept her safe to be everything she could possibly want.

And tonight, she was his.

IN THE MORNING, Yihui realized two very difficult things.

The first was that they had not used a condom. The second was that it was not enough. Yihui was deeply in love with Max, and she wanted to be his forever.

It wasn't possible. He was still a mandarin destined for someone more than a foreign shop girl. She knew it, and it tore her apart from the inside.

When he left that morning, later than ever before, she kissed him as she had every morning—with distraction and adoration mixed together. She begged him to stay in bed even knowing that he would not.

And then she let him go.

Chapter Forty-Four

"**Y**OU CAN'T BE serious."

Max winced at his mother's strident voice as she burst into the library. She was resplendent in her velvet gown, every inch of her declaring her status as a duchess. She wore forest green and gold with rubies dripping from her ears and across her chest. And yet the magnificent effect was spoiled by her disgusted expression.

"Put those away," she commanded. "Save them for the woman you will actually marry." She gestured with disdain at the ancient emerald jewelry set he'd spread out on his desk.

He bristled at the words. "Yihui is my fiancée. These are the gemstones appropriately worn by my bride."

"Exactly! Your bride!" She picked up one of the earbobs and carefully cleaned the stone. "I thought these were safely locked away at the Cornish estate."

"They were. I got them the moment I realized she would be presented at court." Indeed, he'd left the morning after he'd first graced her bed. It had been a long trip, but well worth the effort. He couldn't wait to see Yihui wearing them.

"But if she wears them, then everyone will think she's been accepted as your bride. I thought she was to throw you over."

He folded them up in their case. He had to carefully modulate his tone. He wasn't sure how he felt about the plan anymore. "She can't throw me over if I don't appear to embrace the wedding as Prinny commanded." He looked up at her. "You're the one who decided she should wear green and gold."

"Because they're our family colors and we dressed her," the lady huffed. "That doesn't mean she should wear jewelry." She huffed out a breath. "Think, Max. People need to see a reason for her to throw you over. If we give her the minimum of support—just enough to not be embarrassed by her—then it will make sense when she declares you don't suit. After all, who wants to marry into a family that despises you? But if we give her all the trappings of a future duchess…" She pointed at the gemstones. "Then whyever would she refuse you? No sane woman throws away such an opportunity."

He folded his arms across his chest. "That is convoluted logic, even for you."

"It is the truth of the *ton*, and you men never understand it."

"Because it's nonsense!" This time he made no effort to moderate his angry tone. "Yihui *deserves* a great deal more than these stones. From the beginning, she has acted for our benefit, not hers. She agreed to this ridiculous charade. She could have gone back to China if she'd wanted. Instead, she has worked tirelessly to act as you decree, to learn what you dictate, and to bring honor to this family. And what does she get out of it? Your scorn. And that, mother, is beneath you."

"Have you taken leave of your senses? She killed a man upstairs! I wish she had gone back to China, but she doesn't want to. Instead, you are paying for her shop and bedecking her in emeralds. If you ask me, she has gotten far more out of this charade than any of us."

Max felt his blood settle into a frost that chilled him from head to toe. It was a shock—but not a surprise—to realize that after all this time, his mother did not see Yihui's character. She didn't recognize Yihui's resilience, patience, or her medical skill. Neither did she see Yihui's kindness to the servants and his mother. Damn it, Yihui had even learned English history, not to mention a new language.

All his mother saw was a foreigner, and that, apparently

trumped everything else.

"You are blind, mother," he finally said. "I suggest you keep your opinions to yourself until such time as you can see people for who they truly are."

His mother sputtered in outrage, but Max ignored her. He was already heading to Yihui's bedroom where Millie and Emmaline were helping with her toilette.

He paused outside her door to smooth his clothing before knocking. He wanted to calm his emotions before seeing Yihiu. Placing these jewels upon her body was important, and he had no wish to taint the moment because he was cross with his mother.

He was just about to knock when he heard a burst of feminine laughter. Not raucous, of course, but filled with excited delight. Such a delicious sound, and not just from Millie. He heard Emma's chuckle as well. Thanks to the new butler he'd hired, her daily responsibilities had dwindled. He'd thought she'd come out into the world more, but instead, she'd locked herself in the attic painting.

It was grief, he knew. Every day that passed with no word from Christopher led him to believe that his best friend was dead. He'd gone to a dangerous area of London to confront a dangerous man. It was foolishly noble of him and had likely gotten him killed.

Pain tore through Max whenever he thought of it, but it was nothing compared to how wrecked Emmaline had seemed. And yet, listening at the door, he was sure he'd heard her laugh and that gave him such joy that he felt suffused by it. His sister had giggled like a schoolgirl again and his wife was the cause of it. Or the center of it. Or simply there in the midst of such joy.

He didn't want to interrupt it. And yet, he equally wanted to be part of it. So he rapped twice on the door and waited in gleeful anticipation for his first sight of Yihui in her gown.

The laughter quickly muted and a moment later, Millie opened the door. She curtsied to him as did Olivia from her place near the dressing table.

"Max! Don't you look handsome," Emmaline said.

He didn't answer. His gaze was on Yihui alone.

She was dressed in his family colors, rich green silk with gold accents. Her hair was pulled up in an elegant sweep of ebony strands accented by gold filigree. But it was her face that caught him. He realized now how often her face had been obscured from him. He recalled the beads that had blocked his view of her the first time they met. Other times, her face had been dirty from work or with her hair always across her cheek or dipping low across her brow.

Not this time. Her hair was pulled up, and he saw for the first time how very elegant she was. Clear skin, raised cheekbones, and dark, exotic eyes that had been accented with kohl.

"I do believe my brother has been struck dumb."

"I…I have," he confessed. Yihui was a rare beauty who now flushed dusky red at his words. "You are exquisite."

"It is the clothes," she said humbly. "The dress—"

"What dress? It's you, Yihui. You look…" Ravishing? Beautiful? Words failed him.

His sister laughed. "Wonderful? Stunning?"

"Yes," he said as he stepped forward. Then he found the word.

"Regal." He caught her hand and bowed over it.

"Well, she should," Emma said. "She's supposed to be a Chinese princess."

"I am the luckiest of men. It will be my honor to stand beside you tonight."

Yihui didn't answer. She seemed tongue-tied until she finally whispered, "Thank you, my lord."

"But there's something missing," he said, and her head shot up.

"Oh no," she murmured, her eyes wide with horror.

Her hands went to her face as if to hide, but he caught one and gently flipped it over. Then with a grin, he poured the emeralds into her palm.

She gaped at them. And then she gaped at him.

Emmaline straightened up from her place on the bed to see what he had done.

"Ah yes, the emeralds. Very good."

"But—" Yihui gasped. "But—"

"But nothing," he said as he gently disentangled the necklace from the pile. "My fiancée must wear these."

He laid them across her neck and carefully set the clasp. The earbobs came next. He struggled with those. He was not used to putting those on a lady.

"There is not much call for an apothecary to wear finery." Her words were near whispers, but he heard them nonetheless. So once her earrings were set, he stepped back.

"Tonight, you are my fiancée, soon to be Lady Artanges and then afterwards, my duchess."

He could hear the echo of his words, unspoken but so loud between them. This was for *tonight*. Just as he had loved her on other nights, this was for now, and for the rest of the week before she cried off on Friday.

A lump formed in his throat, and he struggled to speak around it.

"One more jewel," he said as he picked up the ring. It was a heavy thing. A huge square emerald set in gold and encrusted with diamonds. It didn't fit her hand. It was meant to be worn above a glove. And yet he put it on her finger and then drew it up to his lips. He kissed her ring as if she were a queen. And with his fingers, he stroked her palm in a slow caress.

"It doesn't fit," she said.

"It will," he answered.

He wanted to kiss her. The urge burned in his body. His blood pounded, and his cock thrust forward. He already knew how she tasted, knew how she would feel. In this moment, she was his duchess in heart, in body, and in soul.

But not in fact.

He stepped back.

She looked down as the ring flopped on her hand. "I will lose it," she cried.

"It goes over your glove."

Millie stepped forward, quick to hand Yihui her long gloves. Together they quickly set her to rights. He watched, his heart in his throat. He didn't even move until his sister shoved him aside.

"Get out of the way, you lummox. And yes, brother, I do look stunning. Thank you for saying so. But I need to get my wrap, so get out of my way."

He did because she gave him no choice. And then he waved Olivia back when she stepped up to carry Yihui. Though it had been over a month since her initial injury, Yihui's feet could not easily bear weight without risking further injury. Not to dance and certainly not to stand for hours on end, awaiting the prince's pleasure. Mr. Torres recommended at least two more weeks before she stressed them. Privately, Max determined to carry her for another month.

Or he would have, if she weren't set to throw him over at the end of the week.

"I'll carry her now," he said to Olivia while emotions churned within him. "But I won't be able to in the palace, so that will fall to you."

"I am pleased to do so, my lord," she answered formally, using more words than he had ever heard her utter before.

"And you look wonderful in that uniform. You will put the palace guard to shame."

Olivia was a contradiction in body and form. She was very obviously an Irish woman and a lovely one at that. But instead of a gown, she wore the livery of a man in his household. She was the one who was there to carry Yihui wherever she was meant to go inside the palace. And as such, Olivia had the position of status among the four other footmen who would carry Yihui's litter into Buckingham.

"You won't mind using the palanquin again, will you?" he pressed Yihui as he carried her downstairs. "I had it remade. It's quite sturdy now—"

"I saw. It's lovely."

"You'll ride in the carriage with me. The palanquin is for when you enter."

"I know."

"You're every bit a Chinese princess, Yihui." He looked down at her face. "I hope you enjoy tonight. You are to be celebrated at every turn."

She looked into his eyes. She was still in his arms held close enough that he could see the dark striations in her pupils and the sweet red of her lips.

"Max…" she whispered. He waited, but she said no more. Just his name and a longing he felt echo in his own soul.

He wanted to give her a compliment then. He wanted to tell her what she meant to him, what this night presenting her to the *haut ton* meant in his world. She was at the pinnacle tonight, and he was stunned by how gloriously she shined. Stunned and proud.

But the words didn't come. And then his mother interrupted them with an exasperated groan.

"Whatever are you thinking, Max? Put her down. Your clothes will be a disaster. Why isn't that Irish woman carrying her? Isn't that—"

"Her name is Olivia, Mother, and she is coming."

With that, he nodded to their new butler who swept open the door with the pompous grace of a duke's butler. That he was also young and grinning in no way detracted from Max's delight.

"Thank you, Butler," he said, still amused by the irony of the man's surname. His butler was named Butler.

"Have a good evening, my lord, Miss Wong."

"Our evening shall be splendid. Absolutely, amazingly, wonderfully superb."

"My goodness," Emmaline chuckled behind him. "Setting your sights a little high, aren't you brother?"

"Never."

Chapter Forty-Five

S O MANY FEELINGS coursed through Yihui that she was dizzy from the experience.

They arrived at Buckingham Palace, a building so large, she thought surely it was as great as what stood in the Forbidden City. Throughout the carriage ride, the duchess continued to remind her of one thing or another. She heard none of it. All she felt was Max's thigh pressed against hers and his ring heavy on her finger.

If only her family could see her now. She who had slept on her brother's floor, who had been servant to her father and barter for the Wong cohong. She would be carried before the English prince and greeted by great men and women.

Tonight was her triumph. It was also her heartbreak.

Tonight, she would end things with Max. If she could keep him, she would. If she could serve in his household, she would. If she could slip into his bed at night, she would.

But all these things were denied her, not because she couldn't find a way to achieve it. After all, she had already pulled him into her bed. But because he was a great mandarin in England. And like all men of power, their choice in bride was never their own. It was why the Chinese had concubines. The first bride was chosen for political reasons. Sometimes even the next brides. Eventually, a great man would marry the woman of his choice, pulling her into his household as a concubine. She could have a little or a lot of power, depending on the situation. But she would also have him.

Yihui would have readily accepted such a situation. She loved Max that much. But because the English did not have concubines, that was not an option. The only thing she could do, the only action allowed that would show her love, would be to set him free.

And the best time to do it would be tonight.

The carriage stopped and a footman opened the door. She and Max waited while Emmaline and the duchess climbed out. And then he slid his arms beneath her and squeezed her tight.

"You're going to be magnificent."

She didn't have the strength to answer. Too many emotions choked off her words. Indeed, she feared she would soon lose her command of English if she didn't get a hold of herself. She simply nodded while Max scooped her up and gently carried her to the waiting palanquin.

The remade carrier was everything she could wish for. And his footmen were strong and steady as they lifted her and headed inside. He walked beside the litter, resplendent in black, white, and gold. A single huge emerald glittered in his cravat, a reminder of when she had told him to wear more colors. She did not know the English names for his clothes. Only that they emphasized the breadth of his shoulders and the length of his leg. Unlike the many layers of garments that the Chinese men wore, his was tight across the belly to show his trim figure. And if she wasn't required to sit absolutely straight, she would gaze at him as she would a sunset or a mountain.

Instead, she watched his every step from the corner of her eye. And she resolved to be exactly what he wanted. Magnificent.

She entered the palace on a litter meant for a princess. The doors of the palace were thrown wide as she was carried inside. They did not wait with the others who stood in line to enter the main reception. They were pushed to the side as she was carried in.

She heard gasps and whispers, and knew the sound of jealousy. She felt her lips curl in delight. Let them look, let them seethe in their envy, for she had Max in a way most of them never would. She had had him in her bed, in her arms, and in her body. And they could only look on and wish for such a thing.

She was carried into the throne room and down a long red carpet, then introduced by a majordomo with a booming voice. Finally, Max pulled the door to the palanquin wide.

The Queen of England sat in her throne, her lips pursed in interest. Her son Prinny sat beside her, his attention well and truly caught. The mad king was miles away being treated by his doctors.

The next step was hers, and so she performed it to the best of her ability. Fortunately, she had practiced it with Olivia, who scooped her up and carried her easily forward.

"Your Royal Highnesses," Yihui said, her voice gratifyingly strong. "I am injured and so I cannot greet you in the English way. Therefore, I shall have to show my respect in the Chinese way."

At that, Olivia gently lowered her to the ground. The woman was extraordinarily strong to manage it, even with Yihui helping as best she could. Olivia set her down on her hands and knees, and then Yihui dropped flat into a kowtow, banging her forehead on the carpet loud enough that the dull thud could be heard.

Once, twice, thrice.

She would not do the Grand Kowtow because these royals did not rule China. But three kowtows were enough for the prince regent and the queen.

She heard the shocked gasps of the people around them, but mostly she was surprised that Max made such a sound as well. Did he think that she would embarrass him? Or had she miscalculated?

When she straightened up from the floor, she scanned the room to see if she had erred. Most of the courtiers were whispering their surprise. The prince, however, was obviously pleased. And even the queen's lips curved in secret delight.

"Yes, yes," the prince said. "Extraordinary. Wonderful. Get her up, Max, and bring her over there. I've set a place for us to chat."

Olivia knew her business and bent down. They had done this dozens of times throughout the last few weeks, so the movement was easy despite the layers of clothing. Olivia wasn't Max by any means, but she did very well and Yihui was grateful.

Soon Yihui was seated in a chair. Max stood beside her, and a larger, more imposing chair was brought for Prinny. Then, to everyone's shock, a second even larger chair was set for the queen.

Yihui waited to be addressed before she spoke. She waited politely, then answered the questions put to her, adding a bit of flattery because all kings and queens liked that.

Yes, she found London to be a wonderful city.

The palace was extraordinary, and she'd never seen its like before.

The duke and duchess had been most kind. She hoped that the duke recovered from his illness soon.

The duke had indeed been drinking special teas that she had mixed herself. She credited them with the improved function of his right side.

Chinese medicine had been studied for five thousand years, carefully analyzed and tested. She was but one of many practitioners in China. That skill was why she had been chosen by the Wong cohong as a gift to the English. It was believed that England might benefit from her medical knowledge. This was a lie. No man in China had respected her skills.

And then the last, most important comment. If the English doctors could not benefit a patient, what did that man lose by consulting with the Chinese?

She could see those words settle into the queen. She knew that no English doctor had aided her husband, the king. It was several minutes of more talk, more questions before that lady pierced her with a long stare.

"I should like you to walk with me. Now."

The queen stood up and the others, including her son, fell back. Olivia rushed forward to lift her, but given how far the queen had already moved, it would be difficult for one person to carry her that far. Fortunately, Max was there with equal speed. Together they lifted her up, making a base on which she sat while they followed behind her royal highness.

It was a long walk.

Through back rooms and hallways, past gilt mirrors and long tapestries, and then, at last, to a door protected by two guards. At the queen's direction, the men pulled it open and led the way into the king's bedroom.

Chapter Forty-Six

MAX HAD BEEN in the king's presence several times when he was younger, but never in the man's private chambers. Since the onset of the king's madness, few were allowed here except his doctors and the guards who kept the royal safe.

So when the queen said, "You will utter no word of this to anyone," all three of them were quick to nod their understanding. "The king is at Windsor Castle," she said firmly. "We discussed Chinese medicine as it pertains to… to…" Her words failed her.

"Grief, Your Highness," said Yihui. "I have a few teas that support a woman as she grieves a child's death…or a husband's madness. Such things are very hard on a woman's heart and body."

The queen was silent a moment before she nodded. "You may send those to me on the morrow."

"Of course, Your Highness."

Contrary to what they'd just agreed to say, the king was not in Windsor Castle but sitting at his writing desk muttering as he scribbled furiously in a book. A quick peek showed that it was, in fact, a printed book and not blank pages. The King of England was furiously scribbling across what Max thought was a book of sermons.

The very sight punched Max in the gut. He remembered George III as being a man of towering presence. Unlike his father who kept his wits but was losing his body, the king's mind was fractured while his body seemed hale, though he'd lost his sight.

It was a sobering realization.

Meanwhile, a man he recognized as Dr. Francis Willis looked up from where he'd been reading on a nearby couch.

"George," he said calmly. "The queen has come for a visit. George, will you say hello to her?"

The king did not look up. If anything, he hunched closer to the paper, though it was clear he could not see anything. He simply scribbled while muttering to himself. The quill he held was nearly broken in half, and the nub was dull and without ink.

His king was completely blind, and yet intent on whatever he was writing.

Meanwhile, Max whispered to Olivia who nodded and passed Yihui into his arms. A moment later, Olivia placed a chair next to the king so that Max could set Yihui down. It was damned awkward, but he managed it. And he even gave her an encouraging squeeze in the process.

If she felt it, she didn't react. Her attention was centered on the king. It was an odd thing for Max to experience. Normally, Yihui seemed very aware of her surroundings. But this was Yihui as a medicine maker. Every part of her was focused on the patient.

She didn't say anything as she watched the king. Dr. Willis, however, was extraordinarily upset. "Who is this woman? Why is she here gawking? This is most upsetting to the king!"

The only one getting upset was Dr. Willis. The king didn't seem to notice anything but his scribblings.

"I must protest—" he continued.

"Be quiet!" the queen snapped.

Dr. Willis straightened with a furious sniff. Then, rather than speak, he headed toward Yihui. Max quickly stepped forward, blocking the man's path. A moment later, Olivia joined him and together they created a hard wall that kept everyone else away from Yihiu and the king.

And once she was protected from interference, Yihui began to talk.

"Hello," she said to the king. "May I touch your wrist?"

There was no reaction except that the king turned a page and began writing on the fresh one. Yihui moved excruciatingly slowly as she gently placed her hand on the king's left wrist, appearing to take his pulse. He didn't react beyond a subtle twitch.

"His heartrate is accelerated," Dr. Willis growled. "Any fool could see that."

No one responded, not even Yihui who continued to hold her hand lightly upon the king's wrist. She watched him closely, never interfering with his work, but twisting around to see his face or perhaps his eyes from a better angle. And in her movements, she made a noise that penetrated the king's madness.

"Why you?" the king demanded. "Why you?"

"I told you this would upset him!" Dr. Willis all but shouted.

The queen rounded on him with a furious glare. "You will be silent!"

"I must protest!"

"Then you will leave." She glanced at the guards who stepped forward ready to grab the man. Dr. Willis folded his arms together and glared. Fortunately, his mouth stayed closed or Max would have done the guards' work for them.

Meanwhile, Yihui smiled at the patient.

"Hello, George. May I see your writing?"

"Economy of effort. Economy of effort. No one sees. No one hears!"

The king spoke very fast, but Yihui seemed unfazed. She listened as he continued to spew nonsense words. She nodded as if it made sense. If it made a difference, Max could not see it. And in time, even the queen lost patience.

"Miss Wong—" the queen began.

Yihui's hand shot up to quiet the queen. The blind king could not see it, of course, but still Yihiu gestured behind her back in deference to the patient. And if Yihui heard the gasps of shock from the others in the room, she made no comment.

"She is a charlatan, Your Majesty," Dr. Willis snorted. "Take her away. She is only making matters worse."

Thankfully, the queen was not yet swayed. She shot the doctor an irritated glance.

Meanwhile, Yihui waited until the king paused in his muttering. Then she spoke softly and slowly to him.

"Thank you. You were very helpful," she said.

The king straightened, his madness seeming to clear for a moment. "You're welcome, young lady. Do send for tea."

The reaction from everyone in the room was stunned surprise. This was a clear moment of lucidity. Everyone, that is, except for Yihui who answered pleasantly.

"I will. Thank you." Then she turned to Max who quickly picked up her and carried her to another part of the room, sitting her down in the very spot that Dr. Willis had been in when they'd arrived.

The queen was quick to come to her side, but Yihui wasn't ready to report yet. She looked at the nearest footman. "You will send for his tea?" she asked.

The footman looked to the queen who nodded. But of course, Dr. Willis had to interfere again.

"This is not the time for his tea. His stomach is delicate."

Yihui narrowed her eyes. "Delicate how? Have you made a study of his food and his body's reaction?"

"Of course, I have!" the man huffed.

She held out her hand. "Please let me see it."

"I will not! You are an ignorant savage who has—"

The queen cut in. "You grow tiresome, Dr. Willis."

He turned to her. "Your Majesty, do not be fooled—"

"I have heard your diagnosis. I should like to hear hers." She gestured to the guards who again moved forward.

"You insult me. And you insult all the good, hardworking men who toil on your behalf!" He jerked on his lapels as he spun on his heels and stomped out of the room.

Just as well. Max could see he was about to be thrown out

anyway. But that left Yihui to search for answers without Dr. Willis' information. Fortunately, that didn't seem to bother her.

"I assume he has been given medicine. May I see it?"

The queen made a gesture and a footman brought over a vial pulled from the doctor's large bag. "This and this," he said as he set down the bottles. The man didn't exactly sneer, but his tone wasn't cordial.

Yihui sniffed the first bottle and quickly set it down. "Laudanum," she said as she looked at the frenetic king. "Does it have much effect?"

"Not without a very large dose," the footman answered.

Yihui nodded and set the bottle aside. She opened the second bottle and tipped a tiny drop onto her finger which she set upon her tongue.

Then she spit it out straight into a handkerchief.

"This is poison!" she cried, obviously shocked. "For rats!"

The queen nodded. "Dr. Willis said that in the right proportions, it has greatly benefited other patients."

Yihui nodded. "Yes, there are times when I use such a thing." Her gaze went to the king. "But it will not help him."

The queen lifted her chin. "What would you do?"

Yihui took one last look at the king then focused completely on the queen. "My father had two such patients in Canton. One was a man, the other a woman." She frowned. "But neither was blind. That is something unique to the king."

"What did your father prescribe?"

"We balanced the channels of energy. We calmed when the patient grew excited. Energized when the patient was overwhelmed with sadness. I can make medicines for this."

"And did it cure them?"

Yihui shook her head. "No. The moods remained, but not as severe." Then she frowned. "This blindness, however, seems a bad addition. I can prepare soaks for him." She made a gesture of setting a wet cloth on the eyes. "It may help."

The queen's lips compressed. "But they most likely will not," she guessed. "Tell me, Miss Wong, what use are you to me?"

Yihui lifted her chin, meeting the queen's gaze with a steady one of her own. "I would like to give him a special medicine. It is the same brew that saved my life."

The queen shook her head. "He does not have broken feet. It is his mind that rebels—"

"This medicine is very strong. I have seen it cure many different ailments." She sniffed as she pointed at the bottle of poison. "And if you wish to settle his stomach, stop feeding him poison."

The queen stared at Yihui, clearly undecided. To the side, the king was growing agitated again. He had completely broken his quill and now threw it away with disgust. His mutterings were louder and his gestures more expansive.

"Do you have someone who sits with him? Who listens when he speaks?"

"He speaks nonsense!" the queen huffed.

"A girl, perhaps, who knows how to be patient? Or a religious man whose energy is calming?"

"No," the queen returned. "I think you are making things up."

"Please, Your Majesty. At least let him try the strong tea. The one that cured my infection."

The queen looked back at her. "You believe it is an infection?"

"I believe that when one is poisoned a little every day, the body becomes weak and cannot defend against many things."

It took a while. The queen was clearly distraught, especially as her husband started shouting, standing up hard enough to bang the desk with his shins. He howled in distress and no one, not even the footmen went to his aid. It was Olivia who made a mew of disgust and crossed to the king. She spoke in a sing-song tone, and he began to quiet to listen. As did everyone else.

It was a lullaby, Max realized, in Gaelic.

The king rocked back and forth to the sound.

It didn't last long. Eventually the king grew bored and wandered to another corner of the room in search of something. He had returned to muttering to himself, but apparently, the interlude had been enough to convince the queen.

"You will bring the strong medicine here tonight." She looked at Olivia. "She will stay to serve it to him."

Olivia turned back, her brows high in surprise. She didn't speak, but she did bow deeply to the queen. As did Yihui, though it was awkward given her seated position.

"Right away, Your Majesty. Shall Olivia stay here now? Or—"

"She will stay. I wish to speak with her." The queen dismissed them with a turn of her back. She didn't even look to see the way Max and Yihui acknowledged her commands. And a moment later, Max was lifting up Yihui and praying he could carry her through the entire palace. She was light, but it was a very long walk.

Or perhaps it wasn't. As he picked her up, she tightened her arms around him. She gripped him with the kind of strength he felt only when she was in the throes of passion. It startled him. By everything he'd seen, she had impressed the queen. She and Olivia both, which was not easy to do. Better yet, the queen had asked for her medicines, not just for the king but herself as well.

That was an unmitigated success.

"What is the matter?" he asked. "Do you fear you can't help him?"

"No," she said as she pressed her face to his cheek. "I can help the king, if they will let me."

"Then what?"

She didn't answer. She just clung to him so hard that her arms began to tremble.

"Yihui," he said, growing alarmed. "What is it?"

She didn't answer as he wended his way through the palace. They were led by a footman and followed by another. Neither offered to help, and indeed, he wouldn't have released her even if they had. She was his, and whatever the matter was, he would hold her. He would take care of it.

"We'll talk tonight," he said. "After you get the medicine to the king."

She shook her head. It might have been a slight tremble of her jaw against his shoulder, but he didn't think so. And damn it, they were heading back into the party. There would be no conversation now.

As expected, the door was thrown open. The noise of several dozen courtiers swelled and then receded. They all wanted to know what had happened with the queen. Max could already see Prinny heading their way.

"Yihui," he began, but she interrupted him.

"I love you," she said. And then she straightened in his arms.

He thought to carry her the rest of the way. Apparently, a footman had called for the palanquin which was wending its way through the room now. Damn it, what idiot wanted such a display right in the middle of everyone? But the more he tried to support Yihui, the more she wriggled away from him.

And then to his shock, she stood upright before him. She tottered on her heels, and she winced in pain as she grabbed the nearby wall. He saw her scan the room, her gaze landing on his mother and sister where they stood with Lady Kimberly.

"Yihui—" he began, but she shook her head.

When she spoke, it was with growing strength. She started in a near whisper, but by the time she was done, everyone in the room heard her words.

"Max, it is time for this charade to end. I am honored by the patriotism of your actions. The prince showed kindness to me, and you honored his regard."

Honored his regard? What the hell was she saying? It was like she was reciting a speech. "Stop this," he commanded. "Whatever—"

"Thank you for your indulgence." She braced herself against the wall as she pulled off the necklace and held it out to him.

"No." His voice was loud and ringing.

"I am a woman of medicine," she said, at last sounding more

like herself. "The queen herself has seen my worth. But…" Her expression was breaking, even as her chin lifted. "But I cannot wed."

Oh good God. This was his mother's doing. This was the public refusal of their marriage. It included flattery of the prince, a repetition of the royal command, and then a plausible excuse for her to throw him over.

"You can wed," he said, fury starting to color his tone. "You can be both."

She shook her head, still holding out the necklace. Well, she could stand there all night like that. He would not take it.

But apparently, his mother would. She darted forward, exclaiming loudly, "Oh you poor dear. Of course, of course, we understand your customs. Medicine women in China do not marry. Not allowed. Not in their customs."

"That's not true," he snapped.

It didn't matter. His mother was already grabbing the family emeralds, pulling the earbobs right off Yihui's ears.

"This is ridiculous," he growled as he started forward, but Emma was there blocking him. She grabbed onto his arm and pulled him back.

"Don't fight this," she hissed. "It's better this way."

"Emma, stop it!" She was like a clinging vine and while he was trying to set her aside, his mother enlisted the help of the other footmen. Faster than he thought possible, Yihui was set in the palanquin.

Finally, he got past Emma, only to be stopped by his mother. And then, to his shock, even Lady Kimberly blocked his way. Three women all telling him to quiet down, to let it happen. This was only logical.

"Stop this!" he commanded, but they wouldn't listen. Worse, Prinny had also stepped into the breech. Max might be able to bypass the women, but he couldn't avoid the prince.

So he let it happen. He couldn't punch out his own mother, much though he wanted to. And though he had gotten past

Emmaline, Kimberly stood before him with her arms crossed and a look of challenge. She didn't need to speak. They'd known each other so long, he could read the question on her face.

What was his plan?

He'd never intended to marry Yihui, so what was the point in making a scene now?

Why follow her in a grand display of lovelorn fury if he could not finish the act?

And then Prinny made it to his side and clapped a heavy hand on his shoulder.

"Didn't know she was a medicine woman. Seems they don't marry. Strange idea to us—a woman who cannot marry—but they're like nuns, I suppose. Married to medicine." He chuckled loudly at that thought.

"Your Majesty, that's not true—"

"It seems pretty clear it is," the prince boomed. "Well, that's done then. You can't marry her. Best you look to someone closer to home." He grinned at Lady Kimberly. "My lady, I believe Max has partnered with you for this next dance." Then he clapped his hands before bellowing at the musicians. "A waltz!"

There wasn't a dance floor set up. There was only the space where the palanquin had been. The musicians weren't ready either, but at the prince's command, they scrambled to obey. The first strains of a waltz began, and the prince backed away as he gestured at them.

"Go on. Dance!" He looked around the room. "Everyone! Waltz!"

And so he did. He took Kimberly's hand and pulled her into a dance. He watched as his mother secreted the emeralds away in her overly large purse. Damn it, why hadn't he realized she'd planned this? There was no other reason for her to bring such a large thing to the palace.

"Don't scowl, Max. This was *your* plan."

And that was the hell of it. That was why he hadn't shoved them all aside and run after Yihui. That was why he hadn't defied his family or his prince.

He could never marry Yihui. A future duke could not have a foreign duchess. Especially not a Chinese shopgirl so different from anyone he had ever known. One did not marry foreign, not because she came from far away but because she was so fundamentally different from everything he had ever known.

Unless, of course, different was exactly what he wanted.

His steps slowed, losing tempo with the musicians. Ever tuned to him, Kimberly slowed as well.

"You once told me that purebred dogs are weaker than mutts. They have known ailments that a mixed breed just doesn't."

"Yes," she said, trying to push him back in tempo. "But mutts are just dogs. They're not special in any way."

He stopped dancing all together. "Special just means weaker. Why would anyone want a weaker dog?" He looked around the room. Others were slowing as well, some even coming to a complete stop to stare at them. "Kimberly, why do we go to other countries? Why do we want spices from the Orient or silks from China?" He didn't wait for her answer. "Because they do some things better than we do. So we trade with countries around the world."

"Yes. Our ships are unmatched. We explore, we—"

"Bring the strengths of other countries into our own. Why not their people, too? If they know things that we don't, if they cover our weaknesses and make us stronger?"

She dropped her hands from him, shaking her head in dismay. "We learn from other countries."

"No, we don't. We take their product, but we don't learn. We buy their silk but can't make it for ourselves. Not as well."

"We will."

"Yes, we will. Because learning from other people makes us stronger. Because breeding with other humans covers our weaknesses."

"Max, we are not dogs!"

"We're not perfect either!" He looked around, seeing people he had known all his life. Every one had weaknesses, every one could benefit from a larger understanding of the world around them.

Kimberly's gaze became frantic. "Max, this is who we are. It's what it means to be English."

"Weaker. Stupider." He thought of the king, the product of generations who married their own cousins. "Blind."

She threw up her hands. "We should all be mutts then?"

"I don't know about you, Kimberly," he returned, "but I want my children to be strong. I want them to have the best of two worlds."

"You can't be serious."

He grinned, his resolve growing. All his life, he had been told that England was the best. They were the smartest and the most resilient people in the world. And as a future duke, he was the greatest of the great.

Now he saw the arrogance in that statement. Other countries had gifts, other people had strengths. And if England failed to understand the value of other countries, then it was headed toward the downfall of every overly confident fool. And if he didn't value other cultures, other skills, then he was in danger of losing the best thing that had ever happened to him.

The love of his life.

"Thank you, Kimberly. You are indeed the best of England, but I already have that." He laughed. "I am that. Now I want the best of China."

Chapter Forty-Seven

YIHUI COULD BARELY function, but the duchess had made sure she didn't need to. While the woman had taken the ducal jewelry off Yihui, she'd whispered, "The carriage is out front. Go quickly. Do not stop for any reason."

She hadn't. She knew that if she looked at Max again, she would change her mind. She would stop the palanquin and beg for a place—any place—in Max's life. She still might do it. After all, a mistress could have a good life, assuming Max would ignore his wedding vows.

That was a big assumption.

Yihui had spent a great deal of time learning about English wedding customs. She knew that Christian husbands promised to love, honor, and cherish their wives. They considered it dishonorable to have congress with women outside of the marriage bed, but few in the aristocracy kept such promises.

Unfortunately, Max was a man of honor. He wouldn't break his wedding vows, and she didn't think she could share him with another woman.

Which meant that this was the end, and no amount of begging would change it. She held back her tears through force of will. She would not cry in front of these people. She would not cry in front of anyone. She would focus on her work and on creating medicine for the king.

As soon as the palanquin cleared the palace doors, she saw the carriage set there to whisk her away. She told it to go directly to the duke's stables. Blue was there, and she knew Max would not begrudge her use of the pony.

Especially given what she had to do.

It was difficult to maneuver on her heels as she transferred from litter to carriage, but she managed it. And then, once inside the dark vehicle, she allowed the tears to fall.

She allowed herself to double over with pain, to clutch her sides and moan, to weep as if her life were over. How could turning away from a man be so much more devastating than leaving her entire country?

They arrived at the ducal stable too soon. She felt the carriage jerk to a stop and rushed to clean her face. Thank goodness it was dark. They need not see her red eyes or the dark kohl smeared down her cheeks.

Thankfully, one of the footmen was kind. He helped her wobble into the stable and he even saddled Blue for her. With his help, she mounted the pony, and she tried not to compare his hands to Max's sure grip. Someday, she promised herself, some other man would feel as safe, as smart, and as wonderful as Max.

Or she would be exactly as she had declared—alone for the rest of her days with only her work to comfort her.

With that thought fixed in mind, she guided Blue out of the stable. She headed home as fast as she was able. She did her best to ignore the stares of people on the street. In truth, most were already used to the sight of her on Blue. She made it home, instructed Druina on what was to be made for the queen, then grabbed a collection jar. The ducal stables were too clean for what she needed. She headed to the public stables and the dark, moldy corners there.

If it was hard to transfer from palanquin to carriage, it was even harder to dismount from Blue, strip out of her finery, and then crawl in her shift through the muck to gather mold. She had already created a place in the apothecary shop to nurture the mold she needed, but for now, all she could do was gather it this way and hope it worked for the king.

She had just finished collecting what she needed when she heard a man come in. Damn it, she had paid a street boy a full shilling to keep everyone away until she was done. She had no defense while she was in there. She could barely stand, and she wasn't even fully dressed.

Her only hope was to hide, and so she shrank down behind the water trough and damned her skin for showing in the moonlight. Fear flooded her body, triggering memories of Weed and Pervert, of the raucous laughter of men and brutal hands. She tightened herself into a tiny ball, but that shifted the weight from her heels to her toes, and she gasped at the pain. They had smashed her feet. They had held a sword to her neck. They had drugged her and beaten her and laughed as they made her feel small. And the one man who had been kind, who had cared for her as no other, was destined for someone else. Not because the woman was better, but merely because she was English.

The cruelty of the world weighed her down, compressed her into the horse shit as if she were of no account. Little girl crying in the corner with—

"Yihui! My God, what are you doing there?"

Strong hands grabbed her arms, and she struck out on instinct.

"Yihui! It's me. Max!"

Reality burst in on her. Not just his voice, but the sight of his boots. Bright-black boots splashed with muck. How they had laughed as they'd fought to get them off him that first night together. Those were his boots, his voice. That was his strength surrounding her and his body bracing her as she was lifted out of her hiding place.

"Max." The word was a whisper, but it was no less potent. She threw her arms around him and gripped him with all the fear and pain in her body. He was her rock, and if she released him, she would drown.

"What are you doing?"

"The king's medicine."

"Yes, I know. I knew you'd come here. But why are you undressed?"

"I could not damage the silk. Not the green silk that is your color."

"So you undressed in a public stable?" There was no accusation in his tone. Merely incredulity.

"I paid a boy—"

"Yes, he tried every way he could to delay me. Yihui, a street boy is not the protection you need."

No, what she needed was him. "I will do better next time."

"You will send for me next time. Or better yet, send someone else here."

She nodded. At that moment, she would promise him anything if only he would stay with her for a few more minutes. She needed her heart to stop its frantic tempo. She needed to feel safe once again, if only for a few minutes.

"Come on. Let's get you dressed and home."

"The mold—"

"Yes, I see it. Have you gathered enough?"

"Yes."

He set her back on Blue and then passed her the gown. But when she looked at her knees and arms, she saw how dirty she had become. Not just her own body, but her shift was a disaster. She could not put silk on that.

"Max, I can't."

With a grunt, he pulled off his coat and wrapped it around her. Suddenly she was not held in his arms, but she was surrounded by his scent and his warmth.

"Thank you," she whispered.

"Let's get you home. I should like to speak with you."

She shrank down until his coat all but buried her. She did not want to have this discussion. She did not want to hear how he could not have a mistress when he wed. The duchess had already told her he would marry a proper Englishwoman as soon as possible because of the scandal Yihui had created. As if any of this were her fault.

She knew he would say all these things because the duchess had made that clear while she was grilling Yihui on English history, on English customs, on English manners. A future duke must marry within his own caste.

"No, Max," she finally managed. "We do not need to talk. I know you will not see me again. Your mother has explained—"

Her words were cut off by his blistering curse. And then he glared down at the dirty floor. "I blame my mother completely," he said. "Not you, of course, but because of her, this shall be done here and not at all in the proper way of things." Which made him chuckle a bit. "Which means, I suppose, that it is all the more appropriate."

She did not know what he meant. There was too much misery this night, and she still had more to accomplish. She could not take any more.

"Max—"

He grabbed her hands, or he tried to. She would not release her hold on his coat, and so he could only capture one. He held it tight as he looked in her eyes. When he spoke, it felt like the words came through his hand, his eyes, indeed his whole body.

"I love you, Yihui."

She blinked, tears spilling from her eyes. She knew this. She knew they loved one another, but the world was never kind to lovers.

"I wish to spend my life with you. I want my children to be our children. I want my home to be your home."

What a beautiful picture he painted.

"And so, Yihui, my heart…" He began to sink in front of her.

"Max!" she exclaimed. At first she thought he was hurt, but then she realized he was going down on one knee.

"Yihui, will you do me the greatest honor and become my wife?"

He was kneeling before her in the stable muck. He was destroying his clothes. He would destroy his standing among the

English. They would revile him for this. Not to mention…

"Your father will never allow it."

"My father has no say in this. I want you, Yihui. I love you. Please say you'll marry me. We can fight the dragons together because I cannot do it alone. I need you as much, I think, as you need me."

She blinked. He couldn't have said what she thought. And yet her heart had already answered.

Yes. Yesyesyesyesyes!

Her whole body sang the word, but she could not force it out between her lips. Instead, different words came out. Different fears.

"Will you take away my apothecary shop?"

"What? No! If you wish to work there, then you may. You should. But I shall demand that you come home to me every night. Indeed, I insist that I be the one to escort you because this…" He looked about them and shuddered. "This is not what I want for you."

"I will be your wife?" she whispered. "And have my shop, too?"

"If you say yes."

It was true. He was the best of men, and she was the most fortunate of women. She was so overwhelmed with the knowledge that she couldn't speak.

"Yihui?"

"Yes! Yes, please!"

He straightened up out of the dirt and wrapped his arms around her. She was no less fast as she threw herself into his arms. And then they kissed as they so often did, with lips and tongues and their spirits fully intertwined.

Sometimes, she realized as she pressed her body to his, Heaven takes everything away just to give it back a thousandfold and in an entirely new way.

Chapter Forty-Eight

CHAMPAGNE POPPED WARM and sweet in Benedict's blood. It was barely nine in the morning, and yet he was misty-eyed and maudlin at his friend's wedding.

Everything had worked out for Max when it should have been a disaster of epic proportions. The wedding at St. Paul's Cathedral had gone off exactly as Prinny had once decreed. Indeed, when the prince had learned of Max's intention to wed Yihui, he proclaimed that he had known it all along. He also declared that he would honor the couple by serving as Max's best man.

With so royal an endorsement, the duke and duchess had no choice but to accept the match. Even Emmaline had appeared joyous, though Benedict could see the shadows that still darkened her expression. Still thinking of Lord Christopher, no doubt, who was certainly dead and gone. Benedict had brought all his considerable network in on the search and found nothing. Which meant the man could not to be found short of dredging the river Thames.

As if to bless the day, the queen sent news that the mad king's bowels were markedly improved. The bride explained that it was because of her very strong tea. Privately, Benedict believed it was because they stopped forcing arsenic on the king. Either way, it was good for the bride and her Chinese apothecary shop.

All of that was to say that Max had come out of this disaster smelling like a rose. Prinny cheered the nuptials, the queen was a known customer of the apothecary, and…and none of that appeared to make the least difference to Max.

Why? Because the man was besotted with his wife, and she appeared to be equally enraptured. Happiness like that was impossible to fake, and Benedict ached to experience that for himself.

Clearly it was time for him to find his own wife. Well past time to sire his heir. His gaze wandered to Lady Emmaline and Lady Kimberly. Good women to be sure, but his mind was caught up with Lady Janelle as she skulked about London in her secret profession.

He loved the idea of a wife with a mystery. Better yet, it proved she had a flexible mindset for his own secret passions.

His courtship would be more difficult than Max's. He had no benefit from royal attention. And if either of their secrets were exposed, then the results would be calamitous. But he had every faith that it could be accomplished.

And so he drained the last of his glass of champagne and looked to Major Gabriel Lance, his right-hand man.

"It's time," he said. Thankfully, the major understood what he wanted.

"You'll propose?"

"Tomorrow night. Can you have all the details in place by then?"

The major nodded. "Everything will go just as you want."

How he *wanted*, not how it *ought to be*. Because what Benedict intended was not in the least bit proper.

"Then let it begin."

About the Author

Flirty, dirty and fun! That's how Katherine Lyons likes her love stories. One would think that would lead her to contemporary romance, but she's always loved the witty dialogue and hot, sexy humor of regency romance. She's a big fan of *The Bridgertons, Big Bang Theory* (even though it's over), and her favorite movie is *The Avengers* because she loves the MCU. Stop by her website to sign up for her newsletter, special contests, and geeky giveaways!

www.katherine-lyons.com